Isabelle Broom was born in Cambridge nine days before the 1980s began and studied Media Arts at university in London before a twelve-year stint at *Heat* magazine. When she is not travelling all over the world seeking out settings for her escapist novels, Isabelle can mostly be found in Suffolk, where she shares a home with her two dogs and more books than she could ever hope to read in a lifetime.

To find out more about Izzy and her books, as well as read excerpts, view location galleries and gain access to exclusive giveaways, you can sign up to her monthly newsletter via her website, isabellebroom.com.

Also by Isabelle Broom

My Map of You
A Year and a Day
Then. Now. Always.
The Place We Met
One Thousand Stars and You
One Winter Morning
Hello, Again
The Getaway
The Summer Trip
The Beach Holiday
The Orange House

Isabelle Broom

The French Guesthouse

HODDER &
STOUGHTON

First published in Great Britain in 2025 by Hodder & Stoughton Limited
An Hachette UK company

This paperback edition published in 2025

The authorised representative in the EEA is Hachette Ireland, 8 Castlecourt
Centre, Dublin 15, D15 XTP3, Ireland (email: info@hbgi.ie)

1

A CIP catalogue record for this title is available from the British Library

Paperback ISBN 978 1 399 72115 8
ebook ISBN 978 1 399 72116 5

Typeset in Plantin Light by Hewer Text UK Ltd, Edinburgh
Printed and bound in Great Britain by Clays Ltd, Elcograf S.p.A.

Hodder & Stoughton policy is to use papers that are natural, renewable
and recyclable products and made from wood grown in sustainable
forests. The logging and manufacturing processes are expected to
conform to the environmental regulations of the country of origin.

Hodder & Stoughton Limited
Carmelite House
50 Victoria Embankment
London EC4Y 0DZ

www.hodder.co.uk

To Tom Hinshelwood, for bear hugs, beers, book chat and being an incredible friend. One day, we will write that 'Romaction' novel.

I

The hotel was on fire.

When people tell you that flames lick, they're lying. Flames don't lick, or caress, or dance – they tear, and spit, and roar. Flames shatter glass, crack floorboards, and send great billows of thick, black smoke pouring out into the night. Rooted as if by wet tar to the pavement, I watched as the fire ate its way through my business, my livelihood, my home, and thought about those lies. More in a long line of many.

Surrounding me, noise. Men and women in beige suits and helmets, fluorescent bands around their sleeves. So much shouting, not one word of it decipherable: a code between firefighters. The torrent of water was an unnatural blue, caught as it was in the glow of the engine lights, and as the droplets fell from the sky, I was spirited back for a fleeting moment to my childhood, chin raised as fireworks exploded above, Dad's warm hands resting on my shoulders.

'Look, Fliss – shooting stars. Make a wish.'

The door of the hotel burst open with a tumble of bodies. The sight of one was enough to unfasten my feet from the concrete. I shouted his name, and he swung around, squinting through the mess of limbs, the crowd of onlookers, the paramedics who surged forwards.

'I'm fine,' he proclaimed, baritone lacerating the clamour.

A walkie-talkie crackled, static flared, numbers were spoken. I was jostled, and a large boot connected with my slipper-clad foot, causing a ricochet of pain so intense I saw spots.

'Clear the way,' the owner of the boot said brusquely. 'Get back.'

The smoke mushroomed, its acrid scent abrasive. The evacuated guests stood off to one side, a cluster of mono-grammed terry-clothed robes, hands raised to shield their airways, some barking commentary into mobile phones. Mine had been abandoned amid the chaos – the peal of the alarm, the disgruntlement that soon became panic, the list of names, ticked off one at a time, the scrape of fear as it clawed through my gut.

I reached the ambulance and put my hand on the open door. They were sitting side by side on a cot, she wrapped in a foil blanket, he with a plastic mask over his mouth and nose. His shirt was unbuttoned, blond hair askew, feet bare.

'What happened to your shoes?' is how I greeted him.

Charlie glanced down, then back towards me. When he spoke, he did so through a volley of coughs. 'Took them off, in the bar.'

The paramedic, a tired-looking woman with a steely demeanour, glowered at me.

'Keep breathing through the mask for me, sir. That's right.'

'Were you in the bar, too?' I asked, turning my attention to Madeline. Charlie always referred to her as 'our front-of-house girl', though she was not a 'girl' at all, very much a woman, and her job title was Head Receptionist.

Madeline's eyes grew a fraction wider. 'I was . . . yes.'

'Didn't your shift end at four?'

'Charlie said—' She stopped, glanced at my fiancé. 'It was just a nightcap.'

They must have bumped into each other in one of the bars in the area. Chelsea was full of them. Nondescript doorways leading through into darkened rooms, throbbing music and overpriced cocktails, places to be seen, to network, to indulge in a spot of 'mutual ego-greasing', to quote Charlie. He was a social bee, someone who needed to pollinate, while I was happier in the back office, strategising, filing and overseeing the minutiae of tasks that must be done in order to keep our modest hotel running. It was a partnership that I told myself was working well, each of us playing to our strengths, he free to roam and me understanding his need to do so. On most nights, he was out until the small hours, not back for a nightcap before midnight. Furthermore, I had checked the bar during my final sweep of the ground floor, and it had been empty.

Madeline was looking not at but past me. 'They've switched the hoses off,' she said. 'The fire must be out.'

Charlie lowered his mask. 'Finally. Thank Christ for that. Fliss, why don't you go and find out what's going on?'

'I don't think that—' I hesitated. 'I'm sure they'll keep us informed. Won't they have to go room to room first, and make sure nobody else is in there?'

Madeline suppressed a shudder, the foil blanket slipping down to reveal a skimpy sliver of a dress. She, too, was barefoot, her toenails painted a bright, coral red.

Charlie coughed, earning himself a concerned look from the paramedic. 'Do they have key cards?' he managed.

I nodded. 'I gave someone the master.'

His eyes narrowed as he moved the mask back up, though with satisfaction or annoyance, I couldn't tell. I dropped my gaze, studied his toes instead, which were large, and far paler than one would expect, given his ruddy complexion. I loved this man, though acknowledging it had begun to feel more like a habit than an emotion. On my hand, the symbol of our mutual devotion: a large diamond so sharp that it sparkled even in the dark.

'Felicity Fitzgerald?'

I turned.

'Crew Commander Hinshelwood – call me Tom.' He made no move to shake my proffered hand, and I withdrew it meekly as he removed his helmet and tucked it under one arm. 'And you're the owner, are you?'

I opened my mouth to reply, but Charlie beat me to it. 'Officially, my folks own the biggest share of the place,' he said, 'but it's our business, mine and Fliss's here. We run it, live on the premises.'

I watched as the firefighter took this in.

'And you're Mr Fitzgerald, are you?'

Charlie coughed out a laugh that sounded painful, and from beside him, Madeline emitted a whimper of sympathy. I looked at my fiancé, knowing what he'd say next, what he always said when someone made the assumption that we were married.

'I'm Charles Fitzsimons,' he said. 'I know, right? What are the chances of the two of us having such similar surnames? Pals tend to call us "The Fitzes"' – he made the inverted commas – 'and it's actually how we came up with the name for the hotel, you know, "The Fitz".'

The fire officer frowned. 'I assumed it was a play on The Ritz,' he observed, to a guffaw from Charlie.

'We have a smidgeon of the luxury of that place, but it's a lot more fun here. That's what the "F" in Fitz stands for, you see – fun.'

I closed my eyes briefly.

The crew commander, to his credit, dredged up a smile from somewhere, though it was short-lived.

'Sorry,' I said. 'We're straying off topic here, aren't we? How can we help you?'

'Well, the fire is out; that's the main thing.' He folded thick arms across a broad chest and focused his attention on me.

'We got here quickly, and structurally the building's remained sound. I received the all-clear a few minutes ago.'

It sounded like encouraging news, but his expression remained sombre.

'Do you know how it started yet?' I asked. 'There's strictly no smoking in the hotel, so I'm guessing it was some sort of electrical fault. All our appliances have been checked, and our fire-risk assessment is up to date.'

'Fliss is on top of all that sort of thing,' chimed in Charlie. It sounded as if he'd swallowed a handful of sand. I turned and saw Madeline place a hand on his back, tapping it ineffectually. It was easier to look instead at the firefighter, though now I detected pity in his expression.

'We do have an idea of what happened,' he said, 'but it's a bit tricky to explain. Could you . . .?' He moved backwards a few paces, beckoning for me to follow.

I glanced at Charlie, and he shrugged. He couldn't very well accompany me, not anchored as he was by the oxygen mask, the determined paramedic, the sympathetic touch of a woman who could not meet my eye.

I followed Crew Commander Hinshelwood across the street, pausing by the hotel entrance to put on the hard hat he passed to me.

'The roof isn't going to fall in on us, is it?' I said, only to wither at the look on his face.

'Precaution,' he told me. 'Come along.'

I'd only been alerted to the existence of the fire a little over an hour ago – it didn't seem possible that so much had changed in such a short space of time. The Fitz looked familiar, but felt different, the dark walls frowning down at me resentfully.

'I'm afraid the power will have to remain off on the upper floors until we finish assessing the extent of the electrical damage,' he explained, clutching a gargantuan torch in one hand. I'd assumed we would be heading straight upstairs, but instead he led me past the bar, along the carpeted corridor, and into the office beyond. The overhead light cast an artificially white halo around the room. My laptop was on the desk, the safe beneath it untouched. I'd asked Charlie once if I should lock my engagement ring in there, and he'd laughed at me.

'You're supposed to wear it, Fliss – that's the whole point of the thing.'

But it felt heavy on my finger, a great weight of responsibility, an object worth more than my parents had paid for their first house. I loved it, but it was obscene. Mum had worn a ring – a gold band with a blue glass flower adornment – one of the only possessions she truly seemed attached to or took care of. I would see her talking to it sometimes, her hand raised to her lips, a faint murmur I could never decipher, tender and considered, so unlike the manner in which she addressed me.

'Mrs Fitzgerald?'

I had been gazing into the middle distance and rushed to apologise. 'It's Ms,' I corrected automatically. 'And please, call me Fliss.'

'Fliss.' The briefest uplift at the corners of his mouth. 'I had a look at your CCTV.'

'Oh?'

We had inherited the rather antiquated closed-circuit television cameras with the hotel, deciding not to splash out on a more high-tech system right away. It was not password-protected, and from the deft way Crew Commander Hinshelwood was now spooling through the footage, it was apparent that he'd used this particular software many times before.

'We know the fire originated on the top floor,' he said. 'Room twelve, correct?'

He didn't need me to confirm it, but I did so anyway, nodding as the air began to constrict inside my chest.

'That's why I assumed it must be an electrical issue,' I said, 'because room twelve is – was – unoccupied. There was an issue with the plumbing in the en suite. We've got someone coming to look at it tomorrow, although I suppose I'll have to cancel that now. God,' I said, contemplating the to-do list that was beginning to unspool in my mind, 'there's so much to do, to sort out.' I pressed a hand to my chest, felt the rapid machine-gun fire of my heart.

The firefighter stared at me for a moment, then lifted his radio and instructed someone to bring a cup of sweet tea to the office quick-sharpish. 'Take a seat,' he added, motioning to a chair.

'I'd rather stand,' I said, fearing that if I sat, I would not get up again. I felt unsteady – even my voice was strange, a tremor running through it that made me sound off-kilter.

Crew Commander Hinshelwood turned to the screen on the wall, his hand on the keyboard, and tapped a button to restart the video. It showed the narrow hallway leading to rooms ten, eleven and twelve, the stair banister intersecting the bottom corner of the frame, and a fire extinguisher tucked into an alcove below a painting of the Fitzsimons' long-ago deceased Labrador, Champ. Charlie's parents had been so devoted to the dog that they'd named their son after it, bestowing him with Charles but nicknaming him Champ from the moment he was born. It was a moniker that had endured, though one I never used. He'd always been Charlie to me.

Two figures came into view on the screen, a woman and a man, the latter of whom threw a furtive glance over his shoulder. My blood stilled, curdled, burned.

Not 'in the bar', then.

'We can't be sure, obviously, until we ask him, but it looks to me as if that's a cigar tucked behind his ear.' Crew Commander Hinshelwood paused the footage and pointed at the blurry image of my fiancé's head.

The night Charlie and I slept together for the first time, he'd made a show of bringing out a cigar to smoke afterwards. 'The PCC,' he'd proclaimed, as he ran the stick of fermented tobacco along his upper lip, explaining after I'd raised an enquiring brow that the acronym stood for 'post-coital cigar'. Enthralled as I was then, I had deemed it a charmingly idiotic Chelsea-boy trait, and told him sweetly that he stank. 'It's my one remaining vice,' he'd replied. 'But I'll give it up for you.'

But he hadn't given it up – not the cigars, nor the smoking of them after sex, apparently. There were no cameras inside room twelve, but it was glaringly apparent what had gone on behind that closed door. Charlie had taken Madeline upstairs, the two of them had enjoyed themselves together, fallen asleep, and forgotten to put out the infernal 'PCC'.

'Do you know for sure that the cigar started the fire?' I asked, marvelling at my own ability to remain calm.

The firefighter shook his head. 'Not definitively, but we have traced the origin of the flames to the curtains, and, as you know . . .'

'The bed is beside the window.'

He waited for me to continue, though I couldn't locate any coherent words. It would affect the insurance claim – it had to. Charlie wasn't an errant guest breaking the rules. He was the boss, the person who was supposed to set the boundaries, not defy them. My hands started to shake, and I curled them into fists.

'Shame you had to find out this way,' Crew Commander Hinshelwood said, his gruff tone softening a fraction. His stoicism, which had been coming across as impersonal, was, in fact, strength, and it took a great deal for me not to simply collapse against him and wail. But wailing would not solve the problem; crying gets nothing useful done at all. Instead, I drew in a long breath, used it like a sail to steady myself, and told him not to worry, that it was fine, that I would sort everything out.

Another firefighter arrived with a Styrofoam cup of tea, Charlie following in her wake.

'There you are, Fliss,' he said, pausing in the open doorway. 'I thought that— Oh.'

His gaze slid from me to Crew Commander Hinshelwood, before settling on the small screen behind us.

'I can explain,' he said.

2

Time alone to think.

That was what I told him, though in truth, there hadn't been much time in which to say it. The paramedic, having pursued Charlie through to the office, insisted that he simply must accompany her to the Royal Brompton Hospital. Smoke inhalation was dangerous and, given what had been revealed to me about the goings-on inside room twelve, so was I in that moment. When I tersely pointed this out, Charlie had, for once, done the sensible thing and allowed himself to be ushered away. There was nothing more I could do at The Fitz, not once all the guests had collected their belongings and been rehoused at nearby hotels, and rather than remain onsite, I went instead to the same bolthole to which I'd fled many times as a teenager, pulling up in a taxi to find my aunt Angela waiting in the open doorway.

'Oh, lovey,' she said, pulling me into a hug. Her dressing gown smelled strongly of fabric conditioner, and the cheek that she pressed against my own was soft. As I always did when I looked at her, I thought of my dad.

'Sorry for barging in like this,' I said, head hanging.

Angela tutted. 'Barging in? What tripe. You're always welcome here, you know that. Doesn't matter if it's' – her eyes searched around, eventually settling on the old carriage clock that sat on the hallway table – 'five in the morning. I was up anyway.'

'Liar.'

'I was! The boys are here this weekend, and they've all gone off to the Brecons this morning – some endurance challenge or other.'

I glanced towards the stairs. 'Patrick, too?'

Patrick was Angela's husband of over thirty-five years, and my uncle, in his early sixties but still marathon-fit, determined to keep up with his two sons. My cousins Jono and Rich were both in the military, engineer and field-army divisions respectively. They were robust, kind and partial to banter. As a family unit, the four of them were more tightly knitted together than silk.

'You know Pat,' Angela said, as we made our way along the carpeted hallway to the kitchen at the back of the house. 'He never could resist an opportunity to roll around in mud. If there's any truth to those theories about animal reincarnation, I hope for his sake that he comes back as a hippo.'

I realised a moment too late that I was supposed to laugh.

'Don't apologise,' Angela said, cutting me off mid-flow. 'You say sorry too much.'

It was true, I did. Not three hours ago, I'd said sorry to Crew Commander Hinshelwood for placing him in an awkward situation, sorry to the paramedic for delaying her transportation of Charlie to hospital, and sorry to the other firefighter for having had to bring me a cup of tea. The apologies I'd dutifully reeled off to our displaced guests had been endless, and I had even said sorry to Charlie.

'Sorry, but I just can't talk about this now.'

'Sorry, but I think you should go.'

Sorry, sorry, sorry.

'You might be right,' I told Angela. 'But you, at least, deserve a sorry.'

She made a clucking sound, then turned her attention to the preparation of coffee – 'Shall I make it in the fancy cafetière thing you bought me?' – turning her back to fill the kettle. For a moment I simply stood, watching the wobble of her greying topknot, the deft way her small hands flitted from cupboard to drawer. When she moved away from the sink to reach for two mugs, I crossed and stared out through the window.

The sky had lightened on the drive over, but it was a dreary, ashen colour. May had begun wet, and was ending washed out, the promised balm of summer still far from reach. London was bleak in the winter, and barely tolerable even during the warmer months. The truth, much as I tried to deny it, was that with every passing year, I found something new to dislike about the capital, another piece of me that wouldn't fit into the Fliss-shaped gap I had whittled out for myself. At least here, in the suburbs of the city, there were gardens with flowers. Angela took great pride in hers, and what it lacked in size, it more than made up for in sheer range of blooms. Of the few happy childhood memories I had, a great many of them featured this garden as a backdrop.

I turned at the contented sigh of the plunger being pressed down inside the cafetière, and went to join Angela at the kitchen table. Together we sipped, and sat, and shared a silence that felt to me as if it were teetering on the edge of something – a torrent that, once unleashed, would be impossible to stop. In the end, it was Angela who leapt off first.

'What will happen now?' she asked. 'With the hotel?'

I dragged my palm across my face, groaning as I remembered the scene of devastation I had discovered on the top floor of the hotel: the patterns of black on the walls, the gaping cavity in the ceiling, the coiled springs of a burnt mattress where, hours before, the man I loved, had built a life with, had lain with another woman.

'It has to remain closed, at least until everything is fixed. I'll have to go back in a few hours and start cancelling reservations.'

'Will Charlie help with that? Where is he, anyway?'

I lowered my cup to the table, knowing that the next part would be tricky. 'He's in hospital,' I said, adding quickly, 'Don't worry – he's fine. He was in the hotel when . . . They were concerned about the smoke, you know? Just a precaution.'

Angela's shrewd blue eyes found mine. 'He was in the hotel, but not with you?'

'That's right.'

'In a different room?'

I drew in a breath. 'Yes.'

'Oh God.' She raised a hand to her lips. 'He wasn't— He hadn't passed out drunk or something, had he?'

The subject of Charlie's drinking, of his swan dive off the wagon mere weeks after we'd taken ownership of The Fitz, was a delicate one, and when I didn't reply straight away, Angela continued talking.

'I have to admit, lovey, it was a shock to see him get so out of it the last time the two of you came over for Sunday lunch. He drank two of the three bottles of wine we'd got in by himself, didn't he? Paddy had to raid the good stash he keeps in the garage.'

'He'd had a row with his dad that day,' I protested weakly.

'Be that as it may—'

'And he didn't pass out drunk in the hotel,' I interrupted. 'He fell asleep, that's all.'

Angela took a sip of her coffee, her eyes narrowed above the rim of her mug. I knew what she'd say if I told her about

Madeline – it would be a no-nonsense 'dump him and run' – but life was not that black and white.

'I'll make sure he pulls his weight,' I promised her. 'Charlie needs the hotel to be up and running every bit as much as I do.'

'I just worry that he's not supporting you,' she said. 'Not properly. There should be a balance when it comes to looking after each other, and with you two, it's increasingly starting to feel as if you do the lion's share of the taking care.'

I had finished my coffee, the caffeine already working its way through my bloodstream, causing my pulse to quicken, my fingers to start tapping.

'Charlie does take care of me,' I said. 'I haven't wanted for anything since the night I met him. Without him, I'd still be working sixty-hour weeks at someone else's hotel, lining some fat cat's pocket. He's given me freedom and agency – and he loves me,' I added. 'He might not be at his best at the moment, but I know he'll get back to being that person again, and he's a damn sight better than a lot of others, a damn sight better than—' I stopped abruptly, my throat swollen.

Angela leaned forwards and covered both my hands with hers. 'I only want you to be happy,' she began, but I shook my head, let out a strangled laugh.

I'd heard the same sentiment so many times. Did she think that happiness was a choice? One that I was choosing not to make?

'I should go,' I said, making to stand. 'There's so much to do at the hotel and—'

'Don't go yet.' The tone of her voice had changed. She was not asking, but telling.

I sat.

'There's something I need to tell you,' she said.

Not more bad news. Not now. Not today.

'You're not ill, are you?'

She shook her head.

'And Patrick, he's—?'

'Paddy's fine. The Volvo of men, that one; he'll go on and on. We had a bit of news,' she said. 'Yesterday. A letter came.'

What kind of news constituted the sending of a letter nowadays, when so many people used email, text message, or reached out through social media? A letter reeked of bureaucracy – a bill or a summons, the bank or the tax office. I searched her face for clues, using the same technique I had honed as a child, when I had been perpetually convinced that the adults were hiding things from me. It had frustrated me then – and it infuriated me now.

'A letter from whom?' I said pressingly. 'About what?'

'Well, it had a French postmark.'

I should have known.

'Oh, so her?' I said, slumping back in my seat. 'What's she done now? Been evicted for not paying rent? Got herself arrested for being drunk and disorderly? Whatever it is,' I went on, rebuffing Angela's attempt at a reply, 'I don't want to know. Nothing that woman does is of any consequence to me. She gave up the right to my concern a long time ago.'

Angela's eyes moistened, and I immediately looked away, staring past her at the jar of raspberry jam that had been left on the worktop, the loaf of sliced white bread half tumbling out of its wrapping, the butter knife beside it, coated in crumbs.

'I mean it,' I said. 'I don't want to know.'

Angela's face was pinched as she replied. 'I'm so sorry, Fliss. I'm afraid this is something you *have* to know.'

'So, what, she's sick, is she? I can't say I'm surprised. What's the matter with her?'

'Your mum isn't sick,' Angela said, and when her voice cracked open, I knew.

I shut my eyes, but blocking out the world did not prevent me from hearing what came next.

'She died.'

3

The train clattered across the tracks, a steady percussion to the phrase that was repeating itself over and over inside my head.

My mother is dead to me.

I had thrown the words out so many times, had spent more than fifteen years saying them, leaving nobody who asked in any doubt about the state of our relationship. But throughout all that time, my mother had not actually been dead – she had still been alive, existing in the world, a tangible somebody towards whom I could channel all my resentments.

Hearing that she had gone struck me utterly dumb, impervious to the squeeze of Angela's fingers, ignorant of the box of tissues she'd pushed my way. I'd had no need of them, because there were no tears, only the persistent ring of disbelief.

A tannoy system crackled into life and an announcement filled the carriage: a woman's voice, clipped and precise, listing destinations and issuing safety warnings, first in French and then again in English. I looked out at the rapid blur of countryside. Clouds framed the undulating hills, and distant, gold-stone chateaus perched like checkmated kings on the fringes of patterned vineyards. The scenery was beautiful, though the view did not stir me, not as it undoubtedly would have done had I been travelling from Bordeaux to Libourne for reasons unrelated to death.

The letter had been in the pocket of Angela's dressing gown, the envelope warm.

'I don't think I can,' I'd told her, as I held it in my hands, and so she read it aloud to me.

Chere, Madame Angela,

My name is Benoit Chapdelaine, and I am sorry to say that I am writing to you with sad news. Your friend, Delilah – or Lilah, as I knew her – passed away two weeks ago, here in Libourne. It was sudden, unexpected, and I do not believe she suffered. The funeral was held a few days later, as is customary here in France, and it was not until this morning that I began to sort through her belongings and discovered several letters from you. She told me many times about her daughter, Felicity – are you in contact with her? I did look for her online, but I could not find anything. If you could please pass this letter on to her and inform her that there are things she needs to collect, and also some paperwork she needs to sign, that would be a great help. It is very important that Felicity comes here, to Libourne, as soon as possible. I will explain everything as soon as she arrives. If that's not possible, please write back to me at the below address to let me know.

With my deepest sympathies again for your loss.

Toute mon amité,
Benoit

'He doesn't say how she . . . How it happened?'

'No.' She shook her head.

'And, what, he just expects me to up and go to France? I can't do that. The hotel can't spare me, especially not now, and things with Charlie— I can't. No, I won't go.'

Angela folded the letter back into its envelope 'Why don't I come with you?' she offered. 'I can rearrange my shifts – someone will fill in.'

'No.' I had been adamant – had *felt* adamant as I rebuffed her. 'Nobody is going. This is Delilah we're talking about, which means the "things" in that letter likely mean rubbish, "paperwork" probably amounts to unpaid debts, and "very important" is a simple case of "hurry up and pay us what we're owed".'

My cheeks had turned hot, so hot that I'd felt compelled to press my splayed fingers against them.

'It doesn't sound like that to me,' Angela had insisted. 'This Benoit fella, whoever he is, clearly cared about her.'

'More fool him.'

It was then that Charlie had decided to call, and I had been relieved to see his name, to hear his smoke-ravaged voice asking if I was OK.

'Listen, Fliss, I'm really sorry about—'

'My mother died,' I'd blurted, and only then had the tears begun to fall. After extracting myself from a concerned Angela, I'd made my way back to meet Charlie at The Fitz, allowing him to comfort me, console me and convince me to give our relationship a stay of execution.

'It was a one-off, Fliss. A stupid, selfish mistake.'

'But the fire,' I'd wailed. 'All this damage.'

'My balls-up, so I'll be the one to fix it, liaise with the insurance company, whatever I have to. I know I've been drinking too much; I know that. I'll get it under control again.'

His promises had barely registered.

'Angela thinks I should go to France . . .'

'And so you should,' he'd said with a surge of enthusiasm. 'You go and do what needs to be done. I'll have the place back up and running on all cylinders in a week or so. These hands are very capable,' he'd added, flapping them in the air. 'And you never know, there might even be a big payout waiting for you.'

'That,' I'd told him, 'is about as likely as you ever smoking a cigar indoors again.'

'Ouch. Guess I deserved that.'

'Yes,' I'd said dully, 'you did.'

Sensing that my anger had begun to crack, he'd moved in more closely, fixing his gold-flecked eyes on to mine, though I could not bring myself to receive or bestow any further affection. If the fire had never happened, would he ever have told me about Madeline?

'You're not forgiven, Charlie,' I'd said. 'Not yet.'

That had been four days ago, and now, I was in France, on my way to a town I had vowed never to visit. I stared again at Benoit's letter, which I'd taken out to read for what must be the twentieth time. I had searched for him online as he had for me, using the name he'd provided, though I'd found no trace. Perhaps that was the reason why my nerves were so shredded? If I knew what he looked like, or had a sense of who he was, then I would have been better able to prepare myself. All I knew for certain is that he would have questions, would surely want to know why I hadn't seen or spoken to my mother for so long. If I were him, those were exactly the kind of things I would ask.

The train began to slow, a 'Libourne' sign coming into view on the platform outside. Stuffing the letter into my pocket, I lifted my bag from between my feet, hurried down the steps and stepped through the doors. Nobody else disembarked, and I stood still as the carriages trundled away, one after the other, after the other.

'You're very brave,' Angela had said, when I'd reiterated my decision to come to France unaccompanied. Though now, as I waited for the sound of the departing train to fade, any courage I might have been carrying drained away. All of a sudden, I found myself overwhelmed by how sad it felt.

To be completely and utterly alone.

4

A balmy sun greeted me as I made my way out of the station. Squinting, I raised a hand to shield my eyes.

The linen dress I'd worn for the journey was crumpled after hours of sitting, of crossing and uncrossing my legs, of restlessly fidgeting. I paused to remove my denim jacket and put on my sunglasses. Having already copied the address from the letter into the Maps app on my phone, I followed its directions through a car park and over a small roundabout beyond.

The pavement was narrow, the modest houses on either side tightly packed together, some shabby, others freshly painted. I passed a café, caught the distinctive tang of fresh coffee, looked down and saw not takeaway cups but porcelain crockery, small cups with even smaller handles, side plates dotted with flaky croissant crumbs, ashtrays containing thin, white butts. Dogs panted in the shade below the tables, flies buzzed, and pigeons wobbled on unsteady feet. A waiter stopped beside me, offered a '*Bonjour*,' but I backed away, shaking my head, trying in vain to recall the French words for 'sorry', and 'no, thank you'.

Hurrying away, I allowed myself only the most fleeting of glances through shop windows. There were some I recognised – H&M, Yves Rocher, Sephora – but most were independent, a mix of clothing boutiques, gift shops and florists. There were more cafés, a burger bar, an exquisite patisserie with a green frontage that wouldn't have looked out of place in Belgravia. Now that June had arrived, I had expected to see more evidence of tourists, but if there were any in Libourne, they were well hidden.

The map steered me along a side street, before the route banked sharply left, and a few steps later I found myself at last on Rue Montesquieu, standing opposite the house from Benoit's letter. Only, it wasn't simply a house – that felt like too insufficient a word. It was something far more substantial. I had to crane my neck to see all the way up to the third storey, and each tall window had its own ornate balcony, wrought from twisted curls of iron. For all its grandeur, however, the building appeared neglected. Paint peeled from shutters that were cracked and rotting, watermarks stained the cream-coloured stone exterior, and there was what looked to be some kind of courgette or marrow plant sprouting from a drain by the front steps.

I could still change my mind, turn and flee, catch the next train back to Bordeaux, and from there a bus to the airport. Chances were, I could potentially have been back at The Fitz before midnight – but then what? I had come this far.

Drawing in a fortifying breath, I pulled back my shoulders, lifted my chin, and crossed the road. The large brass knocker was in the shape of a kingfisher, and it made a resounding thud.

Nothing happened.

I tried again, rapping harder this time, yet still nobody came. Pressing my ear to the wood, I strained to hear the sound of footfall, but could discern only a faint scratch of music, something classical perhaps. Leaning closer, I was surprised when the door swung open against my weight, and very nearly tumbled over on to my knees. Inside, the hallway was dingy, dusty, high-ceilinged. I peered up and saw a lone bulb hanging from a frayed cord, the glass tarnished black.

'Hello,' I said, though it came out as more of a rasp. I cleared my throat, attempted a timid, '*Bonjour*,' followed by an even more tentative, '*Excusez-moi?*'

A muffled snore drifted out from the bowels of the house, followed by a thunk and what sounded like a bottle rolling across a hard floor.

I froze.

Another snore, louder this time. I stepped carefully across the tiled floor towards a door at the far end of the hallway. How could a house with so many windows be this dark? I knew a little about architecture, having spent the majority of my adult life in London hotels, and guessed the house to be nineteenth-century, or thereabouts. The front had impressed me; the interior, less so. Nobody had bothered to sweep, vacuum or mop the floor for several weeks or even months. And then there was the smell – something sweet and pungent, reminiscent of rotting fruit.

When I reached the door, I could hear the music more clearly. The room beyond was vast – so much so that I took a step back in order to survey it, my gaze drawn instinctively upwards, to where an old-fashioned chandelier was throwing out a muted glow. On the far side were glass doors and several elongated windows, the shutters half-closed. In the space between those and the doorway in which I was hovering, there was clutter: tables of various heights and sizes buried beneath piles of paper, yellowing magazines, and vases of dead flowers. A record player crooned from the corner, and I counted three chaises longues, all of which were obscured by mounds of blankets, discarded shirts, a stained towel. The most notable element, however, and one that sent a roiling churn through my stomach, were all the bottles. They littered every available surface, lay sideways against the furniture, and jostled for position on a make-shift bar trolley, upon which teetered a collection of dirty glasses.

That was the scent I'd detected – alcohol. This was the house of an alcoholic.

One of the mounds of blankets moved, and another snore thundered into the room. It was so animalistic that I half expected a slumbering warthog to emerge – an image that caused nervous laughter to break through my dismay. I was about to make my approach when I heard a banging coming from above. At least whoever it was upstairs was awake, and presumably not some kind of wild pig with tusks. Easing the door shut behind me, I went back into the hallway and made for the stairs. They were uncarpeted stone, the wrought-iron banisters festooned with cobwebs. Was it too much to hope there would be a box at the top, labelled with my name? Something I could pick up and spirit away, without having to speak to anyone.

It was less murky on the upper floors; the doors and shutters had been propped open. Someone had painted a hideous mural on the landing wall, depicting cherubs and birds set against a blue sky – only the cherubs were proportioned all wrong, the birds more like bats, and the background daubed with drips and patches of yellow that the artist had missed. Creaking floorboards were shrouded by threadbare rugs, the patterns so worn as to be indecipherable. There were fewer empty bottles scattered around up there. There was, however, more junk – acres of it, including in a bath-room, where I also discovered another bizarre mural, this one with an underwater theme. A pot of green paint stood in the bath, a brush poking out, more drips on the enamel. Needless damage, pitiful desuetude.

I advanced to the floor above, skirting around an uncurl-
ing sheath of wallpaper, behind which the plaster was pockmarked with holes. The sour aroma of wine had followed me,
and I tried not to picture my mother in amongst all this chaos,
did my best to ignore the tap-tap of my senses, telling me
she'd been here, privy to this sorrowful existence – or, worse,
had been its co-creator. The promise I'd made to myself years
ago, to never again set foot in her world, had broken the
moment I crossed the threshold of this ruinous abode, and
now there was no going back.

I paused on the final step and listened for signs of life.
There was something, a low, scuffling sound that seemed to
be coming from the closest room. Given all the mess, I
wouldn't have been in the least surprised to discover a family
of rodents ensconced under one of the beds.

'Hello?' I called, wincing at how loud my voice sounded.

No reply.

I crossed the landing and pushed open the door. A
bedroom, only this one was pristinely tidy, the wooden-
framed bed neatly made with clean, white linen; the window
glass gleaming and the floor swept. Tall built-in wardrobes
banked along one wall, each gloss-painted panel immaculate,
and folded towels had been set aside on a chair. For the first
time since I'd entered the house, I felt able to put down the
heavier of my two bags, and did so with relief. I was about to
inspect the view through the open shutters when one of the
wardrobe doors creaked open. The man who stepped out did
so backwards, and didn't see me until he turned around, his
yelp of surprise clashing with my own. There was a hammer
in his hand, and he was wearing headphones that he promptly
pulled from his head.

I took in a fringe of dark curls, belted jeans, bare feet.

'You're not going to hit me with that, are you?'

He looked from my enquiring face to the tool in his hand. 'Oh,' he said. 'No – sorry. I was in the middle of putting up a rail when— I didn't mean to frighten you.'

'You're English,' I said, and a smile flickered across his face.

'So are you.'

He looked to be around my age, mid-thirties, a suggestion of lines around his eyes, a few grey strands on his temples, average height and build. All this I absorbed as I stood and stared at him, unsure of how to respond.

'Let me guess,' he said. 'You're Felicity.'

'Yes, I am, which I'm guessing makes you . . .'

'Benoit.'

'Oh,' I said, momentarily thrown. 'I wasn't expecting you to be— I thought that— Who's the person snoring like an idling bus downstairs?'

He cocked an eyebrow in amusement. 'That would be Etienne, my uncle.' There was an undertone of French to his voice, layered in like cream to a cake.

'You sent this?' I said, retrieving the crumpled letter from my dress pocket and holding it up.

'I did.'

'I would've called ahead, rather than show up unannounced like this,' I went on. 'But you didn't include a phone number.'

'No.'

'And I couldn't seem to find you online.'

'Ditto,' he replied, putting the hammer down on the bed. 'We are a man and woman of mystery.'

'I'm not,' I countered. 'I actually have two Instagram accounts – a personal and a professional.'

Benoit frowned.

'I run a hotel called The Fitz, in London. It has its own account.'

'But there's nothing under your name – Felicity Sanderson?'

'That was my mother's surname, not mine,' I bristled. 'I'm a Fitzgerald.'

'Married name?' he asked, dark blue eyes straying down to my hands, to where the ring and its diamond sparkled.

'Fitzgerald was my father's name. I'm not married – not yet.'

'Good to know,' he murmured.

My skin felt suddenly hot. 'Your letter mentioned belongings? Paperwork I need to sign.'

He nodded, hair falling across his forehead. When he lifted a hand to brush it away, I saw a tattoo on his forearm: a fork topped with a twist of spaghetti and splatters of sauce.

'There's no desperate rush, is there?' he said.

'I'd really rather get on with it.'

'But you'll stay tonight?'

I folded my arms. 'I booked a hotel near the train station.'

'Here?'

'In Bordeaux.'

'You can't go all the way back there today.' He glanced down at my bag. 'And you have your luggage.'

'I was too early; they wouldn't let me leave it for some reason.'

Benoit did not look remotely surprised by this. 'I had it in my head that you might like to stay here,' he said. 'I've spent the best part of a week getting this room ready, in case you showed up. The wardrobe rail was my last job, so you can move straight in.'

The empty bottles, the lingering odour of alcohol, the dirt, the mess.

'I can't,' I said. 'It'll be far too late to get a refund on the other place.'

Benoit's brows knitted together. 'Listen,' he said, leaning back against the bedframe, 'I think we're getting off on the wrong foot here. I should have started by saying sorry.'

'Sorry for what?'

He looked at me steadily. 'For your loss.'

I started to retort, to say something flippant, to brush off his pity, but all that emerged was a hollow laugh. Moving away, I crossed to the window, turning my back on him. A cloud trailed lazily across the sun, and the view dimmed. I would not cry for her, not again.

'Are you— Can I get you anything?' Benoit's tone had softened, and I closed my eyes, wished I could close my ears, too. 'A glass of water?' he went on. 'Something to eat? Coffee, or something stronger? There's a bottle of whisky in my room—'

'I don't drink.' I turned to look at him. 'I haven't touched a drop since my eighteenth birthday.'

'That is ...' He thought for a moment. 'Unusual. Isn't eighteen the age most people start?'

'Not me.'

Benoit's forehead creased, and I got the sense that he was aware of having overstepped. Before he got the chance to say more, however, an almighty crash rang out. His eyes met mine and widened, and then, without another word, we both raced towards the door.

5

Etienne was on the floor, struggling to his hands and knees as Benoit and I hurried into the room.

The music had stopped but the record player was still switched on, its repetitive scratching setting my teeth on edge. While Benoit crouched to help his uncle, I picked my way over the piles of junk and set the needle back in its cradle.

'Thanks,' Benoit said distractedly. Then, as he levered Etienne into a sitting position, he added, '*Mon Dieu*, there's blood everywhere.'

Etienne reeled backwards against the chaise longue, clutching his left arm against his chest. '*Mon chéri*,' he lamented. '*Ma belle chérie.*'

'There's broken glass on the floor,' I said, wincing as a dark stain began to spread across the front of the older man's smock. 'Do you have a first-aid kit? Or some cotton wool and antiseptic?'

'In the kitchen,' Benoit said. 'Shall I go, or . . .?'

'It's OK; I can stay with him a minute.'

He hesitated.

'Go,' I urged. 'It's fine – honestly.'

Turning to Etienne, I saw the anguish in his features, the tear stains on his flushed cheeks. Benoit stood and murmured something in French, which seemed to calm his uncle down. Nodding, bottom lip wobbling, the older man attempted to focus on me, but I could see it was a struggle. He was over-wrought, more than likely inebriated.

'It's OK,' I said, wishing I was able to communicate in his first language. 'Can I take a look?'

I gestured to his injured arm, and after a moment, Etienne let me prise it away from his chest. There were a number of cuts, the deepest of which was on his palm, and he sucked air in past his teeth as I prodded the skin around it.

'Don't worry,' I told him. 'We'll have you patched up in no time.'

'*Ma chérie,*' he mumbled, though it was unclear whether he was talking to me or to himself.

Benoit returned, carrying a bowl of warm water and a roll of toilet tissue, a green first-aid box tucked under one arm.

'There isn't much in there,' he admitted, as I snapped open the lid. 'Restocking it is on my to-do list, and, well, it's a fairly long list.' He glanced around the room as he said this, jaw set, shoulders hunched.

I located a gauze pad and dipped it in the bowl. 'First, we clean,' I said, dabbing the smaller wounds, 'and then we dress.'

'You look as if you know what you're doing,' Benoit observed.

'I was a St John Ambulance cadet for a few years growing up. First-aid training goes with the territory.'

Benoit passed me a second pad of gauze. 'I've done basic first-aid training, but it was a long time ago now. I'm a chef,' he added. 'I guess when you're working with knives and fire, it's a good idea to know how to deal with minor injuries.'

The tattoo on his arm made more sense now.

Etienne cried out as I pressed the damp pad against the largest gash on his hand. His bloodshot eyes were the same colour as Benoit's – a deep, almost indigo blue. Once upon a time, before alcohol had ravaged his body, he must have been a handsome man. I took in the wild grey hair and stained teeth, the crepe-like drag in his skin, and felt only sympathy. It was all so avoidable, this needless self-destruction.

'Do you know when he last ate?' I asked, tearing open a packet of antiseptic wipes. 'I'm just wondering if it might be a good idea – after this, I mean. It might help sober him up.'

Benoit looked doubtful. 'No harm in trying, although he hasn't been eating much, not since . . .'

Etienne began to weep. Raising his good hand, he began bashing himself on the side of the head. The wound I'd just finished cleaning burst open, and droplets of bright red blood splattered across the folds of my dress.

'*Merde*,' said Benoit, moving to calm the old man.

'It's fine,' I told him, even though it wasn't. Nothing that was happening could ever have been described as 'fine'. There was so much about the house that reminded me of my past – a life I'd closed the door on a long time ago. Tending to Etienne had been a reflex, but what I didn't want was to be pulled into a trap of caring for him. No good could ever come of that.

I waited until he was docile again, then continued the process of blotting, wiping and applying antiseptic cream. The smaller cuts and scratches, I covered with plasters. Then I pressed a fresh wedge of gauze on to the larger gash and secured it with a bandage.

'Impressive,' Benoit said, as I smoothed down the final strip of tape.

Etienne peered at me through watery eyes, then surprised me with a dry-throated, '*Merci*.'

'You're welcome,' I said, standing up as he sank back against the cushions. The floor was still littered with glass, though when I started to push the broken pieces into a pile with my foot, Benoit rushed to stop me.

'I can do this,' he said, through a tentative smile. 'Why don't you go and unpack, freshen up? I'll make us all a light supper. Steak *frites*?'

'The *frites* part suits me, but I'm afraid I don't eat meat.'

His smile grew wider. 'Not a problem – omelette *frites*?'

'Only if you're sure? I can eat somewhere else.'

Benoit narrowed his eyes. His brows, like his hair, were thick and dark. 'I'd be offended if you did. Chef, remember?'

'Will we be eating in here?' I asked with some trepidation, closing the lid of the first-aid kit and casting around for somewhere to set it down. Every surface was covered, and most of the floor, too.

'Definitely not,' Benoit said, taking the box from me. 'We can eat in the kitchen. Go through the door, there, into the courtyard, then it's the last door on the left. Actually,' he went on, 'I'll set a table and chairs up outside. It's too nice an evening to be stuck indoors. Give me half an hour?'

I hadn't formally agreed to stay, nor was I any closer to knowing why he'd needed me here in Libourne, in person. None of the questions I'd lined up to ask had been answered, and yet for some reason, I found myself relenting. Perhaps it was inherent British politeness, or because the thought of travelling all the way back to Bordeaux felt suddenly nonsensical, or maybe I was simply hungry. It had also been a long time since anyone had cooked me a meal. There was a kitchen at The Fitz, where I'd throw together breakfast or a quick lunch, but Charlie had always preferred to eat out or order in. Neither one of us had time to prepare dinners, worn out as we were by the daily running of the hotel, and for me, especially, food had become fuel, nothing more.

'You're not going to take no for an answer, are you?'

Benoit smiled. 'Nope.'

'I guess I'd better cancel my hotel reservation then,' I said. 'Probably too late to get a refund.'

'Would you like me to call them for you, work some of my French charm?'

'French charm?'

'A natural endowment, born and bred into me by my mum, Océane. She's Etienne's younger sister – his only sister, as it happens – and I'm his only nephew.'

'Océane,' I repeated. 'What a beautiful name.'

Etienne chose that moment to lurch to his feet and stumble between us, making for the double doors that led outside.

'Something I said?' I asked.

Benoit looked regretfully after his uncle. 'He and my mum, they don't speak,' he said. 'It's a bit of a sore subject.'

'Happens a lot,' I replied, and he turned back to face me. 'Families, you know. Complicated at the best of times.'

He said nothing to this, and the silence soon became uncomfortable.

'I'd better go and—' He gestured towards the courtyard. 'Thirty minutes, *oui*?'

That, at least, was a French word that I understood.

'*Oui*,' I agreed.

6

Fully unpacking would feel too much like admitting I was going to stay, but I did change out of my blood-splattered dress and rinse it off in the basin of the tiny en suite, wrinkling my nose at the smell of fresh paint. Unlike the bathroom one floor down, there was no unsightly mural on the wall here, though I did wonder if perhaps there might have been a week ago, before Benoit plastered emulsion over it.

He'd mentioned having his own room, so it was safe to presume he lived here. Though if that were true, why had he let the other areas of the house fall so dismally into disarray?

This I pondered as I cleaned my teeth and brushed the knots out of my hair. There were no messages on my phone, but I fired off a few lines to Charlie and Angela in turn, letting them know that I'd arrived safely.

My aunt replied immediately, a flurry of questions, asking if I was OK, if I'd found the house, if Benoit was nice. I sent back three affirmative yeses, and told her I'd call once I had more news.

It took Charlie longer to respond.

'Any news on possible £££ yet?' he'd written.

Typically imprudent, though he didn't mean to be. His brain worked as a pogo stick might, bouncing around from one subject to the other. I'd actually asked him on our third date if he had ADHD, and he'd laughed before quipping,

'Well, I got no As at all at school, mostly Ds, so perhaps you're half right.'

My mum would almost certainly have liked Charlie, especially once he'd deviated from the path of sobriety; she would've declared him 'fun' and told me to lighten up when I rolled my eyes at his antics. It was one of her preferred phrases: 'Lighten up, Fliss – it's only a gin and tonic'; 'I was only an hour late to collect you, lighten up'; 'Yes, I stole your paper-round money to buy vodka – so what? Lighten up, won't you?'

The memory left an acidic taste in my mouth, and I texted Charlie, 'Not yet,' adding two kisses before deleting them. My thumb hovered over the button; it felt too curt. I scrolled through the menu of emojis instead, eventually settling on one of a shrugging woman, then pressed send.

That would have to suffice, at least for now.

Downstairs, I found the messy lounge deserted, and the broken glass swept up. It looked as if Benoit had cleared away some of the dirty glasses, though there were still empty bottles everywhere, and the air remained fuggy with the scent of spilled wine. I was glad to push open the glass doors and go out into the courtyard, where a table and two chairs had been arranged in the shade of a pergola. The wooden structure was practically groaning under the weight of a huge and sprawling wisteria, its pendulous lilac petals in full, heart-lifting bloom. Finally, something I could genuinely love about the place.

I was still staring up at it when Benoit emerged from the kitchen a few minutes later, two plates balanced in one hand, a bottle and two glasses in the other.

'You know, it is possible to walk through a door forwards,' I said, as he manoeuvred himself around in a slow half-circle.

'Hey,' he replied. 'That wardrobe only has limited space.'

'Etienne not joining us?' I asked.

Benoit's gaze flickered upwards. 'Sleeping it off,' he said. 'I left him snoring like – what was it, a tractor?'

'An idling bus,' I said. 'But either works.'

A flurry of sudden movement caught my eye as a dozen or so birds flew overhead in a high, screeching arc.

'Swallows,' he said, putting down the plates. 'This is the best time of day for them to catch insects. They'll carry on until it gets properly dark.'

'None for me,' I said, putting a hand over my wine glass.

Benoit paused midway through easing out the cork. 'Of course – you did say. Sorry.'

I started to say more, to offer some justification, but he spoke over me.

'You don't need to explain. I'm not judging you, nor would I. To be honest, I could do with cutting down myself. I'll go and fetch us some water, unless you want a Coke or something?'

'Water's fine. I can go?'

But Benoit was already heading back across the courtyard. 'Needed to go anyway,' he called. 'I forgot the cutlery.'

A wisteria petal dropped on to the table, and I picked it up, rubbed its delicate membranes between my fingers. The omelettes Benoit had made were fluffy, soft and oozing butter, and crystals of salt had been sprinkled liberally over the thin-cut chips. A low growl sounded in my stomach.

'This looks great,' I said when Benoit reappeared. He'd brought a jug of water with him, and added ice, mint leaves and wedges of lemon. 'You shouldn't have gone to so much trouble.'

'You're right,' he mused. 'Egg and chips are the epitome of fine French dining.'

'This is finer than any egg-and-chips dish I've had before,' I said, suppressing a moan of pleasure as I sliced into the rolled omelette and melted cheese oozed out.

'It was one of the first dishes I was taught,' he said, spearing a forkful of *frites*. 'My mum's never been a professional chef, but she probably could have been. She's far more adept than me, and I've got fourteen years of training in my back pocket.'

'My mother was a terrible cook,' I said as we sat down, and Benoit chuckled.

'You can't mean Lilah – she of the leathery scrambled eggs?'

'Served on burnt toast that'd been ripped apart by cold slabs of butter, with ketchup as a side.'

Benoit had taken a sip of water, and choked as he laughed. 'Her signature dish, I believe she told me once.'

I tried and failed to smile along. She would have sat here, beneath this pergola, watching the swallows fly overhead. Did she ever think of me in those moments? Was there even any space for quiet contemplation in a mind as sozzled as hers? I cut myself another slice of the omelette, but it seemed to have lost all its flavour.

'I don't mean to be morose,' I said, lowering my knife. 'I know I brought the subject up, but talking about her, it's . . . it's not easy.'

'I get it,' he said, though did he – really? He, with his doting mother and easy charm. Benoit struck me as someone for whom life had been a series of sunny days; there was no discernible darkness within him, no shade where demons might be lurking.

'What did she tell you about me?' I couldn't help but ask.

He mulled this over, jaw working to demolish another forkful of *frites*. 'That you had made a success of yourself; that she'd heard you were in love, and happy.'

Happy. The word felt abrasive. What would she have known?

'My aunt, Angela – the one you wrote to – she must have passed that information on, but she'd have been overstating.'

'So you're not successful?' Benoit asked. 'Or you're not in love? Or neither?'

'Success is a sliding scale,' I said. 'And love is . . .'

'A fool's game?' he suggested blithely. Benoit wore no ring, had mentioned no significant other, and while I was loath to make assumptions about people I barely knew, my instincts were telling me that he was a single man.

'Let me guess,' I said. 'Your ex left you for someone with four Michelin stars after their name.'

He picked up a napkin and wiped a dribble of butter off his chin. 'If only it had been that simple. Are you going to finish those *frites*?'

I glanced down at the food I had abandoned. 'They're all yours.'

'*Merci*.' He lifted my plate and tipped everything that was left on to his own. Evening had drawn in since we'd sat down, the visible gap of sky a rich, profound blue. Light from the downstairs rooms of the house fell in warped patterns through the tall windows and across the paving stones. I drew in a slow breath, the sultry air flooding in to fill my lungs, swell my chest and ground my emotions.

'You know, when I first read your letter, I assumed you were my mum's partner,' I said. 'It was quite a shock to get here and realise I was completely wrong. I mean, would Etienne even have bothered if it had been left up to him?'

Benoit didn't answer. He was watching me, his expression serious.

'How did it happen?' I asked, more serenely than I'd have thought possible.

'How did what happen?'

'My mum,' I clarified. 'You didn't provide any details in the letter.'

Benoit lowered his knife. 'It was her heart,' he said. 'She'd been ill for some time, but I didn't know how bad things had become, and neither did Etienne. It came as a huge shock when she collapsed.'

'Did it happen here?'

He shook his head rapidly. 'Not in the house, no. She'd been to pick up a few things from the Carrefour – that's the name of the supermarket here – and it just . . . happened. One moment she was waving to Monique at the flower shop, the next she'd gone. They tried to get her back, to help, but . . .' He stared at the table. 'A lot of people tried.'

I could not risk speaking; instead I nodded, my lips set in a hard, tight line.

'Etienne was asleep,' Benoit went on, leaning back in his chair and stretching his arms. There was a gentle crack as his muscles contracted, and he sighed and lowered them again. 'Slept through the whole thing, *vieux fou*. I've wondered since if sleep is his defence mechanism, you know? His way of escaping from a world that's become too much for him.'

'He's lucky he has that luxury,' I replied, more bitterly than I'd intended. 'Most of us have no choice but to face whatever the world feels inclined to throw down.'

Benoit's brow wrinkled. 'He's a good person,' he said gently. 'Tomorrow, when he's sobered up, you'll see how wonderful he is.'

I had to battle not to scoff.

'Seriously,' he said, as I stood to stack the plates, refusing to meet his eye. 'I'm yet to encounter a single person who hasn't fallen in love with Etienne once they got to know him. You'll be the same.'

'With all due respect,' I said, as Benoit gathered up the jug and our empty glasses, 'I doubt that. I doubt that very much indeed.'

7

Having refused Benoit's offer of dessert or coffee, I excused myself, feigning exhaustion, and left him in the thankfully extremely clean kitchen, before making my way up to my room.

The dress I'd left hanging up by the open window was already dry, but even more creased than it had been after my long journey. Unzipping my bag, I removed all my belongings and laid them out on the bed. Perhaps they would offer some modicum of comfort, a reminder of home that would feel reassuring? It was a paltry collection: ten pairs of knickers, two bras, a heap of balled-up socks, a nightshirt, decanted bottles of shampoo and conditioner, a tiny pot of moisturiser, a nail file and a travel-sized perfume atomiser. I spritzed some on to my pillow, and promptly sneezed. It was a heavy scent, chosen for me by Charlie, whose gift range was yet to extend beyond fragrance, lingerie and jewellery. He'd given up asking me what I wanted after our first Christmas together, when I'd protested that I didn't 'need' anything.

'It's not about *need*, though, is it?' he'd said – and what had I offered in return? A shrug, a noncommittal murmur, a reiteration that he shouldn't bother to buy me anything.

'I don't deserve nice things.' That's what I wanted to say – but didn't.

Feet sounded on the stairs, a steady tread that stopped when it reached the other side of my bedroom door.

Benoit.

I waited, breath held, and after a moment he knocked, very gently.

'Fliss?'

I swallowed, untensed. 'Hello.'

'Do you need anything?'

'No, no,' I trilled. 'All fine. Thanks again for dinner.'

'You're welcome. I'm going to head on up, watch a movie.'

'OK,' I said. Was he was issuing an invitation, or . . .?

'Feel free to come up,' he added, 'or, you know, if you need anything. I'm on the top floor. Doesn't matter what time.'

I smiled at the door, charmed by the sentiment of his words, and the clumsy way in which he'd delivered them. 'I'll be fine,' I told him.

'OK. *Bonne nuit*, Fliss.'

A warmth settled over me. '*Bonne nuit*, Benoit.'

I listened to the renewed tread of his feet on the next set of stairs, then strained my ears and made out a faint click as he opened and closed a door, casting my eyes upwards as the ceiling creaked. He was in the room above mine.

Angela had asked me once if it was strange living in a hotel, knowing that you were surrounded on all sides by people you didn't know, but I'd always found the proximity of others a comfort. A hangover of being an only child, of growing up wishing so hard for someone else to be there, someone who would understand how it felt to be a child in that house. On the hardest nights, when I'd pull the pillow over my head to block out the caterwauling from below, I would get the sense that someone was there with me, a vague, faceless figure just out of reach in my subconscious, more fully formed than a dream but not solid enough to be a memory, only the shadow of one. If I looked carefully enough,

I could still see them, even now, that faceless friend I would never forget.

My phone buzzed. Another message from Angela.

'Just checking in ☺.'

I hadn't the energy to call and so messaged instead, filling her in briefly on the day's events. I glossed over the incident involving Etienne and the broken glass, not wanting to worry her, and explained that I was having an early night. I still hadn't told her about Charlie's betrayal, the need to unburden far less pressing than the desire I felt to shield myself from judgement – or worse, more sympathy. There was also the small matter of my pride, which had been severely dented.

Hating myself, I checked Madeline's Instagram account. It was full of glossy-looking selfies, holiday snapshots, artfully arranged cocktails and various incarnations of avocado on toast. She'd added hashtags to many of the posts, benign clichés such as #lifeisforliving and #makethedayscount. Scrolling further, I stiffened at an image of Charlie, his head thrown back, mouth open in a laugh, the top few buttons of his shirt undone. It was dated five weeks ago. What would I have been doing when it was taken? Working, most likely, hunched over the desk in the back office, wrestling with a staff rota or invoice.

'We could hire a manager,' Charlie had offered, but I'd been reluctant, argued that it would save us money if I simply took up the mantle myself. 'Money' worked as a magic word to my fiancé – it was his 'abracadabra'. Beneath the photo, Madeline had simply written 'The Boss' and added a single black heart. No hashtags, no further explanation, and only one comment below, from the man himself. Charlie hadn't bothered with words; he'd simply opted for the emoji with a closed zip for a mouth.

I sat down heavily on the edge of the bed, missing the mattress and jarring my spine on the wooden base. Tears sprang from my eyes, and I bit down to stop myself from crying out. Charlie had clearly been cheating on me for far longer than he'd claimed on the night of the fire. And I'd known it, hadn't I? Deep down, I'd known that he was getting restless, that our dwindling sex life would have repercussions on our relationship.

I closed Instagram, watched the screen until it went dark, then got up to use the bathroom, hobbling slightly due to my bruised back. The house was quiet, and no sound was filtering in from outside. After years of living in a busy London borough, the silence felt almost claustrophobic, and I cringed at the loud flush of the chain. Having closed the door of the en suite behind me, I heard a grunt on the landing and crept out to look.

'Jesus!' I cried, as Etienne staggered towards me, hair an electrocuted nest, dirty smock hanging down over bare knees.

'Lilah,' he slurred, reaching for me.

I stepped swiftly to one side and his hands landed on the wall behind me.

'I'm not Lilah,' I said, ducking as he made another grab. 'I'm Fliss, remember. *Je m'appelle Felicity.*'

He squinted at me, close enough that I could taste the warm tang of his breath. Instantly, I was sixteen again, leaning over my supine mother, my fingers going into her mouth to make sure she hadn't been sick. The smell of that, of her – it was there in the corridor, emanating from him, polluting the air. I pushed him gently but firmly away from me. Etienne looked down at his chest in confusion. Then his features crumpled.

'Oh no, don't start crying again.'

Wobbling backwards, he veered towards the dark stairs.

'No, you don't,' I said, grasping him by the shoulders. Wheeling round, he stumbled through into my en suite, and a few seconds later, I heard the toilet seat bang against the cistern. A great torrent was unleashed, more than I could ever have thought possible from such a diminutive man, and he punctuated it with a volley of decidedly sad-sounding farts.

I gazed up at the cracks in the hallway ceiling, but there was no solace up there amongst the cobwebs. Etienne did not flush, and neither did he wash his hands. When he re-emerged and once again headed for the stairs, I was ready.

'*Non*,' I scolded, gripping his arm. 'Come on, time for bed.'

He turned, blinked, sniffed. '*Merci, ma chérie*,' he mumbled, patting my hand. I led him back to his bedroom, which was almost as messy as the lounge, and helped him clamber up into a vast four-poster. The sheet he had been using was damp with sweat. After opening several drawers, I eventually unearthed a moth-eaten blanket and spread it across his lower half. Had my mother done this? Had she spent the last few years of her life caring for Etienne, as I had once cared for her? It should have given me a sense of satisfaction, of karma having been delivered, but all I felt as I trudged back to my room was sad.

For him.

For her.

And for myself.

8

Morning arrived, and with it the chime of bells. I counted each one as I lay on my back, eyes wide open as they had been since the small hours.

When the seventh peal had sounded, I sat up, groaning as my bruised coccyx protested. I was going to need coffee, and a lot of it. Charlie had sent a message at around two a.m., a quick, 'Miss u' and a peach emoji to signify my bottom. He was a 'bottom man' – a fact he never tired of telling me – and was fond of congratulating me on the shape of mine, as if I'd had something to do with the construction of my own anatomy. I had inherited its shape from my mother, who'd once told me her grandmother had 'a bum you could rest a wine bottle on'.

Trust her to use that particular analogy.

Charlie, in fact, had seen my rear end before he saw my face. I had been bent over at the time, my head in a low cupboard in the kitchen of Carlton Community Centre, searching for extra teabags. Part of my role as a local volunteer was to make sure my elderly group was well refreshed after our weekly nature walk, and whoever had hosted the session prior to mine had used up the last of the PG Tips. Aware of someone behind me, I'd turned expecting to see an octogenarian, and was surprised to find it was a man of my own age. Charlie introduced himself the old-fashioned way, with a handshake that lingered a few seconds longer than was strictly necessary, and asked me if he could help with anything.

'Not unless you happen to have a box of teabags up your sleeve.'

He shook his arms in an exaggerated fashion. 'Damn. They must've fallen out on the way here.'

'I'll have to pop to the shop,' I'd replied, eyes straying to the clock on the wall, but Charlie had insisted that he would go.

'That's why I'm here,' he'd said, when I began protesting. 'To help.'

Where, I thought, as I slowly finished getting dressed, had that version of my fiancé gone? But it was a redundant question. I knew where – and I knew why, too.

Rather than heading to the kitchen, I tiptoed along the dark hallway and made my way outside on to the street, relieved to escape the confines of the house, with its strange scent of decay, and properly stretch my legs – although in which direction, I was not yet sure. When a white-haired man pushing a bicycle wandered past and issued a '*Bonjour,*' I decided I may as well follow him and set off across the cobbles.

It was going to be another warm day, that much was clear from the absence of clouds, and I lifted my chin to greet the freshly hatched sun, admiring the tall windows of the surrounding houses, the primrose stone and cracked wooden doorways. Each dwelling had some unique feature or other that marked it out as different to the rest, be it an arched entranceway, old-style lanterns fixed to outside walls, or the trailing tendrils of a climbing plant. I was no horticulturalist, but I did recognise both clematis and jasmine, the latter of which smelled so heavenly that it drew me across the road. Chelsea was all clipped topiary and shiny gloss, whereas Libourne felt untamed. I'd heard many people describe 'rustic French charm' before, and thought I might now understand what they meant. It was rustic here – and I was charmed.

The further through the streets I wandered, the more people I encountered, and with every polite exchange of '*Bonjour*,' I felt more at ease, less like the proverbial sore thumb – or sore bum, if I were to use a more accurate description. It took only a few minutes to reach the town square – Place Abel Surchamp – where I discovered yet more towering, blond buildings, a striking town hall complete with turrets and gargoyles, and, fortuitously, an open café with plenty of empty tables. Moments later, I was sitting in a patch of sunshine, legs crossed at the ankles, head tilted back, and a café au lait beside me.

There was little to no breeze, but the heat was pleasant enough. It might even have been a moment to savour, if my thoughts weren't continuing to swirl, anxiety leapfrogging from one subject to another. I took a sip of the coffee and blinked hard at its strength. Pouring caffeine this potent on to an already edgy mood was akin to hurling gasoline over a bonfire, and yet I had no intention of stopping. I would do what I always did and worry about it later.

'*Excusez-moi, Madame, cette place est-elle prise?*'

I looked up to find a man beside me, his hand on the back of the unoccupied chair at my table.

'Sorry,' I said, flustered. 'You want to take it?'

'*Oui, s'il vous plaît.*' He cocked his head to one side. 'You are German?'

I smoothed a hand over my blond hair, all of a sudden self-conscious under the scrutiny of this man, with his chiselled jawline and dark, turned-down eyes. 'I'm English.'

'Ah!' he exclaimed, and then, before I had time to react, he pulled out the chair and sat himself down on it.

'Erm,' I began, only to be drowned out as the man raised two fingers to his lips and whistled. There was a short bark, a clatter of paws, and a slim grey dog appeared from behind one of the other tables.

'*Viens*,' said my new companion, slapping his thigh.

The dog skidded to a stop and pushed its long snout into his hands, its furiously wagging tail a blur.

'This is Madame,' the man said, bending to plant a kiss on the dog's nose. 'Madame, this is . . .?'

'Felicity.'

'Ah,' he crowed. 'Did you hear that, Madame? This lady must have French blood, the same as you.'

'Isn't she an Italian greyhound?'

'*Exactement*. But she was born here, and so, she is French.'

'She's beautiful,' I said, as Madame regarded me through wide, watchful eyes.

'If you give her your biscuit, she will fall instantly in love with you.'

'This one?' I picked up the plastic-wrapped Biscoff from my saucer and held it aloft. Madame immediately lowered her bottom to the ground and raised a begging paw. Her claws had been painted with a scarlet nail varnish that complemented her diamanté collar. I broke the biscuit in two, and she accepted a half carefully.

'Do you have a dog of your own?' the man asked, and I gave in to a wry smile as an image of Charlie came to my mind. With his uncontrollable hair, boisterous nature and predilection for drooling in his sleep, my fiancé was undeniably canine – although the apparent lack of loyalty suggested otherwise. As quickly as it had lightened, my outlook clouded over once more.

'No dog,' I said. 'I work long hours, so it wouldn't be fair.'

'Ah,' the man replied, only to interrupt himself by calling out to a passing waiter. Once he had ordered himself an espresso and established that I didn't require a refill, he asked me what I did for a job.

What was it with these French men and all their questions? I settled on 'hotelier'.

'I could never leave Madame at home by herself,' he said. His English was precise, yet heavily accented. 'If I did, she would cry until the neighbours broke down the door.'

'You take her to work with you?'

'Of course.' The way he said it made it sound obvious, as if there never had been an alternative option. Madame had finished her biscuit, and now leaned back against her master's legs as he stroked her silky head. The audacity he had displayed in sitting down uninvited, coupled with the brazen way in which he continued to probe me for information, would have raised red flags in any other scenario, and yet I found I was closer to feeling bemused than irritated. When a man is bad, there will always be a feeling, and I did not have that feeling.

'Are you going to open a hotel in Libourne?' he asked, and I laughed – a single short, sharp bark that caused Madame's ears to lift.

'That's not why I'm here,' I told him. 'It's not a work trip.'

'Ah.' His espresso arrived and he thanked the waiter. 'You are on holiday.'

I waited while he took two sachets of brown sugar from the pot on the table and began tapping them against the back of his hand.

Two sugars – in an espresso?

When he looked up expectantly, I shrugged instead of elaborating. There was no straightforward way to explain what I was doing in Libourne – and certainly not to someone whose name I didn't yet know.

'You never told me what you do,' I said. 'Your boss must be very understanding if they let Madame go to work with you.'

The man considered this as he fished a pair of mirrored sunglasses from the neck of his T-shirt and slid them on. The sun had moved, its path unencumbered by cloud. Had I ever seen a sky so blue? If so, I could not recall when. The buildings that encircled us seemed to be basking, the clay-tiled rooftops ember-hot. I pulled the fabric of my blouse away from my chest and used a hand to fan my face. Madame had curled up in the small patch of shade provided by the table, though her eyes remained open, alert.

'She wants to chase the pigeons,' the man said, in a doting tone. 'And they are so dumb, she could probably catch one.'

'You were about to tell me what you do for a living,' I prompted.

'I think, in English, the word is carpenter. I do not have a boss – I am the boss.'

'And what do you make?'

He spread open his hands. 'Whatever you ask me to make. I can work with old wood, new materials, make adjustments, build furniture . . .'

'There is a lot of wooden furniture in Libourne,' I remarked, thinking of the heavy dresser back at the house, buried beneath Etienne's mess, the bedframe that had bruised my spine, the chairs Benoit had dragged out into the courtyard.

'I will give you a business card,' the man said, shifting position to reach into the back pocket of his jeans. 'In case you ever need something made for your Libourne hotel.'

I was about to retort, to reiterate the fact that I was not planning on, nor had any desire to, open a hotel here, when the bells began to chime out the hour. Eight o'clock: time to get back and face whatever the day had in store.

'*Merci*,' I said, slipping the card into my bag without giving it more than a cursory glance and craning my neck in search of the waiter. At the sight of a face I recognised, I waved a hand unthinkingly, but it was not the man who'd brought me my café au lait, but Benoit. Seeing me, he made a beeline towards us, weaving through the tables at a speed that would have put Madame to shame.

'Felicity,' he said, and then, glancing at my new acquaintance, burst into a torrent of spirited French.

'You two know each other?' I prompted, as Madame jumped up, her painted claws coming to rest on Benoit's knees, tail practically spinning with joy. He ruffled her head, leaping from side to side, making as if to chase her before dropping to a crouch so she could lick his cheeks. How many biscuits would I have to shell out in order to get that kind of welcome?

'You know Benjo?' the man said, and Benoit gave him a friendly shove.

'He knows I hate that nickname.'

'I was just about to pay,' I said, fumbling for my bag.

Benoit scanned the table. 'One coffee? Let him pay for it, he's rich.'

'Oh, no, I couldn't possibly—'

'It is OK.' The man grinned, showing off two rows of teeth than were even whiter than Madame's. 'If you are a friend of Benoit, you are also a friend of mine.'

All this talk of friendship.

'I don't even know your name,' I said, to which the men exchanged a look.

'Adélard,' they said at the same time, and Madame began to spin around on the spot, yipping in excitement.

Benoit turned to me. 'We need to go,' he said, to a chorus of disapproval from his friend. Adélard began to tug at the leg of Benoit's shorts, urging him to stay, joking that he could sit on his lap. Benoit batted him off before reverting to French. He gesticulated far more in that vein than he did in English, the rich language animating him, adding a flourish to his movements, a flair to his words.

Adélard listened, then turned grave eyes towards me. '*Je vous offre mes condoléances.*'

I said nothing.

'He means—' Benoit began, but I shook my head.

'I understood. Thank you,' I said flatly.

Adélard glanced at Benoit, who raised his shoulders.

'You said we needed to go?' I asked.

Benoit nodded but didn't smile.

'Lilah's will,' he said. 'Someone is coming to read it.'

My body suddenly felt as if it was in danger of shutting down. I took a breath that felt unnaturally ragged.

'When?' I managed, and Benoit glanced at his watch.

'*Merde,*' he said. 'In about ten minutes – come on.'

Grabbing my hand in his, he pulled me towards him, and although I wanted to resist, to delay, to hide from the strangeness of this new reality, I let myself be taken.

9

The executor, Monsieur Dupont, was small and sharp-edged, with pointy features and a pair of wire-rimmed spectacles he wore so far along his nose that they must be a prop. He either spoke no English or did not feel inclined to do so, which left Benoit with the unenviable task of translating everything he said.

Etienne, who was dishevelled but had at least put on proper trousers and a clean shirt, barely acknowledged me from his position on the chaise longue. Clearly, he had no recollection of the previous night, of me helping him back to his bed, and that was fine. The atmosphere in this hot, untidy room was awkward enough already.

Monsieur Dupont looked at me beadily, muttered something, and clicked his fingers.

'He needs to see identification,' Benoit explained. 'Two kinds, ideally.'

Having rooted through my purse, I was able to hand across my driving licence, though had to hurry up two flights of stairs to fetch my passport. The executor took his time examining each, and then examining me in turn, eventually nodding his approval and handing back the documents. He had not, I noted, pestered Etienne for proof of identity, despite him presumably being the main beneficiary. It was highly unlikely that my mother would have left me anything of value. If our roles had been reversed, she'd have got nothing from me.

Benoit touched a hand to my arm, mouthed an 'Are you OK?', to which I nodded. The two of us were perched side by side on another beaten-down chaise longue, while our guest had opted for one of the hard-backed chairs pushed under a cluttered dining table. I averted my eyes from the empty bottles stacked on top of it, second-hand embarrassment flame-hot on my cheeks.

Monsieur Dupont cleared his throat, waiting until he had our undivided attention before launching into an opening spiel. Benoit muttered the highlights to me under his breath, though I didn't need him to translate my mother's name.

Delilah Love Sanderson.

The 'Love' part had always felt crushingly ironic.

Etienne dragged a hankie from his shirt pocket and began dabbing at his eyes, his sobs evident yet unobtrusive. I glanced at Benoit; he was looking across at his uncle in sympathy, mouth set in a grim line. The stubble across his jaw was denser today, and there were dark smudges beneath his eyes. It must have irked him to wake and find me gone, and to have had to race through the streets in search of me. I'd apologised numerous times, but the guilt still lingered, my stalwart companion of old.

Monsieur Dupont had begun droning on in legal jargon so complicated that even Benoit was struggling to make sense of it.

'Don't worry,' I murmured. 'I don't need to hear every word.'

There was a rustling of paper as Monsieur Dupont began to shuffle through a manilla folder. Having extracted a single sheet, he held it at a distance, eyeing each of us in turn.

'This is it,' Benoit whispered. 'That's Lilah's will.'

I wrung my hands together in my lap, pushing down on my knuckles until they cracked.

'To my beloved Etienne,' Benoit said in an undertone, 'I leave my flower press, and the items of jewellery bestowed on me by him, including but not limited to, one antique diamond ring, a gold bracelet and a locket bearing our photograph. Please treasure them, as I treasured you.'

I jolted in my seat as a loud wail echoed around the room. Etienne had buried his face in his hands, his shoulders shaking.

'*Mon Dieu*,' Benoit said, going swiftly to tend to him. I assumed Monsieur Dupont would pause proceedings, but he carried on. Benoit's head was down as he bent over his distraught uncle, though he must have been listening intently all the while, because a moment later he froze, his eyes finding mine and widening. Slowly, almost mechanically, he stood up and made his way back to sit beside me. Monsieur Dupont had finished speaking and was looking at me expectantly.

'What happened?' I asked. 'What did he say?'

Benoit rolled his lips together, took in a breath, and exhaled as if letting go of something. '*Pouvez-vous relire la derniere partie, s'il vous plaît?*' he said.

Monsieur Dupont grunted, then nodded, and this time when he read from the will, Benoit translated it word for word.

'To my daughter, Felicity Rose, I leave my forget-me-not ring, alongside all other possessions not separately listed above.'

A hollow had opened up in my stomach, though Benoit appeared not to notice. He was staring not at me, but into the middle distance, as he recited the final few lines.

'I also betroth to my daughter, my share of the guesthouse on Rue Montesquieu, Libourne, the deed of which should be transferred into her name, in accordance with French law.'

'What?'

All three men turned to look at me.

'She means this house,' Benoit said, and I shook my head.

'That can't be right. She could never save enough for basic groceries, let alone a place like this. It must be worth millions.'

Benoit frowned. 'I think you're confusing Libourne with London.'

'But it's huge.'

'And rundown.'

'Yes, but still.' I gestured around at the enormous space, the high ceiling with its dusty chandelier, the tall arched windows with their view out into the courtyard, dribbles of wisteria and patterns of light. 'It's . . . beautiful.'

At my words, a smile transformed Etienne's features. '*Oui,*' he said softly. '*C'est beau.*'

A beat of silence followed, lending gravitas to the moment. I was reeling, unable to comprehend what this meant. Why, of all people, would my mother have chosen me? I might be her daughter, but we'd been estranged for so long that it had become a connection in name only. Hadn't it?

Etienne was speaking quietly, though with coherence. He had a rhythmic way of talking, a singsong voice that was both deep and soft. And while I couldn't understand all of what he was saying, I felt compelled to listen regardless, to let the pleasant sound wash over me. It came as a shock when Benoit shot suddenly upright.

'*Non!*' he exclaimed. '*Tu ne peaux pas le penser?* You can't mean it.'

Etienne's smile unhitched, and he nodded gravely. 'I do mean it,' he said, in very deliberate English. 'It is the right time.'

'But . . . But . . .' Benoit had both his hands on his head and was holding it tightly.

I looked at Etienne and received the ghost of a wink in return.

'It is done already,' he said, turning to speak in French to Monsieur Dupont, who nodded, and then he, too, began to talk, this time directly to Benoit, who began to pace up and down, knocking over several empty bottles as he went. His agitation could not have been more apparent, and yet the two older men appeared amused. Getting to my feet, I moved to intercept him, catching his elbows in each of my hands.

'What is it?' I asked. 'What's the matter?'

Benoit closed his eyes briefly, before giving in to a helpless laugh. 'The other half of the guesthouse,' he said. 'Etienne has made it over to me.'

There were stipulations, of course.

The chief among them being that Etienne be permitted to remain in the guesthouse on a permanent basis, and that, during his lifetime at least, it may not be sold on. These points Benoit explained to me, while I sat, mute and dumbfounded, trying to take it all in.

'And there's nothing else?' I asked, as Monsieur Dupont began filing papers away. 'No letter?'

Monsieur Dupont nudged his spectacles up a fraction and fixed me with an unwavering stare. '*Non*,' he said. '*Rien d'autre.*'

'And there's nothing in the house?' I asked Benoit. 'No envelope with my name on it stashed away in a drawer?'

His attention slid past me and around the room, and I knew what he must be thinking. A single envelope? Here? In this junkyard? But there must be something – an explanation, an apology, even a final written chance to twist the knife she had already stuck in. For there to be nothing at all was implausible, not to mention infuriating.

'I'm going to look,' I said, crossing to the dresser. Its surface was barely visible beneath the clutter, and the small gaps of wood I could see were caked in dust. When I attempted to yank open one of the drawers, it snagged on all the detritus inside, and, having spent several seconds tugging at it with all my might, I lost the ability to remain calm.

'What the hell is wrong with the two of you?' I fumed, rounding on Benoit and Etienne. 'How can you live in this . . . in this . . . *filth*?'

Benoit said nothing, though his eyes flared.

'Oh no, you don't,' I said hotly, as Etienne made to reach for an unopened bottle of wine. Weaving through the clutter, I pulled it out of his hands. '*Non!*' I scolded, as he lunged for it. 'You can't just pull the pin out like that, upend two people's lives entirely, then get drunk and pretend it isn't happening.'

'Fliss,' Benoit began, and I rounded on him.

'It's not even ten a.m. yet,' I said, and then, to Etienne, 'I'm trying to help you.'

The older man's Prussian-blue eyes were still moist from his most recent bout of tears, his bandaged hand shaking, its fingernails bitten down to torn stubs. He was a pathetic sight. As it had the previous night, my heart seemed to cave in on itself when I looked at him. The battle was not between me and Etienne; it was one that had begun long ago between him and alcohol, and it was starkly apparent which of the two was in the master suite, and who would be sleeping in the gutter. Defeated, I lowered the bottle and turned away.

The fact was, I would sooner invite a family of rats to live at The Fitz than wait around to watch Etienne drink himself into useless oblivion.

Having snatched up my bag from the chaise longue, I hurried past an ashen-faced Benoit and back out into the street, slamming the front door shut behind me. There was no point calling Charlie, not so early in the morning, and besides, his paintball approach to conversation – a blend of rapid-fire questions and increasingly outlandish solutions – was not what I needed in this situation. What I needed was serenity, clarity, and compassion.

Angela.

I sent her a text message, asking if she was available to talk, to which she replied with a jokey aside that broke through my distress, and a request that we 'FaceTime for once'. I loathed video calls, but my need to see a friendly face overrode any reluctance.

'There you are,' she said, as I was treated to an extreme close-up of her left nostril. 'Just finding somewhere to prop you, hang on.'

I folded down on to the stone steps, elbows on my knees, the phone held out in front of me. Angela had my father's heavy-lidded grey eyes and angular bone structure, features that were softened today by her feathery blond bob and an abundance of blusher. She moved through the house where I'd spent my late teens and early twenties, eventually settling into an armchair in the newly redecorated lounge.

'That's better,' she said, suppressing a yawn. 'I barely got a wink of sleep. It's been that hot here, not that I can say a word about it to Patrick, not without him rolling his eyes and muttering about the menopause. He'll find himself to be a *man-on-pause* soon,' she tutted, though with affection.

'I didn't sleep much, either,' I said.

Not news to her. Angela had long been aware of my persistent struggle to switch off at night, and at one stage had spent several months researching herbal remedies. It was thanks to her that two-thirds of our bathroom cabinet at The Fitz was stocked with magnesium supplements, bottles of lavender oil, and a sheath of CBD gummies, the latter disappearing at a rate that could only mean Charlie was helping himself, though I'd never known him to have any issues when it came to sleeping. If anything, the opposite was true.

'Being in a stranger's house will do that to you,' said Angela sympathetically, removing a cushion the shape of a seashell from behind her and tossing it out of view. I heard the deep rumble of a male voice coming from somewhere off-camera.

'Well, I never,' Angela said. 'Did you hear that, Fliss? Your uncle Paddy's just offered to bring me a cuppa. Now, that doesn't happen very often. I'm honoured.' She trailed off into laughter as Patrick began to protest. 'I'll take a choccy biccy, too, while you're in there – one of those foil-wrapped ones – and a couple of those cheese straws. They're in the tin your mother left here, you know, the one with more dents in it than Muhammad Ali.'

I smiled, but it was watery enough that Angela noticed.

'Oh, lovey,' she said, her teasing tone switching to one of concern. 'You're upset.'

I nodded. 'I think I'm in shock.'

'Someone should be bringing *you* a chocolate biscuit.'

I pictured Benoit, plates of dinner in his hands, last night's genial offer of wine. What had possessed me to be so unnecessarily rude to him?

'I'm not sure that's going to happen. I'm afraid I may have staged a flounce.'

She chuckled. 'Worse crimes have been committed, and under far less extraordinary circumstances.'

'Extraordinary is one way of putting it,' I mused. 'You know what you said a moment ago, about this being a stranger's house?'

'Oh, God. I didn't say it to make you feel worse about your mum, about the estrangement.'

'I know,' I said, watching as she accepted a mug and a small plate of assorted snacks from my uncle. Patrick leaned over until he could see the screen, smiled, and gave me a brief wave.

'Go on, off with you,' said Angela fondly, batting away her husband as he swiped one of the cheese straws. 'You were saying, Fliss, about the house?'

'It's half mine.' I said it so quietly that the meaning passed her by.

'Say again?' she said, bringing the phone closer to her face.

'The will was read a few minutes ago, and, well, Mum left me her ring – remember the flower one? That, and a load of other stuff I haven't had the chance to look through yet. But the main thing is this place. Turns out she owned half of it – so now, apparently, I do.'

My feet were bathed in sunlight. I looked up, part of me expecting there to be clouds – largely of the dark and ominous variety – but the sky remained unblemished, the colour so intensely blue that it felt mocking. There was a spider busy building a web between the back of the drainpipe and the wall behind; another inhabitant with whom I must share this property.

On the other end of the phone, Angela was silent, her furrowed brow telling me she was deep in thought – though not, as I had expected, in shock.

'There was some money,' she said cautiously. 'Mikey had a life insurance policy. I'd assumed Delilah spent it all at the time, but she can't have done.'

Life insurance.

The words slid between my ribs.

'I didn't know she'd even received it until a few years ago,' Angela went on. 'She mentioned it in passing in one of her letters, but not in any detail.'

'I like that she got to be compensated and not me,' I said. 'I lost Dad as well.'

'Of course you did, and I guess that explains why she left you her half of the house.' Angela took a sip of tea. 'You were always owed a share of that payout; Lilah must've known that.'

An ache was spreading out from the base of my skull. I sighed, explaining briefly about the rules, and Benoit being the other beneficiary.

Angela took it all in, lines creasing her forehead, lips a tight bud. 'So, what do you want to do, then?' she asked. 'If you can't sell it.'

'I can't very well live in it,' I pointed out. 'And after the fire, Charlie and me, we're going to need some money. We were struggling as it was, and now we stand to lose a ton of revenue while we get the place patched up.'

'But surely the insurance—' she began.

'It's not that simple,' I said, cutting her off before she could ask too many questions. 'Fact is, there are a lot of useful things I could do if I had some money in the bank. There aren't many useful things I can do with a dilapidated French ruin like this.'

'Hmm.'

'These letters you and Mum exchanged,' I said, batting irritably at a fly that was hovering near my face.

She perked up at that. 'You want me to send them to you?'

'No. I mean, maybe. Actually, no.' I shook my head. 'What did you two even talk about?'

Angela drank some more of her tea. 'Oh, all sorts. Mostly about France, you know – what she was up to.'

'Did you ever talk about me?'

For a moment, she looked stricken, almost as if she might cry. 'Yes, Fliss,' she said. 'Of course, we talked about you. She was so—'

'Stop,' I said, nausea passing over me like a wave. 'Sorry, but I've changed my mind – I don't want to know.'

'But it might help if—'

'No. I just . . . I can't. Not now, not today.'

'OK,' she soothed. 'But the letters, they're here if you ever want to read them. I could even bring them over to France for you. I'd love to see the house, meet Benoit and Etienne.'

'There's no need.'

Angela failed to hide her dismay, and suddenly, I couldn't do it anymore, could no longer stomach her pity.

'There's someone coming,' I lied. 'I'd better go.'

'Fliss, wait a sec—'

I made myself look at her.

'What will you do?' she asked.

What would I do? I knew what I had to do.

The insect I'd shooed away had been caught in the spider's web; I heard its desperate buzzing as it struggled to get free, a distress signal that would do nothing to save it.

'There's only one option,' I said, turning away and brushing the dust from my trousers. 'I'll have to find a way to sell my share of this place, and then get as far away from it as possible.'

11

When I pushed open the front door, Benoit was standing on the other side of it.

'Hi,' I said.

'*Salut*,' he replied.

'I flounced,' I told him. 'I do that sometimes. Thirty-six going on thirteen, apparently.'

The beginnings of a smile greeted this, though he looked beaten down. Was he, like me, puzzling over how his life could have altered so entirely? The two of us had known each other for less than twenty-four hours, and yet we were linked – bound inextricably together by the shared ownership of a property.

'You had your reasons,' he allowed. 'Are you OK now?'

There was no point lying to him. Shaking my head, I stared down at the floor, then back towards him. 'Not really, no.'

'Is it the fact that you've inherited half a guesthouse, or that you have to share it with me?'

I rubbed my face, groaning behind my hands.

'Because you needn't worry,' he went on. 'I'm fully housetrained.'

'Right,' I said, looking pointedly along the hallway, with its acres of dust and stacks of unopened post. A vase of dead stalks that were presumably once flowers sat on a side table. 'You're right – it's completely spick and span in here.'

'It's not all this bad,' he reasoned. 'Have you done the full tour yet?'

'Of the house? No.'

'Come on, then.' He started towards the stairs.

'What, now?'

'*Tout de suite*,' he confirmed, smiling wryly as I followed.

'Who painted the mural?' I asked, when we reached the first floor. I still found it hard to look at the oddly proportioned cherubs and flat-faced birds without wincing.

'That's an original Etienne Chapdelaine.'

'It's original alright. Not that I know much about art,' I clarified. 'It could be a Picasso, and I'd probably have no idea.'

'That would certainly make the house more valuable,' he said. 'Although less interesting.'

'Interesting is an interesting choice of word.'

'Etienne is a fantastic artist,' he said resolutely. 'Or was.'

'What happened?' I asked, though I could guess.

'Alcohol happened. When I was here last summer, he and Lilah seemed better than they had been in previous years. Still drinking, but not drunk, if that makes any sense?'

She had said the same thing to me many times: *'I'm not drunk, Fliss. I'm drinking.'*

Benoit looked pensive as he stared at the mural. 'It was this one night,' he said. 'I'd been out with Adélard and got back late – very late. It must have been three or four in the morning, and I knew straight away that they'd had a row. You know how there's an atmosphere, a kind of friction in the air?'

I did know, only too well.

'Lilah had gone to sleep in one of the other rooms, and Etienne was here, painting over his original mural, crying and saying that he was a failure et cetera, et cetera. I don't know how he managed to paint even this' – he peered more closely at one of the cherub's bulbous noses – 'thing. He could barely hold the brush straight.'

'Did you ever get to the bottom of it?' I asked. 'Their row, I mean.'

Benoit cast sheepish eyes in my direction. 'No,' he said. 'I didn't think it was my place to ask, but perhaps I should have. Maybe I could've acted as a mediator, got them talking again before Etienne destroyed more of his work. I'm guessing you've seen the other mural, the one in the bathroom?'

'No hope of missing that horrorscape.'

'There are more, in other rooms.' He sighed. 'I should have done something about it.'

To disagree would be to belittle him. Instead, I suggested that we continue the tour.

'I know that far room is Etienne's bedroom,' I said, pointing along the corridor.

Benoit looked at me, nonplussed.

'I heard him wandering around in the night and was concerned he might fall down the stairs, so I helped him back to bed.'

'That was kind of you.'

I shrugged off the compliment. 'Happens all the time in my line of work. Steering drunk guests back to their rooms is very much a part of the job – probably too great a part, truth be told.'

'Etienne was probably confused,' Benoit said. 'He's only been sleeping in there since . . . for a few weeks. At least he didn't mistake his bedroom for yours and give you an even worse awakening.'

I noticed the way he said 'yours' – as if I'd been in residence here for weeks, as opposed to hours.

'I'm not sure what I would've done if I'd woken up to find him clambering into bed with me,' I mused, as the two of us

wandered through into a wide, square bedroom. It was decorated almost exclusively in beige – everything from the tatty,
textured wallpaper to the yellowing sheets on the bed. The
floorboards had inexplicably been hidden beneath cheap-
looking linoleum, and a squashy, cream leather chair stood
alone between the tall windows. We were at the front of the
house, and I could see the street below, the distant tips of
church spires, splodges of green where there were trees. A
door to the right of the bed opened into a modest-sized en
suite that was in dire need of modernisation, and I would
happily have taken a mallet to all the fixtures bar the oval
basin.

'This looks original,' I said, running a finger through the
dust on its surface. 'It's marble.'

Benoit moved in behind me to look. 'There are more of
them,' he said. 'I have one that's similar in my bathroom.'

'They go for around four thousand pounds each,' I told
him. 'I know from when we refurbished our place in London.'

'What about the tiles?' he asked hopefully. 'Do you think
those are original?'

I cast a critical eye over the plain white walls and shook my
head. 'Afraid not, although it's nice that they're clean . . . ish.'

We made our way into the second room along, and I began
to map the house in my head. Next door to Beige Basin
Room was Triffid Room, so named for the alarming mural
Etienne had daubed on its walls, which began behind the
iron-framed bed and spread halfway across the ceiling.

'At least he painted on the wallpaper,' Benoit mused, sticking his finger under a corner that was peeling away. 'Means
we can get rid of it easily.'

His use of the plural 'we' did not go unnoticed.

The room Etienne had been sleeping in looked much the
same as it had the previous night, with more obvious dust on

account of the shutters being open. The barge-like four-poster, while not in itself offensive, was far too large for the space, and when I pulled aside the drapes to check the state of the fabric, several moths fluttered out. It was not weeks of neglect I was seeing evidence of, but months – perhaps even years.

'Do you know when it was last used as a guesthouse?' I asked Benoit, as the two of us trooped back out into the corridor and headed upstairs.

'Etienne and Lilah would have friends to stay occasionally, but I don't remember there being any paying customers here for a long while. Etienne's ex-wife, Juliet, she was the one running that side of things. After she left, which was over five years ago now, I guess it all became too much for him?'

'She left him, did she?'

He paused before nodding in agreement. 'Etienne's issues with alcohol pre-date me. According to my mother, he's long been in a cycle of drinking, recovery and falling back off the wagon. Juliet bore the brunt of it, and eventually, she ran out of steam.'

'Everyone has their limit,' I said, and he smiled grimly.

'I guess they do.'

The next room we went into wasn't a bedchamber but a billiard room-cum-library, complete with rolling ladder, faded armchairs, and what I took to be an old-fashioned card table. The billiard table was shrouded beneath a greying sheet, the surface of which was littered with small, dark pellets.

Benoit and I exchanged a look.

'What's the French for mice?' I asked.

'*Souris*,' he said grimly.

'Very apt. It is in a *souris* state of affairs, this room.'

His mouth twitched. 'Did you just make a joke?'

'It has been known.'

Lifting the edge of the sheet, I peeled it back gingerly, but to my relief, the table itself was relatively undamaged. The same could not be said for the larger of the two chairs. Removing a limp cushion revealed a number of nibbled holes, and something had excavated the armrest and trailed horsehair and muslin innards all over the floor.

'Should we open the shutters?' Benoit asked, going towards the nearest window.

'If you want, but they've probably been closed on purpose to protect the books from sun damage. The table, too, for that matter – although we could use some air in here.'

While he busied himself with levering open windows and reclosing the shutters over them, I made my way to the bookcase and ran a finger along the spines. Every one of them was cloaked in dust, as sad and forsaken as Etienne himself.

'Ready to keep going?' Benoit said, and I smiled through my dread.

'Honestly? No. But let's carry on anyway.'

Of the four remaining rooms, three were bedrooms. We began in what Benoit called 'the morning room', but which seemed to be a dumping ground for boxes, broken furniture, and stacks upon stacks of canvases, each one protected by a layer of bubble wrap. The patterned wallpaper sagged, and had come away in places, though the plaster behind appeared intact. Hidden in a narrow alcove, there was a kitchenette area, the sink blotted with spools of rust. I attempted to pick up a plate, but it had adhered itself to the counter with gunk, and there were more mouse droppings inside the drawers.

'Etienne used to paint in here,' Benoit told me, pushing the toe of his trainer across the stained rug. 'It's the only corner room with two sets of windows, and so gets the best light.'

I glanced up to where cobwebs hung down from the brass chandelier, saw more festooned across a folded easel, and was overcome by the tragedy of it all. How unnecessarily dismal this house had become. Creativity must once have thrived within these walls, but now, only misery flourished. As if on cue, mournful strains of music began to drift up from downstairs. Benoit caught my eye, the two of us sharing an exasperated smile, and then he motioned towards the door.

'The room across from this one is the master bedroom.'

I nodded, understanding the tentative warning, appreciating the chance he was giving me to avoid the place where my mother had slept.

'It's fine,' I said, as the boards creaked beneath our feet. 'I'll be fine,' I reiterated, as he turned the handle. Benoit went first, and I followed, sensing the softness of carpet, seeing a glimpse of another mural, this one depicting blossom, the petals intricate, beautiful. A scent reached me, not the mustiness I'd come to associate with much of the house, but something richer, sweeter.

'No,' I said, my body beginning to tremor. 'I don't—sorry.'

My elbow connected hard with the doorframe as I stumbled away, but I barely felt it, didn't stop until my back was pressed up against the opposite wall. It took Benoit a few seconds to realise I'd gone astray, though when he reappeared and saw the expression on my face, his own features softened.

'It's just . . .' I began helplessly, as he closed the bedroom door.

'Too soon. I understand. Don't worry about it. *Ce n'est pas grave.*'

More of the melancholy music filtered up from the ground floor, accompanied by Etienne as he began warbling along.

Benoit went to the banister rail and peered down, before turning back to me. 'Do you want to get out of here?'

'Yes.' I nodded furiously, unable to stop the desperate, strangled laughter that followed. 'Please. Anywhere, I don't care. Just not here.'

He thought for a moment, his eyes lighting up as an idea came to him. 'I know just the place,' he said.

12

Once we were outside, I drew in one deep lungful of air, followed by another.

'Better?' Benoit removed a pair of sunglasses from the neck of his T-shirt and slid them on.

The second of my breaths had been caught by a yawn, and I flapped a hand in front of my face, momentarily unable to answer him.

'If you need a nap, then we can—'

'I don't,' I assured him, blinking moisture from my eyes. 'What I need is to be somewhere clean, and without clutter.'

'The place I have in mind is a bit of a stroll away – are you OK with that?'

'Very much so.'

Extending an arm along the street, he pointed us in the opposite direction to the one I'd taken in search of coffee that morning, and the two of us set off in single file along the narrow pavement. Benoit didn't say anything for a few minutes, though the silence that settled between us wasn't an uncomfortable one. It gave me the time I needed to recalibrate, draw some comfort from the warmth of the mid-morning sun, and he appeared to be in no hurry to interrupt. As far as I had been able to discern, there was very little ego at play with Benoit.

A small restaurant came into view up ahead, and he slowed as we drew level, casting his eye over the chalkboard menu outside. I recognised several of the words, though not with enough confidence to attempt a translation.

'Are those the specials?'

He half-turned, cleared his throat. 'Salmon rillettes, rabbit stew and chocolate-cinnamon meringues.'

'Meringues, yes please. The rest, not so much.'

'Ah, *oui*,' he said. 'You're a vegetarian.'

'I don't think I'd eat rabbit even if I wasn't.'

A waiter emerged in a crisp white shirt and matching ankle-length apron, and immediately Benoit moved away, smiling but shaking his head as the man rattled off a stream of French.

'What did he say?' I asked.

'That the lunch service is full, and they have no available bookings this evening either. It's a popular place,' he added. 'I worked there for a summer, and it was tough going.'

'Only one summer?'

'It was a quite few years ago now.' Benoit cast a final look over his shoulder. 'I was still trying to decide where I wanted to be, and what kind of chef I was.'

'How about now? Are you working somewhere else, or . . .?'

He smiled faintly. 'Or.'

I waited for him to say more, but no further explanation was forthcoming. We reached the end of the street, and I saw the glitter of sunlight on water ahead. A river, low and wide, smooth running. What was it I'd read online about Libourne while I waited in the departure lounge at Heathrow Airport?

'Is that the Dordogne?'

'No.' Benoit smiled reassuringly. 'That's the Isle – it forks off from the Dordogne along there, see?'

I squinted into the distance and was just able to make out an area where the river broadened before banking away. There was an arched bridge over which cars and motor-bikes sped, while along a neatly paved promenade, people sat in groups, ran behind small children, or perched in the shade of several mature trees, watching the occasional boat glide past. Water had power – a lure that proved itself to be irresistible, time and time again. Even Lady Thames, murky and treacherous as she was, had offered me comfort in times of strife.

'Two rivers,' I murmured. 'I might grow to like it here after all.'

'It was Lilah's favourite spot,' he said, and I stiffened. 'She used to sit down on the bank, at the place where the rivers run together, sometimes for hours, watching the water.'

When I didn't reply, he turned to look at me.

'Sorry, I shouldn't have said anything.'

'It's OK,' I began. 'It's just that . . . I hadn't seen my mum for a long time before— I don't honestly know all that much about her.'

Benoit's whole body appeared to slump, but I didn't want his pity, and when he asked if I'd like to see the spot, I shook my head.

'Another time perhaps.'

We crossed the road and followed the Isle away from the centre of Libourne, the newer pathway far easier to navigate than the cracked slabs and uneven cobbles of the old town. On the far side of the riverbank lay one exquisite residence after another, the rear gardens of each stretching down to meet the water below. Small wooden boats were moored against jetties, some slick, freshly painted, others little more than a collection of rotten planks. I saw a flash of white, and a heron burst up from among the reeds, wings open, head held high.

'Stunning,' I breathed, as the bird soared in a high arc.

'I don't come down here enough,' Benoit said. 'It's nice to have an excuse to take a walk.'

'I don't get out half as much as I'd like either,' I said. 'I used to lead walking groups, but that feels as if it was a lifetime ago.'

'Hotel keep you busy, does it?'

'Very,' I agreed.

'How long has it been up and running?'

'Not long,' I admitted. 'Around three months, but there was a lot of work to do before that. What about you? How long have you been living at the guesthouse?'

Benoit thought before answering. 'This summer, only for a month or so,' he said. 'I came not long before Lilah— Before it happened.' He glanced towards me. 'And now, well, you've seen the state Etienne has got himself into. I would have stayed to look after him regardless.'

'That's very selfless,' I said, and he shrugged. 'Is there nobody else in your family willing to help?'

'It's complicated,' Benoit said, snapping a twig off an overhanging tree and breaking it into pieces. 'Most of my family – his family – have given up on him. They still care, but they're tired of being let down, I suppose. People think they can fix Etienne, and become frustrated when they can't.'

'Self-preservation,' I said, and he glanced towards me, smiled fleetingly. 'If your family have given up, it's because they had to, for the sake of their own sanity.'

'I like to think there's a future in which they can be reunited,' he said. 'Divisions like this happen, the years roll past, and before you know it, someone has died and it's too late. I don't want that to happen.'

I was stung by his words, by the implication behind them, and said nothing.

'I have faith,' he went on hesitantly, as if testing the statement for truth. 'I still believe Etienne will change, that once this new pain he's feeling begins to lessen, he'll feel hopeful again.'

I was shaking my head.

'You don't agree?'

'Sorry, no. I wish I could, but I don't.'

Benoit's expression did not change, though I recognised the hurt in his posture, the way he pinned back his shoulders to stand a few inches taller. 'So, you're a pessimist?' he said.

'A pessi-Flisst?'

He raised an eyebrow.

'I would argue that I'm a realist,' I said.

'You don't believe that people deserve a second chance?'

'Of course they do,' I countered. 'Second, third and perhaps even fourth chances – but how many of those has Etienne had? Is he on his second, or his hundredth?'

Benoit chewed his lip. 'There have been a few,' he allowed. 'My mother tried for years, and in the end, it all became too sad. He used to call her in the middle of the night. I remember it from when I was a child. He'd tell her these outlandish stories that she later found out were lies, fantasies, and eventually, she stopped believing anything he told her; the trust was gone. She's sad about losing Etienne, but always tells me she'd feel sadder if he was still a part of her life.'

'Do you ever feel sad about it?' I asked, and he nodded briskly. 'But you're still here?'

We had reached a point where the path ended, a steep set of steps banking up towards road level. Benoit paused with

his foot on the first, turning so he was facing me. I could see
the river reflected in his sunglasses, the same faultless blue as
the sky above.

'Still here,' he confirmed. 'And, unlike everyone else, I'm
not going to give up on him.'

13

While it was no longer possible to look out across the Isle once we were up on street level, the second half of our walk turned out to be every bit as interesting as the first.

Chelsea, with its avenues of multimillion-pound townhouses and designer boutiques, was intimidating in its exclusivity, whereas Libourne exuded more of an 'anyone's welcome here' charm. I was beginning to see beauty in the peeling wooden doorways and wildly overgrown gardens, and found that I appreciated the lack of uniformity: one moment we wandered past the gates of a crumbling chateau, then the next I was peering through the windows of shops. Dwellings varied in size from tiny, two-windowed terraces to mighty, corner-plotted abodes, some of which were pristine while others appeared abandoned. I asked Benoit why so many had been left to the elements.

'I don't think they have been,' he said. 'What is it people call it – shabby chic?'

'Shabby chic sounds about right.'

'These houses,' he went on, 'a lot of them are old, seriously old. To cover up all the cracks would be to erase the building's history, lose all that Libourne magic.'

'Leave cracks long enough, and they become holes,' I warned. 'And holes become damp, and damp becomes—'

'Expensive to repair,' he finished. 'Believe me, I know. The cracks that have become holes are what keep Adélard in business.'

'I thought he was a carpenter?' I said, to which Benoit chuckled.

'Carpenter, plasterer, decorator ... Adélard will do anything.' He had put significant emphasis on the 'anything', and I caught the tail end of a smirk as it fell from his lips.

'Do you two go back a long way?' I asked.

'Quite long. I think we met when I was fifteen, so he would have been around seventeen. He'll tell you that I used to get him into trouble, but it was always him who was the instigator – he still is the instigator, most of the time.'

'Still?'

Benoit diverted my attention by pointing out a small vineyard up ahead. I listened with only half an ear while he explained about acreage and profit margins. The manufacture and distribution of alcohol was of little interest to me, and having elicited little more than a polite 'Hmm' from me by way of response, he dropped the subject. The sun was high, its heat intense, a scouring pad against my exposed skin. I needed shade, a cold drink, another layer of sun lotion.

'Is it much further?'

Benoit seemed impervious to the rocketing temperatures; he was cool and collected, with not so much as a single bead of sweat on his lips, whereas I could feel trails of perspiration running in rivulets down the small of my back and dampening my hairline.

'We're almost there,' he assured me. 'It's the next left, just up ahead.'

The path leading off the main street felt gloriously cool, shaded as it was by vast trees. Loose stones tumbled away beneath my feet, the ground more dirt track than pavement, dappled by shoals of sunlight. Behind the low rumble of traffic back up on the road, and the merry song of birds up among the branches, there was another sound, suspiciously animal.

'We're here,' Benoit said, nodding across to a large sign that read: 'Ferme de la Barbanne'.

'A farm,' I said, as realisation dawned. 'You brought me to a farm?'

Benoit continued to smile benignly. 'I like the peacocks,' he said.

'They have those here?'

'They have all sorts of birds and beasts – come on.'

Chain-link fences bordered each side of the path inside, and I stared through at roosters, hens and, further along, a large number of pheasants.

'Hello,' I cooed, crouching to admire the bright, rich colour of their feathers, the smooth turquoise necks and tawny breasts.

Benoit scooted down beside me.

'I suppose you're dreaming up all the ways in which you'd cook them,' I said.

Taking off his sunglasses, he eyed me as if affronted. 'I'm not that ravenous a carnivore – and anyway,' he added, 'pheasant is better to look at than eat. A lot of the boys I went to school with would boast about going out to shoot them on the weekends, and I always thought it was an unnecessary cruelty – pain for not much gain.'

'Must have been some school you attended,' I said, thinking of the inner-city comprehensive where I'd battled through my teenage years.

Benoit looked grim. 'It was something alright,' he said. 'Something I'd never inflict on a child of my own. My mother got it into her head that in order to succeed in England, you had to enmesh yourself with future politicians and aristocrats, which in my case meant being bundled off to a boarding school.'

'That bad?'

'Awful,' he said. 'I managed two years, after which I begged to leave.'

I studied him for a moment, trying to picture him aged eleven or twelve, gangly in that way teenage boys so often are, no longer children but still a giant leap away from adulthood. I wondered if he had always been so measured and considerate, or if the quietness in him had come from somewhere more unsavoury, an experience or event that had taught him to be cautious. I knew only too well how deep a trench childhood trauma could mine.

We moved along from the pheasants to a pen of goats, all of which propped their sturdy hooves on the fence and nibbled at our clothes in search of food. Benoit scooted out of reach, but I leaned in, stretching over to scratch the coarse fur behind their ears.

'How was school for you?' he asked. 'I assume you did well, given where you are now.'

'You mean the hotel? That had nothing to do with any grades or qualifications. I started right at the bottom,' I told him, wiping goat saliva from my forearm on to the grass. 'Got my first paid job at a women's refuge, then worked at a hostel that housed ex-offenders, primarily women or younger adults. It was tough work, but I enjoyed it, did well there, and then I carried on, went from a small place to a bigger premises. Then from there, I was tempted into hotels. Took me a while to adjust to the new clientele.'

'Which did you prefer?' Benoit asked, and I smiled as I answered.

'The former.'

The goats had moved away from us and begun to strip the leaves from a small tree inside their enclosure. A woman wandered past with a buggy, singing to her dozing infant in French. There was a parasol clipped to the arm of the pushchair, and all I could see of the child was two pudgy legs and a pair of rainbow-striped socks. Charlie had a pair the same.

'You're a grafter,' Benoit stated, rousing me from my thoughts. 'Hit the bottom and you can use it to bounce back up to the top – that's something my father used to say a lot,' he added, as I turned to face him. 'That adversity is a stepping stone to greatness.'

'Now I see where you get your positive mental attitude from.'

'Perhaps so,' he allowed, as we moved across to the next pen.

This one was home to a flock of geese, all of which hurried over to greet us, waddling on their flat feet.

'I started out on the lowest rung as well,' he said, 'kitchen porter at a village pub. Six pounds seventeen pence an hour, if I remember rightly – might even have been more, with a share of tips.'

'You must've enjoyed it?' I said, removing my fingers from the fence just in time to avoid being pecked by one of the bolshier geese. By contrast, the bird that had approached Benoit was seemingly content to have its beak stroked.

'I'm not someone suited to an office job – anything involving a desk and not moving for hours on end,' he said. 'I have to be doing something, moving my body, preferably cooking.'

'What drives you – hunger?'

'Sometimes,' he said, throwing me a sidelong glance, 'but mostly, I do it for others. Preparing a meal, watching people enjoy it – it's a small thing but, I don't know, it brings me pleasure.'

'I know what you mean,' I said. 'The part of my job I like the most is creating a space for people, somewhere they can relax, feel instantly at home, have access to everything they need – plus things they didn't even realise they wanted.'

Benoit smiled, though a few moments passed before he spoke again. 'Earlier on, back at the house, I got the impression that you weren't particularly happy.'

'Whatever gave you that idea?' I said drily.

'And I get it,' he continued. 'You were in shock after the will reading; it was a lot to absorb.'

I could sense a 'but' looming.

Benoit had paused his petting of the goose, though it continued to gaze up at him adoringly while its companion hissed at me.

'In an ideal world,' he said, 'what would you do with your share?'

He wasn't going to like what I had to say.

'I'd sell it,' I said, through a sigh. 'Sell it and walk away.'

Benoit looked as though he had been expecting this – his eyes dulled, and his jaw loosened. 'What if I told you there was a way of doing exactly that?'

My head shot up. 'I thought there were rules.'

'There are,' he agreed. 'The house can't be sold in Etienne's lifetime, but there's nothing in the will stipulating that you can't transfer ownership.'

'You mean . . .'

'We find an investor,' he said. 'Someone to buy you out, a business partner for me.'

Elation blossomed, only for its petals to immediately drop.

'But the state of the place,' I said with a moan. 'It's – well, it's awful, isn't it?'

'Nothing that can't be fixed.' Benoit's eyes flickered to mine. 'If we work together.'

I went very still. 'What exactly are you proposing here?'

'You said it yourself: the guesthouse has potential. And you know better than me how to bring that potential out. If you can extend your stay by a few weeks, we can clear the place out, mend what needs to be mended. and transform it into an enticing opportunity for someone looking to invest. I would eventually like to run it as a guesthouse again.'

I stared at him until my eyes felt dry. 'You're serious?' I said, and Benoit began to bounce on his tiptoes.

'Very serious. It's the perfect solution. Everyone gets what they want, and we all end up happy.'

'You make it sound so easy.'

'Because it is,' he insisted. 'A few weeks, that's all I'm asking, and then you can walk away and forget all about this place and everyone in it, if that's what you want.'

'I don't know what I want,' I said, flustered. 'There's stuff going on in London; it's not ideal.'

Benoit cocked his head to one side. 'Tell me what is,' he said. 'This is what life is like, Fliss – one snagged fishbone in the throat after another. It's up to you whether you're going to swallow, or if you're going to let it choke you.'

'I don't let anything choke me.'

'There you go, then.'

'That's not a yes,' I said sternly. 'I'll need to make some calls first.'

'OK.' He beamed at me, a smile so wide that I was in danger of falling right into it. 'But I really believe this could work, that we could work well together – don't you?'

'Maybe,' I said, though privately I had no such qualms. Was it truly possible to feel so at ease with someone I barely knew? I couldn't deny there was something distinct between Benoit and me, our pieces moving together like magnets on a board – though what it meant, I did not know, could not say.

I only knew that it must mean something.

14

It was late afternoon when we returned to the centre of Libourne, but rather than taking the road back past the restaurant, Benoit led me further along the river, towards the bridge he'd pointed out earlier in the day.

I knew I should call Charlie, fill him in on what had happened at the will reading and talk to him about the possibility of extending my stay in France, but the resentment was still there, crackling away inside. Several times during the walk back, Benoit had asked if I was OK, observing that I seemed quiet. I couldn't confide in him about Charlie, though. I was too embarrassed, ashamed to admit that my fiancé had gone elsewhere in search of affection.

'I'll make us something to eat when we get back,' he said, as we waited at a crossing for several cars to pass. 'Anything in particular you're craving?'

I was not remotely hungry, and settled on an 'Up to you,' distracted by the vibration of my phone inside my bag. Not a notification bearing Charlie's name, or even Angela's.

The blood drained from my cheeks.

'Can we talk?' Madeline had written.

'No,' I muttered aloud. 'We bloody can't.'

'What was that?' Benoit dipped his head towards me as I tapped at the screen, deleting her message in irritation. A car horn sounded and, stowing my phone, I hurried over the road. There was a bar on the corner ahead, not far from a small roundabout, its outdoor seating area alive with activity. As we skirted the furthest edge, someone called out, and I turned to see Adélard waving at us.

'*Salut!*' he called. 'Come and have a drink.'

'Do you want to?' Benoit asked. It was clear he wanted to, and I had no real reason to refuse.

Adélard greeted me like an old friend, leaping from his seat to kiss each of my cheeks.

'*Biere?*' he offered. '*Ah, non – vin. Rouge ou blanc?*'

'A Diet Coke is fine, thanks.'

'*D'accord,*' he said, and wheeled off inside.

Benoit fetched an empty chair from a neighbouring table, and we both sat. The air in the seating area was thick with cigarette smoke and the easy chatter of well-versed friends.

I stared around, feeling oddly conspicuous. Bars were not somewhere I found myself very often, not since work had taken over my social life. I explained this to Benoit, and he nodded in understanding.

'When I was cheffing in London, there was a drinking culture that went alongside it. If you didn't go out with the staff after your shift ended, you were seen as *le freak*.'

'Decompression time,' I said. 'I've worked near enough hotel kitchens to know how chaotic they can be.'

'They can,' he allowed, 'but I do my best decompression alone – a long walk, a bit of music or a podcast. I did a lot of pavement pounding during my London years.'

'For me, it was the teenage years,' I told him. 'My dad volunteered as a walking guide at weekends, and I started to go with him – anything to avoid being at home.'

Benoit looked as if he wanted to reply, but the two of us were interrupted by Adélard, returning with two vast goblets of beer and my soft drink clutched between his big hands.

'*Santé*,' he said, crashing his glass against ours. 'And how are we?'

Benoit steeled himself for a moment and threw a glance in my direction.

'It's OK,' I reassured him. 'Go ahead and tell him what happened.'

This Benoit did, though in French rather than English. I watched as Adélard's face registered first concern, then open astonishment, followed by what looked to be enthusiasm.

'What was it that I said to you this morning?' he crowed to me. 'About opening a hotel. Turns out I was right, *non*?'

'Maybe,' I said, sipping my Diet Coke. It was swimming with ice, and there was a bedraggled slice of lime floating on its surface.

'Ah, but you must,' he insisted. 'And we must celebrate. Felicity, what will you have? Champagne?'

I had just taken a gulp of my drink, and so responded with a vigorous shake of my head.

'*Pourquoi pas?* This is a special occasion.'

Benoit put a hand on his friend's arm, murmuring to him in French.

Adélard's eyes widened. 'Ah, you are teetotal?' He pressed a hand against his cheek. 'Sorry, sorry.'

'It's fine,' I said, keen to squash the subject. Adélard fanned away a hovering wasp. 'It's not a big deal.'

Why did I always do this – diminish a subject that was important to me, that I felt so strongly about? I knew why. Because talking about sobriety meant talking about my reasons for it, which meant talking about *her*. Adélard was scrutinising me, and I looked away, past the boundary of the seating area towards the glittering surface of the river. His concern scratched at me, wire wool against my resolve not to feel weak. What I wanted, and needed, was to remain strong.

'Where's Madame?' I asked, peering beneath the table.

'She is at the salon,' Adélard said.

'Don't ask,' Benoit said lightly, as I caught his eye. 'That dog's beauty regime would put most supermodels to shame.' As he spoke, his hands worked, wiping the condensation off his glass, turning it around on the tabletop, drumming his fingertips against the wood.

'How long ago did you quit?' I asked, and he looked at me askance. 'The cigarettes,' I went on. 'I can recognise a fellow former smoker when I see one.'

'Four months ago,' he said. 'I thought I was doing well, and then summer started . . .'

'I get it. It's so much harder to avoid temptation at this time of year.'

'I tried to stop last summer,' he said.

'And you would have succeeded,' put in Adélard, 'if it was not for Cé—'

'That had nothing to do with it,' Benoit said, cutting across his friend. Then, turning to me, 'How long ago did you quit?'

'Almost three years ago now. I made a pact with my partner: if he gave up cigars, I would give up my beloved Marlboros.'

'Cigars?' Benoit very nearly choked on a mouthful of beer. 'Who are you dating, Tony Soprano?'

'He might have been less trouble,' I replied drily. 'But no. To the best of my knowledge, I am yet to date a mobster.'

'Well, there's always time.'

Adélard was observing our exchange with open amusement. He had got almost to the end of his beer, and now leaned back in his chair, trying to catch the attention of a passing server. The noise level had continued to rise at a steady rate since we'd sat down, and having tuned in to it, I was struggling to zone back out again. Benoit's lips were moving, but I couldn't make out what he was saying; my head was too full, senses overstimulated by the clamour around me.

'I'm going to go,' I said, standing abruptly.

Benoit reached for his glass. 'I'll come with you.'

'No, please don't. You stay. I know the way back from here.'

He looked as if he was about to argue, but before he could get a word out, my phone began to ring, and I held it aloft triumphantly.

'I should get this,' I said, forgetting until a moment too late about Madeline's message, her plea to talk that I had ignored. My stomach dropped for a few awful seconds, skin clammy with dread at the prospect of a confrontation, of yet more bad news. But it wasn't my fiancé's lover at the other end of the phone; it was the man himself.

15

As first dates went, ours had been anything but conventional.

Given that he was doing his best to stay away from the temptation of alcohol, and I openly abhorred it, Charlie had surprised me by suggesting we meet at the Blue Anchor pub in Hammersmith. He was standing outside when I arrived, clutching a Waitrose bag for life, out of which poked two plastic sticks.

'Felicity,' he'd said, bending to kiss me shyly on the cheek. 'Thanks for coming.'

It had been hard to wrangle myself a Sunday afternoon off, but the smile he offered me made it feel worthwhile. Instead of leading me inside the pub, Charlie had gestured to a path leading down towards the River Thames.

'I thought we could go litter-picking,' he'd said, to which I blinked at him stupidly.

'Litter-picking?'

'I bought you a grabber,' Charlie raised the bag, 'so you won't have to use your hands.'

'It's not that . . .' I had stared at him, trying not to laugh, hopelessly touched by his attempt to find common ground with me. It made sense, after all, given where we'd met.

'If you don't want to, we can do something else,' he'd said then. 'Clean graffiti from under the bridges along Camden Canal; stand at crossings and wait for old people to escort across?'

I had laughed then, for what felt like the first time in a very long while, and let myself relax into the rhythm of him, enjoying his compliments and relishing the attention he bestowed upon me. As we collected discarded plastic bottles, nappies, make-up wipes and crisp wrappers from the muddy bankside, Charlie had opened up about his childhood, explaining how he'd struggled at school, how he tried to please his stern father, how his need to be liked had led him inevitably towards drink and recreational drugs, and how bad those problems had become.

'Volunteering was my sister's idea. She's barely ever wrong about anything, is Olivia, and she thought it would do me good to be a bit humble for a change. Do something good, you know? Give back. Turns out, it's rather good fun, and' – he'd turned to me, reached for my hand – 'the women are far sexier than I'd dared hope they'd be.'

When he then moved in to kiss me, I'd been only too thrilled to kiss him back, had marvelled at having encountered such a man, whom I felt at the time had been designed purely for me.

It was this version that I held in my mind as I talked to him now – the sober version, the selfless version, the version I yearned for him to be again.

Charlie, once filled in about all that had happened, responded far better than I had expected.

'And you think it's salvageable, this guesthouse place?'

I pictured the marble basins and sturdy walls, the pergola with its canopy of wisteria, Benoit's pristine kitchen, the intricate pattern of painted blossom glimpsed through a half-open door.

'I do, yes.'

Below me, the river churned. Instead of going back towards the house, I'd headed from the bar to the bridge to continue my call. The promenade was still teeming with groups of people. A section of the smooth concrete had been painted in rainbow stripes, and two young girls were taking it in turns to hopscotch across them. A yearning sensation was building inside my chest – but yearning for what? To be young again? Definitely not. To be a mother with children of my own? That one was trickier. We had discussed it, Charlie and I, but only in passing, a conversation during which we'd both assured the other that becoming parents was part of the eventual plan. He'd said it, I was sure, because he'd meant it, whereas my motivation was more dubious.

'How many weeks are we talking about?' Charlie asked.

'Two – maybe three. We won't know how much needs patching up or replacing until we clear out the majority of the junk.'

'Do you remember how bad The Fitz was when we took it over?' he said. 'All those packing cases full of rubbish.'

'I still feel awful about that,' I said. 'I can't believe the family didn't want them.'

The boxes we'd discovered, crammed into a closet in the largest bedroom, were full of handwritten cards, letters and photographs. Charlie had been borderline ruthless, insisting we 'toss the lot', but I had gone through each one with pains-taking patience, selecting a few of the more captivating photos to frame and hang in our modest lobby.

'We don't even know this person,' he'd said, nonplussed, as he stared at an image of a young woman, in 1960s attire, smiling shyly for the camera as she cuddled a rabbit in her arms. But someone knew her – or had known her.

'How are things at The Fitz?' I asked, and Charlie sighed.

'I spoke to that fire guy – what's his name again, Hinch something?'

'Hinshelwood,' I reminded him. 'Crew Commander Hinshelwood.'

'Well, according to him, we can't reopen to customers until we have a new fire-safety certificate, and we won't get one of those until the majority of the repairs are done. Why we can't simply rope off that area and carry on as normal, I don't know. Seems a bit harsh.'

'Safety first,' I said. 'I'm sure that—'

'Costs keep going up,' he interrupted. 'Seems the roof is damaged – the insulation can't be patched. It needs replacing.'

I balked at that. 'How much are we talking?'

'Oh, a few extra thou.' The way he said it made it sound as if four zeros amounted to pennies. 'I'll bung it all on the Amex, and we can pay if off when you find your investor.'

The two girls had stopped their game of hopscotch and were now crouched together on the steps, below where I was sitting, one plaiting the other's hair while they sang a nonsense song.

It was my inheritance he was casually talking about using: money belonging to me, being used to fix a problem that he had created. I had been cheated on, and now I was the one who must pay for it. The unfairness fizzed amid the still-festering resentment.

'Have you been drinking?' I asked.

Charlie grunted. 'Well, I'm not drunk right this minute, if that's what you're getting at.'

'But you are still drinking?'

When he sighed, I matched it with one of my own.

'Charlie . . .'

'Fliss . . .'

'You said you'd try. After the fire, you promised.'

'And I have been. But all this, it's been pretty bloody stressful.'

'I knew coming here was a bad idea,' I said. 'You shouldn't be by yourself if—'

'Flickster, it's fine.' Charlie's voice had become staccato. 'I'm not by myself. I have people helping me.'

A breeze swept in across the water, lifting strands of my hair. 'People?'

'Staff,' he said cagily.

'Oh, Charlie,' I said, failing to hide my impatience. 'We talked about this. Madeline has to go.'

'I can't very well sack her, can I? We'd be leaving ourselves wide open to a lawsuit if I did that.'

Again with the 'we'. It was he who had done this; he who had gone behind my back; he who'd been unable to control himself. For all the mitigating factors he'd impressed upon me – how I neglected him, how work came before him, how he needed alcohol to do the job he did, bringing in customers and therefore revenue – I refused to accept that it was entirely my fault. We were both guilty of coasting within the relationship, but he had gone further than I ever would have. Being unfaithful was so basic, and tawdry.

Someone was smoking a spliff, the sharp, herbal scent uncomfortably reminiscent of my teenage years: school nights spent huddled under the slide in the park, burn holes in the fabric of my anorak, nails painted white with Tipp-Ex, illicit roll-ups passed from one grubby hand to another. I never wanted to go home when my father was at work, was always the last to leave the recreation ground, often forced to climb over the locked gates to get out.

'Can't you talk to her?' I said, thinking again of Madeline's earlier message. 'Surely she must see that staying on is impossible?'

He made a noncommittal noise.

'If not, I suppose *I* could call her.'

'No,' Charlie said with feeling. 'I mean, you've got enough in your trough.' This Charlie-ism would probably have made me laugh under any other circumstances. 'I'll tell her tomorrow,' he went on. 'Encourage her, very kindly, to resign – consider it done, sorted, swiped left.'

I drew in a breath, exhaled it slowly. 'Remind me again why I put up with you?'

'Because you're kind,' he said, 'and you believe in me. Plus, you know I couldn't do any of this life stuff without you. Seriously,' he went on, 'you're the pin keeping it all in place – pull you out and I'll sag like a deflated Space Hopper. Bloody hell, Fliss – I know I don't deserve you, not even close, but I am doing my best. I'm trying.'

'I know you are.' I sighed heavily. 'I know that.'

'Hang on a tick, do you want me to come out there?' he asked, instantly energised by the notion. 'I might be able to help.'

It was my turn to say no. 'It's not because I don't want to see you,' I added. 'I do – I just think one of us has to stay at The Fitz and oversee the repair work. It's too important to leave in anyone else's hands.'

Charlie considered this. We had planned the redecoration together before I left for France, agreeing to stick to the original palette and simple-yet-sophisticated décor. He'd been all for painting the walls a dark red colour, but I'd steered him gently but firmly towards the same salt-white shade we'd chosen for the other bedrooms, disregarding his plea of: 'This is our chance to try something different.' Trusting him not to stray outside the lines of this plan had been a decision I'd had no choice but to make. The fact that he was seemingly keen to pass it into the hands of someone else concerned me.

'You *are* overseeing the work, aren't you?' I said. 'You're at The Fitz now?'

'Of course I am.'

'Because we can't afford for anything to go wrong – as in, we literally can't afford it.'

'I know that,' he said, only to immediately temper his tone. 'Sorry, Fliss, it's—You can count on me, you know.'

'Can I?' I looked away from the water, down at my hand gripping the railing, the ring on my third finger sparkling as it caught the light. The sun was egg-yolk yellow, sliding down against its backdrop of sifted cloud.

'You have to,' he said. 'If this is going to work, if we are going to work, then you need to trust me. You do still love me, don't you?'

I readjusted the phone against my ear. 'What kind of a question is that?'

'A valid one,' he said. 'You've been so cold with me since the fire.'

With bloody good reason.

I closed my eyes briefly. 'Everything will be fine,' I said, and heard him exhale.

'OK, and you do love me?'

I hesitated, my mind holding up picture cards of litter-picking and first kisses; of proposals and promises made, of a future spent with the man I knew Charlie could be.

'Of course,' I said, turning my back to the sun. 'Of course I do.'

16

The first thing I became aware of when I woke the following morning was a scraping noise.

I lay still for a few moments, listening. It was as if something was trapped inside the walls of the room, clawing to get out. Not a mouse, but something larger, more substantial.

Rubbing away the grit that had settled hard as sand in the corners of my eyes, I got slowly out of bed. The scraping continued as I tugged a sweater on over my pyjamas, though less insistently, more of a whisper than a cleared throat. One of the shutters was open enough to reveal a crack of pale daylight. It was early, not yet seven, and I had stayed up until the small hours, scrolling mindlessly through my phone as I chewed through the Brie and rocket baguette I had picked up from the Carrefour. If Benoit had returned from the bar, he must have done so after I fell asleep, and that would have been long after last orders.

The bedroom door clicked shut behind me. The light in the corridor was muted. The scraping turned into a loud rip, and a swarm of dust rose up from below.

'Is that you, Fliss?' called a voice, and I looked down to see Benoit's face peering up at me through the banisters.

'Morning,' I said, coughing out the word through a clog of sleep. The floorboards creaked in protest as I made my way along the landing and down the stairs to join him. For someone who had presumably been out drinking until the small hours, Benoit looked positively perky. He had a flat-edged tool in one hand and a high colour in both his cheeks. I took in the blue jersey shorts and faded Fleetwood Mac T-shirt, the bare feet and curls of fallen wallpaper.

'You've been busy,' I said. 'How are you feeling?'

'Surprisingly, not hungover,' he said. 'Adélard kept me out late, but I switched to water when he wasn't looking.'

'Smart,' I said, 'though it doesn't explain why you're up so early.'

He grinned. 'Never have been a late sleeper. I also forgot to switch off my regular alarm. I was on the way to make myself a coffee and' – he gestured to the wall behind him – 'as usual, I had to dodge an overhanging flap of wallpaper – only this time, I decided to pull it off.'

We both looked down to where a pile of torn shards littered the stairs.

'Once I'd done the first few pieces, I got a taste for it,' he went on. 'So, I dug out this scraper and carried on. I've only been here about fifteen minutes, and look how much I've done.'

'It looks a lot better already,' I agreed. 'Quite the achievement.'

'I was inspired after our conversation yesterday,' he said. 'Getting this place in order is something I should've prioritised weeks ago. Consider this my attempt at making up for lost time.'

'Sounds as if you could use a hand,' I said, and his smile broadened.

'Does this mean . . .'

'Yes,' I said slowly, breaking into laughter as Benoit let out a gratified 'whoop'.

'You're going to stay?'

'For a few weeks, yes – but only a few.'

'A few weeks is great,' he enthused. '*Incroyable!*'

'But we're going to need a plan,' I said. 'I agree that we should tear down every mouldering piece of old wallpaper, but we should do it strategically. Work our way through the house, one room at a time, one task at a time, in an order that makes sense.'

Benoit stuck a hand into his shorts pocket, a studied expression on his face. 'Sounds to me as if that's a job for you,' he said. 'You make a plan, and I'll put it into action.'

I shook my head. 'I'm not letting you do everything. You might think I'm just some hoity-toity Chelsea hotelier, but I'm not afraid to get my hands dirty.'

Benoit laughed. 'Hoity-toity?'

'What would the French call it?'

'Hoity-toity,' he repeated, only this time with a thick French accent.

'Very funny.'

'I thought so.'

For a brief moment, we stared at each other. I could see the dance of humour in his sloe-blue eyes, and it lifted me, loosened the perpetual grip of my anxiety. Here was a man I didn't have to battle against, someone with the same goals as me, and someone whom instinct told me would be support-ive first and combative only if an extreme situation demanded it.

We began by going from room to room, compiling lists of what needed to be done in each, and how much, if anything, we would need to spend in order to achieve our aims. In most cases, I calculated that no materials more extravagant than Polyfilla, paint and wood varnish would be required, though several of the bathrooms required new fixtures, and we would also need the largest skip that Libourne had available.

The only rooms we didn't venture into were Benoit's, on the top floor, Etienne's, and the master bedroom that had once been my mother's, though I told myself I'd have to soon – that eventually, I'd have no choice but to face it.

Etienne emerged from his lair at around midday and stood for a while on the landing in his greying vest and pants, watching as Benoit and I scraped off the final patches of wallpaper. The older man's skin was sallow, the shadows beneath his eyes purple, as if bruised. He was difficult to look at, so I avoided doing so, bestowing a brief smile before turning my back.

'*Petit-déjeuner?*' Benoit offered – though, by rights, it was far too late in the day for breakfast.

Etienne grunted out a '*Non, merci,*' and shuffled into the bathroom, the sound of his peeing echoing out into the stairwell.

By tacit agreement, Benoit and I were working on the basis that any obvious rubbish could be thrown away, while other detritus, such as paperwork, ornaments, photos and assorted trinkets, would be put on one side to be organised at a later date. All I knew about hoarders was what I'd gleaned from watching documentaries about them, but I recalled that sensitivity was key. Neither of us wanted to upset Etienne, though neither could we realistically keep every item of junk he'd collected.

'I don't mind the books,' I said to Benoit, when later that afternoon we found ourselves in the library. I'd dragged him inside to reinspect the state of the billiard table, and discovered a crammed cupboard I hadn't seen before. 'But is there really any need for' – I paused to count – 'seventeen packs of playing cards?'

Benoit rolled a ball across the table, where it clunked satisfyingly against another. 'That does seem a bit excessive,' he allowed. 'What else is in there?'

I extracted a long, thin box. 'Dominoes,' I said, blowing a layer of dust off the wooden lid. 'And an extortionate number of jigsaw puzzles.'

'Never saw the point in those,' he said, coming across to crouch beside me. 'And is that French *Scrabble*?' He withdrew the box and shook it. 'Sounds as if there are only about ten letters in here.'

'Enough to spell out "Throw me away"?' I asked hopefully.

Reaching further into the cupboard, I encountered something that was both hard and soft, probing it for a few seconds before recoiling in disgust.

'What?' Benoit rocked back on his heels. 'Not a spider? If it's a spider, I'm leaving.'

I pressed my lips together to quell my laughter. 'You're happy to pet a goose, but you won't let a spider crawl on you?'

'Don't even say it,' he said, affecting a shudder. 'I feel like there's one on me.'

'I fear it's worse than a spider,' I said, removing more boxes. 'Ah, yes – see.'

There was a distinct tightness to Benoit's expression as he peered into the gloom. 'Oh no, is that a—'

'Desiccated mouse? Yes. Yes, it is.'

'*Merde*,' he muttered. 'And you didn't even scream.'

'Not my first time.'

Benoit rolled his shoulders violently. 'Do you think there are more?'

'Oh, yes. Where there's one, there are generally more – often hundreds more.'

'Hundreds?'

'They breed every few weeks. It's actually quite impressive.'

He paled, and, putting up a hand, began to back away.

'Don't worry,' I said, suppressing a grin. 'This one definitely won't be mating anytime soon.'

Benoit's cheeks bulged, a choking sound beginning in his throat as I ferried the tiny corpse to a rubbish sack.

'I'm going to go and wash my hands,' I told him. 'And then, I'm going out to buy mouse traps.'

17

Accustomed as I was to cold-shouldering intrusive thoughts, I nonetheless became aware of their circling menace as the day wore on, half-expecting to glance up and find them swarming above me like a plague of locusts.

It helped that there was so much to do. Concentrating on the house, and the practical tasks of clearing and organising, meant that dwelling time was kept to a minimum, and rather than being crushed by the pressure, I thrived, my sense of purpose reactivated. Traversing the corridors, stairways and rooms in bold strides, I held my chin high and body taut, scribbling notes as I went, creating a checklist to be ticked off, an endless means by which to sidestep the looming grief. Still, I supposed, it would catch up with me eventually.

It was several hours later, having ducked into my bedroom to answer an urgent email from Charlie regarding an issue with the hotel booking system, that I emerged to find Benoit jogging up the stairs.

'There you are,' he said. 'Dinner's ready.'

'Dinner? What time is it?'

Benoit slid his phone from the pocket of his shorts. 'Almost eight.'

As if in answer, my stomach growled. 'Is Etienne joining us?' I asked, rubbing it. 'I haven't seen him for ages.'

'Not tonight.' Benoit stretched across to pick at a scrap of wallpaper he'd missed. 'Some friends of his invited him over for supper. He wasn't going to go, but I managed to persuade him. He's barely left the house since' – his eyes darted to mine – 'since the funeral.'

'Oh.' A lump formed, and I swallowed it. 'Right, well, good for you – for him.'

'I hope you like *le fromage*,' he said, his bare feet making barely a sound on the smooth stone steps. The spaces on the banister where he'd placed his hands were still warm to the touch when I slid my own across them.

On the table beneath the pergola sat a vast wooden platter piled high with food – a charcuterie board, though without any cured meat. Instead, Benoit had arranged slices of apple, grapes, tomatoes and radishes around a large baked Camembert, flecked with flakes of chilli. A wedge of soft Brie was flanked by an assortment of crackers, and he'd sliced carrot sticks to dip into a bowl of creamy aioli. There was also a dish of baba ghanoush, several types of olive, and a still-steaming white baguette, fresh from the oven.

'You've gone to a lot of trouble,' I said.

'The cornichons aren't a step too far?'

By way of an answer, I popped one into my mouth.

Benoit passed across cutlery and a chipped plate patterned with birds. 'I put a lump of Cheddar on there as well,' he said, 'to remind you of home.'

'You know I live in London, not Somerset?'

'If you don't want it, we can put it in the mouse traps,' he said. 'How many did you buy, in the end?'

'Twenty,' I said, through a mouthful of ripe fig. 'I've set every single one, so hopefully by the morning we'll have twenty fewer furry guests staying with us.'

'You got the humane ones, didn't you?' he said airily, spearing the Camembert with a breadstick.

'I tried, but nowhere seemed to sell any.'

Benoit continued chewing.

'We probably won't catch any,' I went on, pulling a black grape off its stem. 'French mice are likely far smarter than their UK counterparts – and far more stylish, too, with their tiny berets.'

'Don't do that,' he pleaded in mock despair. 'Don't human-ise them.'

'Not berets, then – Berettas. Made especially for rodents, with seeds in place of bullets.'

'So, not only do these mice have opposable thumbs, but they also use them to blast seeds out? Meaning they are essentially gardeners, saving the world one planted flowerbed after another?'

I started to laugh. Benoit joined in, only to stop abruptly.

'That reminds me,' he said, sitting forwards and patting at his pockets. 'Must've left it in the kitchen – back in a sec.'

Expecting him to return with another dip of some kind, or perhaps more cheese, I was taken aback when he presented me with a small velvet box.

'You're not about to get down on one knee, are you?'

Benoit rolled his eyes. 'I came across it today,' he said, 'when I was helping Etienne find something to wear that wasn't an old smock. It was in his old bedroom, the one he shared with Lilah.'

The box was not much bigger than a conker; it disap-peared when I closed my fingers around it.

'Is this what I think it is?'

Benoit crunched on a radish. 'That depends.'

'It's my mother's ring, isn't it?'

Benoit nodded. 'I recognised it,' he said, 'and then I remembered about the will, and thought that—' His Adam's apple bobbed. 'She wanted you to have it.'

'I don't know why,' I said, aware of a tightening sensation in my stomach. 'She used to whisper things to it, you know – even kiss it sometimes.' I blinked the image away, forcing a smile as I put the box back on the table. 'Anyway, whatever. None of that matters anymore.'

Benoit carved a hand through his dark fringe. 'She kissed it – why?'

'Because she was drunk,' I said, feet beginning to tap beneath the table. 'Or mad, or both.'

Deliberately avoiding his eye, I cut myself a slice of Brie, using the same knife to smear it across a cracker that promptly crumbled into pieces.

'There's not much point asking me anything about my mum. You probably knew her far better than me.'

'How long had it been since . . .?'

'Fifteen years.'

'Oh.'

'Oh,' I intoned. 'Almost half a lifetime ago.'

Benoit's gaze fell to his lap, and the silence that followed chimed like a struck gong. I picked at what was left on my plate; the Brie had melted, obscuring a section of the china's patterned surface, the white smudges making the birds appear sickly.

'We can talk about her,' he said. 'If you want to.'

'I don't.'

'But if you ever do.'

I cut him off with a sigh. 'I appreciate the offer,' I said, in a voice brittle enough to shatter glass. The box containing the ring was still on the table, a morbid talisman I had neither asked for nor wanted. 'But there's honestly nothing I want to say. Nothing good, anyway.'

Benoit's eyes seemed to have doubled in size.

'Listen,' I went on, 'this was delicious, but I'm stuffed. I think I might go up to bed soon, if that's OK with you?'

'Of course,' he said, hand coming up to rub the back of his neck. 'I'm sorry if the ring upset you, I just thought that— I can clear all this away; you go on up.'

Tears pressed at my eyes as I turned and fled, snatching up the small velvet box as I went, crushing it against my palm. I would not cry in front of him. Not for her – never for her. Once upstairs, and without bothering to do much more than remove my shoes, I collapsed on to the bed and fell almost instantly into a deep, cocooned slumber – though it was fated not to last.

At some point in the early hours, I woke, acutely aware that someone was in the room. Whoever it was was moving across the floor towards me, and I froze, eyelids pinned and heart loud, ready to scream the moment I felt an inevitable hand reaching for me.

Would Benoit hear if I called for help? How fast would he get here?

Whoever was intruding began to scrabble around underneath the bed, searching for something – or someone? With a roar, I threw back the sheet and stamped down as hard as I could, my heel sinking into the soft flesh of the trespasser's buttock. I heard a grunt, followed by a sharp snap, and then a bellow of pain.

Stumbling in my haste to get away, it took a few seconds for the realisation to land.

'Bloody hell,' I exploded, snapping on the light. 'Benoit?'

He didn't answer, but swore with gusto, and having shuffled up on to both knees, began to vigorously shake his right hand.

'What the hell are you doing? Is that . . . Oh!' I clamped a hand to my mouth, a strangled laugh bursting out as I took in his stricken expression, puce cheeks, and the mouse trap attached to his pinkie.

'Can you help me?' he begged. 'It really hurts.'

'Here,' I said, kneeling beside him. 'Hold still while I . . . Hang on.'

The mechanism had jammed, its cheap metal spring twisted in on itself.

'It's OK.' Benoit gritted his teeth. 'It's not like I needed that finger.'

'Just stop wriggling,' I said, drawing his trapped arm forwards until his hand was nestled against my chest. 'Keep this part steady, and I'll force it open – ready?'

'As I'll ever be . . .'

Once I'd prised apart the trap and set him free, Benoit did what so many people with an injury do, and started blowing frantically on his bruised finger.

'Let me see,' I said, taking his hand in mine. 'Can you bend it? Good. And this way.'

Our elbows touched, and a rush of heat radiated between us. I got unsteadily to my feet while Benoit remained where he was, good hand flat against his thigh, muscle playing in his jaw.

I waited until my heart rate slowed to pose my next question. 'Why on earth were you crawling around in here in the dark?'

'I would've thought that was obvious.'

'Enlighten me.'

'The mice,' he said simply. 'I couldn't bear the thought of them getting killed. I've just spent the past few hours searching the house for traps. This one' – he held up what remained of the battered contraption – 'is number twenty.'

A smile tugged. 'I thought you were an intruder, some madman come to kill me.'

'Sorry about that.' His gaze travelled the length of me. 'I hoped you wouldn't hear me.'

'I had no idea you were such a softie. I would happily have shown you where the traps were, if you'd only told me.'

Being careful not to put any pressure on his injured hand, Benoit stood up. '*Je sais*,' he said, and then again, in English, 'I know.' He went as if to touch my cheek, then thought better of it. 'You're dressed.'

I glanced down at my crumpled dress. 'Tiredness over-came me. I don't know why. I just – when I came up here, I felt utterly drained, as if I'd run a marathon or something. I thought I'd just rest my eyes for a few minutes, but clearly, I passed out.'

'Probably the after-effects of shock,' he said, nodding sagely. 'I shouldn't have dropped that ring on you like I did, without any warning. I'm sorry.'

'That's OK,' I said, though we both knew it wasn't.

'Lilah told me she hadn't seen you for a while, but I had no idea how long that while was. If I'd known, then—'

'It's not your fault,' I said, sitting down on the bed.

'Can I?' he asked, and I patted the mattress beside me.

'Be my guest.'

Benoit sat, close enough that his knee brushed against mine. The finger was beginning to bruise, and what looked to be a blood blister was blooming beneath his nail.

'You should put some ice on that,' I said.

'Probably should,' he agreed.

'I should probably put on pyjamas.'

Benoit inclined his head. 'Probably should,' he said again, adding lightly, 'Or not.'

I looked at him in surprise and he laughed.

'Sorry. Not sure where that came from – must be all the crawling around on all fours. The blood has gone to my head. I'll go, let you get undress— I mean, go to bed. I mean— *Merde*. I'm going.'

I couldn't help but smile as he got to his feet, waiting until he was at the door before asking my question. 'If there ever was a real intruder in this house, would you come if I called?'

Benoit paused. His gaze when he looked back at me was direct, unwavering in its intensity.

'Nobody is going to hurt you, Fliss,' he said. 'Because I won't let them.'

18

Libourne had come to life.

For the first time since I had arrived, there was a hive of activity happening out on the street, with chatter, the grind of engines, and the general hubbub of a crowd filtering over the courtyard wall. It was not yet eight, but already the air was soupy with heat. Behind the distinctively sweet scent of the wisteria, I caught the aroma of something salty, a brininess that put me in mind of the sea.

The kitchen was deserted, light falling in across a scrubbed wooden table and dribbling down on to the terracotta tiles below. At one time, flowers would have been hung up to dry from hooks on the exposed beam ceiling, alongside strings of garlic, onions and chilli. Admiring a lemon-patterned ceramic bowl, the vase of pink tulips on the table beside it, and the glossy surface of a vast range cooker, I stood on tiptoes to run a finger along the spines of recipe books, all of which were neatly arranged on a built-in shelf above the worktop.

Hankering for tea rather than my usual dose of coffee, I unearthed an ancient-looking box of Twinings from behind a packet of pasta shells in one of the cupboards and readied a mug. The kettle had not long boiled when Benoit appeared, dark hair awry and a smudgy expression on his face.

'Up too early?' I said, as he almost dislocated his jaw with a wide yawn. 'How's the finger?'

'Sore, and barely functional.' He held it up to show me. 'At least I don't need it to chop.' He heaped coffee into a cafetière, poured over the hot water and stirred.

'I've been thinking about which jobs we should tackle today,' I said. 'I don't suppose there's any chance of the skip arriving on a Sunday?'

'Zero chance,' he confirmed. 'But that's OK, because by rights, we shouldn't be working – not on market day.'

'So, that's what all the noise is about.' I gestured towards the outer door. 'Sounds lively.'

'Busiest day of the week,' he said, over the rim of his cup.

'Every day is going to be busy for us, if we're to stand a chance of clearing this place out in two weeks.'

Benoit pulled a face. 'This afternoon, I'll do whatever you tell me,' he said. 'But not this morning. This morning, we're going to the market.'

'I'm coming, too, am I?'

'On this occasion,' he replied, 'I'm going to have to insist.'

Twenty minutes later, the two of us were walking towards Place Abel Surchamp, Benoit a few paces ahead of me on the narrow pavement. The first set of stalls we passed were towards the end of the street. Locals and tourists clustered around them, nattering away to the vendors and each other, wicker shopping baskets propped on hips.

'Oysters for breakfast?' Benoit suggested, as we stopped beside crateloads of the things. A few had been cracked open and arranged on plates around wedges of star-cut lemon, their slippery innards exposed for all to see.

I wrinkled my nose. 'My vegetarianism has never been more of a blessing.'

'I'll get some on the way back,' he said. 'After we've stocked up on vegetables.'

Having meandered past a stall selling bunches of fabric peonies and another sporting an array of colourful straw hats, we reached the boundary of the square and were soon drawn in amongst the slipstream of shoppers. Accustomed to doing the majority of my own food shopping at the nearest Tesco Metro, or via an app that saw a delivery driver bring it to the back door of The Fitz, it made a pleasant change to see so much fresh produce in one place. Never had I known strawberries to be so plump, oranges to be so firm, or tomatoes to be available in so many shapes, sizes and shades. Radishes snuggled together in frothy handfuls of pink and green, juice dribbled from enormous smiles of watermelon, and white asparagus stood to attention in close-knit bundles. Benoit made a beeline for the latter, running a discerning eye over each batch as the seller called out prices.

'It's late in the season for these,' he told me, 'but I can never resist them when I see them.' He accepted his paper bag with a cheerful, '*Merci*.'

'You may judge me for this,' I said, 'but I've never been a fan.'

Benoit gasped in mock horror. 'You don't like asparagus?'

'I don't like the stringiness.'

He ushered me away from the vegetable stall towards another selling woven baskets.

'If it's stringy, you're not cooking it right. How do you do it?'

'If I ever did cook it, which is highly unlikely, then I'd boil it,' I said, to which he grumbled in French.

'Asparagus needs delicate handling.' Extracting a spear, he ran the thumb of his uninjured hand along the stem. 'You need to remove the tougher ends and then peel away the outer layers.'

'And then you boil it?'

'*Mon Dieu!* Forget about the boiling. Asparagus is full of essential vitamins. Boil it too long and you'll be left with barely any of that inherent goodness, not to mention flavour.'

'Would I fry it, then?'

'Better,' he allowed, 'but you get the best results from roasting. Hot tray, splash of good-quality olive oil, bit of salt on there.' His hands moved as he spoke, mimicking the action of sprinkling. 'I'd do these with a simple sweet-sherry dressing, throw in some shallots, garlic, mustard, half a spoonful of brown sugar.'

'Stop or I'll start drooling.'

'I'll cook them later,' Benoit said. 'Perhaps with a saffron risotto – or a mushroom one. Which do you prefer?'

'Both sound delicious, but I can't let you cook for me every single night. It must be my turn by now. Although,' I added, unable to miss the glint in his eyes, 'I'd have to insist we ate out, so as not to humiliate myself.'

'You can prepare the asparagus,' he said. 'I'll teach you how.'

Throwing me a knowing grin, he strode away before I had time to respond, pausing only briefly in front of a rotisserie chicken stall, before continuing on towards the Fromage de Montagne cheese counter, and a fishmonger selling all manner of crabs, prawns and – Charlie's favourite – scallops, each one sitting proudly inside its open shell. For a moment, I was caught by the vacant staring eyes of fish, its mouth fixed open in imitation of a scream. The sign beside it read: '*Lieu jaune entier.*'

'Whole pollack,' Benoit translated. 'A great fish to cook with. The flavour's subtle enough that it doesn't dominate, but complex enough that it can sit beside stronger *accompagnement*, such as lemon, fennel and artichoke.'

'I'll take the latter pair and leave the former.'

'Have you always been averse to meat?' he asked, bending to examine a net of mussels.

'For as long as I was given the choice to be. Even before I understood what it was, I disliked it. My dad said I used to spit it out and, as you know, my mum wasn't the most creative or skilled of cooks. I began making my own meals from the age of about ten onwards, and mostly that constituted a jacket potato hardened to a rock in the microwave, topped with a cheap tin of baked beans. It's a wonder I didn't get scurvy.'

'Where was your dad?' Benoit asked, declining the vendor's offer to sample a curl of smoked salmon.

'Working late,' I told him, adding, with a measure of defensiveness, 'He had to. My mum could never hold down a job for more than a few weeks at a time, and the more of them she lost, the harder it became for her to find another one. Nobody wants to hire an unreliable drunk.'

Benoit turned his head, but not quickly enough to mask his grimace.

'You think I'm too hard on her.'

'No.' He took off his sunglasses. 'I'm not judging you, Fliss. That's not who I am.'

When I didn't answer, Benoit jabbed me gently with an elbow.

'Listen, I'm going to be here a while,' he said, tagging on to the end of a long queue. 'This is the best boulangerie for miles, and everyone who comes here knows it. Don't feel you have to keep me company. I'll find you once I'm done.'

'Oh, well, OK then,' I said, stung by the dismissal. 'Guess I'll do a lap of the square.'

I set off, soon finding myself on the corner of Rue Victor Hugo, with its rows of grand houses and myriad shops.

There was a small jewellery stall sandwiched between two others, its wares treasure-chest bright against a bottle-green cloth.

'*Bonjour*,' I said, only for the woman vendor to reply in a stream of French. When I merely smiled helplessly in response, she hesitated.

'*Es-tu Anglais?*'

'Yes.' I replied. 'I'm afraid I don't speak much French.'

'That is OK.' She tossed her head in a Gallic shrug. 'I can speak in English; it's not a problem.'

'You put me to shame,' I told her, meaning it.

Ignoring the remark, she wafted a hand over a display of necklaces. 'I can change the length for you, and everything you see is available in gold or silver.'

'It's all very nice.' I selected an opal pendant, angling it to catch the light.

'That's a nice ring,' she observed. 'Is it a diamond?'

I lowered my hand, felt the familiar reddening burn as I nodded.

'Can I take a look?'

I had curled my fingers into a fist and had to straighten them again. The woman's brow furrowed as she moved my fingers first one way, then the other. Petite, with wide-apart, watchful eyes, sleek brunette bangs and a tiny rosebud mouth, she was dressed in red culottes and a black-and-white striped vest. Effortlessly chic. My own outfit – the same linen shift I'd worn to travel in, since washed but not yet ironed – made me feel as if I were a potato, and the dress my sack.

'*Bonne*,' the woman declared. '*Très intéressant*.'

I murmured a polite thanks.

'You are here on holiday?' she went on, as I examined a pair of earrings in the shape of origami birds.

Adélard had asked the same question, yet I still didn't have a ready answer to roll out.

'Visiting,' I said. 'My friend told me I had to see the market, and he wasn't wrong.'

'It is the best thing about Libourne,' she agreed. 'This, and the lake. Have you been?'

'Not yet. I did go to the farm, though.'

'Ah, *oui*.' She rolled her eyes. 'Turkeys and sheep – *très excitant, non?*'

It was easy to smile; I did so every time I recalled the hour I'd spent there.

'Well, I should go,' I said, mildly surprised to find Benoit a few paces behind me, a straining carrier bag in his hand.

'Oh, *c'est toi*,' drawled the woman. '*Salut*, Ben.'

Benoit's trainer began to tap against the cobbles. '*Salut*, Céline.'

I looked at each of them in turn, taking in the flush on her face, the narrowing eyes on his.

'Benoit is the friend that you mentioned?' Céline said, folding her slim arms across her chest. 'He is the one who told you about the market?'

'Er, yes,' I said. 'He and I, we're—'

'Cousins,' Benoit said brusquely. 'Or, as good as. Felicity is Lilah's daughter.'

Céline's hands fluttered into motion. 'I am very sorry,' she said. 'Lilah, she . . . It is very sad.'

Cousins?

'Thank you.' I took a breath. 'And how do you two know each other?'

'We were together,' she proclaimed, at exactly the same time as Benoit said, 'We're old friends.'

Céline began to pluck at the material of her striped top, muttering under her breath. Benoit didn't appear to notice, his focus solely on me. Was there anything more that I wanted to see? No. Then did I mind if we headed back to the house? Not once did he look back, though I could not resist a stealthy final glance over my shoulder as we walked away.

Céline stood immobile, eyes fixed in our direction, a look of pure and potent fury on her face.

19

Adélard was waiting when we got back, his tanned limbs draped across the front steps of the guesthouse.

'You are blocking my sun,' he droned, when our collective shadows fell over him. Opening one eye, he clocked the bag in Benoit's hand, and asked, '*Pain frais?*'

'Fresh from the market,' Benoit agreed, going around his friend to open the door. 'But I'm saving it for lunch.'

'*Trouble-fête*,' Adélard grumbled, standing up and brushing dust off the back of his shorts.

The three of us trooped inside, swapping the dazzling morning sunshine for the gloom and cobwebs of the hallway.

'Where's Madame?' I asked.

'In bed.' Adélard flashed me a wolfish grin. 'A guest spent the night, and now they are together in my apartment.'

Benoit turned in amusement. 'A guest?'

Adélard's reply was a throaty rumble of laughter, although it ceased abruptly when we reached the lounge and heard the scratch of the record player being switched on. A few seconds later, to our collective horror, the breathy opening words of Serge Gainsbourg's 'Je t'aime – Moi Non Plus' filtered out into the hallway. Etienne immediately began to sing along, hopelessly out of time and in the kind of slurring warble that indicated inebriation. It was not yet ten a.m. – the older man must have got stuck into the bottle early. Benoit and I exchanged a look, and he sagged against the wall.

'I can take these through to the kitchen later,' he said, putting his bags on the floor.

'*Mon Dieu*,' murmured Adélard, as more strangled lyrics rang out.

Without conferring further, the three of us quickly made our way upstairs.

'That song is so bad,' Benoit said a few minutes later, closing the door of the billiard-room-cum-library behind us and leaning against it.

'Terrible,' Adélard agreed. 'It is like listening to somebody having sex in the next room.'

'Somebody you really dislike,' I put in, and both men roared with laughter.

Adélard crossed to the bookshelves, his head on one side as he examined the titles. 'Are you going to keep all of these?' he asked, pleased when Benoit and I said 'Yes' in unison. 'This is, in actual fact, a very good construction,' he went on, running the ladder along on its wheels. 'Often, I am asked to mend pieces that are broken because people use cheap materials, and then, of course, things begin to fall apart. It is better to spend more now to spend less later, no?'

'There's a small problem with that theory,' Benoit said. 'What if you have no money to spend? We need to do some repairs, but our budget is . . .' He glanced towards me.

'Negligible,' I said.

Adélard frowned. 'Do you have a vision for the house? A way that you want people who come inside to feel?'

'Comfortable,' I said.

'At home,' agreed Benoit.

The two of us had yet to discuss aesthetics, not in specific detail, and I was glad he wanted the guesthouse to have a congenial feel.

Adélard sighed and rolled his neck. 'What you should want is to wow people,' he insisted. 'Blow off their hats!'

'Can't we achieve both?' I said, but Adélard wasn't listening.

He was striding around the room, inspecting furniture, opening and closing shutters and cupboard doors. 'You will have to pay some attention to the *portes-fenetres*,' he mused. 'Rot has got into the wood. I can help, sand them down for you and prime them, but it will take some time.'

'*Portes-fenetres?*' I asked.

'That's the name for these types of tall windows,' Benoit explained.

Adélard danced his slender fingers along the places where the panes had begun to split.

'What a shame,' I said. 'I like how they look. This crumbling effect, it's attractive, and feels authentic.'

Adélard narrowed his eyes. 'It is disordered,' he said flatly. 'If you are planning to paint the walls, then you must also paint the window frames and shutters.'

'How long would it take?' Benoit asked. 'To do all the windows? And how much would you charge us?'

Adélard considered, then quoted a number that sent my eyebrows into my hairline. 'However,' he went on, as I struggled to regain my composure, 'as we are all friends, I will give you a special price. If you cover the cost of materials, I will complete the work for two thousand euros.'

A generous mark-down, given that his original estimate had been four times the amount. Benoit's expression was studied.

'I don't have enough in my savings to cover the full amount,' I admitted. 'Everything I had went into the hotel in London. I might be able to stretch to five hundred?'

'Don't worry.' Benoit fingered the cracked shutter. 'I have it.'

'But—' I began, as the two of them shook on it. 'I want to contribute something at least,' I said.

'I will begin today,' Adélard said. 'But first, I must go home and change. While I am gone, you should discuss which colours you want to use. You will need to choose some paint for me.'

'Fliss?' Benoit came towards me.

'Sure, fine,' I said distractedly, opening a banking app on my phone as Adélard disappeared through the door. 'I just need to check how much—What the hell?'

The joint account I shared with Charlie contained a balance of only four pounds. It must be a glitch. Logging out, I entered my password for a second time – and swore under my breath.

Not a glitch.

'Everything alright?' Benoit touched my arm, but I turned my back on him, tapping furiously at my phone, closing the first banking app and opening a second to check my personal account.

'No!' I gasped, collapsing down on to one of the mouse-eaten armchairs. My balance wasn't simply low, it was in arrears – to the tune of two thousand, five hundred pounds. My overdraft limit was set at three thousand, but I hadn't used it for years, had not got anywhere close to using it. With a hand against my temple, I scrolled through my recent outgoings. There was my coffee at the airport in London, the train ticket from Bordeaux to Libourne, a payment for thirty-eight euros at the shop where I'd purchased the traps, and there, only a few hours ago, a transfer payment of over four thousand pounds to a Mr C. Fitzsimons.

Charlie. Charlie had robbed me, and undoubtedly cleared out the joint savings account at the same time. I checked, and there it was: another fifteen hundred pounds moved to his personal account. White-hot fury seared through me, and I rose swiftly from the chair, almost knocking over a hovering Benoit in the process.

'Whoa!' he exclaimed. 'What's happened?'

'Nothing. I need to— I'll be back in a minute.'

I had left the shutters open in my bedroom, and it was stifling, the sun having crept around the rooftops until it was glaring in through the window. I began to pace up and down, shielding my eyes as I located Charlie's number.

He didn't answer.

'Charlie,' I said to his gratingly chipper voicemail, 'I've seen the accounts. What the hell is going on? Call me back.'

Hanging up, I immediately tried Angela, the angry words like hot fat in my mouth, demanding to be spat out. My stomach hurt as if I'd been punched, every fibre in my body pulled taut and rigid. I got her answerphone and sobbed, jabbing at the screen to end the call, blinking as the diamond on my finger caught the light. A symbol of love and fidelity? It may as well be a lump of coal. Dragging off the ring, I slammed it down on the bedside table, accidentally knocking off the velvet box Benoit had given me the night before. It rolled across the floor. Cursing, I bent to retrieve it. The ring was nestled inside, a faded gold band with its blue glass flower, the petals mattified from years of wear.

My heart stalled at the sight of it. I felt my legs weaken, and moments later, I was on the floor, powerless to prevent the tears from erupting. I closed my eyes, and saw my mother, sitting on the end of my bed, a storybook open in her hands that she had stopped reading halfway through. I was six, or maybe seven, accustomed by then to what my dad called her 'disappearing acts', and so, with my pink stuffed rabbit on the pillow next to me, I waited for her to bring herself back from wherever she had gone.

'Mummy,' I said, when several minutes had passed with nothing. 'Mummy!' Louder, more insistent. She didn't respond, did not even look at me. 'Mummy!' I kicked her.

'What the hell do you think you're doing?' Mum's neck turned a mottled red. 'Don't you dare do that. Don't you dare kick me.'

'But you weren't answering me.'

'It's always about *you*, isn't it?' The way she'd said 'you', grinding the word out as if her teeth were metal cogs in a machine, set my bottom lip trembling. I brought my knees up to my chest and wrapped my arms tightly around them, shutting her out, wondering why she didn't look at me like the other mothers in the school playground looked at their children, as if they were precious angels. I might as well have been a smear of muck on the bottom of her shoe.

I did not get to hear the end of the story. Instead, I heard the slam of fridge door as it banged against the worktop, the clank of a bottle as she helped herself to wine. 'Mummy's adult juice', she called it; but it wasn't juice, it was poison. It turned happy people into sad people, quiet people into shouty people, and kind people into mean people. It did all those things to my mum, but still she drank it every day – sometimes first thing in the morning, out of a mug so Dad wouldn't see. She thought I didn't know, but I did. I always knew.

My sobs were becoming difficult to mask. I stuffed my fist into my mouth and bit down; skin hot and wet, throat swollen and sore.

There was a loud creak, and the bedroom door opened.

20

It was not Benoit, but Etienne.

'Don't,' I said, burrowing my head against my shoulder. 'Please, I don't want to see anyone.'

Etienne ignored me, letting out a grunt of effort as he lowered himself down next to me. The skin around his bloodshot eyes was lined and papery thin. I took in the grey whiskers and cracked lips, recognising neglect yet sensing compassion. He sat with his legs crossed, a childlike pose at odds with his advanced years. There was a scab on his ankle.

The ring box was still clutched in my hand, and Etienne stared at it for some time, his eyelids growing heavy. Was the burden of his own memories weighing him down? His love for my mum seemed to be a broken faucet that was destined to keep trickling – the drip, drip, drip of the damned.

'Do you want it?' I said, in a voice I barely recognised. 'The ring. You can have it.'

Etienne's unruly grey brows knotted together. '*Non, chérie*,' he said. 'It belongs to you – it is a part of you.' He tapped his chest, speaking slowly, coherently, no trace of the drunken singing from earlier.

'I don't want it,' I said. Wiping away tears, I pushed it into his hand. 'Take it.'

Etienne closed the lid and set the box on the floor by my feet.

Isabelle Broom

'I mean it,' I said. 'All it does is remind me of all the things I'd rather forget.' Lifting my foot, I kicked the box away as I had kicked my mother as a child. It tumbled across the rug and skidded to a stop against the skirting.

Etienne did not react.

'The woman you knew,' I said, my voice trembling, 'she's not the same as the woman who raised me. Do you under-stand that?'

He nodded gravely. 'I understand.'

'This whole' – I gestured with wildly flailing arms – 'situa-tion. It's surreal. The only reason I'm still here is because I want to help with this house, make it beautiful again. I want to—'

I panted, coughed out another sob.

Etienne uncrossed his legs and stretched them out. He was barefoot, which reminded me of Benoit. They were similar in so many ways, yet fundamentally different in others.

'I am happy that you decided to stay,' he said.

I sniffed noisily.

'And Delilah, she would be happy also.'

'I find that hard to believe,' I said, eyes stinging as I stared at the slivers of paint criss-crossing his long, black smock. There was paint under his fingernails, too, and more drying in splodges across his bandaged hand. 'My mum didn't *do* happy, not when I knew her.'

Etienne wriggled his toes. 'We tried very hard to make each other happy,' he said softly. 'There were good days, and there were bad days. In that way, we were the same. Sometimes, our bad days coincided, and that was difficult, but there were many good days – a great many of those.'

I wanted to know why. Why had he turned to alcohol? What cataclysmic event had sent him along the path of self-destruction? People did not simply wake up one day and become addicts. I'd posed the question to my mum only once, as a strident teenager, and she'd refused to answer. Even my father, who'd promised never to lie to me, had changed the subject when asked about it. My mum was a drunk, in the same way that she was a blonde, and a terrible singer, and someone who drank straight from the carton without using a glass and stuffed envelopes from British Gas behind the radiator. She was sad, had been sad in every memory I had of her – but it stood to reason that the misery inhabiting her could not have been there from the start. It wasn't a freckle, or a birthmark. Anguish was a product of trauma. She and Etienne might well have bonded over their shared desolation, but their catalysts could not be the same. Because no matter what I'd been told to the contrary, I knew that I was the one who'd caused my mother's torment. She was happy – until she had me.

Etienne did not say anything more, though he did put his hand over mine. A pigeon landed on the windowsill, and the bells began to chime out across the rooftops. I jolted at the crash of the front door, heard Adélard's voice as he bounded up the stairs, followed by a shrill barking.

'Madame,' I said, reaching for the hooded top that lay on the bed and wiping my eyes on the sleeve.

Etienne shuffled on to all fours and groaned.

'Here.' I stood and offered him my hand. 'Let me help you up.'

For a fleeting few seconds, I thought he was going to hug me, but he settled on patting my cheek. '*Belle fille*,' he said. 'Beautiful girl.'

I could not have felt less so, and once he'd gone, I fled to the en suite, blinking in dismay at my blotchy face and trails of wept-away mascara. Charlie had not called me back, and I scowled into the mirror as I considered my empty bank accounts, the nonchalant way my fiancé had sought to appropriate any funds I managed to secure from the guesthouse, the casual 'I can explain' in response to almost burning down our hotel. Since he'd begun drinking again, Charlie had become not only a cheat, but also a thief, an opportunist – a person so far removed from the man with whom I'd gone litter-picking three years ago as to be a stranger.

Why had I stood by and simply watched it happen?

Out in the corridor, I found Etienne coming up the stairs, a tin of paint swinging from one hand.

'Where are you off to with that?' I said.

Etienne grinned, showing off slightly stained teeth, and nodded towards the main bathroom, home to his nightmarish underwater mural. It hardly mattered if he added in a few extra deformed fish or lumps of mangled seaweed; Benoit and I had agreed to paint over it in due course.

When I pushed my way into the library a few minutes later, I didn't notice Madame curled up on the floor inside the door.

'Oh no!' I wailed, as the dog gave an indignant yelp. 'Sorry, darling,' I said, dropping to my knees to check on her.

'*Que s'est-il passé?*' Adélard cried, clumping over in his workman's boots.

'I trod on her,' I said. 'She was right behind the door.'

Adélard scooped the dog up into his arms. Madame wriggled, then licked his nose.

'She's fine,' Benoit said from behind me, as Adélard tested each paw in turn. 'I've done exactly the same thing a million times,' he went on. 'One of these days, she'll learn not to lie down in stupid places.'

'Do not listen to him, *ma petite fille*. You are not stupid,' Adélard crooned. 'Bennie, he is the stupid one.'

'I'm really sorry,' I said again.

'Are you OK?' Benoit looked at me more closely. 'You look upset.'

'I'm fine.' How many times was I going to tell him the same lie? 'Looks as if you two have been busy.'

As if in answer, Benoit used his arm to waft away a cloud of dust and nodded across to where an industrial sander had been plugged in. A pair of plastic goggles hung from a strap around Adélard's neck, and he cursed as Madame's paws became tangled up in them.

'Shouldn't we have moved out the rest of the furniture first?' I said to Benoit in an undertone. 'Taken away the books, at least?'

'Probably,' he agreed, with a sideways look towards his friend. 'But Adélard wanted to get on with it, and given that he's doing us a favour, I thought it made more sense to let him.'

A wet snout nudged my knee. Madame stared up at me, dark eyes soulful, slim body quivering.

'Does this mean I'm forgiven?' I said, bending to stroke her.

Adélard was reaffixing his goggles, and said something in French to Benoit, who nodded.

'We're being kicked out,' he told me. '*Allez*, Madame.'

The dog cocked her head.

'Downstairs?' Benoit suggested, when the three of us were on the other side of the library door. 'I was about to make a start on clearing out the lounge – that was at the top of the list, wasn't it?'

'Needs must,' I agreed.

Of all the rooms in the house, the largest ground-floor space was undoubtedly in the worst state, so far as junk was concerned. While Madame hopped up on to one of the chaises longues and spiralled herself a makeshift bed out of a ratty old blanket, Benoit nipped to the kitchen and returned with a roll of bin bags and several empty boxes.

'You don't seem yourself,' he observed, tearing off a bin bag and passing it to me.

'Don't I?' I said, my attempt at chirpiness landing somewhere close to brittle.

Benoit was about to reply when my phone buzzed with a message. It was Angela, telling me she was 'lunching with Sue', and would call me later this evening. The swell of my anger having dissipated somewhat, it now struck me as faintly ridiculous that I'd rung her at all. The situation with Charlie was my problem, not hers.

'Everything OK?' Benoit asked. 'You haven't blinked for about five straight minutes.'

'Sorry,' I said, shoving my phone away.

'Sorry,' he repeated. 'Sorry for what?'

'For not blinking.'

'Fliss . . .'

I scrunched my face, then relaxed it, torn by indecision. On the chaise longue, Madame opened her jaws in a wide yawn.

'There might be a small delay,' I began, 'with getting you some money. There's been a, um, misunderstanding.'

'A misunderstanding?'

'Yes. That is to say, a mistake. Not mine, but – all you need to know is that I'll get you the money, as much as I can. I just need to speak to my partner.'

'You don't need to worry about the money thing,' he said. 'It's handled. Adélard has already been paid.'

'I do need to worry,' I said, picking up a bleach-stained towel with my fingertips and transferring it to a bin bag. 'Trust me, I do.'

'Fliss,' he said again. 'If there's something you need to get off your chest—'

'It's gone,' I said, through a burst of agitation. 'My money. Charlie – that's my fiancé – has cleared me out.'

'I see.' Benoit nodded slowly. 'Can I ask why?'

'I don't know *why*,' I exclaimed. 'I can't get hold of him to ask.'

'Has he ever done anything like this before?'

'No,' I said, hesitating as a memory snagged. 'Oh no, wait. There was an incident with his sister Olivia, once. She told me that when they were teenagers, she took on a summer job working at a stable, mucking out and grooming the horses, that sort of thing, and saved all her earnings. It was supposed to be a top-up for her gap-year fund, and she stuffed all the cash into a jar in her bedroom. September rolled around, and she came home one day to find the whole lot gone. She said Charlie had taken it, blown the lot.'

'Did he pay her back?' Benoit asked, eyes widening when I shook my head.

'Their parents did. The family is fairly wealthy, so . . .'

'So?' Benoit looked mutinous. 'Not a very good lesson to teach, is it? "You go ahead and steal, son, we'll bail you out."'

'Not the best,' I agreed. Retrieving one of the cardboard boxes, I moved to the dresser and began to fill the box with empty bottles. 'I'm hoping that in this case, it's a misunderstanding. There must have been a cost relating to the hotel, something he needed the money for.'

'Such as?'

The next bottle went into the box with a loud clunk.

'We're doing some repairs at the moment,' I said breezily. He did not need to know about the fire.

Benoit sighed heavily. 'And does this fiancé of yours make a habit of doing things like this? Going behind your back, I mean.'

My cheeks burned at the thought of Madeline. 'He's never done anything specifically like this to me before,' I said – which was, at least, the truth.

'And you trust him?'

A simple question, and one that should have been easy to answer. I lifted the hair off my neck. 'It's so stuffy in here – can we open one of the doors?'

Benoit gave me a quizzical look, but he did as I'd requested. The breeze that filtered in from the courtyard was barely cooler than the stifling air indoors, though it brought with it a sweet, floral scent. Having filled my box, I began stacking up glassware.

'You didn't answer my question,' Benoit said, tugging at some old leaflets that were adhered to one of the low tables by Christ only knew what.

'You asked if I trusted my fiancé – of course I do.'

'Uh-uh.'

'OK, so maybe he's tested my trust today, but I have to give him the benefit of the doubt – that's my job, isn't it?'

'Your job,' he recited drily. 'Can I tell you what I think?'

'If I say no, will it make any difference?'

'Obviously, I've never met this man, and I've only known you a few days,' he began, 'but from what you've said, it sounds to me as if you're doing an awful lot of the heavy lifting in your relationship. And that's fine, if it's a dynamic you're happy with. But if it's not . . .'

I prised a rock-solid paintbrush off the top of the dresser and, after a moment's deliberation, tossed it into the trash. 'Neither Charlie nor I are perfect,' I said. 'He's done some stupid stuff, but so have I.'

'I find that hard to believe.' Benoit gave up trying to peel the leaflets off the table and tore them apart instead.

'Why?' I asked.

'Because,' he said, '*tu es une fille géniale.*'

'In English?'

'You're a great girl.'

A smile crept over my face, the first in what felt like hours. 'Am I?'

'I'd say so.'

'Not a grumpy, hypocritical bint who thinks it's acceptable to boil asparagus to a pulpy mess?'

Benoit grinned. 'I said great, Fliss, not perfect.'

21

When she eventually rang back, Angela was incandescent when I told her about the transferred funds – angrier than I could recall her being in a very long time.

'How dare he?' she kept on repeating. 'How bloody well dare he?'

'You know Charlie,' I said weakly. 'Once he gets an idea in his head . . .'

'Obviously, I don't know him,' she said, and then promptly offered me a loan. 'I have a bit put by in the Christmas pot that you can borrow – just say the word, lovey.'

'It's OK,' I said, watching Benoit carry our scraped-clean lunch plates across the courtyard. He'd thrown together a peppered tofu salad, complete with butter-drenched new potatoes, tissue-thin slices of avocado, and a creamy dressing that made my taste buds zing. 'I'm sure Charlie will transfer everything back once I manage to get hold of him.'

'*I'd* like to get hold of him,' she said ominously. 'But how's everything else going? Have you been through any of your mum's stuff yet?'

I shook my head, but didn't say anything.

'Too soon?' she guessed, to which I made a small noise of agreement. 'Well, there's no rush, is there? All in good time.'

'I'd better go,' I said, as Benoit came back into the lounge. 'Please don't worry about me.'

'All OK?' he asked as I hung up, and I nodded.

'That was my aunt.'

'Angela?'

I stared at him blankly.

'The letters,' he reminded me. 'I wrote to her. Now, shall we put on some music?'

Once he'd selected a record from Etienne's sizeable collection – an album of jaunty French numbers that he intermittently sang along to as we worked – the two of us agreed a system whereby Benoit would sort through paperwork, letters, documents and the like, while I removed grime from the windows, stains from the furniture and dust from the corners. The conversation continued to flow back and forth, though we played it more safely this time when it came to subject matter, discussing films we liked, books we'd read, and who we'd invite to a dream dinner party. I chose famous hoteliers – men like William and John Astor, César Ritz and Conrad Hilton, while Benoit reeled off the names of famous chefs, including Alain Ducasse, Joël Robuchon and Anthony Bourdain.

'No women at your table either?' I mused, and he thought for a moment.

'If you insist, I'll have Claudia Schiffer, Michelle Pfeiffer and Marilyn Monroe.'

'The gentleman prefers blondes.'

Benoit didn't miss a beat. 'Always have,' he said, as my fingers inched up unbidden towards my own fair hair. 'Always will.'

The next few hours sped by, the two of us diverted by an ongoing game of what Benoit dubbed, 'Haven't Got a Cluedo', in which we uncovered strange ornaments or pictures, and challenged one another to guess what the hell each was supposed to be. By early evening, my sides ached from laughing, my throat was parched from furniture polish, and I was more than ready to collapse face down on to one of the now-far-tidier chaises longues.

'No, you don't,' said Benoit, knotting the last of the bin bags. 'I'm teaching you how to roast asparagus, remember?'

I groaned at the same time Madame's head shot up, her whine of delight heralding the arrival of an extremely dusty Adélard.

'I have done three of the rooms,' he announced, wiping his hands on the front of his overalls. 'But now, I must go.'

'You won't join us for dinner?' I said, as he bent to clip a lead to Madame's diamanté collar.

'Not today. I have a date.'

'Who with?' Benoit asked. 'Eloise?'

Adélard shook his head.

'Romilly?'

'Madame did not like her,' Adélard lamented. 'And she is the boss.'

'Louvel?'

'Ah, Louvel,' he said, baring his teeth with relish. 'My little panther.'

I coughed behind my hand.

'If it is Louvel, then we won't expect you early tomorrow,' Benoit teased. 'The two of you together are . . .' He whistled.

Adélard continued to grin, as a T-rex might at a meat buffet. 'Louvel is a lot of fun, but he is in Paris, visiting his mother.'

'Oh, I know,' Benoit went on, 'is it the woman you met in Saint-Émilion last weekend? The American. What was her name – Sophie someone?'

'Sapphire.' Adélard sighed dreamily. 'She is very beautiful and very . . .' He paused, taking the time to look meaningfully at each of us in turn. 'Demanding. I am sure, that if you wanted to join us, she would not mind.'

I stammered out a laugh.

'What is funny?'

'Nothing. It's just that I'm not— I wouldn't—'

'You never know,' Adélard said, 'you might enjoy yourself.'

At a loss for how else to respond, I laughed again.

Adélard steepled his fingers together. 'Or perhaps, the two of you have something private planned?'

'Oi,' Benoit interrupted. 'Don't stir.'

'There is something between you, *non*? A certain ... frisson.'

My cheeks, throat and ears felt impossibly hot.

'Only a friendship,' I said forcefully.

'Fliss is engaged,' Benoit reminded him. 'Last time I checked, that means a person is getting married soon.'

'*Vraiment?*' mocked Adélard, a lascivious glint in his eye. 'If that is true, then why have you taken off your ring, Felicity?'

I clutched the offending hand to my chest, turning away as Benoit marched Adélard out of the lounge, Madame trotting demurely after them. The ring had completely slipped my mind. I hadn't thought about it once, all afternoon.

'That man is an animal,' Benoit said, coming back into the room.

'Apparently, so is this Sapphire woman,' I replied. 'I thought it was the French who were renowned for being passionate, not the Americans.'

'What about the English?'

'We're known for our sarcasm, and maybe our stinginess,' I said. 'Definitely not for our sexual prowess.'

Benoit laughed. 'Thank goodness I'm half French, in that case. There's hope for me yet.'

'I'm sure you get along fine,' I mumbled, rubbing at a stubborn stain with my cloth.

'Sex is like cooking,' he said. 'Get the ingredients right, spend a little time, taste as you go, and you'll end up with something delicious.'

'On that note,' I blurted, seizing at the opportunity to change the subject, 'do you think the asparagus will keep until tomorrow? I don't think I could lift a vegetable peeler if my life depended on it.'

'*Reine du drame*,' he joked. 'Shall we go out instead?'

The door into the lounge opened with a swing, and Etienne appeared, grey hair awry and blue paint splatters across the front of his smock. Taking in the stack of bin bags and gleaming surfaces, his eyes bulged. Benoit and I exchanged a nervous glance.

'We haven't thrown anything of value away,' I said hastily, as Benoit ushered his uncle further into the room, showing him the filed-away paperwork, and where he would find all the errant brushes, palette knives and other art paraphernalia we'd unearthed. Etienne said very little, though fidgeted incessantly, scratching his chin, his arms, behind his ears.

'We were just about to head out,' I blurted. 'For a walk, maybe some food. Why don't you come with us?'

Etienne grumbled something unintelligible in French and, with a meaningful look up at the ceiling, shuffled off in the direction of the kitchen.

'He told us to go ahead,' Benoit said. 'Something about wanting to finish his painting.'

He faced me, a smile playing on his lips. The charge sparked by his casual mention of sex had yet to fade, and my mind kept returning again and again to the phrase he'd used.

Spend a little time. Taste as you go.

'You still want to head out?' Benoit said. 'I can cook if not.'

'No,' I said, resisting the nagging urge I had to touch him. 'It's about time that you, my friend, had a night off.'

22

Situated a short way along from where the Dordogne ran off into the Isle, the waterside eatery L'Embarcadère had the feel of a pop-up, comprised as it was of a large trailer, canvas awning, and a scattering of outdoor furniture.

We chose a high table that provided an unblemished view of the river, and while I clambered up on to a stool, Benoit fetched menus. Music pounded out of speakers, chart hits I recognised but which appealed to me less than the eclectic French records we'd listened to back at the guesthouse. I could not fault the evening, however – it was temperate and serene, the sky not yet dark but aglow with the promise of night; birds flitting down across the water, diving between the reeds.

'We seem to spend the majority of our time sitting, eating and talking,' I said to Benoit, once the two of us had placed our orders – half duck and fries for him, burrata salad for me.

'Well, we are in France.' Benoit raised his beer and clinked it against my Diet Coke. 'And you forgot cleaning – and stripping.'

'Stripping?'

'Of wallpaper, young lady,' he exclaimed. 'Honestly. And here I was thinking that Adélard was the one with the most sordid mind.'

'How do you think his date's going?' I asked.

'Energetically,' he said, and I snorted into my glass.

'Would you say he's your closest friend?'

'Probably,' Benoit agreed. 'Certainly my closest Libourne friend.'

'Remind me where you grew up again – was it France or England?'

'Buckinghamshire,' he said, 'in a village called Hambleden. Think brick and flint cottages, fêtes at the local church.'

'Sounds a lot quainter than south-east London.'

'I didn't appreciate it. I don't think any child or teenager does until they grow up. All I ever wanted was to live somewhere more exciting. London was my dream, the place where I wanted to work my way up the ranks in restaurants. Which I did – for a while, anyway.'

'What happened to make you stop?'

Benoit took a slug of his beer, the shadow of something passing across his eyes. 'It wasn't for me,' he said. 'I decided to go abroad; I worked the ski season in Val-d'Isère, then took a job on a luxury yacht – that was an eye-opening few months – before going to Paris to try my luck there. I hadn't been back to Libourne for a good few years at this point, but then I heard from my mother that Etienne had met someone new and fallen in love, that he claimed to have quit drinking and wanted to see his family again. I was the nearest, geographically, and so I got the train here and ended up spending the whole summer.'

'And that was last year?' I asked, and he nodded.

'I spent the winter back in Paris, but it's a difficult city to work in – and to live in, for that matter. I missed the pace of life in Libourne, found myself daydreaming about settling down here, perhaps one day opening my own restaurant. When I told Etienne, he insisted I take the attic rooms at the guesthouse, and I agreed. That brings us up to a month ago, not long before Delilah . . .' He threw me a nervous glance.

'It's OK,' I said. 'I won't disintegrate into pieces if you say the word.'

Our food arrived. Finding slivers of cured ham on the top of my salad, I forked them off on to Benoit's plate.

'Take some of my chips.' He tipped a few towards me, only to scrabble them back. 'Actually, don't – they've most likely been cooked in duck fat.'

'All I need is cheese,' I sang, to the tune of 'All You Need Is Love' by The Beatles, and pierced my olive oil and cracked pepper-topped burrata ball with a knife.

'Let it cheese,' Benoit sang back, his own rendition of 'Let It Be'.

Picking up an errant chip from the table, I lobbed it into his lap. 'So, what was it about Libourne?' I asked. 'Other than the sleepy pace of life?'

Benoit finished his mouthful before replying. 'I guess it's that I always felt at home here,' he said. 'Safe in a way I haven't anywhere else – not in Paris, and definitely not in London. Granted, Hambleden isn't unsafe, but whenever I'm there, I spend the entire time clock-watching, waiting until I can leave again.'

I understood, felt similarly whenever I visited Angela and Patrick. Their Essex home had been home to me too, for more than three years, yet I'd remained on the periphery, never putting a single picture on the wall or inviting over any friends or boyfriends. Not that I'd had many of either during that period.

'Delilah said the same thing to me once,' Benoit said.

I reeled. It was as if the string of a balloon had been snipped inside my chest. 'Oh?'

'She told me Libourne – and specifically the guesthouse – was where she'd felt her safest.'

The wet mound of creamy mozzarella seemed to curdle as I stared at it.

'What about you?' Benoit asked. 'Where's your safe place – the London hotel?'

'Hardly,' I said, taunted by an image of the small bedroom with its plug-in travel kettle and minuscule fridge, of demanding guests, and Charlie bouncing around like a popped cork, sleeping with a staff member, starting accidental fires and now, apparently, emptying bank accounts. 'To be honest, I don't think I've ever felt safe anywhere.'

Benoit paused mid-bite, then continued to chew slowly.

'Everything in my life feels transient,' I rambled on, 'as if it could be snatched away at any minute. I can't ever afford to become complacent, because if I do – if I take my finger off the pin – it's all going to blow up in my face.'

His mouth turned down at the corners, and I looked away from him, out towards the water. The deepening blue of the sky was reflected in its rippling surface, while lights shone out bright from under the bridge. I heard the drone of a motorbike engine as it sped over the top.

'Fliss.' Benoit's eyes were the same colour as the darkening sky. 'Do you think that maybe your mum understood that feeling? It could be why she left you her share of the guesthouse, because she knew how important it was to have a home, a place you could feel safe.'

I put my knife and fork together. 'It's not my home,' I said. 'I can't imagine it ever being, not when it's been tainted by her.'

'Tainted?' Benoit frowned. 'What do you mean by that?'

'My whole life has been tainted by her. You saw what she was like – the drinking, her inability to stop drinking, the behaviour when she was drinking, the way she prioritised her drinking over everything else, over holding down a job, or doing the housework, or brushing her teeth, or being a mother—' My voice cracked, and I took a deep breath, counted silently to five.

Benoit reached across, placing his hand on the knot of my tightly folded arms.

'I could cope with it, with her, while my dad was still there. Me and him, we were a team. But when he wasn't—'

The pain still took me by surprise; the physical nature of it, the way it made my guts roil. I leaned back on my stool, and Benoit's hand fell away.

'You've really been through it,' he said.

I braved an approximation of a smile.

'If you ever want to talk about it—'

'I don't,' I said, tucking a fallen strand of hair behind my ear.

'I'm a good listener.'

'We should head back soon,' I said, pushing my salad towards him. 'Find out what it is Etienne's been working on all day.'

'I know you don't believe me,' Benoit said, forking up my rejected radicchio, 'but Etienne really is a genius. Behind all the bluster—'

'And the booze.'

'Yes, and the booze, he's a serious artist.'

'A serious piss artist,' I retorted, and though Benoit laughed, I put my head in my hands. 'I shouldn't have said that. It's not as if the situation is remotely funny.'

'Ah, but humour is a coping mechanism,' he pointed out. 'I got the giggles at my grandpa's funeral – to such an extent that I was asked to leave the crematorium. My mother was appalled, but I think old Pierre would've been amused by it. He always was *le coquin*.'

'You sound as if you're very fond of your family.'

'I am.' Benoit drained what was left of his beer. 'I only wish they weren't so stubborn, that my mother would agree to see Etienne, find a way to forgive him. There's so much anger there on her side, and she's never given me a satisfactory explanation as to why. All she'll ever say is that he's selfish.'

'Alcoholics generally are,' I said wearily. 'As disorders go, addiction is up there with the most widely devastating. The ripple effect when someone becomes dependent on alcohol is far-reaching.'

Benoit pressed his palms hard against his cheeks.

'Please don't do that,' I said. 'Don't look at me like that, as if you feel sorry for me.'

'Would that be so bad?'

By way of an answer, I stood and reached for my bag.

'You're not leaving?'

'I'm tired.'

'I'll come with you.' Benoit ran a paper napkin across his mouth and pocketed his phone. 'There's something you need to see, back at the house.'

'Will I like it?' I asked, and he smiled.

'This,' he said, 'you're going to love.'

23

Etienne was in the lounge when we got back, fast asleep on a chaise longue, his knees bent and paint-splattered hands tucked together under his chin. Benoit crossed the room to lift the needle from the record player and switched it off at the wall.

'Should we wake him?' I whispered. 'Help him up to bed.'

'Let's not.' Benoit tipped his head to one side. 'He looks so comfortable. Like some sort of giant mouse.'

'Don't tempt fate,' I murmured.

Having switched off the lights and closed the courtyard door, Benoit gestured for me to follow him up the stairs, both of us stepping carefully around the bin bags we'd piled in the hallway. The skip was due to arrive first thing the following morning, though one would surely not be enough. We had only cleared one room so far, and there were acres of wallpaper yet to be torn down.

'You'll have to excuse the mess,' he said, producing a key from his pocket as we reached the door to the attic. 'When I realised what the old fool had been doing, painting over his good murals and destroying old canvases, I went on a bit of a scavenge around the house and hid everything of value up here.'

The first thing I saw was the moon, shining in through one of two small dormer windows. A lattice of exposed beams decorated the vaulted ceiling, wrapped with strings of tiny lights, only half of the bulbs still functioning. There was a corner sofa crowded with cushions, a simple, wood-framed bed, neatly made, a clothing rail and, pushed into one of the alcoves, a freestanding rattan egg chair. Other than a modest pile of books, a laptop and a set of speakers, all of which were arranged on a low desk, the rest of the space was taken up with stacks of framed paintings.

'How many did you rescue?' I asked.

'Forty or so,' Benoit said, dropping his keys on the desk. 'Etienne's never mentioned them being missing. Either he hasn't noticed, or he doesn't care. I'm not sure what's worse.'

'Is the egg chair yours?'

'It is. A moving-in gift from Adélard.'

'Because he's trying to tempt you into becoming a swinger?'

Benoit applauded me with a slow, bemused clap. 'Help yourself,' he said, as I idled my way across to it, letting out a squeal as the chair rocked backwards and very nearly deposited me on the floor.

Benoit slid his phone from his pocket, and moments later, the opening bars of 'Landslide' by Fleetwood Mac trickled out from the speakers. I began to hum along, closing my eyes briefly, swept away by the sweet roughness of Stevie Nicks's voice.

'This,' I said sleepily, as the chair rocked me gently from side to side, 'was well worth climbing the extra flight of stairs.'

Benoit's lips lifted a fraction. 'I'm glad you like it, but the chair isn't what I wanted to show you.'

Leaving his phone on the bed, he crossed to the far wall and pushed the rail of clothes to one side, exposing a narrow door that I hadn't seen at first glance. It was all very Agatha Christie, a secret second space inside a locked attic room, and, having taken care to step rather than tumble out of the egg chair, I went to join him. Benoit opened the door and switched on the light, and suddenly, I could see vineyards backed by azure skies, stone archways, gold-stone chateaus and a vast lake banked by cypress pines. The landscape was rendered so realistically that it took me several seconds to comprehend that I was looking not at a view, but a painting.

Benoit smiled in triumph. 'I told you he was a genius.'

'Etienne did this?'

'Who else?'

'But it's incredible,' I said, my jaw unhinging as I studied the series of murals more closely. Everything, from the grout between the bricks of the buildings to the black cat sunning itself on a window ledge and the sunlight cascading across the hillsides, had been depicted with minute attention to detail.

'There used to be more like this,' Benoit said. 'But after Lilah . . . After she died, Etienne painted over every single one of them. He drank until he was incoherent, then sat up all night, painstakingly eroding one mural after another. You've seen how bad the new ones are, how skewed and distorted.' He shook his head. 'It's why I keep this door locked, and why I've brought so many of his other works up here. To protect them.'

Other than the murals, there wasn't much inside the hidden room, aside from a scatter of large cushions and a thick, green rug.

'I come in here to read sometimes,' Benoit said. 'Or just to think. It's a good place to escape the world for a while.'

'Do you often get that urge?' I asked.

'Probably more than I should. You?'

'Same.'

He huffed in amusement. 'What a pair we make.'

'What's in there?' I asked, noticing a cardboard box pushed against the wall. When he didn't immediately answer, I knelt to look and discovered a series of framed photographs.

'Is this you?' I asked, lifting one out. Despite the picture being faded with age, the courtyard it showed was instantly recognisable as belonging to the guesthouse. The young boy beaming for the camera was wearing a paper chef's hat atop his halo of dark curls.

Benoit crouched beside me. 'Whatever gave it away?' he said, taking the photo from me. 'If I remember rightly, I'm about eight here, and was waiting for my first-ever cake to finish baking.'

'Is that why you've got flour all over your shorts?'

'And often still do, to this day.'

The next photo down was also of a young Benoit, this time flanked by two adults, a vaguely familiar man and a strikingly beautiful woman.

'My mother,' Benoit said. 'Now you see where I got this hair from.'

'And is that your dad?'

'That's Etienne.'

'No way.' I brought the picture closer to my face. 'But he's so . . .'

'Handsome? He was – still is, underneath all that grey fuzz he refuses to have cut.'

'You're a lot like him, you know. The eyes, the shape of the jaw, those straight brows.'

'Huh.' Benoit took the photo from me. 'I suppose we are quite similar. My father looks nothing like me – he's about a foot taller, with ginger hair and freckles.'

'Who's in this one?' I reached for the next photo, only for Benoit to put his hand over it.

'You might not want to,' he said, as I attempted to pull it away.

'Why – are you naked in it?'

The laughter shrivelled in my throat as I stared at an image of my mother, undoubtedly her and yet nothing like her, completely unlike the woman whose eyes I'd last glared into across a hospital waiting room fifteen years ago, that spectre from my past, the ghoul that tormented my thoughts. This woman was smiling; she was clean. Her grey-blond hair was brushed and her swirling dress was alive with colour. The picture had been taken at the café in Libourne's main square, and Etienne was with her, his hand grasping hers, a softness in his gaze, casually but smartly attired in a pale blue shirt and dark trousers, his hair tied back off his face, and no whiskery beard to speak of.

'I took it last summer,' Benoit said. 'It was the first weekend in June, so almost exactly a year ago, and Lilah was celebrating the fact that May was over. I remember thinking that was such an odd thing to say. Most people love May, don't they? The spring sunshine breaks through, flowers are blooming everywhere, the evenings draw out, and there's that feeling of possibility, of things growing, starting over. But she hated it. I never did find out why.'

'I know why,' I said.

Turning the photograph over, I brought it down hard on the floor. There was a crack as the glass shattered, and Benoit rocked back on his heels.

'Oh, God,' I said, instantly appalled. 'I don't know why I did that. I'm so sorry.'

'Don't worry,' he said. 'It's nothing that can't be fixed.'

My hands began to shake. I raised them to my face, pressed my fingers hard against my temples.

'Don't,' I said, shying away as Benoit moved as if to touch me, my tone desperate, strangled. I shut my eyes, pushed harder against my head, felt the tension spread from my shoulders across my back. And then another sensation: that of strong arms encircling me. I resisted for only the briefest moment before giving in and collapsing against him, my head on his chest, the steady rhythm of his heart loud in my ears, the murmur of his lips, so close to my own.

I could not recall ever being held in this way, with such comfort and lack of judgement. Had I not already been on them, Benoit's kindness would have brought me to my knees.

I shuddered violently, and he responded by squeezing me tighter, the warmth from him flowing into me; he rocked me gently, soothing me until I stilled.

Beyond the boundary of his arms lay the murals, each one crafted from a heart yet to be poisoned by grief.

'That's it,' I murmured, and Benoit released his grip, dipping his chin as I tilted my own.

'What's it?' he said, with such tenderness that I wilted.

'The murals,' I said, through lips that felt suddenly dry. 'They are what we need to make this house unique, to captivate guests and keep them coming back.'

With infinite care, Benoit brushed a few errant strands of hair off my face. 'But Etienne isn't— He hasn't painted anything like this for years.'

'Then we have to help him,' I said, sitting up a fraction straighter. 'Find a way to make him care enough to try.'

Benoit's gaze did not falter. 'And what about you, Fliss? Are you going to let us help you in return?'

I started to protest, only to fall silent as he lowered his face towards me, resting the tip of his nose against mine.

'I want to help you.' It was barely a whisper. 'I want to—'

My phone rang, startlingly loud and sudden. Benoit's arms dropped away as I got hurriedly to my feet. It was a video call – Charlie, at last. Fearing he would stage another disappearing act if I didn't answer, I swiped at the screen, just as Benoit stood up behind me, the two of us caught together in the frame.

Charlie did not miss a beat 'Who's that?' he said, as I bolted from the room.

'It's nothing,' I said, plastering on a smile. 'Nobody.'

24

'Seriously, Fliss – who was that?'

'That was Benoit,' I hissed, almost slipping in my haste to get down the attic stairs. 'I told you about him – he inherited the other share of the guesthouse.'

'I thought he was an old drunk?'

I angled the phone so he could see me glaring at him.

'What?' Charlie stuck out his bottom lip. 'I'm supposed to be happy with the fact that you're spending time alone with some good-looking Frenchie, am I?'

I ignored that. 'Thanks for finally calling me back,' I said sarcastically. 'Did you get my messages?'

He should have done. I'd left four.

Charlie put on his best thinking face while I hastened down the final flight of stairs and headed for the front door, keen to put some distance between the house and the conversation I was about to have. The warmth of the day had cooled into a night that was tepid and still.

'Are you outside?' said Charlie, squinting into his screen. 'Weather's been bloody awful here – I got drenched waiting for an Uber earlier.'

I walked quickly, only half-listening as he filled the silence with small talk, and having crossed the near-deserted Place Abel Surchamp, I banked down Rue Fonneuve and found an empty table outside Le Cartel, a wine bar I'd spotted on an earlier meander. No sooner had I sat than a woman emerged with a menu. She had a soft, open face, and smiled encouragingly as I ordered '*une petite eau gazeuse*' in painfully clumsy French.

'Right,' I said, propping my phone against an ashtray. 'What were you saying?'

'That I wasn't ignoring you on purpose. I was summoned for lunch with my folks, and you know how they feel about phones at the table. I've only been back about an hour, and had to get straight in the shower on account of the rain.'

He was in our bedroom at The Fitz; I recognised the paisley print on the headboard.

'Are you already in bed?'

'No. Well, yes, I suppose in a literal sense I am, but I'm not going to sleep. This is just a pitstop before I head out. Gregster and Jazz are insisting I join them at The Beauf.'

'Insisting?' I said drily, breaking off to thank the waitress for my sparkling water.

Charlie's lip was protruding again.

'We have to talk about it,' I said. 'The joint account is empty, and you've moved thousands out of my personal account. How did you even gain access?'

'You told me the password once,' he said, nostrils flaring. 'You said, in case I get hit by a bus, all my online passwords are either MikeyFitz69 or FitzMikey69, for your dad.'

'You can rest assured I'll be changing them.'

Charlie didn't reply, instead going into our en suite and propping the phone by the sink as he applied wax to his hair.

'What did you take the money for?' I asked. 'Repairs? The plumber? A bill I missed?'

'You think I can get away with a side-sweep fringe?'

'Charlie!'

The phone slid down, and I was treated to a view of the spotlit bathroom ceiling. A headache was beginning to take root.

I sipped my water, looking past my phone for a moment towards the other tables. There were three couples, as well as a gaggle of women who looked around my age. As I stared, one of the party turned away from her friends to spark a cigarette, and in the flash of the lighter, I recognised her as Céline.

'Lost you there for a second.' Charlie was back, tweaking a section of hair, twisting another.

'This is serious,' I said. 'You've left me with barely a penny, and there are things I need to pay for over here, jobs that have to be done on the guesthouse.'

'But we should be prioritising the hotel,' he said. 'What about all the work that needs doing here?'

'What happened to "We can use the insurance money for that"?'

Charlie's eyes flickered to the right of the screen. 'You know insurance companies. They'll do anything to get out of paying. It's how the brokers all get so stinking-pig rich.'

A great weight settled on my chest. 'They're not going to pay out for the fire damage?'

He grimaced.

'But that's ridiculous. What reason did they give?'

'Something about clause this or clause that,' he grumbled. 'It wasn't clear. All that was made abundantly clear was the fact we aren't getting a bloody penny out of them.'

'It was an accident, though. It's not as if you set the place alight on purpose.'

'I told them that. The issue, I think, is that it was me in that damn room. If a guest had done it, that would've been different, but because it was me . . .'

I swore loudly enough that the couple at the nearest table exchanged a wide-eyed look. 'I'll call them,' I said. 'Send me the number.'

'Won't do any good. We went with Taylor's, remember? The owner is an old colleague of Pa's. It was him I spoke to, in fact, and they're not budging. I'm sorry, Fliss. I screwed up.'

'Is that why you took our savings, then – and mine? To make up the shortfall?'

Charlie was clad only in a towel, and, stepping back from the vanity unit, he let it drop to the floor. At the sight of his flaccid penis, I slammed the handset down on the table, fury mounting as the tinny sound of laughter filtered out. Raising the phone, though not enough that the screen would be visible, I leaned forward and hissed at him to stop messing around.

'Fine,' he said, and when I looked again, he'd put on boxers and was buttoning up his shirt.

'This still isn't adding up,' I said. 'There are no invoices for any repair work – I checked the email account. So where has the money really gone?'

He sighed. 'Fine. I used it to pay a few credit card bills. Happy now?'

'A few? I thought we only had one, for the business.'

'*We* do. But I have some personal accounts.'

It was as if someone had dropped a breeze block into my stomach. I watched as though dazed as Charlie went back into the bedroom. I caught a glimpse of a whisky bottle beside the television, its lid unscrewed, the glass beside it half full of amber liquid. He was drinking again as well. Anger smouldered inside my chest.

'How many is "some", Charlie?'

'Oh,' he said casually, 'four or five.'

Four or five?

'And how much on each?'

'The limit on one is only five grand, so that's manageable. Then another is twelve, and there's a ten and' – he coughed – 'an eighteen.'

I did the maths, blood draining as rapidly as the bubbles were rising in my *eau gazeuse*.

'So, what? You're forty-five thousand pounds in debt?'

He winced. 'Networking doesn't come cheap, you know – especially not in Chelsea. You barely ever come out with me – and you never mingle in the bar,' he continued. 'You sit there squirrelled away in the office, while I go out and entertain, like I'm Bingo the bloody Clown.'

Where was the man I'd met? It was as if I'd planted tomato seeds and ended up with a patch of thistles.

'Squirrelling away is what I have to do,' I told him. 'Someone has to do all the mundane tasks that you complain are dull. If it wasn't for me, the hotel wouldn't function at all.'

'And if it wasn't for *me*, it wouldn't have any guests,' he threw back.

A beat passed during which all I could do was glare at him, and him at me. This wasn't who we were, or it hadn't been until we went into business together. Had I been naïve to think that the two of us could work and live side by side? Angela had expressed her doubts at the time, but I had disregarded her, bullishly sure that we would thrive, that I could make it work.

'All we need is one large injection of cash,' Charlie went on. 'Then we can clear all the debt and start again with a clean slate, us and the business.'

He climbed into his trousers and pulled them up.

'You should have told me sooner,' I said despondently. 'The insurance company know about the outstanding debt, I presume. It provides a rather compelling motive for arson, wouldn't you agree?'

At this, finally, he looked shamefaced. 'They can't honestly think I'd try to burn the bloody place down for a measly fifty grand? It's worth well over a hundred times that amount.'

'And what about the drink, Charlie?'

He froze in the motion of fastening his shirt cuffs.

'I can see the bottle.'

He moved it instinctively. 'It was only one. I needed to take the edge off. I made it through an entire lunch with my parents on nothing more exciting than Perrier.'

'It's never "only one", though, is it? You know how this works, Charlie – alcohol leads to bad decisions, and—'

'Don't do that,' he interrupted curtly. 'Don't talk to me as if I'm a teenager. I know I have to quit, OK? I bloody well am trying.'

'Doesn't look much like it from where I'm sitting.'

A stalemate silence settled, him glowering, me tight-lipped with exasperation. I wanted to run, to rage, to punch, but I was paralysed, vision tunnelling, voice shaking as I muttered my next three words: 'This isn't working.'

Céline and her friends had moved inside. I could see them clearly through the large front windows. She was at the bar, talking to a well-built man with a full beard, a hand placed coyly on her hip. I would once have stood in front of Charlie in that way, laughing as he regaled me with stories about the mishaps he and his friends had got caught up in, blushing when he told me I was the most beautiful woman he'd ever seen, daring to hope it was all true, and that I could, at last, embark on a new chapter of my life, and leave the past to wither and die.

'What?' Charlie had turned pale. 'Fliss, what do you mean, "This isn't working"? You can't mean us?'

A rogue tear burst the ramparts of my self-control. 'The hotel,' I said, wiping my cheek. 'I thought we could handle it, I believed in us making a success of it, but it's not working – *we* are not working.'

'We are!'

'No.' I shook my head. 'If you can't do the job without drinking, then you can't do the job. It's all such a mess, Charlie, don't you see? The fire, Madeline, all these debts, the lies. I think it's time we accepted reality.'

'You mean give up?' he said, blinking in amazement. 'No fucking way. Sorry, Fliss, but you don't get to bail at the first sign of trouble – that's not how relationships work. We're engaged to be married, or had you forgotten that?'

Instinctively, I glanced down at my bare finger. In taking off my ring, had I subconsciously made my decision? Had I, in fact, been making it ever since I heard the peal of that fire alarm going off?

'You're catastrophising,' he went on decisively. 'Panicking because of the money. But I've given them enough to keep the wolves from the door, and once you find your investor, we'll be back in the game. All I'm asking for is a chance. If the roles were reversed, I'd do it for you. I'd bail you out in a heartbeat.'

I took a large, fortifying sip of sparkling water. It had gone flat in the time we'd been talking, and tasted slightly metallic. 'I know you would.'

Or rather, his parents would. It made me queasy to think about how much his family had already invested in us.

'Well, then.' Charlie's triumph was grating.

'Well nothing,' I said. 'I need some time with this, and you should take some as well. We should both think about what we want, and—'

'I don't need to think,' he said petulantly. 'I know what I want, and it's you, us, this place, a wedding, kids, a future, maybe even a dog, one day.'

It was everything I had wanted to hear, once. Misery felled me, and I slumped in my chair. 'I'm going to go,' I said. 'Please, pour what's left in that whisky bottle down the sink. I'll call you in a few days, OK?'

'Not OK,' he said. 'Very bloody far from it.'

And with that, the screen went black.

I slid a five-euro note beneath my half-empty glass and returned slowly to the guesthouse, stopping outside for a few minutes to stare up at its crumbling façade. Light glowed around the edges of the top-floor windows, and I thought of Benoit inside, of the way he had held me, comforted me, and how safe I'd felt in his arms.

Blinkering my mind, I went inside and headed straight to my room, thinking only of sleep, of solitude, of oblivion. The sight that greeted me when I switched on the light stole the air from my lungs. All the way around the walls, sprouting up from the floorboards and above the skirting, someone had painted hundreds and hundreds of bright blue forget-me-nots.

25

When I heard the creak of feet on the stairs the following morning, I was ready.

'Check this out,' I said, gesturing at the mural. 'Someone's been busy.'

Benoit rubbed sleepily at his eyes. He was wearing another faded band T-shirt over grey tracksuit bottoms, feet bare and curls awry. The stubble across his jaw had gone from scratchy to soft, with a small pale patch where his Cupid's bow dipped.

'Well I never,' he said, crouching to get a better look.

'Do you know if Etienne was drunk yesterday? Was he sober when he did this?'

'As far as I know,' Benoit said. 'Though he did start singing along to one of his more mournful records after you went out last night, which he usually only does if he's had a few.'

'I didn't hear anything when I came in,' I said. 'Maybe he passed out in the lounge again?'

Benoit stood up, his arm brushing against mine. 'How are you feeling today? You were pretty upset when I saw you last.'

'Yeah.' My breath felt sharper suddenly. 'I'm sorry about that. I hadn't seen a photograph of my mum in a long time, not for years, and it was a shock more than anything.'

He tugged at the neck of his T-shirt. 'I'm the one who should be sorry.'

'You tried to stop me,' I reminded him. 'There's nothing to apologise for.'

'And everything else?' he said. 'Was that Charlie on the phone last night?'

I smiled grimly.

'Was it a misunderstanding, about the money?'

'Ish,' I said, blowing air out through my cheeks. 'But don't worry, it's my problem. Honestly,' I went on, when he eyed me doubtfully, 'I actually woke up today with a renewed sense of purpose. This new mural . . . I don't know, it made me believe more in the potential of this place. That potential has always been there, but seeing the mural last night was the first time I felt it, and now I'm raring to get going.'

Benoit broke into a smile as I mimed rolling up my sleeves. It was far too hot to wear any – I had dressed in a vest and shorts, tying back my hair in preparation for the day's work.

'One mural changed your entire mindset?' he said. 'Impressive.'

'Should I even be calling it a mural?'

'Well, if you want to pretend that you're French, we should call it *une fresque*,' Benoit replied, tongue rolling languorously over the words.

'Oh,' I said, enthused. 'How about we go one step further and name this place La Fresque Hotel?'

'Technically, it would have to be L'Hotel Mural . . .'

'Hmm. OK, in that case, let's ignore the hotel part, and stick to La Fresque.' I stuck out my hand, and Benoit removed his own from the pocket of his tracksuit bottoms to shake it.

'La Fresque it is,' he said.

We parted ways – he to fetch coffee and check on Etienne, me to begin tearing down more wallpaper in the corner room upstairs. We'd agreed to rendezvous outside once the skip arrived. I began on the back wall, tucking a scraper behind the ripped and sagging paper, though it required little encouragement to come down. Within the first forty-five minutes, I'd cleared almost half the room. Through sheer grit, I banished thoughts of Charlie, of the mountain of debt he'd accumulated, of my mum's former bedroom, still yet to be excavated, instead concentrating on how I would further transform the space I was in. The kitchenette area meant this room had built-in potential to be more of a studio, in which future guests could prepare their own simple meals. We would need to source a table and chairs, and I made a mental note to ask Adélard about the best locations for buying second-hand furniture.

With my arms and shoulders aching in protest, I stood on my tiptoes to reach a section of paper that was barely still adhered to the wall. I gave it a single, firm tug, stepping back as the lot came slithering down.

'No, no, no,' I groaned. Black mould coated the back of the paper, clumps of plaster had fallen with it and, most concerningly of all, there was a large patch of damp on the exposed wall. When Benoit came into the room a few minutes later with coffee, Adélard and an oven-warm croissant on a chipped blue plate, he found me rooted to the spot, still staring.

'*Merde*,' said Adélard. Crossing to the window, he heaved up the sash and peered out. '*Merde*,' he said again, shaking his head. 'The guttering out here, it is destroyed.'

Benoit put down the croissant.

'Destroyed' was not a word you ever wanted to hear while renovating a property – especially not in conjunction with guttering. I joined Adélard at the window and felt my throat close up – there were cavernous holes in the iron piping, mounds of moss and cracks clogged with detritus. Benoit, who had come to stand behind me, swore quietly to himself.

'It must have been like that for ages,' he said. 'Can it be fixed, do you think?'

Adélard began rhythmically tapping his fingers against the wall. 'Anything can be fixed,' he said, 'but a job like this, it is going to cost you a lot.' He turned away as he said it, a single finger raised to silence us as he brought his phone to his ear and began speaking in rapid French. Benoit remained half-in and half-out of the window, palms pressed against the sill, sunlight turning his curls copper bright.

'I have a friend who will come now to take a look,' Adélard said, after finishing his phone call. 'He'll give you a fair price.'

I nodded as the blood drained from my cheeks.

Benoit ducked back into the room, his expression every bit as grim as my own. 'This one is going to sting,' he said.

'Almost certainly,' I agreed.

'But you must do it.' Adélard was matter-of-fact. 'If you leave it, the damage will become worse, the problem bigger, and the eventual cost will be far higher.'

'Whose idea was it to rip down wallpaper anyway?' I said feebly.

Neither man so much as smiled in response. Adélard touched the wall and visibly shuddered, while Benoit wandered away and began inspecting a stack of canvases on the other side of the room.

'What are you looking for?' I asked, going to crouch beside him.

He shifted position, knee warm against mine. 'I was worried the damp might've got into the paintings, but they seem to be unscathed.'

Swathes of blue, green and gold flashed past, as he flipped from one exquisite landscape after another, pausing at one depicting Libourne from the opposite bank of the Isle. Etienne had added gold leaf to the surface of the water, and the sky was a swirl of sunset pastels. Below the artist's signature was a date: "Juin, 1973".

'How old is Etienne?' I asked.

Benoit thought for a moment. 'He was born in 1955, two years before my mother, so . . .'

'He'll be seventy this year,' I said. 'Or is already?'

'Not yet; his birthday's in August.'

'Twelve years older than my mum,' I said, more to myself than him. 'That means Etienne must have painted this when he was only seventeen. When I was that age, all I ever drew were doodles along the edges of essays I was supposed to be writing.'

'I didn't do the doodles or the essays,' Benoit said. 'I was always more of a hands-on man.'

'The same as me,' Adélard chipped in from across the room.

Benoit and I exchanged a wry smile.

'Etienne did a series of gold-leaf landscapes,' he went on, using the hem of his T-shirt to wipe dust from the picture frame. 'I think only six or seven in total, and highly sought-after once he'd made a name for himself. I should take this one upstairs,' he decided, 'keep it safe with the others.'

'Do it later,' Adélard said, leaning through the open window. 'Bernard's arrived.'

A moment later, knocking echoed through the house.

'I will go to fetch him.' Adélard disappeared into the corridor, tread heavy on the wooden boards.

'I'm starting to get the sense that this place is crumbling to pieces around us,' I said.

'It's survived this long,' Benoit said. 'And I don't believe anything is too broken to be fixed. That extends to people as well, although . . .' He stopped, cocking his ear. 'I think that's Etienne on his way up. I'd better get this out of here,' he added, holding the painting more closely against his chest, 'just in case he—'

The door swung open and Adélard marched straight past us, ushering his friend, Bernard – a broad-shouldered, thickset man of around fifty or so – towards the damaged wall. Etienne, who'd brought up the rear, stood and gazed around in awe, as if seeing the room for the first time. The tatty smock was gone, replaced by a faded polo shirt and jeans. He looked younger somehow, less the eccentric artist and more the kindly uncle. When he saw me, he smiled with what felt like genuine warmth.

Bernard muttered something I could not decipher to Adélard, who chuntered in agreement.

'What are they saying?' I murmured to Benoit.

'Nothing good. A lot about special materials, scaffolding and neglect.'

Adélard broke away and came to join us, motioning for Etienne to do the same. The four of us huddled in the kitchenette area, Benoit still clutching the painting.

'Bernard has a gap in his schedule, and he can do it,' he said. 'That is the good news.'

'And the bad?' I asked.

Adélard pressed his thumb and forefinger into the corner of each eye and blinked as if clearing dust. 'The quote is six thousand. He cannot go any lower. It's not only this area of the guttering that needs to be replaced,' he went on, as my jaw went slack. 'He must check all of it.'

'That is . . . fine.' Benoit took a breath. 'I can do that.'

'Isn't there a way we can take out a loan?' I protested. 'Against the house? Something short-term, until we find an investor.'

'No need,' he said briskly. 'Don't worry about it.'

'But I *do* worry about it. I worry that you're bearing the brunt of all the costs.'

Etienne made a comment, which Benoit dismissed with a slight shake of his head, before stooping to prop the painting against the wall. Adélard had returned to where Bernard was now scribbling away in a small notebook. The two men began pointing, frowning, measuring with their hands, putting into motion a task exorbitant enough to leach all discernible colour from Benoit's face.

'However much it ends up costing, I'll pay you back my half when we find a buyer,' I said.

Etienne's head snapped around.

'Oh no,' I said, 'we're not selling the whole place.' The words were becoming garbled in my haste to reassure him, to mend the crack I'd inadvertently opened – a metaphorical one to join the legion of actual fissures.

'It's OK,' Benoit said, 'he knows what we're doing. Turning to Etienne, he added, '*J'ai expliqué.*'

'*Oui,*' the older man agreed, though he sounded unsure to me.

'Please, don't worry,' I said, as with a grunt of effort, Etienne crouched to look at the painting. 'We'll figure something out.'

'Bennie,' Adélard called. 'Come and join us.'

There was no way I was going to allow myself to be elbowed out of proceedings, and after a moment's hesitation, I crossed the room, listening as Bernard rattled off a long spiel, which Benoit then translated back to me in snatches. It was strange, being the one on the periphery. During the refurbishment of The Fitz, it had been me who liaised with the London-based equivalents of Bernard; Charlie was content to eschew what he deemed the 'nitty gritty'. My ability to project-manage did not intimidate him; he did not assume that he could do better, simply because he was a man in a man's world. In that small way, he'd reminded me of my dad – both had professed to seeing good in me that I struggled to believe was there.

The three men had begun to talk over each other in French. I moved away, towards the window, stared out at the cloud-brushed sky beyond the rooftops, felt the hot breath of sun against my skin, and tried not to see my father's face on a hospital bed, pale and waxy, nothing left of him but the vessel in which he had taken on the world and lost.

It was a while before I could trust myself to turn back around, my attention straying past the huddle of still-debating men to the space behind them, empty now of its previous occupant.

Etienne had gone, and he had taken the gold-leaf painting with him.

26

My instinct was to go after him, and so I did.

For a man of nearly seventy, Etienne was remarkably sprightly, and by the time I'd gathered my wits enough to hurry out on to the landing, he had reached the ground floor. A moment later, I heard the front door open. Gripping the banister, I propelled myself down, taking the stairs two at a time before racing outside. Etienne was at the far end of the street, heading in the direction of the main square. He had the painting tucked under one arm, and there was a buoyancy to his stride wholly unlike the shuffling gait with which he usually wandered the house. It was a walk that signalled purpose and determination.

The sun was high and bloated, the street ahead flecked with patterns of light and shade. Bursts of green adorned the walls and pavements: crawling ivy, untamed weeds and tufts of hardy grass. Libourne was becoming familiar, a jumble of life laid out in haphazard tableaus that somehow fit together to make a whole. Accustomed to being the outsider in most scenarios, the sense I had of belonging, the feeling that I could become one of this small French town's many puzzle pieces, was hard to grasp. I didn't feel the same way about London, and I had been born there.

Etienne reached the end of the road and paused to read-just the painting in his arms before crossing on to the square. I kept him in sight as he hurried along the covered arcades, occasionally nodding distractedly to those he passed. Shoppers congregated outside gift shops and sat together at café tables, spectators of life's minutiae. The Carrefour blew out a frigid blast of cool air through its automatic doors as I passed, dodging a sparrow that was plucking crumbs from between the cobblestones. Not once did I allow Etienne to slip out of sight, tailing him along Rue Thiers to a modest-sized, glass-fronted building that bore a sign reading: 'Maison Galerie Vanessa Montagne'. I ventured closer, stopping when I saw my own reflection in the glass: hair in dire need of a brush, hollow eyes and pale skin, no make-up. A far cry from the put-together image I had learned to maintain at home.

An acrylic print of tulips was suspended by wire in the window, the canvas wide enough that it provided me with ample space behind which to lurk and watch as a woman rushed out to greet Etienne. She was tall, her slender figure encased in a cerise jumpsuit and her grey hair pinned up in a chignon. They exchanged a customary kiss of greeting, and Etienne turned the painting around, prompting her to raise a pair of glasses hanging from a chain around her neck. Almost immediately, an expression of wonder spread across her face, and, having checked her watch, she ushered Etienne through an open door at the back of the shop and closed it behind them.

I waited on the opposite side of the street, my back against the cool stone wall, its texture rough beneath my fingers.

'*Patience is a virtue,*' Dad often told me. Mikey Fitzgerald had been a big fan of idioms, tossing them like fish food across the waters of my young, developing mind. '*Rome wasn't built in a day,*' he'd say, when the Lego structures we constructed toppled and fell. '*Look after your pennies and the pounds will look after themselves,*' he'd gravely proclaim as he pressed a shiny pound coin of pocket money into my palm. '*Curiosity killed the cat*,' was his preferred phrase if I asked one question too many. He had been right, about all of it. Patience was an essential skill in our household, and mastering it was a non-negotiable must if you hoped to survive. His had never wavered, unlike my own.

I stared down at my hands, which had curled into fists, and beyond to the warped shape of my own shadow. A memory swam into focus, vague and faceless, leached of colour: a hard yet malleable ball, pressed hard between my finger and thumb; sweetness on my tongue, and another sensation, just out of reach. If only I could take hold of it, force my subconscious to stencil it back into being, then this feeling, and the certainty with which I knew I was missing something vital, would merge into understanding. So many times I had experienced the same sense, and on each occasion, I went no further towards understanding it.

The door to the gallery opened.

'Ah,' Etienne said, sounding not in the least bit surprised to see me there. 'You are here.'

'I am,' I said. Then, noticing his hands were empty, I asked, 'Where's the painting?'

'It's gone,' he said, with a grin so mischievous that I could not help but smile in return. 'Madame Montagne has a collector. Within a week, it will be sold.'

'Sold? But wasn't that the last one?'

'Oui, it was the final *Ville Lumiere* work. *Viens*,' he continued, 'let us walk.' Taking my hand, he drew it through the crook of his elbow.

'But why now?' I persisted. 'It must have meant something to you, for you to have kept it all these years.'

'Something,' he allowed, 'but not everything. There are more important things.'

A young woman in a long flowing skirt strolled past us, a chihuahua prancing delicately along beside her. '*Bonjour, petit chien,*' Etienne said with a chuckle.

'This is about the guttering, isn't it,' I said. 'At the house?'

He smiled broadly and patted my hand. 'Very clever. *Fille très intelligente.*'

The square opened up ahead of us, and Etienne towed me across to a florist, relinquishing my arm so he could inspect the bouquets of yellow, white and red roses, elegant fragranced lilies and frothy pink peonies bound together with twine.

'Aha,' he said, lifting a bunch of sunflowers and offering them to me. 'Felicity flowers.'

'Not much that's sunny about me,' I said. 'And since I saw the mural you painted in my bedroom, I think I prefer forget-me-nots.'

Etienne put the bouquet back in its bucket, and once again fed my arm through his. 'The favourite of your mother also,' he said, and my smile faltered.

'Yes, I remember.'

We continued to amble, and Etienne talked, explaining how Libourne had inherited its chessboard layout from its Roman origins, and pointing out details he liked, such as the wrought-iron balustrades of the surrounding houses, and the corbel balconies above them.

'It's no real wonder you became an artist,' I mused. 'There's so much here to inspire you.'

'Libourne is' – he put his head on one side – 'my home. I believe you can always find beauty in the things, the places, the people, that you love most dearly; those that live in your heart. You must feel the same way about your home, *non*?'

'London is a fascinating city,' I said carefully. 'I'm sure it is beautiful, to some people.'

'But not to you?'

'I don't get out enough to look, not anymore.'

Etienne dug in his shirt pocket and produced a cloth handkerchief, dabbing it against his forehead.

'Will you paint more murals?' I asked. 'The one you did for me, and the scene you created in the attic, they're incredible. Benoit and I, we thought you might like to do some more . . .' I trailed off when I caught sight of his expression. 'Why not? You're so talented.'

Etienne sighed, his grip on my arm going slack. 'Art does not work this way, *chérie*. It is born not of demand, but inspiration.'

'If that's true, then why did you paint over the murals you'd already finished with ones that are, well, not quite the same?'

He stopped and looked at me in bewilderment.

'Benoit told me,' I said. 'He said that after – what happened, that was when you—'

'I was sad,' he interrupted dolefully. 'I am sad still. Nothing is beautiful; everything is pain.' He could have been describing the past version of me, my feelings, my life.

'The forget-me-not mural is beautiful,' I told him. 'Are you telling me that creating it felt painful?'

A smile found its way back to his lips, though it was fleeting. '*Non*,' he said slowly. Turning to face me, he took each of my hands in his. 'You are so much like my Lilah. The way that you move, how you speak, and your light, whatever is inside that draws others towards you – it was there in her, and it is there in you.'

I stiffened. 'I'm nothing like her,' I said, so acidly that he withdrew from me, stepping back and dropping my arms so that they fell to my sides. 'My mum was weak, and she was selfish.'

Etienne crinkled his dark blue eyes. 'She was afraid,' he countered softly. 'And she was angry.'

'She didn't have anything to be afraid of or angry about. She drank because she was weak, and the drinking made her care about nothing but herself. I know,' I insisted, as he continued to gaze steadily at me. 'I was there.'

'Felicity,' he called, as I hurried away. We had almost reached the guesthouse. I could see the cracked paint of the shutters, the still-open window on the upper floor.

'Don't,' I said. 'I don't want to hear it.'

Etienne caught up with me on the steps. 'The alcohol is what we use to forget,' he said, the words heavy with lament. 'It is what Lilah did to forget.'

'To forget what?' I demanded. 'That she was a mother, that she had responsibilities, that she was supposed to turn up for work, wash my school uniform, make even the slightest bit of effort to prove that she felt anything other than hatred towards me?'

I breathed hard to stop myself crying, shying away when Etienne attempted to console me.

'It was to forget her sadness, *chérie*. You must try to find some forgiveness for her.'

The white noise of incredulity fizzed inside my head.

'Me, forgive her? No, I won't. I can't. I don't want to.' I stared up at the house, a symbol of her past and my future. I'd worked so hard to extricate myself from all of it, and now here I was, entangled once more in the mess that had been my mother.

Etienne touched a hand to my shoulder. 'You do not have to *want* to,' he said. 'You only need to try.'

27

The door to my mother's old bedroom was closed.

I stared at the brass handle, a gamut of options unspool-ing. I could do this on another day, or I could decide never to do it; I could pack up and go, forget I had been to this place, met these people, been forced to confront my past.

My fingers encircled the metal. I gripped, then pushed. A creak as the hinges folded, the soft whisper of wood against carpet, a sprawl of delicate blossom, painted by a skilled hand. The shutters were closed, and the air was dense, scented with stale perfume and a trace of something sharp, medici-nal. Averting my eyes from the unmade bed, I crossed into the en suite. A bottle of nail-polish remover stood on the edge of the basin, its lid abandoned in the chaos of face creams, toothpaste, ancient pots of make-up and foil packets of aspi-rin. Scant greys trailed from a hair toggle on the windowsill, and I stared at it for a long time, recalling how I used to curl my mother's hair around my fingers as she read to me, twist-ing the golden strands around and around. I was young enough, then, to be oblivious to her apathy, the monotonous way in which she went through the motions of caring for me. As I grew, that same coldness penetrated, going right through into my bones, and the more I craved an escape from it, the less she seemed able to offer. Had I ever loved her? I was sure that I must have; could still feel the remnants of a love so all-encompassing that it frightened me to look too closely. I had lost something, that I knew, and there was no way of getting it back.

With a sigh, I returned to the bedroom. Cobwebs hung from lampshades and clothes littered the floor in front of overstuffed chests of drawers. A wicker basket had split beneath its cargo of dirty washing, and a hairdryer lay plugged in on the floor beside a full-length mirror that was murky with dust. There were more clothes in a built-in wardrobe, a few of Etienne's smocks but mostly bold-print dresses in shift or kaftan shapes. Tossed into the bottom were few tatty pairs of sandals, and a pair of black ankle boots, the heel of each worn down, the soles cracked.

In the drawer of a narrow bedside table, I unearthed a nest of necklaces and several pairs of gold clip-on earrings. Alongside a half-empty packet of tissues, an old leather bookmark and a tin of lip balm, was a jar of hand cream so old that the label had all but rubbed off. I unscrewed the lid, inhaled soap, vanilla, an undertone of orange blossom.

She can't have been drinking as much, not if she was bothering to paint her nails and apply moisturiser. The woman I remembered was unwashed more often than not, her hair lank and complexion pallid; breath sulphuric when she hissed in my face to leave her alone. I challenged her once to look at me, properly *look at me*, and she couldn't, not even when I clasped her head between my hands and held her steady. She had closed her eyes, screwing them tightly shut; she had shaken, screamed and shouted, the mere sight of me enough to make her hysterical, yet she refused to tell me why. Nobody ever told me why.

I dropped the hand cream back into the drawer and cast around, searching for a task, a distraction, anything to reel my mind back from venturing further towards the past. I hadn't brought any bin bags upstairs, and the small wastepaper bin in the corner was full to overflowing. Clearing up would have to wait, but I could strip the bed, gather up the clothes on the carpet and tackle the basket of washing.

The duvet cover was threadbare, the sheet below it creased from use. My gaze snagged on the indentation in the mattress, the space in which she would have rested, and dreamed, and made love, all the while unaware of what lay around the corner, of the end that fate had in store. In some regards, she was lucky to have been spared the agony of a long illness, though to die so abruptly, without the chance to do or say what you might want or need to, was far crueller to those left behind. I recalled what Benoit had said by the river, his suggestion that my mum had understood enough about me to know what to bestow should the unthinkable occur, and how I'd been so keen to dismiss it. Could he have been right? Only one person knew for certain, and the chance to ask her had passed.

I shook my head, snatching up one of the pillows and tugging off the pillowcase, only for it to slither through my fingers.

'Well, thank you very much,' I grumbled, stooping to retrieve it and noticing as I did so that something was sticking out from under the bed – a canvas bag that I was sure I'd seen before. It had been my dad's, the one he used when he and I went away to visit Angela and Patrick for the weekend. Mum rarely came with us. There was always some excuse: she had a job interview or wanted to do a spring clean – laughable – or she had a cold, and didn't want to pass it on. I knew, just as my dad did, that all she really wanted was time alone to drink. Alcohol was always her priority.

I slid the bag towards me, wiped a sheath of dust off the top and eased apart the zip, only to rock backwards in surprise. My favourite childhood toy was nestled inside, a stuffed bunny with pink fur and a sewn-on button for a nose. I had believed it lost a long time ago.

'Hello, Thumper,' I murmured, breathing in its mildewy scent. I'd chosen the name after watching the *Bambi* movie, enchanted by the rabbit who teaches the young fawn how to survive after his mother is killed, and for a time, I could not sleep without it, loathed being parted from it when I went to school. On the days Dad collected me, he would often bring Thumper with him and make it wave to me. The joy I'd feel would distract me from what his presence at the gate meant: that Mum was having one of her 'wobbles'.

I put down the rabbit, only to find a second inside the bag, this one yellow and in far better condition, the same style yet totally unfamiliar. Didn't parents sometimes keep a reserve version of toys in case of loss or breakage? Though if that were the case here, wouldn't they have selected a second pink bunny? A gift, then? One that had never found its way to me? Angela might know.

I returned to the bag, drawing out a thin sheaf of photographs that I hurriedly upended. The first was an image I knew well, as it had sat on the mantelpiece of our family lounge for the entirety of my childhood. A wedding photo, Dad in a brown suit and Mum in understated white, both self-conscious but aglow with happiness, her fingers wrapped tightly around his. Below it in the stack was another of my father, taken a few years later, sideburns long and shirt collar pointed, grinning up towards the camera from a picnic blanket spread across our old lawn. My mother must have taken it – he never smiled at anyone the way he did at her.

I flicked through several more, all taken in the era before I was born, my parents laughing, relaxed, full of the life that I had so yearned to see in my mum. The pain came then, scraped its way through my guts, but I couldn't stop. I pored over each captured moment, examining it for details, biting back tears at seeing my parents so young and carefree.

In becoming my mum and dad, they had been broken. I had broken them, and so it came as little surprise to discover only three photos of myself. One taken on my third birthday, chocolate icing spread across my face and more smeared in my golden pigtails; a second where I was perched between my parents on a stony beach, Dad smiling in his red shorts, me holding up a great mound of seaweed for the camera, knees knobbly below my yellow swimsuit. On the back, someone had scribbled: 'Chesil, Dorset, July 1997'. A holiday of significance for my mum? Nothing came to mind, but then, every positive memory I had featured my dad in the starring role. Mum was little more than a smudge in the background, a brooding sense of disquiet.

In the third photograph, I was a baby, all pudgy legs and soft cheeks, sitting in an old-fashioned pram with large, spoked wheels and a fixed hood, another infant beside me. The shock of hair was so blond, and the features so similar to mine, that it had to be Jono. My cousin was only a few months younger than me, and still blonder than a dandelion. In all likelihood, his mum, Angela, was the one who'd taken the picture.

Feet sounded on the stairs, and I turned as Benoit came into the room. It took a moment or two before he spotted me on the floor, the innards of the bag spread out around me.

'I thought you might be hungry.' He held up a plate covered with cling film. 'It's only a cheese sandwich, but the relish is an original Chapdelaine concoction.'

'That's kind of you,' I said, as he came towards me. 'A croissant this morning and now this?'

'Food is what I do,' he said, scooting down next to me. 'Every time I'm peckish, I assume everyone else must be as well.'

'A fair assumption.'

'You disappeared.' He nudged the plate towards me.

'I went after Etienne – did he tell you about the painting?'

Benoit plucked an errant piece of fluff from his sock, feet for once not bare. 'He did. I told him to go and get it back.'

'And what did he say to that?' I asked, though thought I could guess.

'He told me, in no uncertain terms, to *se taire.*'

'Does that mean "shut up", by any chance?'

Benoit responded with a single mirthless laugh.

'He's selling it to help us fix this place,' I pointed out. 'The deed might not be in his name anymore, but he still lives here, will live here for the rest of his life. It makes sense that he'd want to invest in keeping the house standing.'

'True,' Benoit allowed, 'but satisfaction doesn't always follow logic.'

'Amen to that,' I replied drily, helping myself to a bite of the sandwich. It was, as I'd predicted, utterly delicious, the onion relish sharp and sweet against the salty, nutty cheese.

'So,' Benoit said, as I took another bite, 'you finally came in here.'

I nodded through my chewing.

'Hang on a minute,' he said, reaching around me to pick up a photo. 'Is this you?'

'Afraid so. A regular little creature of the deep, complete with seaweed boa.'

'Cute,' he observed. 'And is that your dad?'

I stared for a moment at the wedding photo. 'That is the late, great Mikey Fitzgerald,' I confirmed.

'He looks so young – they both do.'

'They were. My dad had just turned twenty when they got married – Mum was only nineteen.'

'Different times,' he said pensively. 'Nobody seems to get married young anymore. Oh, is this you as a baby?' He was pointing at baby Jono.

I slid his finger across to the right place. 'That's me. You can tell from the grumpy expression.'

'You haven't changed a bit,' he joked, and I rolled my eyes. 'But the other baby looks like you, too.'

I swallowed more of the sandwich. 'That's my cousin.'

'Huh.' He squinted more closely at the picture. 'The two of you could be twins.'

I pushed the plate away as Benoit continued to sift through the stack.

'Lilah looks beautiful in these,' he said. 'Not that she wasn't still an attractive woman when . . . More recently.'

'A bit rougher around the edges, no doubt,' I said. 'That's what a lifetime of hard drinking will do to you. You know, I can't recall ever seeing her eat, not even at mealtimes. My dad had this thing about dinnertime; he always wanted us to sit down as a family, no TV on in the background, nothing like that, just conversation. Mum would sit there with her glass of wine and an empty plate in front of her, and it was all so weird and fake. I'd set the table while Dad cooked, and I'd always lay out a placemat and cutlery for her, then later, I'd put everything away again untouched. Dad never said anything, at least not in front of me, and I hated it.' I shook my head. 'Once, when I was about thirteen, I plucked up the courage to ask her why, and she couldn't even answer. She just got up from the table and walked away from me.'

Benoit's face was lined with sorrow. 'That must have been difficult.'

'Infuriating is what it was. And when I got nowhere with her, I turned on my dad. I thought he should push her harder, but it was as if he was scared she'd break. Most of the time, he treated her as if she was made of spun sugar – it drove me mad.'

'Can I ask how your dad died? Lilah never talked about him.'

I stared down at my hands, which had begun to shake.

'It's OK,' he said quickly, 'you don't have to tell me.'

So few people knew the truth, the part I had played in it all, the stain it had left on my life. Not even Charlie knew everything; I hadn't wanted to tell him. But with Benoit, the compulsion to omit the truth was not as ingrained. Perhaps because, with his calm unflappability and tendency towards compassion, he reminded me of my dad. And so, despite barely knowing him at all, I trusted him, trusted the instinct telling me that I should.

Selecting the photo of my dad in his ridiculous seventies shirt, I found my way to a smile, and, with a final deep breath, began to tell him my story.

28

'It happened on my birthday,' I said. 'My eighteenth, to be exact.'

Benoit, who was leaning against the bed with his knees bent, made a small noise of dismay.

'Tenth of May, 2007. That was the day. I'd actually woken up in a more positive mood than usual. I think I was hoping that, somehow, things might be different, that me becoming an adult would change how my mum felt about me – or that she might, for one day at least, put my needs ahead of her own. Of course, she did no such thing.' I glanced towards him. 'If anything, she was behaving more erratically than usual, goading me before I went to college, snapping at me when I asked if she'd bought me anything. Dad had been paying for my driving lessons for months, but he still went out and bought things for me to open, token stuff like bath bombs and comedy socks. I'd asked for money towards a holiday as well, and he'd slipped a hundred pounds into my birthday card. He was the sole earner, running the house, covering all the bills – he must've had to save for ages. It was only later that I appreciated quite how hard he worked, how much he sacrificed. I was too self-involved to see it then.'

'What teenager isn't?' Benoit said gently. 'Selfishness is part of growing up.'

'I should have known better,' I said, closing my eyes briefly as I remembered how that money was eventually spent: the wreath I'd bought, the word 'Dad' spelled out in white flowers.

'And Lilah didn't get you anything?'

'Oh, she did,' I told him. 'She bought me half a litre of vodka. Told me I should be grateful, because it was the good stuff.'

Benoit raked a hand through his hair.

'As you can imagine, I didn't say thank you. I took the bottle straight to the kitchen sink and tossed the lot down the plughole. She wasn't very impressed by that, and we got into a row. Dad had to intervene. I can remember him pleading with me to stop – just stop. In the end, I told them both I wanted nothing more to do with either of them, and stormed out. Jesus,' I said, letting out a long breath. 'I was awful.'

'You were young.'

'I was vile.'

'You were provoked.' Benoit was looking at me intently. 'Seriously, Fliss – everyone has their breaking point, a line past which a normal reaction becomes impossible, and you were pushed way past yours.'

'It wasn't my dad's fault, though. He didn't deserve to be spoken to like that, not after he'd made such an effort to ensure I had everything I wanted for my birthday.'

I looked again at the photograph that had been taken on the beach and saw nothing but hope in my dad's expression. Like me, he had believed things might improve; unlike me, he had never given up on that hope.

'I brooded all day, was snappy to all my friends – most of whom had also bought me presents – and downright rude to my teachers. A horror, in other words. They were all glad to see the back of me when the final bell rang. Dad had arranged dinner out, and left work early so he could go over to the restaurant and set up balloons, drop off the cake he'd had specially made.' My chest constricted around the recollection, and for a moment, I couldn't speak.

Benoit passed me the pink bunny, his fingers brushing against mine, though he said nothing.

'I went to the off-licence on my way home, bought myself a bottle of white wine and drank it in my room while I was getting ready. I hated alcohol, usually did whatever I could to avoid being anywhere near it, but that night – I don't know. I was on a mission to be as bad and as stupid as it was possible to be. I wanted to hurt my parents, and hurt myself, too, I suppose. Of course, Mum was drunk, too, and when Dad got home, he found us in the midst of another argument. I can't even remember what it was about. Probably nothing' – I sighed – 'or everything.'

Benoit had his head resting in one hand, elbows propped on his bent knees, attention focused on me.

'We all piled into the car, Dad driving, me in the back. Mum had a thing about always sitting up front, claimed she got motion sickness, although I never saw any sign of it. I wasn't done having a go at her, so I carried on, and at first, she ignored me, acted as if I wasn't even there, which was typical, and wound me up even more. I started hitting the back of her seat, banging my fist against the headrest, yelling at her to turn around, to look at me, to listen.'

I pressed my face into my hands and rubbed them up and down, digging my fingers into my scalp, pulling hard at the skin. Benoit touched my shoulder.

'Sorry,' I said, in a muffled voice. 'This next bit is hard.'

'It's OK,' he said. 'Just take your time; there's no rush.'

I shivered, an iciness stealing through me as I pictured those final few minutes: the blur of streetlights through the windshield, the concern in my dad's eyes when they met mine in the rearview mirror, the chipped black of my nail polish as I continued to hit out.

'I wouldn't stop, couldn't stop. I kept on hitting that seat, until Mum finally snapped. She turned around and tried to grab my hands, screaming at me while my dad shouted. He had one hand on the wheel and was trying to restrain her with the other, and then suddenly there was this sound, this roaring sound, and we were rolling, the car was rolling over and over, glass smashing everywhere and—'

Benoit's grip tightened on my shoulder.

'We'd gone through a red light, and a lorry had hit us. Dad's window was down, and he—' I had begun to cry, hiccups making it difficult to speak. 'The impact was . . . There was nothing anyone could do. I broke my arm, had some cuts and bruises; Mum had whiplash, but Dad—'

I forced myself breathe.

'Dad died at the scene. The doctors said he broke his neck, so it was instant. They told me that like it would make me feel better, as if he hadn't suffered every bloody day for eighteen solid years already.'

Benoit inched closer. 'Can I give you a hug?' he said.

I couldn't reply, but managed to nod.

Sliding his arm around me, he pulled me to him. 'God, Fliss,' he said. 'I'm so sorry.'

'The stupid thing is, he was the good one,' I said, my voice wobbling. 'Of the three of us, he was the kindest, the sweetest, the most patient. When he was gone, there was no "us" anymore. You should have seen the looks on the faces of the police, and the doctors, when they saw the state of me and Mum. I knew what they were thinking – and they were right to think it.'

Benoit's body was solid, warm against mine. I had finally stopped shivering.

'My aunt Angela was the first to reach the hospital, and as

soon as I saw her, I lost it. They had to sedate me. Nobody wanted me to go home with Mum; they could all see how toxic things had become. My uncle Patrick said it would be best if I went with them, which I did. And that was that.'

'You never went home again?' Benoit asked.

'Never. Angela collected everything for me, and I refused to speak to my mum. The only other times I saw her were at Dad's funeral and at the coroner's court, and on both occasions, she had been drinking.'

'Did you speak?'

I shook my head against his shoulder. 'I told myself that we were both to blame for what happened that night, but that's not true. It was my fault. I was the one who lost control, the one who distracted him from the road.'

'No,' Benoit said. 'That's not true. It was an accident.'

'An accident I caused.' Moving out of his embrace, I used the pillowcase to wipe my eyes.

'What are you going to do with all this stuff?' Benoit asked, as I stared down at the fanned-out photos and stuffed toys.

'I don't know.' I shrugged. 'Keep it all for now. I'll certainly keep the pictures.'

'There's something else in the bag,' he said, reaching inside before passing me a small, brown envelope. 'More photos?'

He had guessed correctly, although the pictures were not of the holiday snapshot variety. I studied the grainy black-and-white images in turn, taking in the overly large heads and minuscule hands, the tiny turned-up noses and neat chins. They were pregnancy scans. On the back of the first was scrawled 'T1, Dec '88' and on the second 'T2 Dec '88'.

'Must be me,' I said. 'I was born in May 1989.'

Benoit squinted to get a better look. 'Guess so,' he agreed. 'I wonder what "T1" and "T2" mean. Maybe an initial? Were they always going to name you Felicity?'

'I don't know,' I said. 'I think so – my dad's favourite grandmother was called Felicity.'

'Not an initial then,' he said.

I wasn't listening. The scan photos had sparked something, ignited the awareness I'd long had of a door being closed on me.

'Don't,' I said, catching Benoit's arm as he went to put the pictures back into the bag – pictures that had been kept, hidden from view but within easy reach, by a woman who wore motherhood as if it were a mighty ball and chain. There had to be a reason for it all; there had to be questions that I should ask, secrets that must be uncovered, some meaning perhaps, a light in the dark.

'Are you OK?' he said. 'Is there anything I can do?'

I turned, put my hand out towards his cheek, almost touched him. 'Thank you,' I said. 'But this next part, I have to do on my own.'

29

The painting sold the following day.

Etienne announced the news while Benoit and I were in the kitchen, sharing a breakfast of yoghurt, homemade granola and freshly brewed coffee, sunlight strung in like bunting across the wooden tabletop.

'There is a collector,' he explained, plucking a banana from the fruit bowl and giving it a cursory sniff before putting it back.

'Croissant?' Benoit was already on his feet.

Etienne gestured for him to sit. '*Non, merci*. I have to go to the gallery. Call Bernard, tell him to begin the work today.'

Benoit and I exchanged a look, something between relief and consternation passing between us. Neither one of us wanted to accept Etienne's money, but what choice did we have?

'Can I ask how much it sold for?' Benoit said, switching to French when Etienne did not immediately respond. '*Combien?*'

The older man suppressed a smile. 'Try to guess.'

Benoit took his empty bowl across to the sink. 'I don't know,' he said. 'Five thousand?'

'*Plus haut.*' Etienne bobbed his hand.

'Six?'

He shook his head.

'Eight?'

'*Plus haut*,' he repeated, clearly enjoying himself.

'Twelve thousand?' I called out.

'Ah,' Etienne beamed. 'You are getting closer.'

'Fifteen?' Benoit said, though in disbelief. 'Surely not more than that?'

The hand bobbed higher.

Benoit's eyes widened as he whispered, 'Twenty?'

'*Non!*' Etienne was triumphant. 'Twenty-five.'

Twenty-five thousand euros.

'Wow,' I breathed, as Benoit whooped. 'That's incredible. How do you say "congratulations" in French?'

'*Félicitations!*' both men chorused.

'Tonight, we will drink champagne,' Etienne declared, heading out into the courtyard. I looked at Benoit.

'It is a special occasion,' he said.

'Hmm,' I said, pressing my lips into a disapproving line.

'I agree with you that he drinks too much, Fliss, but telling him so won't make a difference. The decision needs to come from him, and he's not going to make it today.'

'No,' I agreed. 'But tomorrow, there will be another reason to drink, and again the next day. Alcoholics always find a reason.'

'Then we'll have to help him find reasons to the contrary,' he said. 'Gentle persuasion, applied little and often.'

I sighed as I stood up from the table. 'You really believe that will work?'

'I don't know.' He spread his hands wide. 'But I have faith. I'm not going to give up on him.'

'He's lucky to have you – seriously,' I added, when Benoit looked doubtful. 'Really lucky.'

'Maybe,' he allowed. 'I keep hoping that . . .'

'Hoping what?'

'You'll think I'm delusional.'

'Try me.'

Benoit took a deep breath. 'I keep hoping that if I stay here, become a permanent fixture in his life, no matter what he does, or how much he drinks, then it will show him that he's worth something, that he can be loved unconditionally, you know?'

Skewered by guilt, I nodded mutely.

'My mum never talks about her childhood, but I've always had the sense that whatever it is that's haunting her, it also involves Etienne. I know she misses him,' he added, his tone suddenly fierce. 'I think if I could just get her here, so the two of them could talk, then things would improve. When Lilah died—'

He glanced at me.

'It's OK, go on.'

'It just ... It reminded me how short life can be, how suddenly things can change, how it's all so finite.'

'You don't want them to wait until it's too late,' I surmised.

Benoit leaned back against the edge of the sink, his head down. 'I'm sorry,' he said. 'This must be difficult for you.'

Rather than lie, I remained silent. Benoit turned and began to wash up the bowls and coffee cups, the working muscles in his shoulders visible through the fabric of his T-shirt. It was easier to speak when he wasn't looking at me, when I couldn't see the pity and perplexity writ large across his features.

'I don't know if it would have made a difference,' I said. 'If I'd known that she was about to die, I might have wanted to see her, but I can't say for certain that I would. I know I would've been scared, not just of the past being raked up again, but of rejection. Is there a pain greater than being spurned by the one person who is supposed to love you the most? I don't think there is.'

'No,' he agreed, soapy water dripping on to the tiles as he reached for a tea towel. 'There isn't. Except perhaps the regret that you didn't at least try.'

My cheeks and throat burned. He was doing to me what my former counsellor had encouraged me to do for myself. 'If you want to achieve real growth,' she'd said, 'then you must be willing to sit with your emotions, even the difficult ones – especially the difficult ones. If you don't, there will always be a part of you that is shut off, and that will prevent anyone else from getting close to you in the way you deserve.'

I had not wanted to sit with my emotions then, and I didn't want to now, either.

Benoit's gaze was unwavering. He was waiting for me to respond, to admit that I'd failed, and that he was right to keep pursuing his mission to reunite the members of his own family. I was saved from having to say anything at all by his phone beginning to ring.

Benoit wiped his hands and answered. '*Bonjour.*' A pause, and then, '*Oui. Merci.* The skip has arrived,' he said.

'Only twenty-four hours late,' I drawled, and to my relief, he laughed.

When Etienne returned from the gallery half an hour later, he did so with two clanking bags.

'*Salut,*' he called up the stairs, to where Benoit and I were poised, each clutching opposite ends of a threadbare rug.

'That's a lot of champagne,' I remarked, as Etienne went through into the lounge.

Benoit grimaced. 'I guess twenty-five thousand is a lot of reasons to celebrate.'

'I've never understood that approach,' I said, as we carried the soiled rug along the narrow hallway. 'Hooray for good news, now let's poison ourselves.'

'When you put it like that . . .' he agreed.

We heaved the rug into the skip, where it tumbled down to join three others, a huge pile of bin bags, and reams of torn wallpaper. Back in the house, music blared. Etienne had put on one of his French records and was waltzing around the lounge, uncorked bottle of red wine in hand.

'*Danse avec moi,*' he cried, grabbing a fistful of Benoit's T-shirt as he pirouetted past and pulling him forwards so forcefully that he very nearly fell. Etienne held the wine out to him. '*Non? Comme vous voulez.*'

At the rate he was glugging straight from the bottle, he would be drunk very soon. I escaped to the first floor, where there were more accumulated bin bags, and started to ferry them downstairs in batches. On my third trip outside, I met Etienne coming the other way, still holding his wine, but also grasping a broken kettle that I'd deposited in the skip earlier that morning.

'Erm, where are you taking that?' I said.

Etienne ducked his head, scuttling past me into the lounge.

'What's up?' Benoit's head appeared over the middle banister.

'I think we might have a problem.'

Our approach to clearing the house had been mindful thus far. Benoit had shown the items we deemed beyond repair to Etienne, and he'd agreed to us getting rid of them, waving his hand dismissively, as if he could not care less about chipped ornaments, moth-eaten blankets and stacks of ancient news-paper. Now, however, he appeared to be executing a rescue mission.

Before long, the dresser I had spent so long clearing was crowded once more with a hotchpotch selection of objects we had no need of nor room for.

'You can't want to keep that,' I cried, pursuing Etienne and a crushed and torn lampshade along the hallway. 'What would you even do with it?'

'Fix it,' he muttered, in a voice that was becoming surlier as the day wore on. 'It belonged to my *grand-mere*.'

'If he really cared about it as much as he claims, why did I find it shoved in the back of a cupboard?' I grumbled to Benoit, who'd just reappeared with a rancid old duvet.

'It's only a lampshade,' he began, falling silent at the look on my face.

'One lampshade, I could cope with, but he's bringing newspapers back in, and two of those cushions the mice were living in.'

'I'll have a word,' he promised, though whatever it was he chose to say made not an iota of difference. By the time morning trickled into afternoon, Etienne's stash had surpassed the confines of the dresser and was spreading across the floor. It was a relief when Bernard arrived with his son to take more measurements, after which they were talked into drinking a glass of champagne, and then another. Soon, all three men were lounging in the courtyard, singing along to 'Mimi', which Etienne kept putting on over and over again, scratching the record a little more each time.

Benoit slipped seamlessly into the role of host, fetching bowls of crisps and nuts from the kitchen, while throwing me apologetic glances. All four men spoke in French so rapid that even if I had been fluent in the language, I'd likely have struggled to follow what was being said.

'I might go out for a bit,' I said. 'Get some air. I won't be long.'

'Take as long as you want.' Benoit gestured towards the rabble. 'I can't see us getting much more work done today.'

As I turned to go, he put a hand on my arm.

'Do you want me to come with you?'

He looked so sincere, and so handsome, with his sculpted cheekbones, spray of freckles, hair falling into his eyes and a faint smile playing around his lips, that I almost said yes. More and more, I was becoming aware of Benoit, keeping him within sight, straying closer than I knew was right for someone who had agreed to marry another. The bond between us had been there right from the start, and I was allowing it to gain strength.

It was for these reasons, in the end, that I turned down his offer.

30

The river was waiting.

I sat for a time on a bench beneath the plane trees, watching the water turn from blue to grey to fiery orange as the light leaked out of the sky. Music drifted over from the bar on the corner; a dog tugged free from its lead and raced across to greet another; laughter swarmed, and warmth settled. A yawn nudged, and I stretched my arms, easing out cricks and soothing away stiffness. The day had been both physically and mentally challenging, though despite Etienne's interference, we had achieved a lot, the two us.

A daydream beckoned, playing out in snatches as if it were a silent film: Benoit in the kitchen preparing breakfast for our guests, all of whom had come to admire the exquisite murals, sample incredible food, savour our impeccable hospitality. I envisaged trips to the market on Sunday morning, fresh flowers on the tables, French chocolates placed on pillows; cookery lessons, bike rides, wine tours; painting instruction from the master himself, our artist-in-residence, no longer habitually drunk but congenial, the man who'd held my hand as I wept, and shown me the parts of Libourne that were special to him.

I rose from the bench and made my way to the bridge, averting my eyes from the bankside where my mum would once have stood. Traffic rumbled past, tyres turning against tarmac. On the opposite side, I headed past the shell of a former factory, long ago taken by the elements. Ivy snaked through gaping windows, and the chained wooden doors were splintered and dry. Further along were small houses, each set back from the pathway, while closer to the water, residents had set up deckchairs. A man lounged, reading a novel in the last of the light. I sensed his gaze roam over me as I continued, past hawthorn bushes that buzzed with insects, thick clusters of reeds at the water's edge and indigo clouds that trailed the sky. Nature was abundant, thriving, and here I was, inserting myself amongst it, a cumbersome human disrupting the balance, flattening blades of grass and startling birds from the trees.

When a gap opened up in the undergrowth, I left the path and found a patch between the daisies, kicking off my shoes and pressing my bare feet to the earth. Scents found their way to me, carried on a tepid breeze: fauna and honeysuckle; the chalky flavour of the merged river as it skittered across silt.

The envelope of photos had grown moist in my hand. I spread them out before me, drawn once more to the image of me and Jono in the old-fashioned pram. Why hadn't I ever seen it before? That Angela wouldn't have a copy was hard to believe, given that it was her son in the picture. I tried to recall other photos I'd seen of my cousins, taken when they were kids, and then, all of sudden, it hit me – the reason why I'd been unable to shift the snapshot from my mind. The message took less than a minute to send, the reply pinging back moments later.

'You're right,' Jono had written, 'it's deffo not me. I was bald until the age of three, a regular little Dr Evil. No idea who it is, tbh. Ask Mum, she'll know.'

'Thanks,' I typed back robotically, pulse loud and throat dry. 'I'll do that.'

This time, it took far longer for a response to appear, and when it did, I felt punched.

Angela's message read: 'Aww, that's you and baby Jono. One of your mum's?'

I didn't reply. Instead, I rang her.

'Hello, lovey. Is everything alr—'

'It's not Jono.'

Angela stuttered out a laugh. 'What?'

'It's not Jono, in the photo. I sent it to him. He had no hair at that age, and this baby, whoever it is, has loads.'

'Gosh, so it does. Oh well, must be another friend's baby, in that case.'

'Which friend? Mum didn't have any friends.'

'I'm sure that's not true,' she said, but I heard a quiver in her voice.

'Angela, please. If there's something you're not telling me—'

'There isn't.'

'I can tell there is.'

She let out a long, weighty breath. 'Where did you find it, the photo?'

'Under Mum's bed, hidden away in a bag that used to belong to Dad. There were a couple of toys in there, too – that pink rabbit I used to take everywhere, and another yellow one – plus their wedding photo, a couple from holidays we took, some baby scans.'

'Scans? What scans?'

I leafed through the photos on the grass in front of me until I found them: two scans, each labelled differently, almost as if they were not of one baby at all.

'Oh my God,' I said, swallowing rapidly, my voice hoarse as I asked her again who it was in the pram with me. When she didn't answer, I began to rant, pleading with her to tell me, just tell me. Angela begged me to stop, and then, with a muffled cry, she began to whimper.

'It isn't Jono,' I said.

'No.' It was barely a whisper.

'And you know who it is?'

'Yes.'

I closed my eyes, no longer able to face the fiery patchwork of sunset, nor the ripples of dark water or soft fingers of wind. The night my father died had brought an abrupt end to the first chapter of my life. Was a third now about to begin? There could be no going back, not once the words were spoken, the truth let out from its shadowy box.

On the other end of the line, Angela sniffed. 'It's not Jono in the photo,' she said at last. 'It's your twin brother.'

I opened my eyes.

My twin brother.

Another sob. 'His name was Felix.'

Felix and Felicity, named for happiness and good fortune. How hard fate had laughed at that.

'Was?' I echoed, tone featherlight. 'So he's, what, where?'

But I knew. Of course, I knew.

'He died. I'm so sorry, lovey.'

'When?'

'A long time ago.'

'*When?*' I demanded. My legs had begun to tremble.

Angela's voice cracked open on another sob. 'On his second birthday.'

Our second birthday.

'I always said they should have told you,' she said, her voice piercingly shrill. 'A secret like that, it was always going to cause more harm hidden than the truth ever could.'

'And what is the truth?' I said. Then, when she didn't reply: 'Angela!'

There was an abrasive sound, as if she'd put her phone under a cushion, and I heard muffled voices, one high and another far lower. The view was swirling in front of me, black spots obscuring the emerging stars, my breath coming in rapid gasps as I saw flashes of the past, of soft skin and fingers tightly clasped, a cry in echo to my own, the feeling of another beside me, the comfort that came with being one half of a whole.

'Fliss?' Angela was back. 'I'm coming out there.'

'What?'

'Out to France. I've just spoken to Paddy, and he's booking me a flight right this minute.'

'You don't need to,' I began weakly, but she continued to talk across me. 'No arguments. This is simply too important a conversation to be had over the phone. I'll be there the day after tomorrow – can you hold on until then? I promise I'll explain it all to you once I get there.'

I could not dissuade her, no matter how much I begged, or how many tears I wept. I didn't want to need her. I wanted to be strong enough not to need anyone at all – not her, not my parents, nor Etienne, not even Benoit. But at the same time, what I wanted more than anything was to pull them all to me, let them protect me from whatever it was that was coming next.

My phone call ended, and I stayed exactly where I was, staring through damp eyes at the river as it rushed and roared below me. Night came, and the air cooled. A waxing crescent moon leered down, the great sideways grin of a world that continued to mock me. Snatching up a handful of grass, I tossed it into the water and watched as it was swept away.

Piece after piece after piece.

31

The following morning did not begin well.

Waking from a tormented dream that had followed many hours of tossing and turning, I stumbled to the bathroom and caught my toe on the jamb of the door, hard enough to draw blood. There were no plasters in the cabinet above the basin, and in the process of hopping back through to search my bedside drawer, I collected a splinter in the heel of my other foot.

'I'm not usually a clumsy person,' I told Benoit, who had hurried down from the attic when he heard me swearing.

'Come on,' he said, helping me hobble back to the en suite. As I dabbed at the blood with a tissue, he ran back upstairs and returned a few minutes later with the same first-aid kit I'd used to patch Etienne up on my first day in France.

'You don't have to do this,' I said, as he knelt in front of me, a wad of cotton wool and pair of tweezers in hand. I was dressed in pyjama shorts and a thin vest top, while Benoit wore only tracksuit bottoms, his chest and feet bare.

'I don't think you'll need stitches,' he said, cupping my ankle and raising my leg to get a better look at the cut. 'You said the door did this to you?'

'*That* door,' I confirmed, throwing it a murderous glance.

'I didn't see you last night,' he added. 'What did you get up to in the end?'

'Oh, you know,' I said. 'Not much. Sat by the water for a bit.'

The words had come out staccato, and Benoit's eyes flicked up to mine.

'Sorry about the impromptu party,' he began.

'Don't be. I heard you all still singing when I got back. Someone was really going for it.'

'That was Bernard. I believe he was a choir boy in a past life – hold still.'

I winced as he tested the wound.

Benoit, having applied antiseptic cream to my cut, unsheathed several plasters and carefully wrapped them around the injured toe. With a nod of satisfaction, he rested my foot against his thigh and raised the other one.

'How bad is it?' I asked. 'It feels as if half the floor is in there.'

Benoit gave me a sardonic look. 'Tiny,' he said, squinting more closely at my heel. 'Shard of a speck.'

'Can you get it out?'

Benoit ran his finger along the softest part of my foot. 'You have very high arches,' he remarked, inching forwards so that the other foot slid higher up his thigh. He loosened his grip a fraction, jaw set as he manoeuvred himself into position. 'Whatever you do,' he warned, 'don't sneeze.'

I held my breath, waiting for the sting, but none came. Benoit sat back, the tweezers raised in triumph.

'You got it?'

'Snuck in there like a thief.'

'I barely felt a thing. That's some skill you have there.'

'Maybe I should join a splinter cell.'

I smiled weakly.

'It's my steady hands,' he said. 'Fiddly dishes often require ingredients to be plated using tweezers, and when you're doing hundreds a night, often at high speed, you become adept.'

'Let's see if I can walk on it,' I said, but when I attempted to lift my leg from his hands, Benoit held on. Without breaking eye contact, he lowered his head and kissed me, very lightly, on the bridge of my foot.

'There,' he said, a single dark curl falling across his forehead. 'Good as new.'

I should tell him what I'd found out, confide in him. I wanted to. It was right there, on the very tip of my tongue.

A great clanging noise echoed up from below. We looked at each other, and Benoit let go of my foot.

'That'll be Bernard with his team of scaffolders.'

'Great,' I said, though without much enthusiasm.

Benoit studied me for a moment. 'Listen,' he said, 'it's going to be a madhouse here today, what with all the workmen going in and out, and Etienne crashing around the place with a hangover. We got loads done yesterday. Why don't we take the morning off?'

'What?' I was aghast. 'But there's so much to do, and someone has to oversee the work.'

'Bernard will be doing that,' he pointed out reasonably. 'You are entitled to a four-, six- or even nine-hour window during which no work is undertaken, only leisure activities – preferably enjoyable ones.'

My withering look did little to diminish his enthusiasm.

'There's so much of Libourne still to see,' he went on, 'and it's going to be hot today, far too hot for manual labour. Adélard can keep an eye on things here.'

'I don't know . . .'

'Fliss,' he said, getting to his feet and drawing me up from the edge of the bath, 'when was the last time you took a proper day off?'

I went to answer, only to realise I couldn't remember. Before we took ownership of The Fitz, I had been evangelical about taking every Sunday off to volunteer – and so had Charlie. In the chaos of everything that had happened since, I hadn't allowed myself time to register quite how much I missed those days, how much I needed them.

Benoit cleared his throat. 'If you don't know, then it's too long,' he said. 'And you're injured.'

'Hardly.'

All I really wanted to do was get back under my bedsheets and block out the world – but if I told him that, he would want to know why. The waves of shock were still rippling through me, draining me of energy, keeping me from any kind of logical thought. Tomorrow, Angela would arrive with her answers, but until then, I was stuck. Numb. Benoit was right: staying in would only lead to more brooding. What I needed most was distraction.

'Where have you got in mind?' I asked, being careful not to put too much weight on my bandaged toe as I went back into the bedroom.

'You'll see,' he replied, heading to the door. 'Now hop to it.'

'It's not as if I have a choice in the matter,' I grumbled, gesturing to my foot, and heard him laugh in reply.

Fifteen minutes later, having washed, dressed and applied a liberal amount of high-factor sun lotion, I met Benoit coming out of the lounge with a cooler box in hand, and the two of us filed outside, dodging scaffolders as we went.

'Thought we'd take the car,' he said, leading me towards a red Renault Clio parked by the kerb.

'Yours?' I asked, peering through the dusty windshield.

'Etienne's,' he said. 'Although Lilah was the one who drove it most of the time.'

I stepped back. 'We could just walk?'

'With that limp? No chance.'

'It's not that bad.'

'Regardless,' he said, 'it's too far, and too hot, and I'm too hungry.'

'You're very bossy today,' I remarked, clambering into the passenger seat. The interior of the car was at least clean, though dated, with more than two hundred thousand kilometres on the odometer.

Benoit's reply was to wipe his brow in exaggerated relief when the engine started. It took a series of backward and forward inching to free us from the tight space, but he managed it without incident. Behind us, workmen crawled like ants up the front of the house, screwing in poles and balancing planks.

'They're not wasting much time,' I said. 'When we needed work doing on The Fitz, it took weeks to set up, and even then, the progress was painfully slow.'

We had reached the far end of the street, and Benoit flicked on the indicator, hunching over the wheel to check for traffic.

'Bernard is a good friend,' he said, the car vibrating as we drove over the cobbles surrounding the main square. 'From what I remember of London, it's not the friendliest place.'

'It can be,' I said, 'but I know what you mean.'

'I didn't enjoy living in such a big city,' he said, his attention on the road. 'But that was more down to the people I encountered than London itself. I started doing a bit of private catering while I was there, as a way of earning extra money after the pandemic, and the clients were mostly . . .' He paused for a moment at a set of lights, glanced across at me. 'Really bloody awful,' he finished. 'Maybe I got unlucky, but it really coloured how I felt about the elite for a while.'

'The elite?' I said. 'As in, the aristocracy? Or do you mean celebrities?'

'I mean rich idiots with no manners, the kind who think they're better than everyone else, simply because they were born into money.'

'You probably wouldn't like Charlie much, in that case,' I said, as the lights changed. 'He was born into a wealthy family, although his manners aren't actually too bad.'

Benoit unhooked his sunglasses from the neck of his T-shirt and put them on. 'The same Charlie who emptied your bank account without asking?' he said. 'You're right, I'm not sure I do like him much.'

I had very nearly called Charlie the previous night, as I'd sat numb with horror by the river, my thumb poised over my phone. But while he would have undoubtedly been sympathetic about the situation, he'd also have had questions. It was the way his mind worked – gather all the facts, then come up with a solution to the problem – and I had no real facts to share.

'Fair enough,' I said, watching the scenery rush by in a blur: buildings groaning with history; street signs that demanded a roll of the tongue to pronounce; bicycles, baskets and bare legs. When we sped past a set of rusted ornate gates, I made a murmur of recognition.

'Are we going to the farm again?'

'Why, are you missing your goose friend? Want another gander at him?'

I groaned, and Benoit slid his hand over the gearstick, shifting down to second as he navigated a small roundabout and turned left into a wide car park. Ahead of us lay a large, terraced restaurant, while beyond, I saw a glimpse of dappling blue.

'Welcome to Lac des Dagueys,' he announced. 'Manmade, but man, they made it well.'

We parked between a rusted campervan and an SUV with an '*Bébé a bord*' sticker in the window. Benoit retrieved a sunshade from the back seat and rolled it across the windscreen.

The day was as warm as every other had been since I arrived in France, but a light breeze rustled the trees along the bank.

'What would you prefer?' Benoit asked, as we reached a pathway that encircled the lake. 'We can go for a walk around the trail, or pitch up on that beach area over there?'

'Option two,' I said. Inside my sandal, the stubbed toe still throbbed. There were plenty of people dotted around despite the early hour, most of whom appeared to be mothers with small children, though a few teenagers lingered down by the shore, smoking, chatting, scrolling through their phones. There was no natural shade, but a few of the more conscientious bathers had brought umbrellas. I rolled out my towel, and Benoit followed suit, dumping the cooler box between them.

'I might go for a quick swim,' he said, his hands already on the hem of his T-shirt. 'Want to join?'

'Better not.' I nodded towards my bandaged foot. 'I'll stay here and mind our stuff.'

He undressed in a few swift movements, stripping down to a pair of black trunks that were snug against his upper thighs. The muscles contracted in his lower back as he strode towards the water, going in up to his stomach before diving beneath the surface, re-emerging further out, wet hair flattened against his head. He raised his chin to the sun before looking across at the beach, a wide smile taking root when he located me. I tried to smile back, but the gesture felt forced, an imitation of pleasure that was at odds with my still-frozen heart.

I would tell him. As soon as he came back from his swim, I would tell him about the photograph, about the secret that had been kept from me, about the brother I had lost.

A shadow fell across my towel. Startled, I jerked my head up to look, disquiet trickling through me as I saw who had blocked out the sun.

It was Céline, and she did not look at all pleased to see me.

32

'*Salut*,' she said, sitting down uninvited beside me.

I looked back towards the lake, but Benoit was no longer visible, his dark head blending in amongst those of other swimmers.

'*Comme ca va?*' I said, and Céline raised a single, perfectly groomed brow.

'If I answer you in French, will you be able understand me?'

'Probably not,' I admitted.

'*Anglais*, then,' she said. 'And, to answer your question, I am not good or bad. So-so, I guess.' She asked how I was, before noticing and promptly enquiring after my injured foot, then frowning when I explained what had happened that morning.

'That house' – she rolled her eyes – 'it is very dangerous. I fell down the stairs once, when I was there, twisted my knee very badly.' She stretched out her slim, tanned legs, examining them as if for marks. Her skin was smooth and unblemished, whereas my own legs were peppered with scrapes and bruises, sustained as I lugged around bin bags full of torn wallpaper and boxes of empty bottles.

'Have you stayed often?' I asked.

'Of course,' she said with feeling. 'One summer ago, I was there with Benoit every night. I practically lived there.'

She and Benoit had clearly been seeing one another on more than a casual basis. Presumably, things had not ended well. I shifted position on the towel.

'Your mother,' she said unexpectedly, 'She was . . . complicated, *non*?'

'That's one word for it.' I unscrewed my bottle of water
and doused my parched throat, catching sight of Benoit as I
lowered it. He was swimming lengths across a roped-in
portion of the lake, arms rising and arching over, droplets of
water falling diamond-bright around him.

'Can I look at your ring once more?' Céline asked. I had
put the ring back on the previous night in the vague hope
that it might offer some form of comfort, perhaps serve as a
reminder that there was still a future waiting for me beyond
the realm of my current predicament.

When I extended my hand, Céline took it, her fingertips
cool and deft.

'How much is it worth?'

'No idea,' I told her, balking slightly at the impertinence
of her question. 'My fiancé is the one who bought it, not
me.'

She looked at me appalled. 'He didn't let you choose? I
would want to choose.'

'And I'm sure you will one day.'

Céline curled her lip and scrutinised me for a few seconds.

'We have some food, if you're hungry?' I said, removing
my hand from hers.

'I don't think Benoit would like that.'

'Why not?'

She flicked a glossy curtain of hair off her cheek. 'I am sure
he prepared it only for you.'

'Let's ask him, shall we?' I said, as the man himself waded
out from the shallows. Céline looked on unabashed as he
wrung water from his shorts, her cat-like eyes predator
bright. When Benoit drew nearer, she got up to greet him,
pressing a kiss to each of his cheeks.

'Where did you come from?' he asked, wiping water off his legs.

'I followed you,' Céline said, bursting into laughter at the look on his face. 'It was a joke, dummy. I was walking. I always walk here in the morning.'

'Since when?' Having sat, Benoit took a banana from the cooler box, peeled it, and ate it in three successive bites.

'Since always,' she replied, tucking her legs beneath her on the end of his towel. 'You know this.'

He continued hunting through the picnic, eventually withdrawing a rather flat pain au chocolat, which he offered first to me, and then, rather more reluctantly, to Céline. When we each declined, he broke a piece off and put it in his mouth, dropping flakes of pastry on to his chin in the process. I resisted the urge to wipe them away, but Céline had no such restraint.

'What are you doing?' Benoit swerved to avoid her.

'There are crumbs.'

'I can do it myself.'

They continued to snipe and grumble at one another for the next few minutes, Céline lapsing into French as the colour mounted in her cheeks.

'I might leave you to it,' I began, but Benoit stilled me, his hand lake-cold on my arm.

'Don't,' he said. 'Stay.'

'I apologise,' Céline said, in a simpering tone. 'Benoit and me, we are like the canary and the cat.'

'She's the cat,' he said, and she laughed. A thin, glacial tinkle.

'It is true.'

'Shall I start calling you Tweetie Pie?' I asked Benoit, and he responded by shaking water from his hair all over me.

'Look at you two, flirting with each other,' Céline said, in a voice that was no less steely for being singsong.

My blood cooled.

'Is there something going on?' she pressed. 'Are you sleeping together?'

'Céline,' Benoit's tone carried an edge.

'*Quoi?*' she asked, feigning innocence. 'It is a simple question – *oui ou non?*'

'*Non,*' I snapped. 'I'm engaged, remember?'

'Ah, of course.' Céline clutched her head. 'How could I forget? That ring you wear is very convincing.'

'What do you mean by that?' The last thing I needed, on today of all days, was to be goaded. Prod me, and I was liable to bite.

Céline eyed me with open disdain. 'If I wanted people to believe I was not available, then I might wear a ring on that finger as well,' she said.

'You think I'm lying about being engaged?'

'Céline . . .' Benoit said again.

She ignored him, her dark eyes zoning in on me. 'What does your boyfriend think about you being here without him?'

'That's enough,' Benoit barked.

'My *fiancé*' – I enunciated the word clearly – 'trusts me.'

She shook her head, smile hard. 'I think that if he saw what I am seeing, then he might change his mind, *non?*'

'What exactly is your problem?' I asked, slapping far too hard at a bug that landed on my shoulder.

'Me?' She feigned surprise. 'I don't have any problem.'

'Right, of course not. That's why you're accusing me of being a liar and a cheat.'

Benoit banged the lid back on the cooler box and stood, gesturing for Céline to follow him. She threw me a triumphant look and took his outstretched hand, wobbling slightly as he pulled her up. They went down to the water's edge, out of earshot but not out of sight, and while he gesticulated, she glared, arms folded across her chest.

'What was all that about?' I asked, when he eventually returned. Céline had stormed off in the direction of the car park, kicking up great clumps of sand as she went.

Benoit looked up towards the sky. Clouds had moved in as the morning wore on; they looked like enormous lumps of Chantilly cream.

'I don't understand why people do it,' he said.

'Do what?'

He sighed and sat back down. 'Insist on rehashing things from the past – and I don't mean you,' he hastily added, when I said nothing. 'You have every right to feel bad about the way you were treated as a child. With you, there's genuine trauma, but with her . . .'

'Can I make an observation?' I said.

'Go on.'

'It seems to me as if Céline isn't over you.'

The dark blue eyes dulled. 'Whatever gave you that idea?'

I nudged him with my uninjured toe, and he exhaled, long and slow.

'There's nothing there – not for me, not for ages. When I broke things off with her, I did it for good reason, and I stand by that reason.'

'And she doesn't agree?'

Benoit grunted. 'I'd be happy to draw a line under it all and move on, but she won't.'

'I think it's all tied up with regret,' I said. 'Either you regret what you did in that moment, or what you didn't do, and either way, that missed opportunity eats away at you. It taunts you, this image of what might have been. We don't like how the story ended, and so we rewrite it over and over again in our heads. That's probably all Céline is doing – trying to get a better ending for herself.'

A small bird with grey and yellow feathers landed on the sand a few feet ahead of us, its head cocked to one side, beady dark eye fixed on the brown paper bag that had contained the pain au chocolat. Very slowly, Benoit shook out the pasty crumbs, and the bird hopped forwards.

'Is that why you came to Libourne?' he asked. 'To find a different ending?'

'I don't know,' I said, staring out across the water. A group of kayakers had paddled out into the middle of the lake, their life vests a vibrant slash of yellow against the serene blue. 'As far as my mum and I are concerned, I think it's too late. There isn't going to be a different outcome.'

'You can't change what happened,' he said quietly, 'but you do have the power to change how you feel about it.'

'You mean forgive her?'

Benoit's hand went to the sand, his fingers digging through it, creating a shallow trench. 'Do you think you ever could?'

My throat thickened, and I coughed to clear it. 'It's funny,' I said. 'Because when you're young, forgiveness doesn't feel like a choice. When I was a child, I always forgave my mum her indiscretions, and her small cruelties, precisely because she was my mum. For all the other things she was, she remained constant, always there when I woke up, most often the first and final person I saw on each day. To reject her then would have meant rejecting my reality. There is no alternative when you're seven years old, and so you make the best of it. For me, that meant making myself as small as possible, until the person I was had disappeared altogether. It's hard to think about that child version of myself and not feel sad, or resentful.'

'But you're not her anymore,' Benoit said, and I sighed.

'No, but she's a part of me. Aren't all of us made up of the things that have happened to us, the experiences we've had?'

He looked at me, a wistful expression casting lines across his face. Droplets of water had dripped from his hair on to his chest and were pooling on the towel. 'We are,' he agreed, 'and so we can make sense of how we respond to things. But if that's true, then can't we also work on changing those responses? Learn how to stop the past affecting the present.'

'I think to do that, you need to have all the information,' I said, thinking once again of the photograph, of my brother, who had died the day we both turned two. 'There are gaps in my past, and until I can fill them, I don't see how I can heal.'

Benoit considered this, pausing long enough to finish the water in his bottle and dig two oranges out of the cooler. 'Here,' he said, when he'd peeled the rind off one and broken it into segments, 'you must be starving.'

I accepted the fruit but didn't eat it.

'You look as if you want to say something,' he said. 'You're acting as if you're fine, but I can tell you're not. Did something happen last night?'

I lowered my chin.

'You don't have to tell me.' He shuffled forwards until he was next to me, damp trunks against my bare leg. 'Unless you want to.'

The bird had gone, its tiny tracks imprinted in the sand. Every living thing left a mark, from the minuscule boreholes of the gnat to the vast footprints of extinct dinosaurs, laid forever in slowly eroding stone. My brother's life had not been long, but it had mattered. He mattered.

'You were right,' I said, turning to Benoit. 'Something did happen last night.'

And then, at last, I told him everything.

33

We stayed where we were until the midday sun grew too ferocious. I lay on my stomach, Benoit on his back, one arm bent beneath his head, focus solely on me.

'Losing a child,' he said reverently. 'I can't imagine anything more devastating. Poor Lilah.'

My mum, the victim. The mere concept felt alien.

'I've been trying to make sense of it all,' I said. 'Because in some respects, it explains why she drank, and why she was always so sad, but it doesn't explain why they kept his existence a secret from me. My whole family – all of them.' I shook my head. 'They all lied to me.'

Benoit considered this. 'Your aunt didn't give any kind of indication as to why?'

'No,' I said, picking at a scab on my knuckle. 'She said she'd explain everything in person, once she gets here. The thing is, though, my mum hated me. And I know that sounds like an exaggeration, but that's honestly how it felt when I was growing up.'

Benoit thought for a few moments. 'Felix was your twin,' he said. 'Every time she looked at you, she must have seen him and been reminded of what she lost. Grief can warp the mind of even the strongest person.'

'I thought the same thing at first,' I said slowly, 'but why be angry with me? Sadness, I understand, but the resentment? All I can assume is that she loved him more than me, and probably wished I had been the one to die.'

'That's not true.' Benoit propped himself up on his elbows. 'Fliss, you can't think like that.'

'Too late,' I said, pressing a hand to my trembling lips. 'Too bloody late.'

We packed up the picnic things. My limbs felt heavy, as if I was moving through water, every movement a struggle. I had forgotten about the pain in my foot, and swore as I put my weight on it.

'Here.' Benoit offered me his arm. 'Let me help you.'

Back at the car park, I slid dolefully into the baking interior of the ancient Renault while he folded away the windscreen shield. For the first part of the journey, neither one of us spoke. I had talked enough, was glaringly aware of having done so, and Benoit's brow was furrowed in thought.

'Thanks,' I said, when a few minutes had passed. 'For insisting I come out, and for listening.'

'You're welcome.' Benoit glanced briefly from the road to me. 'And I'm sorry again about Céline. She had no right to say what she did.'

Céline. I had barely given her a thought since she'd stormed off. That situation felt utterly inconsequential compared to everything else that was going on.

'I won't bear a grudge,' I told him. 'I understand where she's coming from. I'd probably behave atrociously, too, if I'd managed to lose someone like you.'

'Someone like me,' he echoed.

'One of the good guys.'

'You think I'm *un bon gars*?'

'Well, let's see. You're kind,' I said, folding one finger down, 'you can cook, you make the occasional funny joke, you have all your hair, and you're decent-looking.'

'Decent-looking?' He clutched his chest. 'Oof.'

'OK, fine, you're good-looking. Very attractive. Some might even say handsome.'

Benoit twirled his hand in the air. 'You're getting warmer . . .'

'Did I mention your touching levels of self-deprecation, or did I forget that one?'

He laughed. 'Touché!'

Landmarks I recognised were beginning to come into view. Soon, we would be back in the hub of Libourne, at the house with all its cracks and noise. What would happen if I told him to keep driving, past the town boundaries and out into the countryside beyond? To delay reality for just a short while longer? As if to defy me, Benoit accelerated to get through a set of lights before they changed.

'I wonder if the scaffolding is up yet,' I said. 'Hopefully, they'll attach one of those chutes and angle it over the skip. Then we can throw junk out through the windows rather than lugging it all down the stairs.'

'That's if Etienne hasn't brought it all back into the house by now,' he replied, and I groaned.

We parked not far from the space we'd vacated that morning, Benoit coming around to my side of the car and once again offering me his arm to hold on to. As our bodies came into contact, a bolt of adrenaline spiked through me, raising the hairs on the back of my neck. Benoit's sunglasses were pushed back through his curls; he smiled at me, lips slightly parted, and then, very slowly, reached for the strands of hair that had worked loose from my ponytail and tucked them behind my ears.

'*Voilà,*' he murmured. '*Parfaite.*'

I searched his eyes for humour, but Benoit was no longer teasing. He was staring as if transfixed, drawing me in with invisible thread, silencing the voice in my head that was telling me to move away, to sever the connection, to turn it into a joke.

From somewhere close by, a door opened, but neither one of us turned to look. It was only when I sensed a figure approaching that I finally dragged my eyes from Benoit, and when I saw who it was, walking along the street towards us, I felt my legs give way.

'Charlie?' The word came out choked.

Benoit dropped my arm and stepped back, presumably thinking the same thing I was – that my fiancé must have seen us, seen how close we had come to crossing the line.

'Hey,' Charlie drawled, ignoring Benoit and tugging me into an embrace hard enough to crush the air from my lungs.

'What on earth are you doing here?' I asked, squirming to get free.

'Nice to see you, too,' he drawled, holding on more tightly.

The stale sweat smell of him was masked by aftershave, and I detected coffee on his breath behind the mint of his chewing gum. Putting my palms against his chest, I pushed, and Charlie, ever the clown, made a show of stumbling backwards, clutching the wing mirror of the Renault for support. I didn't dare look at Benoit.

'You don't look very pleased to see me,' Charlie said. He'd clearly made an effort with his appearance, putting on the maroon polo shirt I'd bought him the previous Christmas above tailored shorts. His blond hair was neatly styled, signet ring gleaming from the little finger of his right hand.

'I am,' I said, through a strangled laugh. 'I'm a bit surprised, that's all.'

'A good surprise, I hope?'

'Well, yes, obviously it's nice to see you. I just wish you'd let me know you were coming, because then I could have—'

'Aren't you going to introduce us?' he interrupted, staring pointedly at Benoit.

When I did nothing more than flap my hands ineffectually, he stepped around me and extended an arm.

'Charlie Fitzsimons – Felicity's fiancé. And you are?'

'He's Benoit,' I said, cutting in. 'Etienne's nephew, and co-owner of the guesthouse.'

'Yes, of course.' Charlie was still waiting for his handshake, and I threw Benoit a desperate look that he summarily ignored, instead turning away to lock the car.

'Come on,' I said, leading Charlie along the pavement, distracting him with rapid-fire questions about what time his flight landed, how he'd found his way to Libourne, if he'd been in the house yet, and where his stuff was.

Charlie narrowed his eyes in Benoit's direction. 'What's his problem?' he asked in an undertone. 'Bit bloody rude.'

'He's just shy,' I bolstered, though in truth, I was disturbed by quite how standoffish Benoit was being. He followed us down the street, but maintained a distance, his eyes down, mouth set. Unreachable.

The guesthouse door was propped open, Charlie's holdall on the floor just inside.

'Some chap in a high-vis let me in,' he explained. 'Told me you were out, so I went to get a coffee. Pretty quiet around here, isn't it?'

'I know,' I said. 'It's one of the reasons I like it so much.'

Charlie looked at me as if I'd sprouted tentacles.

Voices sounded from above, and we looked up to see Adélard coming down the stairs, Bernard a few steps behind him. I made the introductions.

'This is your *amor*?' Adélard eyed Charlie in the way one might an ancient Greek sculpture. 'Felicity, I am impressed. He is very handsome.'

'Blimey,' Charlie said, cheeks as red as his shirt.

The hallway shuddered as Benoit banged shut the front door. Adélard's eyes rolled briefly to mine, then away again just as quickly.

In the lounge, we discovered Etienne sitting on the floor, unpacking a bag of newspapers he had presumably rescued from the skip. I ground my teeth.

'*Bonjour, monsieur.*' Charlie's French was word-perfect.

Etienne clambered slowly to his feet, a smile ready on his pale, lined face. Before long, they were nattering away as if they'd known each other for years. I stood off to one side, trying not to mind how quickly he'd embedded himself, reminding myself that Charlie's amenability was his talent, and the reason why people warmed to him so quickly.

Benoit stomped past us to the courtyard, his features set.

Perhaps not all people.

'Are you going to give me a tour?' Charlie turned to me. 'I've been dying to see the place for myself.'

We started at the bottom and worked our way up, Charlie's expression registering the same thoughts I'd had during my initial exploration.

'What in God's name?' he exclaimed, upon seeing the cherub and triffid murals, and 'What died in here?' as we stuck our heads around the door of Etienne's bedroom.

I showed him the damp patches and pockmarked plaster, the patches of black mould on the bathroom ceilings and the frayed clumps of wire sticking out from where plug sockets had been. He was wowed by the marble basins, though loathed the intricately carved fireplaces.

'Nice in here,' he said, as I pushed open the door to my room. 'What's with all the flowers?'

I explained about my mother's ring, opening the box to show him. Charlie took it over to the window and examined it in the sunlight.

'I don't think it's worth much,' he said, immediately losing interest. 'Unlike the house. This place is definitely an inheritance worth having – and selling.'

'A lot of work still to do,' I replied, and he pouted.

'Good thing I'm here now to help keep the ball rolling.'

I frowned. 'Why are you here, really?'

Charlie stared blinkingly at me for a moment, and then, in three short strides, he was across the room, cupping my face in both his hands, tilting my head up toward his.

'Because I missed you,' he said, lips an inch from mine. 'Didn't you miss me?'

I pulled away, shaking my head. 'I told you I needed some time to think.'

'Yeah,' he agreed, 'days ago. Meanwhile, I'm doing my best to get The Fitz back up and running, dealing with builders and fire inspectors and irate bloody customers, and you're – what? Dallying around in the French countryside with some bloke.'

'I wasn't *dallying*,' I said, with heavy sarcasm. 'I found out something yesterday, about my family, and I was upset. Benoit was only trying to cheer me up.'

'That's what he called it, was it? And what did you find out?' he asked. When I hesitated, he added, 'So, what? You'll tell some bloke you've known for five minutes, but you won't tell me?'

'Fine,' I said, sitting down on the edge of the bed.

Charlie remained where he was, hand burrowed into the pocket of his shorts, expression flat, unreadable.

'I found some old photos of my mum's, and, well, it turns out that I had a twin brother.'

'Had?'

'He died young, when we were still babies.'

'Oh, God.' Charlie's features softened, and he came to sit beside me. 'That is . . . Christ. What a shock.'

'It was,' I agreed. 'I'm still trying to make sense of it myself. Angela is on her way out here to give me the full story.'

'She's coming here?' Charlie curled his lip. 'I suppose I'm her persona non grata, am I?'

I shrugged.

'Is that why that Benoit bloke won't give me the time of day either?' he said. 'Because you've been bad-mouthing me?'

'I had to tell him about the money, Charlie. The poor man is having to pay for the majority of the repairs. Do you know how embarrassing it is, not being able to contribute a cent?'

'Fine, fine,' he blustered, getting up from the bed. 'I'm getting it sorted. Livvy is—'

'Oh no. Please don't tell me you've asked your sister for a loan.'

'It's that or nothing,' he said firmly. 'The bank of Pa has run dry, I'm afraid. He won't help us.'

Music began to play, the volume cranked high enough that it filtered through the closed door and windows.

Charlie glanced at me, an eyebrow cocked in amusement. 'Sounds like someone's having a party,' he said. 'Your uncle, Etienne, is it? He did mention something about opening a few bottles.'

'He's not my uncle.'

'Stepdad, then – whatever. Shall we go and join him? I could use a drink.'

'What about trying to quit? You said that—'

'It's one drink, Fliss. What's the worst that could happen?'

The worst already did happen.

'Whatever, Charlie,' I said. 'You go ahead. I'll be down in a minute.'

In the bathroom, I locked the door behind me and went directly to the sink, where I splashed cold water across my face. My ponytail was a tangled mess, and I pulled out the toggle and used my fingers as a makeshift brush, before pressing my hand to my forehead, trying in vain to ease the frantic pounding of a heart – which then lurched at the sound of approaching feet, a heavy tread, a knocking that demanded attention.

I opened the door, and Benoit stepped quickly inside, closing it behind him.

'Don't.' I shook my head.

'Fliss.' He reached for me, and I folded my arms.

'Please, don't.'

'I just wanted to make sure you were alright.'

'Alright?' I said, through a laugh that was closer to a sob. 'How could I possibly be alright, when you look at me like that, when you come in here and—'

I turned away, met my own reflection in the mirror, saw the fear and longing.

'Look at you like what?' he said quietly.

'Like you are now,' I said. 'Like you want something from me; like I'm keeping something from you.'

'Are you?' Benoit moved in behind me. In the mirror, our eyes met.

'I can't,' I whispered. 'You have to stop. You have to leave me alone.'

'You don't mean that.' His breath was hot on my neck.

'I do,' I whispered, the words fractured.

'I only want . . .' His hands were a few inches away from my shoulders, eyes never leaving mine. 'Can I just hold you?'

A sob erupted that I was powerless to prevent, just as I was powerless to stop myself leaning back against him, my eyes closing as his arms wrapped around me, his mouth coming to rest in the hollow of my collarbone.

'We can't,' I said, hating the words, hating myself for saying them.

Benoit pulled me further into him. 'We can't not.'

All at once, I was angry. Angry with him, with Charlie, with Etienne, with the whole cruel and senseless world. Pulling roughly away from him, I unlocked the door and held it open.

'Go.'

He dropped his chin to his chest.

'I'm not a cheat,' I said. 'I won't do it; I can't. It's not fair, and it's not right. I can't believe that you would even try, given what I told you today. My head is a mess – can't you see that?'

Benoit's eyes widened. 'I know, but Fliss—' he began.

I cut him off, hands trembling with the need to touch him. 'No,' I said again. 'This, this ... thing, whatever it is, can never happen again.'

And without waiting for a reply, I walked out.

34

I walked down the stairs as if in a trance, scrubbing tears off my cheeks with the back of my hand as I went, and pushed open the door into the lounge. The record player was on, its speakers blaring out a chaotic jazz number, and strewn pages of newspaper littered not only the floor, but several tables too.

Etienne advanced with a glass of red wine.

'Not for me,' I said, swerving away.

He wheeled back around to Charlie, who bashed his own full glass against the older man's with an enthused, '*Santé!*'

Adélard came in through the courtyard, Madame close at his heels. 'Where is Benoit?' he asked, sidling over to join me.

'No idea.'

He snorted. 'You have had an argument with each other.'

'Not at all,' I said, deliberately not meeting his eye.

Charlie and Etienne were side by side on the least tatty chaise longue, the latter talking animatedly, his hands gesticulating with such vigour that large slops of wine kept landing on the rug. Not that a few stains would make much difference. We'd tried to persuade Etienne to let us throw the rug out, only for him to cry, 'It is the first place I made love to Lilah,' which had put a swift end to the matter.

'Did something happen today?' Adélard asked, as Madame sniffed around my ankles.

'We did see Céline. She was at the lake when we got there.'

'Ah,' he said, smoothing a hand through his thick, dark hair. 'That situation is complicated.'

'She is proprietorial over him,' I said, and he frowned.

'I think that he—'

'Fliss!' called Charlie. 'Come over here.'

'I'm going to go.' Adélard pressed his lips to my cheek. 'I have a date, but we can talk about this another time.'

Etienne was at the record player, and there was a screech as he dragged the needle off and slotted another LP into place. It was Joni Mitchell, mournful and sultry, my mum's favourite.

'Earth to Felicity.' Charlie patted the empty space on the chaise longue, sliding his hand over my knee as I sat. My shoulders were rigid, as if a clothes hanger had been slotted beneath my skin.

'We must speak in English now, my friend,' Etienne said, sloshing more wine into his glass.

The smell of it, pungent and slightly peppery, turned my stomach. Vodka had been Mum's poison, and while it didn't have a discerning odour, she did after drinking it. I would detect it the moment I closed the front door and stepped into the hallway, my school bag dangling from my arm, heart sinking down to the waistband of my pleated skirt.

'You never told me your uncle was such a character,' Charlie said, as Etienne began to sing, his hands composing in midair, wine leaving splatters of red on his linen trousers.

'Not my uncle,' I said wearily, wondering as I did so how this singing man could be the same person who'd taken my arm and led me through Libourne only days ago. That Etienne could have been a completely different person.

While Charlie posed numerous questions to Etienne about his past, asking how he'd come to own the house, and what had inspired him to collect so many 'treasures', I sat mute,

ramrod straight against the cushions, passive to the point of
invisibility.

Joni continued to sing, lulling us with her music, lyrics that
spoke of clouds blocking the sun, and the fear of falling in
love. I tuned in for a few verses, sentiment taking over, her
raw voice skewering my heart.

Something made me turn – a sound, or a sense – and I saw
Benoit in the doorway, still and quiet, gaze levelled at me.

I was undone, emotions unravelling like a dropped ball of
string.

Charlie's hand clamped on to my knee, his fingers pressing into the flesh of my thigh. 'Are you OK?' he asked
loudly.

Benoit was moving, across the lounge and out into the
courtyard. He did not look back.

'Fine,' I said mechanically. 'I didn't sleep much last night.
I guess I'm just tired. Might go and lie down for a bit.'

I stood up to leave and he grabbed my hand.

'I'll come with you.' He drained what was left in his glass.
'Pretty pooped myself.'

Back in my bedroom, I closed the shutters and removed
my shoes, being careful to avoid my injured toe.

Charlie loitered by the door. 'You're cross with me,' he
said. 'Is it because I had a few drinks?'

There was a spot of blood on the bandage.

'No—'

'Or still because of the money stuff? Liv is going to lend
me ten grand, so I can transfer the whole lot back to you in a
few days.'

'Fine.' I stood facing him. 'Whatever you want.'

'So, you'll forgive me then?' He clasped his hands together
in prayer. 'And we can get back on track. That's all I want –
you know that, don't you? For us to be OK again.'

'Were we OK before?' I asked. 'Because I seem to remember that before you took my money, you weren't only drinking excessively but also sleeping with someone else.'

'Slept with,' he interrupted. 'Once. And, as you rightly pointed out, I was drunk at the time.'

I flashed him a warning look and he threw up his hands.

'Alright, alright, I know that's not an excuse. But fuck me, Fliss, I was bloody lonely. You're not exactly the most affectionate person. Ever since we got engaged – I don't know, it's as if you're repulsed by the sight of me or something.'

'I'm not repulsed—'

'On the rare occasions we do have sex, it feels as if you zone out, like you'd rather be anywhere else than with me. And I know I've got a big ego, but even I can tell if someone's not into it.'

The truth of his accusation flared hot like a struck match. I turned away, my cheeks burning.

'It wasn't always like that,' I said in a small voice. 'You know it wasn't. It's the drinking, Charlie. I can't bear it – the smell of it, the sight of it, the knowledge that you're doing it every day, that you're sneaking around. If I seem cold, then alcohol is the reason.'

He breathed hard for a few seconds, then, crossing the room, took me in his arms. 'Listen, I'm sorry,' he said, pressing a kiss to the top of my head. 'I know I need to get a grip on the booze again, and I should never have fooled around with Maddie – that was unfair of me. But I only did it to get your attention, don't you see?'

I did see, but that did not make it any more palatable.

Benoit's voice came to me, asking if I'd ever try to forgive my mum. Was my inability to absolve her why I couldn't forgive Charlie for the mistakes he'd made? Was I going to screw up my future with my stubbornness, my brokenness?

Charlie moved closer, pressing the lower half of his body against mine. 'We used to be so good together,' he said. 'We could be again.'

I tried to move away, but he held on tighter, walking me backwards towards the bed.

'Don't you remember how it was in the beginning?' he said softly, lips against the lobe of my ear. 'Before all the stress of opening The Fitz, you couldn't get enough of me.'

He had been my escape, an antidote to long days spent at work, the lure of a fresh start, a new future.

'I remember,' I said, as his hands encircled my waist.

'We are so good together,' he murmured, sliding his fingers lower, lifting the skirt of my dress. His lips parted mine, and I didn't fight him, didn't pull away. I let him kiss me, and I kissed him back, ignoring the taste of the wine, waiting for the moment when my body would respond.

It never came.

My limbs remained leaden, arms two empty sleeves. Charlie's tongue probed more insistently, and then, abruptly, he stopped, staring at me for a beat or two before sitting down on the bed, his face in his hands.

'Don't tell me,' he said, 'it's not me, but it is me.'

I sighed. 'It's so many things, Charlie. It's you, it's me, it's your drinking, it's Maddie, it's this place.'

'You mean him,' he intoned, unable to keep the bitterness from his voice. 'Benoit.'

'He's a friend, that's all.'

Charlie sat up with an incredulous bark of laughter. 'A friend? Right. He's obviously mad about you. And I suppose he's tee-bloody-total, too, is he?'

'He's not,' I said, 'though he certainly isn't alcohol dependent. He doesn't have a problem with it; it's not his crutch.'

'This again.' Charlie stalked away from me. 'I've beaten the booze before, you know. I can do it again.'

'I'm sure you can,' I agreed, 'but I can't be the one who helps you do it. I'm sorry, Charlie, but I can't.'

'Can't or won't? Because there's a difference.'

'Both, alright? It's both. I'm not the right person. When we met, you were sober, and now you're drinking again. What does that tell you?'

'It tells me that I'm weak,' he muttered. 'I should be able to stop; you're right.'

'Why do you think you haven't?' I asked, and he sighed.

'Because, deep down, I don't want to – not really. I like who I am when I'm drinking, and other people do as well.'

'But not me,' I said, and it was such a relief to say it that I almost wept. 'The Charlie I met that day at the community centre was plenty good enough. I fell in love with you because of your strength, because you'd done the thing my mum never managed to do. It was only later that my feelings changed – not because we lived together, or even because of the stress involved with getting the hotel open, but because you started drinking again. When I spoke to you about it, you promised you'd stop, but you didn't. You broke your promise.'

Charlie nodded grimly. 'I had no business making a promise to you that I had no intention of keeping,' he said. 'You're right. I did lie, and I cheated, and the stupid thing is, I don't even know why.'

'Why don't you start by asking yourself why you feel the need to drink in the first place?' I said gently. 'You said before that you like who you are when you're drunk, but do you really? That version of you is why we're having this conversation now, why you're having to borrow money from your family, and why we almost lost the hotel. Alcohol is not your friend, Charlie – it's nobody's friend.'

He began to shake his head slowly from side to side.

'You don't agree?'

'I don't *not* agree . . .'

'But?'

'But I don't know, Fliss – I'm just not ready. Maybe I wasn't ready for any of it. I mean, after we got engaged, stuff seemed to happen so fast. We got The Fitz, we started working together, living in that tiny room. I thought running a business would be a lark, but it's been a total bloody headache, hasn't it?'

'Undoubtedly.' I braved a laugh. 'But I loved it, too. I learned so much, and not just about the ins and outs of running a hotel, but about myself. The things I can and cannot handle.'

Charlie moved towards me, lifting my hand with both of his. 'You're talking in the past tense.'

I slid my fingers through his and squeezed. 'I think we've gone as far as we can go.'

'I want to be angry with you,' he said. 'But I can't, not when I've done this to myself. Christ. I've been an idiot, running around town like the big I am, running up debts and burying my stupid head in the sand about it all.'

'Neither one of us is perfect, Charlie.'

He let out a low moan.

'And debts can be paid back,' I said, extracting my hand from his so I could slide off my engagement ring. 'You can start by selling this.'

I dropped it into his open palm, and he looked at it for a long time.

'About this . . .'

My good foot began to tap against the floorboards. 'What about it?'

Charlie pulled his lips back over his teeth. 'It's not actually a diamond.'

I opened my mouth and closed it again, Céline's words coming back to me, the way she'd described the ring as '*très intéressant*', in her faintly disparaging tone.

Charlie's face was back in his hands, his shoulders hunched. When he spoke, I had to lean closer in order to hear him.

'I was going to replace it for a real one,' he said. 'When I had the money.'

'Charlie,' I said, coaxing him to look at me, 'I don't care about the ring. Truthfully, it always made me nervous, the thought of wearing something so valuable. I actually think I like it more, knowing it's a fake.'

'Will you keep it?' he said, holding it out to me, and smiling.

I took it back, slipping it not on to my finger, but into the small velvet box containing my mum's old ring.

'What shall we do about The Fitz?' he asked, rubbing the heel of his hands into his eyes. 'You could still come back – we can continue to run it together, even if we aren't a couple.'

'No,' I said. 'I think we should sell.'

'Sell?' Charlie turned pale. 'Surely not?'

'It's the only thing that makes sense. Think about it, Charlie. Your whole life, you've been beholden to your parents, forever in their debt as they've invested in this venture and that scheme. They own so much of the hotel that it will never truly be yours, even if your name is over the door. Don't you want something real? A job or a business that is yours alone?'

'Huh.' He frowned, as if the concept had never occurred to him before.

'Sell, pay back your parents, pay back Liv, pay back your creditors, pay back what you owe me. Start with a clean slate and do something that makes you happy.'

'You make it sound so easy,' he grumbled. 'But it's failure. I'm not ready to admit defeat.'

'That's your father talking, not you. Failure is just a springboard to starting again. Real failure would be if you and I carried on as we were before, neither one of us happy, both going through the motions, chipping away at each other a bit more every day, until there's nothing to salvage, not even a friendship.'

'You still consider me a friend?' he exclaimed. 'After Maddie, and the fire, and the fact I bought you the cheapest ring John Lewis had on sale?'

'As a wise friend said to me recently, "You can't change what happened, but you do have the power to change how you feel about it." I'm going to try not to feel angry with you anymore, or sad, or resentful. But I can't stay in your life, not while you're in this spiral of self-destruction. I'll end up getting even more hurt, and I've been hurt enough already.'

'I understand that,' he said glumly, 'but I hope we can at least be friends again in the future.'

I raised a hand to ruffle his hair. 'I hope so too,' I said. 'And I'm sure we will be, one day.'

Charlie's eyes were moist, and he turned away to wipe them.

'One day,' he said, so forlornly that I almost cracked. 'I suppose that will have to do.'

35

I held it together throughout the remainder of the day.

I held it together enough to sleep, my arms around the familiar shape of Charlie.

I held it together as the two of us walked through Libourne the following morning, sharing coffee and pain aux raisins, talking inconsequentially, as if we hadn't just ended our relationship and agreed to sell our business.

I held it together until the train had departed, its final carriage trundling away, taking with it the man I'd thought would one day be my husband, and the dreams we'd shared.

Then, and only then, did it hit me.

I had no Charlie, I had no job in London to go back to, and no home there either. I had no way of knowing if I'd made the right decision about any of it, and no way of going back if I had. Drenched in a sudden cold sweat, I hurried out of the station and collapsed on a bench, my breath coming fast, dizziness swirling. I clutched my shoulders, rocking forwards and backwards on toes that felt disconnected from the rest of my body, hardly registering the dull pain from my injury. Was this a panic attack? I zoned in on a single point, far in the distance, a church spire ripped from the canvas of pale blue sky, and repeated to myself that I was OK, that I would cope, that I had been through far worse things before and survived.

When my phone rang, I barely heard it. A minute later, a message pinged through: 'Train just left Bordeaux. See you soon xx.'

Angela was on her way.

I got unsteadily to my feet and went back into the station, where I bought a bottle of water to dilute all the coffee I'd had. I positioned myself opposite the platform exit. The wait wasn't long, and I spotted my aunt's ash-blond topknot before she saw me. Pink-cheeked and harried-looking, she was wheeling a small suitcase and clutching a limp bunch of freesias.

'Angela,' I said, startling her so much that she almost dropped the flowers.

'You almost did me in,' she said with a laugh, then promptly burst into tears.

'What on earth's the matter?' I asked, ushering her outside.

Angela dug a packet of tissues out of her bag and blew her nose. 'Sorry,' she half-sobbed, 'ignore me. I haven't slept much these past few days, and it was such an early flight. But anyway, none of that matters – you're all that matters. Let me look at you. Oh, lovey, you look dreadful.'

'Um, thanks.'

'Not dreadful, that was the wrong word to use. Tired is what I meant. You look gorgeous, but are you eating enough? You look so slim. Have you eaten breakfast? Shall we go and get some, my treat?'

'You're fussing,' I told her. 'And I've had breakfast, but we can go to a café if you want?'

'Yes,' she said, squinting as she glanced up. 'Can we choose one with outdoor tables, though? Seems silly to be inside on such a nice day.'

I led her towards the main square, filling her in on the past twenty-four hours I'd spent with Charlie as we walked. Upon learning that we had broken up, Angela began to cry again. She could not seem to stop apologising.

'*Café au lait?*' I said, as we sat down at one of the few unoccupied tables.

Libourne was, for once, moderately busy. Locals pushed bikes, many of their baskets laden with bags of fruit and fresh batons, and the flags hanging down from the town hall balustrade were flaccid in the still air. All around us murmured the fog of chatter, while above glared the impish faces of gargoyles, their tongues out and eyes bulging. Shadows stretched long below metal chairs, beneath archways and between the wide, flat cobbles underfoot. Angela stared around, but she didn't appear to be taking any of it in, wasn't able to truly appreciate the ornate details, the way the yellow stone walls sang in the sunlight, or how the clouds were streaked flour-white across the sky.

Despite the heat, I ordered a *chocolat chaud*, wrapping both hands around the cup, giving in to the craving I had for sweetness and comfort. Angela opted for a complicated-sounding caramel concoction, which came with ice and a straw. She stirred but didn't drink it, her fingers drumming across the handbag in her lap.

'Thanks for the freesias,' I said. 'You didn't need to bring me flowers.'

'I know,' she said, 'but they were your dad's favourites, and I guess – I don't know. I wanted to bring him with me to France, as much as I could. I put a bunch on his grave yesterday.'

Dad was buried at Camberwell Old Cemetery, below a dark marble headstone engraved with the words: 'In loving memory. Michael James Fitzgerald – 1966–2007. Always in our thoughts, forever in our hearts.'

We had chosen it together.

'Me and your mum, we talked about this moment. We shared quite a lot in our letters, towards the end.'

'How nice for you,' I said, and she flinched. 'Sorry if that makes me sound bitter,' I said, 'but the fact is, I *am* bitter. I'm bitter that so many people got the chance to share positive moments with Mum, to see glimpses of her that I never saw, to feel affection towards her; that they get to describe her as "funny" and "complicated" and not simply angry or drunk.'

'She was trying to find her way back to you,' Angela said.

'Sure she was.' I pulled my hand away before she could take it.

'Her plan was to get dry first,' she went on. 'Properly, I mean. Prove to you that she'd changed.'

'She never did, though, did she?' I retorted. 'I've been told she was still drinking, right up to the day before she died, although I expected nothing less. She always did care more about alcohol than me – or anyone else, for that matter.'

Angela bit her lip. 'It's all linked,' she said. 'Your brother, what happened, the drinking – they're all strands of the same tragic tale.'

I took a sip of my hot chocolate, the cup crashing down against the saucer, liquid slopping over the sides.

'What happened to Felix?' I said, my tone harsh. 'I want to know – and, hell, I think I deserve to know the truth.'

Angela began to fiddle with a sachet of sugar. 'You're right,' she said. 'You do deserve to know – but it isn't my story to tell. It never has been.'

'Then why come at all? Why are you even here?' I said, only to fall silent as she extracted a small white envelope from her handbag and placed it on the table. The cursive 'Fliss' had been scribbled across the front in an oh-so-familiar hand.

Angela's smile did little to lift her sorrowful eyes. 'Only one other person besides you was there the day it happened,' she said. 'I think it's only right that you hear the story from her.'

36

I sat back against the unyielding cocoon of the metal chair, the letter in my hands. Angela had wandered a short distance away, understanding that this was something I needed to face alone. Only, I wasn't alone; not entirely. My dad was with me. I could feel him, sense his strength, hear his laughter in the whistles of birdsong. And, I supposed, Mum was here, too.

Despite all the past hardship, and our long estrangement, she had reached out after all. Now, at last, it was time for me to hear what she had to say.

To my daughter, Fliss,

I can't tell you how many times I have sat down to write you this letter, and even now, as I'm telling myself that this will be the one I finally send, I find myself in doubt. In doubt that I'll have the courage to be honest; in doubt that I will be able to bear writing the words that I must; and in doubt that sharing it with you is the right thing to do. Do you ever do that, Fliss? Do you doubt every decision you make, so much so that you fail to make any at all? I hope not. I hope you are better than me, and that you've learned to trust your instincts.

There is this saying at AA: 'This, too, shall pass.' It is supposed to remind alcoholics like me that better days will come, and that no matter how bad we may feel, there is always hope. I wish I could say that I believed it, and it is true that here in France, I do have those days, or moments, where the light shines through and eradicates the *darkness. But the shadows always remain. That's what grief is – a shadow. You can never outrun it.*

In all the other versions of this letter that I've started, sorry was first thing I wrote. And there is an awful lot that I need to say sorry for. I don't have to include a list of them here, though, do I? You know them all – except one. The worst one. The one that cleaved my life in two – the Before, and the After. Before Felix, and after him.

Felix.

It feels good to see his name written in my hand, for him to be acknowledged. My son, your brother – and not just any brother, but a twin, another side of the same coin. For the longest time, Fliss, I was so consumed by my own loss that I allowed myself to forget how much his death must have affected you, and that for all my covetousness, you were the closest person to him. I felt his death as a mother, while you must have felt as if a part of you was missing – and, unlike me, you could not name your grief, only suffer it. For that, my sweet girl, I am truly sorry.

Felix was the quieter of the two of you, a pensive little thing, always watching, taking things in. People used to ask me if he was a mummy's or a daddy's boy, and I would tell them neither. He was a sister's boy, his adoration of you unflinching and adorable. You were his Pole Star.

There was a little party the day before you turned two. We had to hold it on a weekend, because all our friends worked full-time, as did your dad. On the following day, which was your actual birthday, I was at home alone with you both, and had left you in the playpen while I went to hang out some washing. May had finally arrived, and it was such a sunny day. I remember that. Five minutes, I told myself. You would be fine for five minutes. Felix loved sitting in there – I think it made him feel safe to be contained in that way – but you were the opposite, always crying to be lifted out, unless you had a new toy or game that you were particularly keen on. At that time, it was a picture book – trees and birds for you, dragons and dinosaurs for Felix. You were both content when I left you.

Your father and I, we'd started this tradition of buying each other a present on your birthday, a kind of 'becoming parents' anniversary gift. That year, I'd bought him a voucher for a family photoshoot, and he'd got me a box of the fancy chocolates I loved. I'd opened them that morning, held them up out of reach when you both came begging. I told you they weren't for babies, though I should have been stricter with you, should've known better than to leave the box unattended.

When you grew bored of reading and peered through those bars in search of more fun, you must have seen those chocolates on the coffee table. I had no idea that you could climb out of that playpen – no idea at all. You made your way across the room and helped yourself to one, and then you decided to give one to your brother, as any doting sibling would, any child who did not understand the danger of a hidden nut, and its ability to become lodged in a tiny airway. It only took a few minutes. Felix was alive, and then he wasn't.

I tried to revive him. I breathed into his mouth, patted his back, thumped his chest. I screamed until the neighbours came. I pushed you away when you ran towards me, your face covered in chocolate. I stopped being able to love in those moments, Fliss, to love anyone or anything. The shock and the anger, and the loss – it consumed everything. It ate me up and spat me out.

Everyone told me it was nothing more than a tragic accident, but I could not accept that. Pain on that level, it feels personal, as if the universe is avenging some misdeed from a past life. I know you understand what I'm talking about. How could you not, given what happened to your dad? That was my moment to become your mother again, to shield you from the guilt I knew would follow, which I knew would likely destroy you, but I couldn't do it even then. I was too weak, too controlled by my addiction, alcohol having become the earth into which I buried my head. Honestly? I didn't feel as if I deserved you. Not before, and not then. Losing you at the same time as Mikey felt like a punishment that I was owed, the universe's way of making me atone for the mistake I'd made. I was a danger to everyone I loved, and

I thought it best to simply walk away. I am a coward, and I have suffered because of it.

The doctors here tell me that my drinking is what's caused irreparable damage to my heart, though the truth is it was broken long ago, and I am the one to blame for it. I let Felix down, I let you down, I let Mikey down, and I let myself down. I have been a dreadful, unworthy mother, and that is what I'm most sorry for, over and above everything else.

I want you to know that I'm not writing this letter in the hope you'll forgive me. I only ask that you try to understand the reasons why I turned into the hateful person you were forced to call Mum. The past cannot be eroded, nor can any of us change what has gone before, but I'm starting to hope that there will be a moment in the future when we can think of each other without confliction, and perhaps even find a new way in which to love.

Because I do love you, Fliss. I always did, always have, always will.
Mum
xxx

I had not heard Angela return, though as I lowered the letter to the table and wept, her arms quickly wrapped around me.

My fault. My mistake. My actions.

I dug my fingernails into my palms, closing my eyes as the world blurred around me. 'I knew it,' I said in a whimper. 'I knew there must be a reason why she hated me so much.'

'Oh, lovey.' Angela hugged me more tightly. 'She didn't hate you.'

'She did – and she was right to, after what I did. No wonder she couldn't bear to look at me. I killed her son, my own brother.'

'No.' Angela gripped my shoulders. 'Look at me, Fliss – it was an accident. Felix died because he choked on a nut. You were two years old.'

'But I gave it to him – me. If it wasn't for me, he'd still be alive. They'd all still be alive – Felix, Dad, Mum. I killed all of them.'

Angela shook me so violently that it stopped my tears. 'I won't have it, Fliss. This is not on you. It's just life. Sometimes bad things happen. Every day, people lose the ones they love, whether through illness or tragic accident. Nobody set out to hurt Felix; it just happened, that's all.'

'Why us, though?' I implored. 'Why did it all have to happen to my family?'

Angela let out a long breath. 'Why does anything bad happen to anyone, lovey? You can't go down the rabbit hole of why; you'll drive yourself mad if you do.'

'Why didn't anyone tell me before about Felix? Why didn't Dad tell me – or you? Whose decision was it to keep him a secret from me?'

Angela fished yet another tissue from her bag and passed it to me. My hands were trembling, skin pocked with goosebumps.

'Here,' she said, inching what was left of my drink towards me. 'The sugar will help with the shock.'

'Whose decision?' I said again, pushing it away.

Angela returned to her seat and took a deep breath. 'It was your dad's,' she said, with a glance at the bunch of flowers. 'You were so young – too little, we assumed, to form any lasting memories of your brother, or of that day, and Mikey thought the kindest thing was to let you forget him. We watched you so carefully in the weeks after it happened, in case there were any signs of trauma, but other than being a bit confused, and looking around for your brother, you seemed to get along with things just fine. Lilah was a mess, obviously, and Mikey . . . It helped him to see you happy. He needed a reason to carry on, and you became that reason.'

'I can understand not telling a two-year-old something traumatic like that,' I said, 'but what about when I was older? I always knew I must have done something awful – I could see it in Mum's eyes. If I'd known why she hated me so much, it might have been easier to bear.'

Angela took a napkin from the dispenser and started tearing it into pieces. 'It wasn't hate, it was hurt,' she said. 'Pat and I agreed you should be told, but Mikey was adamant, and Lilah . . . She wouldn't allow the subject to be so much as whispered about in her presence. Every time I tried, she shouted me down, and her drinking became chronic so quickly after Felix. None of us knew what would happen if we pushed the issue, what kind of reaction she might have had.'

'But I was so unhappy,' I said, fingers against my temples. 'Those teenage years were hell for me.'

'I know,' she said, expression doleful. 'Mikey knew it, too. It's why he took you out volunteering with him so often – he never wanted to leave you alone with your mum, even if he pretended otherwise. In his mind, telling you about Felix would only have made you more unhappy. They'd hidden him from you for so long by that stage that I suppose it felt impossible to dig it all up again. Mikey was scared – you mustn't blame him for trying to protect you.'

'I don't,' I said. 'But what about after he died, and I'd sworn never to see or speak to Mum again – did you consider telling me then?'

'We did.' Angela looked pained by the recollection. 'But in the end, we felt it would be dishonouring your dad's wishes. Like I said, it wasn't our story to tell. It had to come from your mum, and it took her until this year to accept that. When she sent me the letter, she told me I could only give it to you if you came asking, if you somehow found out about Felix some other way. And that's exactly what happened, in the end.'

'Does anyone else know?' I asked. 'Jono and Rich?'

She shook her head once. 'Nobody. Only us, Paddy and Etienne.'

'Etienne knows?' For a moment, I was too flabbergasted to think. 'Are you sure?'

'Very sure,' Angela said. 'From what I gather, Etienne is a big part of the reason why your mum finally wrote you that letter.'

She waited while I attempted to absorb this. Etienne had known, and yet he'd also chosen not to tell me the truth. If I had never found the photographs, would he ever have told me, or would I have remained in the dark about it all? And if Etienne knew, could that mean Benoit did, too? Had he been putting it on at the lake, pretending to be surprised when all along he knew more about my past than I did? My hands were in my hair, and I grabbed great clumps of it, tugging the strands until my scalp burned.

'You had no right,' I said, my voice hoarse. 'None of you.'

The letter crumpled as I shoved it back into the envelope, and cursing, I stuffed both into the pocket of my shorts. I wanted to run away, to hide, to stand by the water and scream. Angela moved as if to comfort me, but I jerked out of reach, the chair tumbling over on to the cobbles. Turning to right it, I cried out as a streak of silken grey rushed towards me. Suddenly, my arms were full of Madame, her tongue rough against my knuckles, dark eyes reproachful.

Adélard, who was sauntering across the square, caught sight of us and waved.

'Your aunt?' he exclaimed, bowing to kiss Angela's hand as I furiously scrubbed at my tear-streaked face. 'Surely, you are sisters, *non*?'

'For God's sake,' I muttered.

'Ah, *bien*,' he went on, eyeing our near-empty cups. 'If you are finished, we must walk to the guesthouse together.'

And without giving me time to reply, he slid an arm around Angela's shoulders and drew her away, leaving me to deal with not only the bill, and the suitcase, but also Madame's trailing lead.

Running away to scream by the river would, apparently, have to wait.

37

Benoit was ensconced in the kitchen when we got back, his dark silhouette moving behind the glass of the interior windows. The thought of seeing him, of having to impart this new and abhorrent development in the ever-disintegrating story of my life, brought a sour taste to my mouth. I did not much want to face Etienne either, though the sight of Angela immediately roused the older man from whatever he was doing at the desk in the corner of the lounge.

'*Bienvenue*,' he cried, kissing each of her flushed cheeks in turn.

Angela let him take her hands. 'Lilah told me so much about you,' she said, and his eyes welled.

'I'm going to take your case up,' I said, hurrying out of the room at the same time as Adélard disappeared into the court-yard. 'I'll be back in a minute.'

The banister was coated in dust, and I ran my finger through it as I ascended the stairs, leaving a dark ribbon in my wake. A pile of crumbled plaster had been swept into a corner on the upper landing, and there was a rainbow-striped feather duster propped against the wall. The thick aroma of paint permeated the corridor, but when I stuck my head around the bathroom door, expecting to see new additions to the underwater mural, I instead discovered that large swathes of the artwork had been obscured in fresh coats of white emulsion.

Benoit had been busy.

There was only one bedroom other than my own clear enough to house a guest, and that was the one that had belonged to my mother. I had been back inside only once since finding the photos, and the bedding I'd laundered was still where I'd left it, folded neatly on a chair. Thanks to a tireless hour spent scrubbing away soap scum and watermarks, the en suite gleamed, though I'd been unable to face packing away Mum's clothes just yet. Opening the wardrobe doors, I pushed them to one side, and made sure there were empty hangers available for Angela.

Numbness continued to hold me hostage. I felt strangely detached, as if I was watching what was going on as opposed to partaking. Shock. I was in shock, and the calmness was disquieting. A typhoon of emotions was going to land right in my centre, and there was nothing I could do to avoid it, no underground bunker in which to cower and wait for the storm to pass.

Overtaken by a sudden need to move, I began systematically hunting through one drawer after another, unearthing packets of tissues, receipts and train tickets, a Loire Valley postcard from someone named Brigitte, a handful of loose batteries and a scratch card yet to be claimed, despite three of the two-euro symbols matching. That was typical Mum.

When I had exhausted the furniture, I began to search beneath it, eventually hauling the canvas bag out from under the bed. The photos, I'd taken away, but the two stuffed rabbits were still inside – pink for me and, I had to assume, yellow for my brother.

I must have been there when it happened. I must have seen him die.

All my life, he'd been there. A smudge on the periphery of my subconscious, the vaguest memories of warm hands in my own, the echo of a dream lost in the moments after waking. The surety I'd always felt of something or someone being missing hadn't been a feeling but a fact – grief so ingrained that it had shaped me.

There was another bag under the bed, a tatty rucksack I vaguely recognised as having once hung in the hallway of my childhood home. I pulled it out, dislodging a small battalion of dust bunnies at the same time.

The backpack was coated in thick dust. I prised apart a zip that was stiff with age and reached inside, my hand encountering a stack of cards, each in their own envelope. None had anything written on the front, no name or address, no postmarks of any kind, and they were all different sizes. A few were coloured, but most were plain white. I tore carefully through the flap and eased out the first card. It was a drawing of a French café, '*Joyeux Anniversaire*' inscribed on a decorative sign. Inside, only a few words, though they turned my heart to stone.

To darling F,
   Happy 36th Birthday. I love and miss you every day.

Mum xxx.

Darling F. Not F for Felicity, as I might have assumed if I'd found them earlier, but F for Felix.

I opened the next card, and then the next, finding more birthday messages, more declarations of love – and of regret.

My angel, F.
   I cannot believe I don't get to be with you on your 21st birthday,
   but know I am thinking of you. I am always thinking of you.

I had spent my twenty-first birthday working, pretending not to care when no message arrived from the mum I hadn't spoken to for three years, telling myself and anyone who cared enough to ask that I didn't need a fuss, that it was just another day, that there was nothing to celebrate.

She had written Felix a card on what would have been his eighteenth, that most awful and devastating day. The message inside read:

You are in my heart today as you always will be.

To the child still living, she had shown only anger and hatred. At least now I knew why.

I cast my mind back to that morning, to the card I'd opened to find a cascade of twenty-pound notes inside. I still had it, could picture it in detail, see the words my dad had inscribed:

To our darling Fliss,
Happy 18th to the best daughter in the world – we are so proud of you.
Love, Dad and Mum.

Written by him, not her. The pride all his, the love limited only to him. Why had he been able to forgive me, while she had not? I still had the letter Angela had given me in my pocket, but a second read shed no further light.

I stopped being able to love in those moments, Fliss, to love anyone or anything. The shock and the anger, and the loss – it consumed every- thing. It ate me up and spat me out.

Were shock, anger and loss reason enough to stop being a mother to your own child? Had she even tried?

I ripped open the remaining envelopes. There was a birthday card for every year bar the first two. The message inside the one with a large '3' on the front was a simple '*I love you so much.*'

Felix had become more than her son and my brother. By dying, he had become an angel, a symbol of purity and perfection that my existence had sullied. Every time she looked at me, she would have seen the space where he should have been. It must have been agony.

The tears came then, and I was helpless to stop them. I sat on the floor, amid the dust and the memories, and wept for my mum, for her loss, and for the chance I would now never have to tell her how sorry I was.

38

I did not go back downstairs.

Angela found me, curled up on my mum's unmade bed, the cards and pages of her letter strewn around me, the pink bunny clasped tightly in my arms. I could not stop shivering, my body convulsing with sorrow, helplessness suffocating the air from my lungs. She clung to me as I sobbed, stroked the hair from my face and wiped away my tears. Later, she fetched tea, hot and sweet and familiar, tucked a soft blanket around me, and told me she would stay for as long as I needed her, that the pain would lessen over time.

I did not believe her.

The day wore on. Bangs echoed through the house; Etienne hummed to himself as he trudged past the door. Twice, Benoit knocked, but at the fierce shake of my head, Angela sent him away. Madame nosed herself into the room and snuggled in beside me, the thud of her small heart a steady reminder that life was still ongoing. Dogs were so present, so utterly unconsumed by their past, or what might be lurking in their future. I envied them for it.

At some point, I must have given in to sleep, because when I next looked towards the window, the sky beyond was the pitch-black of night. I rose slowly, being careful not to wake Angela, who was on the bed next to me, and crept out on to the landing. My limbs were stiff from lack of movement, and I winced as I made my way down the dark stairs.

The doors into the courtyard were locked, but the key had been left in place. It was a relief to step outside and draw in one deep breath after another, taste the fragrant air and count the stars that glistened above. I would have wished on one, if I thought there was any point: wished that I could have been someone else, somewhere else, experiencing something else.

In the kitchen, I helped myself to a glass of water. The surfaces had been wiped clean, every cup, plate and utensil tidied away, tea towels hung neatly on hooks, taps shining as if buffed. When I heard a noise behind me, I knew at once who it would be.

'Can't sleep?' Benoit's hair was tousled, and he wore only a pair of black boxer shorts.

'I was sleeping,' I said, showing him the half-empty glass in my hand. 'Thirst woke me.'

'Angela?' he asked.

'Still asleep.'

'I like her.' Benoit smiled. 'She's a lot like you.'

'Like me?' I crossed to the table and pulled out one of the chairs.

'Sure,' he said. 'Kind, compassionate, but strong with it. Exactly like you.'

'Exactly unlike me. What I am is cruel, bitter, weak and—'

'Careful.' Benoit held up a hand to silence me. 'Say those sorts of things out loud too often, and your brain will hear them and start to believe you.'

'My brain is the thing telling me these things,' I pointed out.

He put his head on one side. 'Where's Charlie?' he said, in a casual tone of pretended disinterest.

'Gone.'

'Gone?' he repeated. 'Gone where? For how long?'

'Back to London, where he'll soon be putting our hotel on the market.'

Could that really have only happened mere hours ago? It felt like weeks.

Benoit's mouth had fallen open, his jaw working as he chewed over what to say. 'I thought that you were—'

I shook my head.

'So, you're not?'

I shook my head again.

He drummed his fingers on the back of a chair. 'Did you and he break up, then?'

'It was the right thing to do.'

Benoit failed to suppress a timid smile as he filled his own glass with water from the tap.

'You don't have to sit up with me,' I said. 'You should go back to bed.'

'Not tired.' He sipped his water. 'Do you know what I do when I can't sleep?'

'Count sheep?'

'Not a *baaa*-d guess.' He grinned. 'But no, what I do is I bake.'

'As in, a cake?'

'As in, something far more exciting than a cake.'

Without waiting for me to reply, he began rummaging through cupboards, then crossed to the fridge, all the while listing ingredients to himself. Soon there was a heap of items spread across the table, along with a rolling pin, two baking trays and a palette knife.

'Here,' he said, passing me an apron before looping the strap of a second over his head. 'In case things get messy.'

'Too late,' I muttered, though Benoit didn't appear to have heard.

He'd crouched down and was levering an earthenware mixing bowl off a low shelf.

'Luckily for us,' he said, as he stood, 'there was a batch of puff already made. Can you get the oven on – crank it up to around one-eighty?'

I did as I was told, while Benoit unwrapped cling film from around a ball of pastry and scattered a handful of flour across the tabletop.

'Do you want to roll, or make the crème pâtissière?'

'What makes you think I'm going to do either?'

'The former, then. Good.'

He wiped his floury hands across the front of his apron. 'Pay attention,' he instructed. 'I need you to roll out the pastry into a thin sheet – not too thin. I'd say about three millimetres.'

'I'll get my tiny ruler out, shall I?'

Benoit emitted a grunt of amusement as he banged a pan down on the hob, pouring in a generous glug of milk before turning the heat to medium. With one eye on the stove, he returned to the table and cracked three eggs on the edge of the mixing bowl, deftly separating each yolk and dropping it in, before spooning in caster sugar. I continued to roll, pressing down hard until the chilled pastry began to yield.

'I used to bake with my dad sometimes,' I said. 'Nothing fancy, just jam tarts, banana loaf cake, the occasional Swiss roll.'

'I'd argue that Swiss roll is moderately fancy,' Benoit said. He'd begun to beat the eggs and sugar, the bowl cradled against his hip. 'He must have had some skills in the kitchen.'

'Maybe that's why you remind me of him so much.'

He glanced up. 'I do?'

'Not in the way you look – that couldn't be more different – but your personalities are similar: the way you see the good in everyone, never give up on them. That's very Dad.'

'I actually spoke to my mum today,' he said. 'Tried again to make her reconsider visiting, explained about you, and what a difference you've made to Etienne since you arrived.'

I stopped mid-roll. 'Me?'

'Of course, you. Think about it – he's drinking less, he sold that painting, did a mural for you, and he's been going through all those old newspapers looking up articles about his past exhibitions. It's as if his inspiration has returned. The sadness is beginning to wane.'

'I don't think any of that is anything to do with me – how could it be?'

'Because you've shown him love,' Benoit said simply. 'You care about the old man. It's OK to admit it.'

I did, it was true.

'I don't know why I'm surprised,' I said. 'You warned me this would happen, that everyone falls in love with Etienne in the end.'

'So I did,' he said, breaking off as he noticed the milk beginning to boil over. 'Just a few spoons of this,' he murmured, slopping a little from the pan into the bowl, 'then we beat.'

'Is this pastry rolled thin enough?' I asked.

Benoit eyed my handiwork. 'More than enough – one sec.'

I stepped aside as he expertly scored the palette knife along each edge, creating a neat rectangle. This he flipped on to a baking tray covered in a layer of parchment, then pricked the surface a few times with a fork before sliding the tray into the freezer.

'Give that a few minutes,' he said, 'then bung another layer of paper on top, as well as another baking tray. That way, the pastry won't expand too much when it's in the oven.'

'Yes, boss,' I said. 'And listen: I'm sorry for not letting you in when you knocked earlier, and for barely speaking to you when Charlie was here. You've been nothing but nice to me, and I've been atrocious.'

'You've been under an inordinate amount of stress,' Benoit said gently, sifting first plain flour and then cornflour into the crème pâtissière mix. 'I'm sorry if I've added to that in any way.'

'You haven't,' I began, but he paused what he was doing and fixed me with a level stare.

'I should have backed off when Charlie showed up, not pressured you into cheating on him. That was a dickhead move, and you were right to be pissed off. I promise it won't happen again.'

The knot in my stomach grew tighter. Benoit's apron had shifted to one side, and the dusky pink of a nipple was visible through his forest of chest hair.

'Don't worry about it,' I said.

The three minutes were up. I removed the pastry from the freezer and tore off a sheet of parchment.

'That goes into the oven now,' he said, adding the remainder of the warm milk to his bowl. 'Fifteen minutes, not a second more.'

'Yes, Chef.'

I crouched to open the oven door, and when I stood, Benoit was right behind me, the crème pâtissière mixture transferred into a saucepan, which he set on the hob.

'We need this to boil, and then thicken,' he explained. 'Tell me if you see any lumps.'

I remained where I was, my back to the kitchen, and to him. It made it easier to ask my next question, though it was a while before I could pluck up the courage. I knew, once this door was open, there would be no way of closing it again. And so I stood, listening to the soft tap of the spoon against the sides of the pan until at last, the words formed.

'Did Etienne tell you?'

Benoit didn't answer for what felt like a very long time, and then he simply said, 'Yes, but not until today.'

Tears stung my nose, and I pinched it between my fingers, breathing deeply to quell the sob that rose.

'You know it's not your fault, don't you?'

I forced out a bitter laugh. 'Don't pretend it hasn't changed your opinion of me.'

'Fliss.' Benoit waited until I'd turned to face him. 'Do you really think so little of me? What kind of man would I be if I judged a person based on something they did as a kid – and not even something malicious, but an act of kindness? Sharing chocolates with your brother does not make you a bad person.'

'He died,' I said harshly. 'Felix died because of me.'

'You don't believe that – you're saying it to me because you want me to refute it. And I do, Fliss, I refute it in the strongest terms. But it doesn't matter what I think; it only matters what you think, and how you feel about it. Can you truly stand there now and tell me that you're the one to blame, and that it wasn't a stupid accident, nobody's fault at all?'

'My mum believed that it was her fault,' I said, and he groaned in exasperation.

'Yes, and look where all that self-loathing got her.'

'But it must change the way you see me,' I said again.

Benoit folded his arms. 'Not remotely.'

The milky mixture was at the point of bubbling over, which felt apt.

'I think it's been fifteen minutes,' I blurted, though when I bent to retrieve the pastry, Benoit pressed his knee against the oven door.

'Still eight minutes to go,' he said, taking his pan off the heat and pouring the rapidly thickening crème pâtissière back into a bowl.

I stood in sullen silence while he added a vanilla pod, taking his time to stir it through. Taking a teaspoon from the drawer, he dipped it in the mixture and held it out to me.

'Taste test?' he suggested, but I hesitated.

'You're the chef,' I said.

Benoit shrugged and slid the spoon into his mouth.

'Delicious, if I do say so myself.'

'Naturally,' I said, giving in to a small smile. 'What's next?'

'We cover this crèm pat,' he said, unspooling a length of cling film, 'and bung it in the fridge to cool. Then, the fun part.'

'You mean all that beating wasn't fun?'

'I definitely gave you the easier task,' he agreed. 'But no – the fun part involves cream.'

As he decanted an entire tub of the stuff into another bowl, I eased the now-baked pastry from the oven and turned it out on to a cooling rack.

'What do you want me to do with this?' I asked, nudging a bar of dark chocolate that was among the ingredients on the table.

'Now, there's a question,' he said, a smile playing around his lips. 'I vote we melt it in the microwave first, and then decide.'

I started to tear the wrapper, aware that his eyes were on me, and that the awful, leaden sorrow that had rendered me numb for so many hours was beginning to lift. Benoit retrieved his bowl from the fridge, removed the cling film, and tested the sauce with his little finger before setting it up beneath an electric whisk and folding through the cream. Droplets splashed up over his hands and speckled the front of his apron. The microwave pinged, and I gave the melted chocolate a stir.

'This is perfect,' Benoit said. He had finished whisking and was cutting the baked pastry in half. 'You got the thickness spot on.'

'I had a good teacher.'

Benoit spooned the crème pâtissière into a piping bag.

'What are we actually making here?' I asked. 'You still haven't said.'

'Mille-feuille, obviously.'

I removed the melted chocolate from the microwave and set it down on the table.

'Come on,' he urged. 'Come over here.'

'You want me to be in charge of piping?'

'You'll enjoy it, and I'll help you.'

He showed me how to hold the bag, and where to aim the nozzle. His hands were warm as they slid over mine.

'We need four separate lines, from the top of the pastry to the bottom, but leave a little room so it doesn't squeeze out the sides.'

The pale gold crème pâtissière glided out, one smooth ripple after another. My first few attempts were uneven in places, but I soon mastered the technique. Benoit stood a few inches behind me, close enough that I could easily have stepped back into his arms.

'Will you still go back to London?'

I had not expected the question, and it took me a moment or two to reply. 'I don't know,' I said. 'Not right away. There's so much to do here, lots of reasons to stay.'

Very slowly, Benoit reached around and laid the second rectangle of pastry on top of the first.

'Same again?' I murmured.

'Same again.'

The wall clock ticked, the fridge whirred. From inside the oven, something clanked.

'Am I one of the reasons?' Benoit's breath was hot against my neck.

'Of course you are.'

The crème pâtissière was almost gone. I had to readjust my fingers on the bag and squeeze to push out every last drop.

'I should prepare the icing,' Benoit said, only moving once I'd crossed to the sink, where I stood and stared out into the courtyard. It was starting to get light, the fallen wisteria petals a grubby mauve colour, the leaves above them near grey.

Benoit tore at the box of icing sugar, his steady fingers for once clumsy. When he came towards me to use the tap, I moved out of his way.

'Go on,' he said, when the mixture was ready, and glad to have a task, I spread the icing across the pastry with a palette knife, while he fashioned a cone out of parchment paper and poured the melted chocolate inside.

'That's so clever,' I said, when he'd piped thin brown streaks across the top and was using a skewer to create the traditional mille-feuille pattern.

'It's all in the wrist flick,' he said. 'Now, let's get this in the fridge so it's chilled enough to have for breakfast.'

I glanced at the clock, astonished to find that it was nearing six a.m. The two of us had been in the kitchen for almost three hours.

'What do we do with all these leftovers?' I asked.

Without once taking his eyes from mine, Benoit stuck his finger deep into the chocolate before sliding it into his mouth. When he held the bowl out towards me, I shook my head.

'Oh, go on – what's the worst that could happen?'

'Fine,' I said, and dipping several fingers into the bowl, I smeared chocolate across his cheek.

'Oh,' he said, 'like that, is it?'

I leapt away as he coated an entire hand. Running around to the opposite side of the table, I snatched up the palette knife, which was still dripping in icing, and flicked it over the front of his apron. Benoit looked down at himself, back up at me, and then he flew into action, hurtling around the kitchen as I shot out into the courtyard. Before I could get the doors that led into the lounge open, he was on me. I wriggled, crying out as he wiped chocolate across my face and neck. Suddenly, we were nose to nose, and then, just as quickly, I had kissed him.

'Sorry.' I jerked away.

Benoit blinked, his eyes searching mine, but before he could do or say anything, I was moving away, stumbling through the lounge, slipping on Etienne's piles of newspaper, cheeks hot with shame, embarrassment and another, deeper, feeling I did not want to acknowledge.

Longing.

39

I took the stairs two at a time, headed straight for my bedroom and locked the door. In the bathroom, I set about removing the smears of chocolate from my face and neck. More had found its way into my ears, and there were splatters of icing sugar in my hair. I quickly gave up on the basin, instead tearing off the dress I'd fallen asleep in and stepping under the shower. The pipes groaned and clanked, but the hot water came in a generous torrent, steam rising over the cabinet mirror, coating the tiles with a fine mist.

Charlie had been gone only a day, and I had kissed another man. I had kissed Benoit, wanted to do more than kiss him. Had done ever since he had taken me in his arms that day in the attic, when my body had been lost in his and everything else had fallen away – the worry, the loss, the regret, the pain – all of it. But how could I trust what I was feeling, when my soul had been crushed by tragedy? Benoit was far too decent to be a mere distraction. He deserved better than the meagre amount I had to give. If I explained, would he understand?

When I went back into my mum's old bedroom twenty minutes later, Angela was awake, sitting propped up against the pillows.

'How are you?' she asked.

I wanted to be as honest with her as I could and took a moment to prepare my reply.

'Numb,' I said. 'Angry, I guess. Frustrated, disappointed, full of self-loathing.'

She patted the bed, and I sat down.

'All understandable reactions, but I wish you'd try not to blame yourself.'

I made a small noise of dissent.

'It was an accide—'

I stood up abruptly. 'Please, I don't want to talk about it anymore. I need a few days of not talking about it.'

'OK,' she said meekly, though I could tell from how flushed she was that I'd offended her.

'You don't have to stay, you know,' I went on, hating myself for being so hostile but unable to rein in my short temper. 'You can go home.'

Angela's scraggly top knot wobbled as she shook her head. 'I'm not going anywhere,' she said. 'I've looked around this place, I know how much work there is to do, and I'm here now, so I may as well stay to help.'

'It's not your responsibility,' I began, but she was already throwing back the covers.

'You would do the same for me,' she said. 'Now, go and get the kettle on while I get dressed.'

Downstairs, I grimaced at the mess that had begun to build up again on every surface of the lounge – crusts of bread on a plate, an empty box of painkillers, a banana skin curled around chunks of orange peel. Etienne's newspapers were spread all over the floor, and the dresser was crowded with empty wine bottles. Half-expecting to see Benoit in the courtyard, standing where I'd left him so rudely and with barely a word, I was relieved to find it deserted, each of the four chairs tipped neatly against the table.

A clunk echoed from the kitchen, and Etienne emerged,

his face transforming into a wide grin when he saw me. '*Bonjour, ma chérie.*'

No exaggerated flourish, or telltale wobble; he wasn't drunk.

'*Bonjour,*' I said, slightly taken aback when he hurried over to kiss me on both cheeks.

'You are still upset,' he said, pulling back to examine me. The top button of his shirt was missing, the gap trailing a thread of pale blue cotton.

Words would not come. Instead, I nodded helplessly.

Etienne cocked his head to one side. 'Do you know that the first time I saw you, I could hardly bear to look?'

'High praise,' I said drily, but Etienne's expression was grave.

'All that I saw was Lilah,' he went on.

I drew in a breath so sharp it scratched my lungs. Etienne placed his hands on my shoulders, his grip not firm but steady. He was making it clear that in this moment, at least, he did want to look. I stared back at the shrewd-yet-tired eyes, their twinkle long since extinguished by time, by sorrow, and of course, by alcohol. The same grey sheen had been present in my mother's gaze, on the few occasions she'd allowed me to stare into her eyes.

'I'm not like her,' I said – words so often repeated that they no longer carried much meaning. The phrase had become my metaphorical hand raised to an incoming blow.

Etienne replied by smiling, albeit sadly, and giving my arms a final squeeze. 'Come,' he said, leading me back towards the main part of the house, 'there is something I want to show you.'

I trailed after him, along the hallway to a room at the very front of the house. Benoit had opened the door only a crack during our initial tour, explaining that the parlour, as he described it, was full to the brim with items that had belonged to his grandparents, and should be exempt from our makeover plans for the time being. I hadn't given the space much further thought since then, though it was clear that Etienne had been making use of it. There was a pathway hewn through the teetering stacks of boxes and lumpy old furniture, which led around to a wide desk, its surface littered with sheets of paper.

'What do you think?' Etienne tapped a finger to the topmost page, and I bent to look.

It was a pencil sketch of what I thought of as the Triffid Room, only in this drawing, he had replaced that image with another I recognised almost immediately.

'It's a mural of the town square,' I said, to which Etienne smiled in genuine delight. The details he'd rendered were small but undeniable, suggesting colour, sound and movement. In the centre of the image, he'd sketched in a couple at one of the café tables. I touched a finger to my lips as I realised the figures were him and my mum.

'And here are more, see,' he said, rooting through the pile and extracting another drawing. This time it was the main bathroom, its underwater mural replaced by one that depicted the wooden jetty at Lac des Dagueys, a blanket rolled out on the small beach beside it. He'd added Mum sitting alone, staring out across the water, a pensiveness in the slight downturn of her lips. How he could capture so much emotion with only a few scrapes of his pencil, I couldn't fathom – it was astonishing.

'How did you get such a good likeness?' I asked. 'Do you use photographs?'

'*Non,*' he spluttered. 'Never. I do not need photographs, I have everything I need in here.' He tapped the side of his head. 'Lilah, I keep her here – and,' he added, his hand dropping to his chest, 'in here also. Always here.'

I looked away, putting the sketches back on the desk. 'And you're going to paint these?' I said.

Etienne's mass of grey hair had been hued yellow by the overhead light, a single valiant bulb partly obscured by cobwebs. He beamed, breath for once not acidulated by red wine, his manner that of a child who knows praise is incoming.

'Showing the drawings to you makes me happy,' he said. 'After Lilah went, I did not know if I would ever paint as I once had again, if I would ever want to try. But then, you arrived here and—'

He looked at me expectantly, but I had no reply. What had I done, really, other than complain about the mess, complain about his drinking, complain that I wanted to offload my inherited share of his home? I had done what I always did; I had focused on the negatives.

'It is different now,' he went on. 'The murals will, of course, be a tribute to Lilah, but I am painting them more for you, so you will understand the love we shared.'

'You want me to see her as you do,' I said slowly, and he clapped his hands.

'*Oui, voilà.*'

But the Lilah he'd known was not the woman I had known as Mum. He had got the good, while I had suffered the bad.

'I don't want to sully what the two of you shared,' I said. 'I know you loved each other, that you still love her, and I'm glad of that, I really am. But I don't want to lie either. I can't pretend that my mum and I . . . that we . . .'

Etienne waited.

'I don't hate her,' I said. 'Sometimes, it felt as if I did, but I think it was only ever frustration – and pain. She hurt me, Etienne. So many times, for so long.'

There it was, bold and unequivocal. *She hurt me.*

I fell silent, waited for him to defend her, perhaps offer a sympathetic platitude that I would brush off the instant it was uttered.

Instead, Etienne merely nodded. 'Nobody hurts us more than those we love, *ma chérie.*'

'But I don't love her – I mean, I didn't. I still don't.'

'That is what you tell yourself,' he said, 'to make the pain hurt a little less. But if you truly do not love her, there would not be any pain. You would feel nothing at all.'

I stared past him, looked beyond his reasoning and compassion. There were more sketches on the desk, each one of them a Libourne scene, every picture built around an image of her.

'It would be so much easier,' I said, 'if I could feel nothing at all.'

'*Oui*,' Etienne said solemnly. 'But if that were true, you would not be human. It is human to love, and so, it is also human to have your heart broken.'

Had my own heart ever been anything but?

I did not remember my brother's death, but it had happened. My heart would have broken at that moment, whether I was aware of it or not, exactly as my parents' hearts had been shattered when they lost their little boy. It was not enough to forgive my mum. I had to find some way of forgiving myself as well.

40

Distraction was what I craved, and the guesthouse delivered.

Throwing myself into the renovation not only provided me with the perfect excuse not to dwell on things or be drawn into a probing conversation with Angela, but it also offered the kind of hard physical work that acted as an antidote to my internal wranglings. On that first morning, I went downstairs determined to take charge despite my sleepless night, and was surprised by how readily everyone else fell into line behind my issued instructions. We had been working out of order, choosing rooms at random to clear of junk, scraping off wallpaper in only half of them, and keeping no record of tasks that had been done or still needed doing. There had to be a system, or the entire project would descend into disaster.

What soon became apparent as I trawled one floor after another was that we needed help. Adélard had done a beautiful job on the shutters, but the meagre budget we had would not extend to paying him to strip and sand the doors and floors. There was no way around hiring a skilled plasterer, but the smaller jobs, such as bleaching, grouting, sealing and painting, would take months if Benoit and I attempted them alone.

'Know anyone who enjoys working for free?' Benoit said wryly, only to recoil in shock as I burst out with an exalted, 'That's it!'

A quick internet search and a lengthy phone call later, I had registered the guesthouse with a UK-based organisation named HandsOn, which specialised in matching volunteers to various renovation projects all over Europe. For the small price of room and board, they would help us, and demand, the woman I spoke to informed me, was extremely high. Within three days, we were joined by a young Anglo-German couple, Hannah and Karl, who'd just begun their gap year, as well as a former Royal Engineer in his late forties, whose name was Clive – but who insisted we call him Clopper.

'It's a nickname,' he explained, red-cheeked below a thatch of even redder hair. 'The lads gave it to me, on account of my size twelves. Put some army regulation boots on those, and people think a cart horse is leading the battle charge.'

The week that we had the trio in situ marked a turning point for progress. Benoit rose with the dawn to make breakfast spreads to 'fuel the troops', as Clopper was fond of stating, while I set up tools, threw down dust sheets and provided each volunteer with a checklist for the day. Adélard was only too happy to act as instructor, and while he oversaw the stripping, sanding and varnishing of internal doors, I borrowed Karl, whose father was an electrician, and the two of us set about rewiring sockets and light fittings. My hands and knees were scuffed, my skin perpetually coated in grime, paint, Polyfilla and cobwebs, and my muscles ached from my neck right down to my toes, but my heart swelled with pride. Thoughts of Felix, of my mother, of what direction my life would take next all faded behind the noise of the everyday, the words of mutual encouragement, the whoops when projects were completed and the laughter shared amongst tired friends as we gathered in the courtyard for another of Benoit's delectable dinners.

Angela took it upon herself to become 'chief declutterer', and it soon transpired that she was a far more skilled negotiator than me or Benoit when it came to convincing Etienne to get rid of things.

'Cut out the articles,' was her reply when he made his case for keeping all the newspapers, magicking a manila folder from a drawer and handing him a pair of scissors. 'And this lampshade really is beyond repair.'

To Benoit, who happened to be passing at that moment with an armful of curtains that had been torn at the hems, she said, 'Don't throw those out. I'll have them sewn up in no time.'

'Your aunt's even bossier than you,' he told me, adding conspiratorially, 'And I couldn't love her more.'

'Such a darling boy,' she said to me, once Benoit was safely out of earshot. 'He has a lovely energy about him, doesn't he? Reminds me of Mikey.'

'Me too,' I admitted, and Angela pressed her lips together.

'I suppose that explains it,' she said.

'Explains what?'

She tapped a finger to her nose, smiled, and then, catching sight of Etienne sneaking back along the hallway clutching a taxidermy weasel half-devoured by mice, cried, 'Oh no you don't!'

The volunteers' final day fell on a Monday, and all three were working through lunch in order to finish clearing the downstairs parlour. Much of the furniture had to be relocated to an empty loft space, which was accessed through a hatch in the morning room, and I could hear the thunder of Clopper's boots on the stairs as he ferried up piece after piece. I was on my way to help when Adélard emerged from one of the smaller bedrooms and beckoned me inside. He was done with sanding the shutters, and now each one needed to be rehung. My job was to hold them in place while he worked.

'*Tiens-le stable,*' he kept repeating, cursing under his breath every time I let the heavy wooden panels slip down. Madame, who had accompanied him, stood whining by my feet.

We had fixed the first and were about to commence work on the second when a sharp rapping filtered up from the street below and echoed through the house.

Adélard leaned over on his stepladder and peered out of the open window. 'Ah,' he said, as I heard the front door being opened. 'It is Céline.'

A torrent of French followed, her voice shrill, Benoit's more measured.

'What's going on?' I asked, but Adélard shushed me.

'She wants him to go with her.' He paused, straining to listen. 'But Bennie does not want to; he says there is nothing left for the two of them to discuss.'

'What actually happened betwe—'

'*Tais-toi,*' he hissed. 'She is telling him off now. He will not like that.'

I balanced one edge of the shutter on the ladder and joined Adélard at the window. Benoit was leaning against the doorframe, only his feet and folded arms visible, while Céline gesticulated on the steps, arms waving, dark bob shining.

'Poor girl.' Adélard screwed up his features. 'Wanting cannot be overcome by thinking.'

'She wants Benoit,' I said.

'*Oui.*'

'And he . . . what?'

Adélard shushed me by flapping his hand. '*Merde,*' he murmured, eyes on stalks as Céline's shouts increased in volume.

I looked towards the street in time to see Benoit hurry down the steps. Céline was walking backwards, away from him, hands raised, face streaked with tears.

'*C'est fini!*' she screamed. '*C'est fini.*'

I was fairly sure I knew what that meant.

Adélard sucked air past his teeth and turned away from the window. 'This is why I never become official with anyone,' he said. 'It gets complicated.'

Benoit was still standing out in the road. Céline had gone, and he was staring into space.

'I'm going on a coffee run,' I said. 'The usual?'

'What about the shutter?' Adélard called after me, but I didn't turn back. My purse was in my bag, which I grabbed on my way past my bedroom. I checked in briefly with Angela and Etienne, then headed straight for the door, pulling it open at the same moment Benoit gave it a shove.

'Whoa!' he said, and then, 'Oh, hi.'

'Come on,' I said, grabbing his hand. 'You're coming with me.'

Outside, the late June day was overcast. Murky white-washed skies backlit by a sun still bright enough to dazzle. I hadn't remembered my sunglasses, and Benoit removed his own from where they had been keeping his dark curls off his face, insisting I put them on.

'They suit you,' he said.

'I don't look like the Terminator?'

'Definitely not.'

'Shame,' I mused, 'I could do with being sent back through time.'

'Where would you go?' he asked.

'Oh, so many places – or perhaps only one.'

'You aren't worried about chaos theory?'

'I thought it was called the butterfly effect?'

Benoit stepped into the road to allow a man walking a small sandy-haired dog to pass. 'Same thing,' he said. 'If you were, for argument's sake, to travel back to the day of your second birthday, and change the outcome of those events, then it would have a knock-on effect upon everything that followed. Worse tragedies could have occurred – a globally catastrophic weather event, or a meteor strike.'

'Sounds a bit extreme,' I said, 'but OK.'

'The point is, the past is the past – you can't change it, so why waste time wishing you could? The only thing we have the power to change is what happens next.'

We had reached the end of the street, but instead of continuing to the main square, Benoit led me in the direction of the river. Explosions of yellow daisies burst out through fissures in the pavement, and I stepped carefully around them, avoiding the handlebars of a moped that had been parked up on the kerb. A woman stood on the opposite side of the street outside a small boutique, legs clad in white jeans, a baby bouncing on her hip.

'What about travelling back ten days?' I asked. 'If I had the chance to redo the piping of those mille-feuilles, they'd have been much neater.'

'You'd mess with the space–time continuum purely to create better custard slices?' Benoit pushed out his lips. 'As a chef, I must applaud your dedication.'

'It would also give me the chance to not kiss you and run away immediately afterwards.'

'Don't worry,' he said, tapping the side of his head. 'My ego survived to be bruised again another day.'

'I didn't mean to,' I said.

'Didn't mean to what? Kiss me, or run away?'

'Both.'

Benoit considered this, holding out his arm to prevent me from stepping into the path of a car. 'Shame,' he said, as we crossed the road. 'I quite enjoyed the former.'

The riverside pop-up where we'd eaten together was in the process of opening, and a man clad in an apron told us to '*Attends une minute*' while he finished setting out tables and chairs.

'I heard you and Céline,' I said. 'I was in one of the front bedrooms with Adélard and, well, I'm afraid we both heard every word – not that I could understand most of it.'

'Céline.' He shook his head slowly. 'She can't seem to stop picking at the wound.'

I removed his sunglasses so he could see the questioning look in my eyes.

Benoit sighed. 'Here comes the next ego blow.'

'Why?' I asked. 'What happened between you both?'

Benoit scratched his nose and looked out across the water. 'She cheated on me.'

'She cheated?'

His head whipped round. 'Is that so hard to believe?'

'I just mean . . . She acts as if she's the injured party, as if she is angry with you, not the other way around.'

'She is angry with me,' he confirmed. 'Because I won't give her another chance.'

'I thought you believed in forgiveness?'

'I do. It's not that I don't forgive her, it's that I don't feel the same way about her as I did. When someone betrays you like that, it changes the way you see them. I can't undo it, and it frustrates her. I think she's actually more annoyed at herself than she is at me, but there's a lot of pride involved. She's never taken accountability, prefers to put the blame on me. If I hadn't worked such long hours, she would never have strayed, et cetera. Why is that funny?' he said, as I let out a helpless laugh.

'Charlie used exactly the same excuse on me,' I said, explaining about Maddie, the fire, and the recriminations that followed.

When I finished talking, Benoit's jaw was slack. '*Mon Dieu*,' he breathed.

'Telling the story makes me realise how bizarre it is,' I said. 'That poor fireman. Talk about an awkward situation.'

Benoit squinted down at me for a second, and then, with infinite care, he removed a tiny yellow butterfly from the front of my T-shirt.

I became suddenly aware of my lips, of a tingle in my hands, of the proximity of our bodies.

'Charlie,' he said slowly, as the butterfly fluttered away, 'is an idiot.'

'He is,' I agreed. 'And so is Céline.'

The aproned man levered open the hatch of the canteen and we gave him our order: espresso for Adélard, *café noisette* for Angela, Karl and Hannah, *café allongé* for me, Clopper and Benoit, plus a *grand café crème* for Etienne.

'Which we won't let him pour brandy into,' I said.

Cups secure in cardboard trays, we made our way back to the guesthouse, talking inconsequentially about whether we'd ordered enough white paint for the downstairs hallway. When we turned the corner into Rue Montesquieu, a man was leaning against the skip, a package in his hands that he asked Benoit to sign for.

'I hope this is what I think it is,' Benoit said, putting the coffees down on the steps and tearing open the box. 'Ah, yes. *C'est parfait.*'

Advancing, I peered down through the mess of torn wrapping to where a smart gold plaque lay gleaming, its cursive engraving bearing the words: 'La Fresque'.

'Oh my God,' I exclaimed. 'It's beautiful.'

'Are you sure?' Benoit looked suddenly uncertain. 'I wanted it to be a surprise, but I probably should've consulted you on colours and styles. We can send it back, if you don't like it? Get another one made or—'

'I love it,' I insisted. '*J'adore!*'

'*Ouf,*' he exclaimed. '*Moi aussi.*'

Lifting the plaque, he held it up against the wall, moving it from place to place, checking to gauge my reaction. The building might still have been half-covered in scaffolding, the skip only three-quarters full of accumulated junk, while the scraped-bare walls inside had yet to be transformed with murals – but somehow, the fact that we had an official name-plate meant it was all going to come together. We were going to create something special, something homely, something a lot like art.

'How many days have you been here now?' Benoit asked.

I thought for a moment. 'Tomorrow will be my twentieth. Wow. When I booked my flights, I assumed I'd be here for a week at most, and now it's almost three.'

He smiled. 'Don't go.'

I looked at him, unsure if I'd heard right.

'I mean it,' he said. 'Stay for good, here in Libourne. Don't sell your half, don't go back to England. Run this place with me.'

Warmth flooded my cheeks, a rush of disbelief spooling out in a laugh. 'Just like that?'

Benoit came down the steps and took my hands in his. 'Yes, Fliss,' he said. 'Just like that.'

41

Stay. Forever.

Tantalised as I was by the thought, I pushed it aside, ignoring the look of dismay on Benoit's face as I allowed his plea to pass without so much as a 'maybe'. It was madness, a fallacy, nothing more than the daydream of a fool. I could not move to France – could I?

It was with bittersweet melancholy that we bid farewell to Karl, Hannah and Clopper the following day, the house ringing with an odd silence as we closed the door behind them.

Benoit, who had just laid on a lunch of goat's cheese salad and chunks of dense, chewy bread washed down with home-made lemonade, muttered something about clearing up, then headed towards the kitchen.

Feeling at a loss, I wandered upstairs, where I found Angela sorting through clothes in my mum's former bedroom.

'Where's Bennie?' she asked.

I shrugged.

'Everything alright between you two?'

'Of course,' I said evenly. 'Why wouldn't it be?'

We were in the process of emptying the final wardrobe drawer when Adélard appeared, displaying the kind of grin that would illuminate a dark road at night, and holding the hand of an impossibly beautiful woman.

'*Bonjour*,' she said, amending the greeting to an, 'Oh, hey,' when she learned we were English.

'This is Sapphire,' Adélard said, puffing out his chest. 'She is with me.'

'Such a lovely name,' Angela said. 'Is it French?'

Sapphire smiled easily. Her rouge lips were the same colour as her silk blouse. 'It was Greek originally,' she said. 'Sappheiros. Then you have the Latin, Safir. Mine actually does come from France, in that I'm named after my grandmother. Her husband was Kenyan, as is my father, but I was raised in the States, down in New Orleans.'

Angela had begun nodding and not stopped.

'Anyway,' Sapphire went on, 'you didn't ask for a family tree. I apologise for running my mouth off.'

'Do not ever apologise for anything that you do with your mouth,' Adélard said, leaning in to kiss her.

I cleared my throat. 'Do you want some lunch? There are plenty of leftovers.'

'No, thanks,' Sapphire replied. She had a deliberate way of speaking, lingering over each word, emphasising the spaces between them. 'Adé was going to show me around, if that's OK with you?'

'Sure. I mean, the house is very much still a work in progress, but feel free.'

When they left, Sapphire's expensive, woody scent lingered.

'Adélard was telling me only yesterday about how he never gets too involved with anyone romantically,' I mused. 'But he seemed pretty smitten just then, didn't he?'

'The *chat* that got the *crème*,' Angela agreed. 'What a handsome pair, though. It's as though they strolled in straight off the end of a catwalk.'

As if she'd heard the word 'cat', Madame, who was curled up on top of the washing basket in the corner, put her snout in the air and let out a long, high whine.

I didn't see Adélard and his glamorous guest again for another hour or so, having been roped into ferrying buckets of water backwards and forwards to Bernard's son, who wanted to test a section of cleared guttering for any further leaks. It was physical work, and my arms and shoulders ached by the time we were done. Benoit, when I located him in one of the larger en suites, looked exhausted. There were shadows under his eyes, and splodges of paint all over his shorts.

'If I never see another roller . . .' he said, and yawned. 'Where have you been?'

I explained about the buckets.

'I thought I heard Adélard's voice.'

'Didn't you meet Sapphire?'

'The American he met in Saint-Émilion?' Benoit frowned. 'She's here?'

'She was earlier, although from the look on his face, I'd put good money on Adélard having whisked her off for a quickie.'

Benoit's eyebrows shot up. 'Don't be so sure,' he said, nodding over my shoulder.

Sapphire hurried forwards when she saw us, her lukewarm tone of earlier replaced by a deluge of superlative enthusiasm. The house was 'a dream', the marble basins 'to die for' and the forget-me-not mural 'so gorgeous, I almost cried'.

'Oh, so you really saw every room?' I said, with a hard stare in Adélard's direction. 'Even my bedroom.'

He offered me a customary shrug. 'It was necessary.'

Benoit reached around me as if to shake Sapphire's hand, remembered his own was covered in paint, and hastily withdrew it. Sapphire's own palm fell through midair, and she faltered for a second.

'You're the other owner,' she said, and Benoit nodded slowly.

'That's right.'

Sapphire glanced towards Adélard. 'I was wondering – well, we were wondering – if I could buy you guys dinner tonight.'

'Why?' I asked, at the same time as Benoit said, 'Yes.'

They all stared at me expectantly.

'It's kind of you to offer,' I said, 'but my aunt is staying, and I can't really abandon her.'

'Bring her along – and the old man, too. We'll have a blast.' Sapphire offered what I took to be her most winning smile. 'I'd love for all of us to get to know each other better.'

Benoit moved beside me, his knuckles brushing my arm.

'It's been a busy week, and we're both knackered,' he explained. 'How long are you in town? Maybe we could all go out tomorrow?'

Adélard let out a loud groan and said something in French that caused Benoit's eyes to widen.

'*Vraiment?*' he said, then, turning to Sapphire, 'You want to invest?'

'Well, hell, I was planning to tell you after we'd shared a nice bottle of something, but sure. I love the place, I think Libourne has a lot of potential, and I've been waiting a long time to find the right business opportunity to invest in over here. When Adélard told me you guys were looking to sell a share, it felt serendipitous. I can free up the funds almost right away.'

It was as if sand had been poured into my ears. I could hear what was being said, though I could not fully comprehend it, my brain working several steps behind my immediate senses.

'I know I'm the first to see it,' she went on, presumably taking mine and Benoit's mutual silence as a green flag. 'So I'm willing to bid high, get in before anyone else has the chance.'

'It is a very generous offer,' Adélard said. 'A lot of money.'

'How much?' I said faintly.

Nobody except Benoit heard me, and he repeated the question, moving closer as he did so, his fingers once again grazing mine.

Sapphire pressed her hands together in front of her chest. 'Well, for starters,' she said, 'how does five hundred thousand sound?'

42

Five hundred thousand euros was not quite half a million pounds, but it was close. And it was a lot.

When Charlie and I had secured The Fitz, I had contributed the sum total of my life savings, which amounted to a little over thirty-three thousand. That, I had accumulated across many years of going without. No socialising outside of volunteering, no car, no holidays, no extracurricular much of anything. I worked, I paid for essentials, and I saved. That was all I did. To be offered such a vast sum, out of the blue, by a virtual stranger, was going to take some time to wrap my head around.

I stood, immobile and blinking, mind racing, my heart rate spiking as if a bungee cord had been dropped.

'Say something,' urged Sapphire.

'Um,' I croaked. 'Sorry, I need a minute here.'

Her face fell. 'You don't want to sell?'

'It's not that,' I said, although it was. Of course, it was. 'You took me by surprise, that's all.'

Benoit slid his fingers around my elbow. 'Can I talk to you for a minute?'

I nodded mutely and threw an apologetic smile over my shoulder as he led me back into the en suite. The smell of paint was overwhelming, but he closed the door regardless.

'Did that just happen?' he hissed. 'What the hell?'

'I know,' I stage-whispered back. 'I'm as shocked as you are.'

There wasn't much space in the small room, which housed a basin and vanity unit, a toilet and an open-sided shower, incongruous with its modern hose and head. Benoit hadn't bothered with dust sheets, and there was an old wooden step-ladder coated in white speckles.

'We haven't even had the place valued yet,' I said. 'It isn't anywhere near finished.'

'You think she's overestimated?' he asked.

'No,' I replied slowly. 'Actually, I think the opposite. The house is worth more – or will be, when it's a functioning guesthouse again. Don't you agree?'

Benoit scratched the side of his head with a paint-covered hand. 'I don't know. This isn't my area of expertise. But value isn't the main issue here.'

I looked at him, knowing what he would say next.

'If you still want to sell your share, then that's one thing, but if not . . .' He widened his eyes, waiting for me to fill in the gap.

I paced to the door, which was two small steps away, then circled back to him. 'Can you see yourself going into business with Sapphire?' I asked, and he frowned.

'Maybe.'

'Really?'

Benoit sighed in exasperation. 'What do you want from me, Fliss?'

'Just the truth.'

'You know the truth,' he protested. 'The truth is I want you to stay. I want us to transform this place and run it together. We make a good team – that's the truth.'

Someone knocked on the door.

'What?' Benoit bark of reply was unusually curt.

Adélard's deep voice filtered through.

'He is asking about dinner.' Benoit glanced at me. 'Do you want to go?'

I grimaced and shook my head, and he nodded.

'We can't keep hiding in here,' I said, stepping past him before he could call back through the door.

Adélard was lounging in nonchalant fashion against the wall, Sapphire a few feet behind.

'Have you given any thought to my offer?' she said as I passed.

'We need more time,' Benoit interrupted.

I closed my mouth, offering her an apologetic half-smile.

'Sure,' she said. 'Of course. You can't rush into a decision like this, I get that. But are you certain you won't let me buy dinner? I've got such a lot of ideas for how we could turn this place around.'

I came to a stop on the landing. 'Turn it around?'

'Yeah.' She spun around, arm raised as if to say, 'look at the state of it'. 'It's in dire need of modernisation. You can't expect people to pay over the odds to stay here unless you up the luxury factor.'

'You sound like my ex-fiancé's mother,' I said.

It was not a compliment, though Sapphire appeared to take it as one.

'I know you've made a start, but it's all pretty basic, isn't it? I think it needs more of a strip-back-and-start-over mentality.'

'I thought you liked the forget-me-not mural?' I reminded her.

'Sure,' she said earnestly. 'We can keep that one, make a feature of it, but one is more than enough. This is a guest-house, after all – not an art gallery.'

I gawped at her. 'Nobody's told you, have they?'

'Told me what?' Sapphire continued to smile. Her teeth were mouthwash-commercial perfect.

Benoit and Adélard advanced along the corridor, each looking harried.

'The rules,' I said. 'About Etienne living here.'

Sapphire's veneer of positivity crumbled a fraction. She glanced towards Adélard, who turned to Benoit.

'That's right,' Benoit said. 'Etienne is as much a part of this place as the walls and roof.'

'But that's absurd,' Sapphire exclaimed.

Adélard issued a low murmur of warning, and I swung round to see Etienne emerge from the stairs on to the landing. He had a smeared wooden paint palette in one hand and a fistful of small brushes in the other, his shoulders stooped and hair awry. Had he heard us? It seemed impossible that he hadn't. A flood of protectiveness sluiced through me.

'There you are,' I said. 'Where's Angela?'

Etienne shuffled his feet, which were bare, against the floorboards. 'She told me to' – he smiled wryly – 'get out of her hair.'

Benoit's phone started to ring. He must be the only person in France, or perhaps the world, who didn't keep their mobile permanently on silent mode. He slid it out of his back pocket, features lifting when he saw who was calling, and hurried towards the attic stairs. I heard him say, 'Hello,' though whatever he said next was masked by the clump of his ascending feet.

Sapphire sidled in beside Adélard.

'*Oui*,' he said, gazing at her upturned face. 'Time to go.'

They sloped off downstairs, and I promptly let go of the tension I'd been holding in. Etienne had disappeared, but it didn't take me long to find him in what had been the Triffid Room. Swamped in a voluminous smock, he was busy sketching out a new mural across the freshly painted wall.

'*Salut, chérie.*' He passed me a stick of charcoal and motioned for me to join him, showing me how to add shadows to the cobbles he'd already drawn.

'Are you sure? I'm no artist.'

'Pah,' he said. 'Everyone is an artist. Art is not about technical skill, it is about feeling, and connection. If you can find a way to show what is in here' – he laid a hand against his breastbone – 'to other people, then you will have created art.'

Charcoal dust floated down on to the floorboards.

'How do you learn to do that?' I asked.

'For me, it was practice. There has always been a reason for me to paint. I began when I was a boy, and it became my way of expressing how I felt, and making sense of the things I could not put easily into words.'

'Benoit told me you left home when you were young,' I said.

'*Oui.*'

'How young?'

'The first time, I was only sixteen. The last time, eighteen. I did not go back again after that.' His voice had thickened as he spoke, but his eyes remained dry, focused on the scene he was bringing to life.

'It must have been bad,' I said, 'for you to leave?'

Etienne licked his finger and buffed the glass of a window he'd sketched. His frown could have been one of concentration or consternation – it was impossible to tell.

'My father was . . .' He stopped, blue eyes narrowing as he turned them to me. '*Un ivrogne.* Do you understand what that means?'

I shook my head.

'It means he was a drunkard.'

'I . . . Oh.'

He returned to sketching, a clock face appearing as if by sorcery beneath the rapid scratch of his fingers. 'He was always *un ivrogne*.' Etienne screwed up his face for a moment. 'I have not a single memory of him that is not tainted by it.'

I ceased my shading as a coldness crept over me.

'I do not believe I was the son my father wanted. He was a big man – strong. I was not.'

'He wasn't that strong,' I said hotly. 'Not if he was a drunk.'

'Physically, he was very strong.' Etienne moved back to examine his mural, shaking his head and muttering to himself in French. Then he said, as if it were as trivial a matter as the weather, 'He beat me up, many times.'

I quailed. 'He hit you?'

'*Oui*.' Etienne smiled sadly. 'With a belt, or his fists – sometimes both. When I was sixteen, I spilled a few drops of paint in the kitchen, and he broke my arm. That was when I ran away.'

A concentrated knot of pain bloomed between my eyes. 'Where was your mother in all this?' I asked.

'Hiding.' He bent and scored a hard line across his rendering of the town hall. 'Weeping. She was afraid of him, the same as me and my sister, Océane.'

'Benoit's mother?'

He sighed and nodded. 'After I ran away, Océane found me, pleaded with me to come back.'

'And you did.'

'For her, yes. My father was upset. He told us that things would be different, that he would be different . . .'

He did not need to tell me the rest. I had lived this story, knew its plotline well.

'During the summer that I turned eighteen, I began to drink. The alcohol, it made me feel less afraid. I began to stand up to him, to protect my mother and sister, but I was still a boy.' He grimaced. 'I was not a true opponent.'

'I'm so sorry,' I said, but he waved away my words.

'I did not care so much about the beatings. Those, I could endure. He could not hurt me in the way he wanted to anymore, but that only made him angrier.'

Etienne's voice had not altered, even minutely, but there was a tremor in his jaw. I wanted to tell him I had suffered the same fate, that although my mother's weapon of choice had been words rather than physical violence, I knew how it felt to be a parent's punching bag.

'How did he hurt you?' I asked. 'You don't have to tell me if—'

'He destroyed my art,' Etienne said simply. 'Took my paintings into the garden and burned them. I watched from the window of my room, and I thought, "If I do not go now, and remain gone, then I will kill this man. He will break me, and I will snap, and I will murder him." And so, I went. Océane has not ever forgiven me.' His face crumpled as, finally, the tears came. Etienne slumped against the wall, then slid to the floor, where he sat with his chin down, heaving out great sobs. It was all such a mess – a hopeless, self-destructive mess. Etienne drank to escape reality; my mother drank to escape grief; both drank because they felt guilty. But drinking had not solved a single problem; it had only caused more.

I crouched and put my hand on Etienne's shoulder. 'Have you ever wondered if the reason your sister doesn't want to see you is not because you left, but because you drink?' I said, and he looked up, blinking through eyes that were wet and raw. 'She grew up in the same house, with the same father, and she saw what alcohol did to him, to your family.'

Etienne wiped his cheeks, smearing them with charcoal.

'If you stop, it might bring Océane back into your life, or it might not – but either way, it will be a positive thing. It hurts so many people; it hurt my mum, it's hurt you, and it's hurt me.'

For a long time, he didn't speak, and then he reached across and took hold of my wrist, squeezing it for a few seconds before letting go.

'I will try,' he said. 'I will try for you.'

43

The evening drew in, and with it came my first taste of Libourne rain. It ran in rivulets down the windows and tinkled out a metallic song on the scaffolding poles. Air hung heavy, thick with petrichor, steam rising in exhalations of heat from sun-baked stone, and when I ducked outside to pull a tarpaulin over the skip, passers-by slipped and slid along the pavement.

Angela was in the lounge, pleased with herself after having dusted off an ancient television set and got it working, and full of plans for the four of us to watch an old movie together. Benoit, she informed me cheerfully, had popped out to get pizzas.

On my way upstairs to fetch a cardigan, my phone beeped with a message from him, asking about toppings.

'Anything non-meat,' I typed back, then added, 'except bananas.'

Benoit made me laugh by sending back a gif of a crying monkey.

With my phone still in my hand, I opened Instagram and began to mindlessly scroll through the stories, flicking past advertisements for wall Pilates, collagen supplements and several other London hotels I followed. Madeline had posted a new video, and I froze as I saw who was with her. Charlie, his arm slung around her shoulders, the two of them stumbling through Leicester Square in central London. I turned up the volume in time to hear Charlie mumble, 'C'mere,' and then he was pulling her face around to his, kissing her so hard that they almost toppled over. More videos followed: glasses being clinked, the unmistakeable clatter of a roulette wheel, shouts of exaltation and a shot where they'd brought their hands together in the shape of a heart. Madeline had pasted a caption over the top that read: 'Marlie reunited <3.'

Marlie?

I went back to the start and watched each clip again, several times, all the while waiting for envy to flare, or pain to ricochet, or disappointment to swallow me whole. None came. I felt nothing at all, save for a slight loosening in my chest. They made sense, the two of them together – much more sense than Charlie and I had ever made. Although a casino did not seem like a wise choice, not for a man with as much debt as him.

I copied the link of the Instagram story and set about composing a message to Charlie's sister, Olivia.

She got back to me within minutes. 'You're right. It is concerning. Leave it with me. L.'

She texted in the manner her father spoke, as if she were issuing a wartime telegram, and the reply made me smile in spite of myself. The Fitzsimons family were nothing if not consistent.

I leapt in fright at a rap on the bedroom door. It was Benoit, putting on a ridiculous accent as he called out, '*Cena per la signora.*'

'You speak Italian as well now?'

'*Sì*,' he said, as I fought to get my arms through the sleeves of my cardigan. 'Do you want to go and watch an old black-and-white film, or one made in the last century upstairs with me?'

I laughed. 'The latter. I'll be up in a minute.'

It made no sense to clean my teeth, but I did so regardless, then brushed my hair and spritzed on some perfume. I counted the attic stairs as I went, feet block-heavy and pulse high, raising a hand to the door only for it to swing open. Benoit bashed straight into me, his chin connecting with my eye, my elbow with his stomach. We both let out an 'oof'.

'Sorry,' he said, righting me on the top step. 'I forgot drinks – what will you have?'

'Water's fine.' I rubbed my temple.

'You go on in,' Benoit said. 'Make yourself comfortable.'

He had lit candles, and fairy lights twinkled from the exposed beams. On the low table sat two pizza boxes, and a slim vase containing a single sunflower. Rain pounded against the roof, speckled the small windows, matched the tempo of my increasingly elevated heart. The TV was off, but music played. 'Teardrop' by Massive Attack. It matched the downpour, the mellow glow, the shooting stars of desire I could no longer outrun, nor wanted to.

I crossed to the egg chair and sat, let the cushioned interior envelop me, closed my eyes as I swung, allowing my grip on the world to slacken, hesitation sliding away: oil on the water of promise.

'Fliss?'

Benoit had returned and was standing in the open doorway, a jug in one hand, two stacked glasses in the other. I lowered my feet to the ground, pressed my toes into the wood, impatient, suddenly, for stillness. It was impossible to read the expression on his face, though he did not once look away from me, not even when he put the water down on the table. My breath quickened and I parted my lips, an unconscious gesture that he mirrored in kind, taking three slow steps towards me; a smile that started shy rapidly grew.

I stood and went to him.

'Don't,' I said, as he started to speak, pressing my finger to his lips.

Benoit's eyes widened a fraction. In the dim light of the attic room, they were no longer blue but the darkest silver.

I moved my hand away, turned it over and stroked my knuckles against his cheek, feeling the gentle scratch of stubble. Benoit brought his own hand up to mine, danced his fingertips across my palm. The song ended and another began, soft drums and the twang of guitars, a male voice softly murmuring.

There were freckles across the bridge of his nose, smudges of the palest fawn, spread haphazardly as if flung from the end of a paintbrush. Beautiful was the word that came to me, but it did not encompass all that he was, could not hope to describe what it felt like to look upon him in this way, to know that what would follow was going to change us, change me.

Benoit's gaze left mine as his hand moved downwards, grazing my collarbone, trailing along my arm, causing ripple after ripple of delicious sensation. He seemed to know that what I wanted was not to lose myself in him but to be seen by him, beheld by him, so that the two of us could meet as equals in this moment, neither leading, nor following the other. I put my hand on his chest, felt the thud of his heart, that big, compassionate centre of him that he wore without ego or performance. A breath, hot; lips finding the hollow of my throat; a crackle of distant thunder. I tilted my head back, arched my body forwards, and he caught me, strong hands wrapped around my waist. Between my hips, all was liquid.

'Fliss.' My name was a breath, his voice trembling.

'It's OK,' I whispered, seeing the reflections of the lights in his eyes. 'I want this.'

I did not need to say more. Benoit took his hands from my

sides and cupped them around my face, his touch gentle, thumbs a teasing caress. I could no longer hear the music, nor the rain; my body yearned to rock and rub, grab and taste, but I held on, each second a tantalising morsel of the pleasure I knew would come, as surely as I had ever known anything before. Sex had always been such a mystery, though all I'd needed to unlock it was true connection. I was alive in a new way, elevated by the conviction that this was right, that we were meant to be together in this way.

'Can I?' I gripped the hem of his T-shirt, damp from the rain, and he nodded, raised his arms, helped me pull it off before stepping out of his shorts, kicking each item away, moving quickly towards me.

His finger slipped below my waistband, a question in the fullness of his lips that I answered by peeling off my top, unhooking my bra, removing every piece of material that barred him from me. Benoit blinked as he took me in, brows raised as if he could not quite believe what was happening. We had stepped back from each other, and he took my hand in his, though he did not pull me towards him, not yet. I glanced over at the bed, and he smiled, his fingers sliding through mine as I moved away. The mattress gave as I sat down on it, raised my knees, moved apart my legs.

The scrape of a drawer and the rustle of cardboard; the shiny packets tossed down like confetti across the sheet. He knelt before me, leaned over, bent and dropped a kiss on my stomach, more across my ribcage. When I took hold of my own breast, he understood and squeezed the other, tongue finding my nipple. A rush of wetness, headiness. I moaned his name as his fingers explored, stroked; a shot of pleasure so intense that I buckled.

'I don't want to wait anymore,' I gasped, sitting up so I could reach him.

Benoit put two fingers inside me, pressed his thumb down hard, holding me tight. I rocked against him, but the sensation was too great; I was too close.

'Together,' I managed, though it burned me to sever our connection, even for the few seconds it took for him to tear open the wrapper and roll down the condom. When he entered me, I cried out, and he stopped, his concern a mask that I kissed away, pushing myself further on to him, spreading myself wider, my body throbbing with each slow thrust. His face contorted and he grasped me harder, burying himself deep before pulling back, almost leaving me entirely before he dived once again, moaning my name, his teeth against my ear, the weight of him across me as we fell back against the pillows.

His pelvis ground firm against me, filling me up with heat, carrying me to a place where there was nothing but feeling. Our eyes were open, and he saw that I was ready, kissed me again, sucking at my lips while he continued to move. I felt him erupt, heard the groan as my world exploded into light, our bodies a slick, shuddering tangle.

The tears came then, and I let them fall, crying for the woman I had been, for the fear that had held me back and, most of all, for what I now understood to have been missing all along.

Love.

44

We ate cold pizza as the candles burned down, breaking off from chewing to smile dazedly at each other. The rain had stopped, and beyond the window, the moon shone bright, a pale fingernail, quartered by cloud.

A blob of tomato sauce dribbled on to Benoit's chin, and I wiped it away, bringing my finger to my lips to lick it clean, laughing as he jiggled his eyebrows at me in a suggestive manner. We were a mess, hair askew, make-up smeared, sweat glistening across bare limbs. My jaw ached from kissing him; other parts of me still tingled, raw from his touch. We had made love on the bed, then lain together whispering, sharing our incredulity, teasing one another with featherlight touches that soon became tugs. The second time was frantic and feverish, the third far slower, more sensual, the two of us side by side, my leg hooked over his, gazes locked, kisses lazy, a gradual wave of pleasure that rose and crashed. I was left panting, incoherent, able only to flop limply into his arms.

'What time is it?' I asked, when the two pizza boxes contained little more than a few crusts.

Benoit scooped them up off the bed, dumping them on the table before checking his phone, a yawn cracking open across his face. 'Almost two,' he said. 'Think how many films we could've watched in that time.'

'I completely forgot about that part of the plan.'

'Understandable,' he teased. 'Do you think Angela and Etienne enjoyed their evening?'

'Probably not as much as us. I'm surprised Angela didn't wander up here in search of me.'

Benoit suppressed a grin. 'I might've said something about needing to talk to you about a business matter . . .'

'So, you're sexy and conniving?'

'Flattery will get you anything your heart desires,' he replied, flopping back down beside me – then, as I moved closer, he added, 'Except that. I need at least another, oh, ten minutes, until I can offer you that particular dish.'

'Ten minutes?' I said, rolling over to plant a kiss on his nose. 'You slacker.'

'*Mon Dieu*,' he drawled, rubbing his eyes. 'I got less grief than this in the restaurant kitchens of Paris.'

'Let's hope you never have to work in one again.'

'I won't have to, not if we can get this place up and running, taking in guests.'

We. I disguised my smile by kissing him again. Benoit parted his lips, wetting them with the tip of his tongue.

'Remember at the start?' I said. 'How we thought – or you thought, more accurately – that it would only take us a few weeks to do the entire renovation.'

'If I'd told you what I really thought the timescale would be, you'd never have agreed to stay, and I wanted you to stay.' He paused, tucked a lock of hair behind my ear. 'Still do.'

'I need some water,' I said, untangling myself and reaching for the almost-empty jug. Benoit slid a leisurely finger along my spine. 'Can I ask you a question?' he said.

I sipped my water but didn't turn around. 'Go on, then.'

'Why now? I mean, why tonight? What happened to make you want to . . . you know.'

I put the glass down on the floor. 'I don't know. It wasn't a thought so much as a feeling. Call it an instinct.'

'Nothing happened?'

I swivelled back around and brought my knees up to my chest. 'Not nothing. I did see a video of Charlie kissing the woman he cheated on me with, but that's not why.'

Benoit shuffled into a sitting position, eyeing me directly from beneath his mop of curls. 'Are you sure?' he said. 'This wasn't some sort of elaborate revenge?'

I recoiled. What a question to ask, when our naked bodies still bore sticky traces of the other.

'None of this is about Charlie,' I said. 'You're not being fair.'

'Then what was it about?'

What had happened was not on me alone – he had been the one who followed me to the bathroom the day Charlie arrived in France, the one who'd chased me through the courtyard, who had kissed me back when I'd kissed him. Benoit took my hand, slipping his fingers through mine, and asked his question again.

'It's like you said before, we couldn't not – *I* couldn't not. And I don't regret it,' I went on fiercely. 'It's OK if you do, but I don't, and what's more—'

'Fliss.' He tightened his grip on me, pulled me towards him. 'Fliss, Fliss, Fliss.'

'You'll wear it out in a minute.'

Benoit rolled the two of us over until we were nose to nose. 'I needed to hear you say that you couldn't fight it anymore,' he murmured. 'Wanted to know if I'd guessed right.'

I nestled into him, my head against his chest, where he would not see my shame. I had been honest about my surface impulses, but I was holding back the murkier incentives: the desire I'd had to eradicate thoughts of my mother, my lost brother, the new reality of myself as someone who had caused the death of another. Benoit, with his tenderness and passion, was another tactic in delaying the inevitable crash.

'Do you ever wish you could hit a pause button on the world?' I said, lifting my chin. 'Stop everything else from moving but yourself?'

'Now, let's see,' he said. 'Either you're asking that question because you'd very much like this moment never to end, or because you want to freeze Etienne so we can put all his rubbish into the skip uninhibited.'

'Pause it for long enough and we could do both.'

Benoit drew me up, kissed my cheeks, my eyelids, the soft corners of my mouth. 'I know which I'd rather do,' he said, and I curled into him, feeling him harden against me, delighting in the response of his body when touched by mine.

'There's something I need to tell you,' I said, as Benoit patted around on the mattress for a condom. 'It's about Etienne.'

'Now?' he said, tearing the packet open with his teeth. I moved my leg so he could slide his hand down, sucking in a breath as he entered me, smooth, full, and fast. 'Can't it wait?'

My eyes were already closing, lids heavy as sensation took over, my words coming in gasps.

Benoit was right: the time for talking was over.

45

I awoke to a faint buzzing sound and opened my eyes to find Benoit asleep beside me, bottom lip protruding, Botticelli-esque bone structure lit up by the first rays of morning light.

We had not closed the curtains, nor cleaned our teeth after devouring the pizza, nor showered after the hours of love-making. I was sated, but stale, and more than slightly grubby. Sneak out quietly enough, and I could wash, change and bring Benoit breakfast in bed before he even realised that I was gone. I had pulled on yesterday's clothes and was half-way down the attic stairs when Adélard appeared on the landing below me.

'Ah,' he said, and then, as realisation dawned, 'Ahhh.'

'I was just—' I began, but there was little point in attempting a denial, not when I was clutching my balled-up under-wear in one hand.

'*Bien sur vous,*' he drawled. 'Good on you.'

The door to my mum's old room opened and Angela emerged, her feet clad in pink slippers. 'Oh,' she said, startled by the sight of us. 'Morning, lovey. Everything OK?'

Adélard rested a hand on the banister. 'When I heard the sound of feet, I thought that it might be Céline,' he said. 'I thought that perhaps she had sneaked into Benoit's bed, like a cat.'

I frowned at that, deflating a fraction. 'Not Céline,' I confirmed, as Angela brightened and said, 'Benoit's bed?'

'They spent the night together,' Adélard told her. 'And I am happy for you,' he added. 'It was about time, *non*?'

Angela pulled her flowered dressing gown more tightly around her shoulders, blinking as she rubbed sleep from her eyes. 'I knew there was a frisson between you,' she said, sounding pleased. 'I could sense it.'

'Me as well,' agreed Adélard, who was thoroughly enjoying himself. 'I told Bennie many times to go for it, and now, he has followed my advice.'

I was tempted to tell him that it was actually me who'd made the first move, but that would only add fuel to his gleeful fire. Instead, I asked if he'd had a nice meal with Sapphire.

'*Très bien*,' he said. 'A very good steak, followed afterwards by very good sex.'

Angela blushed, her mouth a perfect 'O'. I was still standing halfway down the stairs, acutely aware of last night's knickers and bra being visible, and of the no doubt sour reek that must be emanating from me.

'But oh dear, poor Sapphire,' Adélard mused, shaking his head. 'She will be disappointed. After this, there is no hope for her.'

'Does Sapphire have the hots for Benoit, too?' Angela asked. 'Because if so, she's got a funny way of showing it.'

Adélard laughed heartily. 'The hots for Bennie, when she has me?' He preened, making Angela giggle. '*Non*. Sapphire wants to invest in the guesthouse, but after this' – he waved a hand in the air – 'development, Felicity will not think of selling.'

'Erm, pardon,' I said, coming down the stairs until my face was level with his. 'How do you know what I'm thinking?'

Adélard's eyes dropped to my folded arms.

'*I* don't even know what I'm thinking, so I don't understand how you would.'

'I am only saying the facts as I see them,' he said patiently.

'Sapphire wants to invest in the guesthouse?' Angela was several paces behind in the conversation. 'But that's great news, isn't it? Don't you need some money to finish doing the place up?'

'She wants to buy me out,' I explained. 'But according to Adélard, that's no longer an option.'

'Felicity,' he said placatingly. 'Why are you so angry with me?'

'I'm not,' I stormed, so furiously that it negated my point. 'I haven't made my mind up yet, if you must know. I could still decide to sell.'

'And leave?' Adélard went very still. 'But what about Benoit?'

'What about him?'

'You are in love with him.'

'No, I—' I looked to Angela for help, but she shrugged, the pair of them having presumably discussed the situation already, laughed together about how 'in love' I was. Hot, stupid tears welled.

'Don't get upset.' Angela hurried forwards. 'There's nothing to be sad about.'

'Nothing to be sad about?' I said roughly. 'How can you say that?'

'I don't mean about— I just mean that if you're in love, then that's one good thing, isn't it? A spot of colour in all the grey.'

'I'm not *in love*,' I said, grinding out the final two words in hideous imitation.

Adélard took a step back, all trace of languor vanished.

'It was nothing,' I continued. 'A one-night thing, a distraction.'

Too late, I heard the attic door open; too slowly, I fell silent and turned.

Benoit stared down at me. He was clad only in boxer shorts, the two empty pizza boxes tucked under one arm.

'Morning,' Angela trilled.

Nobody responded.

'I might just . . .' she said, and retreated at speed along the landing.

Adélard looked from me to Benoit, who looked ashen.

'What's going on?' Benoit said.

When Adélard immediately began to speak in French, I cut across him.

'It's so rude when you do that.'

Adélard turned, a hand on his chest. 'Me? I am the rude one? We are in France. Perhaps it is up to you to learn how to understand me, *non*?'

I'd had enough, and stormed past him down the final few stairs, heading straight for my bedroom. Once inside, I slammed the door shut behind me, and stood shaking, my breaths coming fast, heart drum-loud in my ears.

'Fliss.' Benoit had followed me. The door handle turned, but the lock didn't give.

'Leave me alone.'

'Why are you being like this?'

'Let him in,' chorused Adélard. 'You are behaving worse than Madame when I take away her toys.'

'*Faire taire!*' Benoit hissed. 'You're not helping, Adé.'

'Both of you, go away,' I shouted, snatching a dress off a hanger and hurling it on to the bed.

From its perch on the bedside table, where I'd left it charging, my phone lit up with a message. I ignored it, glaring instead towards the door.

Benoit continued to knock. 'Please,' he said. 'This is ridiculous.'

I heard another door open and, a moment later, Angela's voice joined those of the two men, cajoling, pleading, encouraging. It reminded me painfully of the weeks after my dad's death, when I'd moved in with her and Patrick, barely leaving their guest room except to wash and use the toilet. Angela had brought up trays of food and left them outside the door; she'd sat on the carpet and talked, reassuring me that I wasn't alone, that I'd always have a home with them, for as long as I needed it. My grief had been such that I could not see past it to hers, which must have been excruciating. I had been selfish then, and I was being so again.

The same buzzing sound that had woken me started up again. It was my phone, vibrating across the wooden surface as it silently rang. I peered at the screen, saw Olivia's name. I should have answered, but there was too much noise already, too much banging, too many voices. One thing at a time. Breathe.

With a mighty sigh, I unlocked the door and opened it wide. Angela had dressed, but Benoit was still only in his boxers, dark curls all over the place, hurt casting furrows across his brow.

'Can I come in?' he asked, and I nodded once.

Angela mouthed an 'Are you OK?' as he passed me, to which I dredged up a smile of reply.

'Where's Adélard?' I asked, closing the door on the departing shape of my aunt.

'I told him to go away,' Benoit said.

'Is he pissed off with me?'

Benoit went to the window. Yesterday's rain had gone, all trace of it evaporated by an implacable sun.

'Not pissed off,' he said. 'Confused. He doesn't understand why you're angry with him.'

'He was goading me,' I said hotly. 'Winding me up about you.'

'That's what he's like. He pokes fun, but not in a malicious way.'

'Maybe I don't appreciate being poked.'

Benoit's eyebrow twitched. 'Are you sure?'

'Very funny,' I said, and then groaned.

'Come here.' He opened his arms, and after a moment's hesitation, I stepped into them. A few hours ago, I would have melted into such an embrace, but the ease I'd felt had abandoned me. When I failed to do anything other than stand stock-still and unyielding, Benoit released me.

'I heard what you said.' He rubbed his jaw. 'Did you mean it?'

'What did you hear?'

'That last night was nothing, a distraction, a one-off. Is any of that true?'

I stared down at the floor.

'Because I was there, Fliss, and I know it wasn't nothing.'

'You're right.' I raised my eyes to his. 'It did mean something – it meant a lot.'

'Then why say it didn't?'

'Because I . . . I don't know, OK? I lashed out.'

'At me.'

'Not at you—'

'But about me. I know I come across as laid-back, but even I have my breaking point. Imagine how you'd have felt if I'd said the same thing to Adélard about you.'

'I would have been devastated,' I said, twisting my hands together, biting my lip.

'Yes,' he agreed. 'You would.'

'I'm sorry.' I tried to touch his arm, but he stepped out of reach. 'The past few weeks, all this stuff about my past, it's warped my mind. I feel as if I'm losing touch with reality.'

'And having sex with me was what – a way of avoiding it all?'

'Not only that,' I began, as Benoit scoffed.

'*Mon Dieu*,' he muttered, shaking his head.

'Don't go,' I cried, as he stalked towards the door. 'I said I'm sorry.'

He turned and looked directly at me, his disappointment so intense that I felt it. 'I know you've been hurt,' he said, 'and that you're still hurting. But it doesn't give you the right to hurt other people.'

My phone buzzed into life. Olivia again. I snatched up the handset and rejected the call, breaking eye contact for only a few seconds, but it was all he needed.

By the time I looked again, Benoit had gone.

46

It was Angela's idea that we spend the day in Saint-Émilion.

'I looked, and it's only six minutes away by train.'

I was reluctant, until I discovered that Benoit had gone out while I was getting dressed, having told Adélard that he wouldn't be back until late afternoon.

'Come on, lovey,' Angela urged. 'You've been flat out; this will do you good.'

We walked to the station together in companionable silence, sipping coffees bought from a café en route, and boarded the next train. Beyond the window, the slow-moving countryside offered little appeasement, and I could not seem to get comfortable in my seat, no matter how many times I readjusted my position. Beside me, Angela radiated serenity, a placid lake alongside my stormy sea.

Once in Saint-Émilion, we exited on to a small platform and followed the trail of other passengers across the tracks and out along the road beyond. To our right, vineyards stretched up across a hillside, while more rippled down into a valley below. We passed gated chateaus, shuttered stone houses and an endless stream of cars, each parked bumper to bonnet along the roadside. The landscape was stunning, picturesque, every single superlative, but it didn't charm me as Libourne so effortlessly had.

Everyone was heading in the same direction, Angela and I at the rear of the pack, each of us content to stroll at a leisurely pace. The wide, smooth road was intersected by a lane as it swept up around a corner, a café coming into view not far ahead, tables dressed in red and white on a covered veranda. Shadows stretched; sunlight shone through scalloped tiles and threw toothy smiles across the cobbles. The flapping of wings drew my eyes upwards, to where a pigeon soared over a canvas of sky sliced in two by thick power cables. Ferns sprung out from gutters, the sand-coloured walls a beach banking sea-hued skies.

As well as numerous gift shops, selling all manner of trinkets, treasures and Saint-Émilion-branded souvenirs, there were numerous wine shops, several restaurants and a bar the shape of a hollowed-out beehive. With no real sense of where to go, we simply wandered, traversing the narrow backstreets in a quiet kind of awe. There were plenty of tourists milling around, yet the atmosphere remained ambient. It was as if they, like us, had been subdued by the rustic beauty of the place.

When we reached a square overshadowed by a vast, monolithic church, we stopped and stood, side by side, heads craning until we could make out the very tip of the spire. Angela dabbed the sweat from her forehead and blew out a 'Phew'.

'Are you OK?' I asked. 'We can go and find somewhere shady to sit.'

She fanned her face. 'Oh no, I'll be fine. Can't get over how hot it is. I always think of France being a similar temperature to England, but it's far warmer over here, isn't it?'

In answer, I burrowed in my bag and produced a bottle of water that I'd swiped from the guesthouse kitchen. It was still cool from having been in the fridge, and Angela accepted it gratefully, unscrewing the lid and gulping down half the contents.

'Do you want to talk about it?' she said.

I looked at her sideways. 'Which part?'

'Any part you like.'

A ring of carved-stone leaves bordered the church arch-way, centuries old yet clean-edged. Saints were depicted below, their halos smooth. I could sense the heat rising in my cheeks as I fussed with my hair, my clothes, the strap of my bag.

'There isn't much to talk about.'

'Well,' she said, clearing her throat, 'there's Benoit, for starters.'

'Benoit is . . . We're friends.'

Angela raised a hand to shield her eyes from the sun. We had yet to move, two statues amid a whirl of activity.

'I'm glad you have someone like him in your life,' she said. 'You know I was fond of Charlie, but he was like a big kid. Benoit is far more stable, and he cares about you.'

'I know he does.'

'And I don't know what went on between the pair of you this morning, but I hope you'll make it up with him.'

'I hope so, too,' I said, and she put her head on one side. 'I care about him, but I don't know – it's just hard. I can't help but think he deserves better than me.'

'Nonsense,' she said. 'And don't you think that's up to him to decide?'

'It's not nonsense.' I turned to her. 'Don't you think Dad deserved better? Wasn't his life ruined the day he met Mum?'

Angela smiled weakly. 'Mikey loved Lilah, and he loved you. Did he wish things could've been different? Of course. Did he ever consider leaving? Absolutely not. He knew why she drank, why she struggled to be a good mum to you after Felix died, and he forgave her. There was sadness there, yes, but never regret, or bitterness.'

'I wish I'd known,' I said, the misery suddenly so heavy that it crushed the air from my lungs.

Angela opened the clasp of her bag and brought out a small sheaf of photographs. 'These are for you,' she said. 'I should have given them to you sooner, but I didn't want to upset you more, set you off crying.'

'It's all I seem to do these days,' I said, dabbing at my eyes as I took the pictures from her.

The first was of me and Felix in the bath, bubble crowns on our matching blond heads; another showed us dressed in red baby-grows, propped on our beaming mum's lap; in a third, we gazed at each other as we lay on a blanket, tiny fingers touching. My dad was in the fourth, a grin on his face lopsided by emotion as he bent over our sleeping forms.

I missed them. I missed all of them so much. Even her.

'Oh, lovey.' Angela put a hand on my arm as a lone tear snaked down my cheek. 'Was I wrong to show you?'

'No, no.' I clasped the photos to my chest. 'I love them. I really do. Thank you. I'll just—'

I was stowing the photos in my bag when my phone lit up with a call.

'It's Olivia again,' I said, holding it up to show Angela. 'She's tried me three times already today. I'd better answer – sorry.'

I pressed the handset to my ear, motioning to Angela that we should sit on the low wall surrounding the perimeter of the vast church. Despite the heat of the early afternoon, the stone was cool beneath my skirt.

'Finally.' Olivia's clipped tone was businesslike. 'I was beginning to think you'd been sucked into a sinkhole.'

'No such luck, I'm afraid,' I joked weakly.

'I thought I'd give you an update on the Champ sitch.'

'You spoke to him then?'

Olivia tutted. 'Did a little more than that. I staged an intervention. Went over to The Fitz last night and found the idiot nursing a sore head in one of the rooms, bloody mess everywhere, bar drunk practically dry.'

'Oh God.'

Angela looked at me in concern, but I shook my head.

'Is he OK?'

'He will be,' Olivia went on grimly. 'I packed him up and out of there. He's at the family pad in Surrey now, licking his wounds like his namesake. It was actually rather touching. Once he'd sobered up a bit, it all came out, you see. He told us about the gambling, the debts – all of it. I had no idea things had got so bad.'

'Neither had I until very recently,' I said. 'I told him to put the hotel on the market.'

'Smart,' she agreed. 'The ball is, as they say, rolling on that score. But I don't want you to worry – we've got him, and we'll sort him out, get him whatever help he needs.'

I started to apologise for having ended things, but she dismissed it with blunt immediacy.

'Bloody hell, Fliss – nobody blames you. Champ told me a bit of what you've been through, with your mother and all that. I had no idea. It all sounds hideous.'

'Thank you,' I managed, through a throat that was swollen tight.

'And the money he owes you is on the way to your account – plus what you put into The Fitz. I know, I know, you were happy to wait until it sold, but this way you don't have to. If what Champ tells me is true about that wreck of a place over in France, you're going to need it.'

I laughed. 'Your first stay will be on the house. I'll be sure to let you know when the wreck is ready for guests.'

'Lovely,' Olivia barked. 'Make sure you do. Must dash.'

Mood buoyed somewhat by the rarity of being told good news, I continued to explore Saint-Émilion with Angela, the two of us pointing out sprigs of wildflowers, vineyard vistas, fresh strawberries bobbing in glasses of crémant, and the sweep of a cat's tail as it disappeared around a curve in the lane. We sought shade in a large antiques market, lunched on feta salad topped with honey and roasted walnuts, enlivened by tangy spheres of red onion, and toasted glasses of sparkling water as if it was the finest champagne.

'How are you feeling now?' she asked, as we wandered back down the hill to the station. 'Any better?'

'A bit.' I paused. 'I'm looking forward to being back in Libourne.'

'You do seem at home there.'

There was an enormous sprawl of wisteria clambering across the walled garden by the roadside and, reaching up, I stroked one of the petals.

'I love it,' I told her. 'The house, the town, the way of life – but I don't know if I can stay.'

'Why ever not?'

'Because it was her place first,' I said, cursing as the delicate flower came apart in my hand. 'I can still feel her there; it's as if she's watching me, waiting for me to mess everything up.'

'But she wanted you to have it,' Angela reminded me. 'She's given you what she couldn't in life – a place to love and feel loved.'

'We'd better go.' I looked past her. 'The train will be here in a minute, and—'

'There are people who can help you.' Angela took my hand. 'I know you tried counselling once before and didn't get on with it, but you were eighteen then. Things are different now – you're different now. It must be worth trying, at least.'

'No.' I pulled my hand away. 'I don't want to. I can't—'

'Fliss,' she said, 'the guesthouse is your home. If you can't be happy there, then what chance do you have of being happy anywhere else?'

A clamminess coated my skin, nettle-stings of unease prickling.

'That's just it, though,' I said. 'I can't be happy; I don't know what that feels like. I'm not even sure if I have the right to feel happy.'

Angela's eyes welled, but she managed not to cry. 'Everyone is entitled to be happy, Fliss,' she said. 'And I don't know a single person more deserving of happiness than you.'

47

The hallway of the guesthouse was blocked by several large suitcases.

Angela and I exchanged a puzzled look as we inched our way around them and went through into the lounge, where we found not only Benoit and Etienne, but two other people, a woman and a man. He, tall with a sparse thatch of ginger hair and a milky complexion, towered over his companion, who was petite and fine-boned, her slight figure encased in a wrap dress the same dusky pink shade as the blossom mural upstairs. She had aged since posing for the photo I'd seen, though not unkindly. There was only the merest hint of grey spidering through her neatly pinned chignon, and her skin glowed with luminous health.

Benoit had done it; he had got his parents here.

'You're Océane,' I said, and she smiled in surprise, glancing towards her son. 'I'm sorry,' I went on, going towards Benoit's father. 'I don't know your name.'

'Angus.' He offered me a hand. 'Ben's dad.'

'This is Fliss,' Benoit said, coming to stand beside his mother.

'It's nice to put a face to the name,' she said. Leaning over, she pressed her dry lips against my cheek.

I introduced Angela, whose, 'Gosh, you're taller than the Eiffel Tower,' remark to Angus made everyone laugh – except Etienne. In the time we had been talking, he had retreated to the far side of the room, ostensibly to hunt through his record collection, though he kept throwing glances in our direction. Benoit seemed to have regained his usual affability, though each time I attempted to catch his eye, he looked away.

Nothing more than I deserved.

'I have been very eager to meet you,' Océane said, drawing me down on to a chaise longue, which creaked and coughed out dust. 'I have been told about your mother. I am so very sorry for your loss.'

Her eyes were the same shape as Benoit's, but the palest green.

'*Merci*.' I swallowed hard. 'I'm so glad you're here. Is the house at all similar to how you remember it?'

'It is' – she wrinkled her nose – 'far less messy. Benoit tells me that is because of you.'

'It's a work in progress,' I said.

When I asked how long they planned to stay, Océane deferred to Angus, who blew air into his cheeks.

'I've told them they're welcome for as long as they like,' Benoit said. 'That's alright with you, isn't it?'

'Me?' I exclaimed. 'Of course. It's not as if you need my permission.'

'You are the co-owner, *non*?' Océane looked at me beadily. 'The woman of the house.'

There was a crash as Etienne sent a stack of records tumbling on to the floor. I leapt up to help, Angela yelped, and Océane rolled her eyes to the ceiling.

'What is the matter, brother?' she called. 'Are you drunk?'

Etienne ignored the barb, though his body seemed to shrink in on itself. Crouching, he selected one LP from the pile that had fallen and slid it from its sleeve. The familiar scratch of the needle was followed by a powerful female voice that filled the room. I smiled as Angus sang along, completely out of tune, and tapped his fingers against the furniture in time to the crashing drums and cymbals.

'What is she singing about?' Angela asked, raising her voice to be heard over the din. 'What's a boum-badaboum?'

'It sounds frivolous,' Océane replied, wobbling her shoulders demurely, 'but actually, Minouche Barelli is making a serious point about the threat of nuclear war.'

'Nuclear war?' My eyes widened. 'That's unexpected.'

Etienne pirouetted from the record player across to the dresser.

'If a bomb had gone off in this house a few weeks go,' I observed, 'nobody would've noticed.'

Angus broke off from singing to roar with laughter. Once again, I attempted to catch Benoit's eye, but he was looking towards the door. A moment later, Adélard and Sapphire strode through it. At the sight of new faces, Madame shot forwards, tail in a propeller spin, and set about licking the blusher off Océane's perfectly made-up face.

'Boum-badaboum!' bellowed Angus.

'I'm going to start laying out dinner,' Benoit said, and Angela shot up to help him, leaving me to introduce everyone.

Adélard, who looked undeniably handsome in dark trousers and a shirt the colour of posh custard, immediately went into a flurry of kisses and French compliments, dropping Sapphire's hand so he could clasp both Océane's in his. The record had got stuck, a hiccupped wail of 'boum' that sent Etienne into a frenzy of headbanging.

I was gripped by a very strong urge to laugh; a glance at Sapphire told me I was not the only one, although my attempts to suppress it were more successful than hers. Before I could gather enough of my wits to cross the room and stop the record, Adélard had picked up a cushion from the chaise longue and flung it at the juddering turntable.

Etienne's appalled cry was almost as abrasive as the screech of the needle. I put my hands over my ears just as Benoit stuck his head around the door and called, 'At the table.'

Angus slapped both his palms against his thighs and stood. He was a head taller than Adélard – who, I was privately amused to see, looked slightly miffed by this fact.

'I'm starved,' Angus said. 'They don't feed you on planes anymore. There was a time when you'd get a cooked dinner even on a short haul, but now the only things on offer are microwavable sandwiches – and you have to pay about seven pounds for the pleasure.'

He led the way out into the courtyard, the others following close behind. I hung back to wait for Etienne.

'Are you OK?' I asked. '*D'accord?*'

He patted my arm. 'Your French is getting better. Bravo, *ma chérie.*'

Given the way in which he'd been dancing, I'd fully expected to detect the fug of wine on his breath but could discern no trace of it, though his hands trembled.

'You must be in shock,' I said. 'Seeing your sister again after so long. It would be hard for anyone to cope with.'

Etienne offered me a watery smile. '*Oui,*' he mumbled. '*Oui c'est le cas.*'

The courtyard had been completely transformed. Where the rickety old metal table and chairs had once been, there now stood a long dining table, draped in heavy white cloth. Eight chairs of various shapes and sizes were set in front of meticulously laid place settings, the forks prong-side down in the traditional French style. Tapered spires of flickering light rose from a brass candelabra, around which were arranged jam jars of lavender and sprigs of fresh rosemary. None of the water glasses or cutlery matched, but that only added to the charm, as did the pile of blankets that had been placed on the ground for Madame. The dog appeared to know these were for her without being told, and as the rest of us deliberated over where to sit, she curled herself up into a bundle of spindly limbs and settled down with a contented sigh.

There was no wine, and nobody asked for any. Instead, Benoit staggered out from the kitchen carrying two large jugs of freshly prepared lemonade.

'How did you do all this?' I asked. It was the first time I'd spoken directly to him since our argument, and for a moment or two, the air between us seemed to crackle.

'It's not a big deal,' he said.

'It is beautiful,' Océane declared, bringing two fingers up to her lips and kissing them with a flourish. Dipping her head towards Adélard, who was seated beside her, she said, 'I taught my son well, *non*?'

'*Très bien,*' he said obediently.

Angela bustled out, cheeks radish pink. 'Starters are plated, Chef,' she said to Benoit, adding to the table at large, 'I hope you're all hungry. There's enough in there to feed an army.'

Angus stood to decant lemonade into his wife's glass. 'Well, that'll do me,' he said. 'Not sure what the rest of you will eat, mind.'

Sapphire unrolled her napkin, which was a different shade of blue to everyone else's, and turned over her fork. Beside me, Etienne had slumped down in his seat and was scraping dried paint off his fingernails.

'How's the mural going?' I asked, but only got a sniff in reply.

The first course was brought out to a chorus of 'oohs' and 'ahhs', each portion of Coquilles St-Jacques baked in its shell.

'Benoit did you a vegetarian version,' Angela said, placing a small dish in front of me. 'Mushrooms instead of scallop, heavy on the cheese and garlic.'

'It looks delicious,' I said – and it was. For a few blissful minutes, the table fell silent as everyone savoured the food. Benoit had positioned himself at the opposite end, as far away from me as it was possible to be. Bread baskets had been set at intervals between the candles and glassware, and I took a slice, tearing it absently into pieces to dip into my sauce.

Etienne was pushing his scallop from side to side in its shell, but had yet to take a single bite. I offered him some bread, asking once again in an undertone if he was alright. The older man didn't even seem to hear me; he was staring intently across at his sister, who had finished her starter and was listening, enraptured, to the story of how Adélard and Sapphire had met.

'I'd ordered myself a glass of wine, and was busy minding my own business, when this handsome Frenchman wanders over, all casual, and pours my wine into the nearest plant pot. Told me I was drinking the crappy tourist stuff, and that he'd like to buy me something better.'

I caught Angela's appalled eye.

'If you'd tried that trick on me,' I said, 'you'd have found yourself wearing the second glass.'

The ghost of a smile appeared on Benoit's face.

'Maybe I'm a fool,' Sapphire said, 'but I thought it was pretty romantic.'

'And now you are together?' Océane asked. 'You will stay in Libourne?'

Sapphire darted a look in my direction. 'Sure hope so,' she said.

Angus, who was sitting on Etienne's other side, asked if he

was done with his Coquilles St-Jacques, beaming as the plate was passed wordlessly across.

It was hard to know where to look, who to focus my attention on, and on whose conversation I should be eavesdropping. Not once had I ever been at such a lively table, and despite the awkwardness with Benoit, and the overwhelming sense of there being an elephant in the room we were all choosing to ignore, I was enjoying myself. Was this what it felt like to be part of a family?

When Angela stood up to clear away the dishes, I pushed back my chair, ready to help, but Sapphire beat me to it. The main course was chicken Francese, served with roasted white asparagus from the market. Benoit had substituted the meat element with tofu for me.

'How did you make this sauce?' I asked.

'Oh, it is a simple recipe,' Océane said, answering for her son. 'Butter, lemon, white wine, a little stock.'

'I used vegetable stock for yours,' Benoit added, returning my smile for the first time.

'Are you not hungry, brother?' Océane said.

When Etienne did not respond, I gave him a gentle nudge.

'Our father was the same,' she went on sourly. 'My mother would spend all day preparing his favourite recipes, then he would arrive home late, and drunk, after the food was ruined.'

I pictured my own mum, arms folded as my dad carved the Christmas turkey, sprouts and gravy congealing on her untouched plate.

'Do you not appreciate my son cooking for you?' Océane needled. 'Can you not even try to be grateful?'

Etienne stared down at the table.

'It's fine,' Benoit began, only to be silenced by a warning look from his mother.

'You told me he had changed, that he was better.'

'He *is* better,' I said. 'He's trying, and he's getting better every day.'

Océane narrowed her eyes at the interruption. Angus, who had finished his chicken and was now mopping up sauce with what was left of the bread, glanced from his wife to me.

'Fliss is right,' Adélard said, lowering his knife and fork. '*C'est vrai.*'

'Lilah hasn't been gone very long, and grief is a tough thing to get through,' Angela pointed out, only to redden as Océane barked out a scornful laugh.

'You think that you are the only one who grieves, Etienne? Who was left to grieve alone after nursing their mother through a terrible illness, only to watch her die?' She banged her hand against the table. '*C'était moi!*'

'Maman.' Benoit's face was devoid of colour. 'Please, don't do this. We are trying to eat.'

Océane pushed away her half-finished plate of food and folded her arms. 'He is not different,' she sneered. 'Not better.'

'But you've barely given him a chance,' I said, aware that everyone had turned to stare at me. 'If you'd only stop attacking and actually let him speak.'

'OK.' Océane fixed me with a steely look and folded her hands together. 'Go ahead, brother – what is it that you want to say?'

But Etienne said nothing. He stood, the chair falling backwards to land with a thud amongst the wisteria petals, and walked lifelessly towards the house.

48

Angela was the first person to speak. 'Oh dear,' she said. 'Shall I . . . Should someone go after him?'

'Leave him.' Océane raised her chin and glared around. 'It is obvious that he did not want to join in.'

Benoit rubbed the back of his neck, a grim twist to his mouth.

'If nobody's going to eat this . . .' Angus said, lifting Etienne's dinner aloft.

Everyone shook their heads.

'You weren't joking when you said you were starving,' Sapphire remarked. 'Can't say I blame you, going in for seconds. It really is great food, Benoit. Someone should award you a Michelin star.'

'Hardly,' Benoit said, spearing a blade of asparagus.

'He really was trying, you know,' I said, unable to thaw the ice from my tone. 'Tonight was a big deal for Etienne. I don't mean to be rude, but you should know that he had no idea you were coming, and the shock of seeing you both again after so long must have been huge. But despite that, he didn't immediately start drinking. He was obviously uncomfortable, but he sat here and let you goad him without so much as a murmur.'

'If he did not want to be goaded,' Océane replied coolly, 'then he should not have abandoned me and my mother.'

Benoit stopped chewing. He did not know this story; I'd not had time to tell him what Etienne had confessed to me.

'What do you mean, "abandoned"?' he asked.

Adélard raised his napkin and dabbed at his lips, while Sapphire took an overly large sip of lemonade, dribbles of it running over her chin.

'Perhaps it's better if we discuss this later, eh?' Angus said, but Benoit was not going to let the matter drop.

'You told me that Granny made him leave because of the drinking.'

Angus's eyes met the table.

'Was that not the case?' Benoit persisted.

Océane sighed. 'It is true that he was drinking,' she said. 'But so was my father. He was' – she smoothed down a flyaway hair – 'violent.'

Benoit stared hard at his mother.

'When Etienne left, we were at that monster's mercy.'

Angela made a small noise of dismay that was matched by Sapphire. Even the usually unflappable Adélard appeared sombre.

I recalled Etienne's words – '*The alcohol, it made me feel less afraid. I began to stand up to him, to protect my mother and sister, but I was still a boy*' – and knew that I must defend him.

'How old was he?' I said, and six faces turned to me in unison. 'When Etienne left, how old was he?'

Océane cleared her throat. 'Eighteen,' she said.

'And how long had he been taking the brunt of the beatings your father dished out?'

Océane's pale green eyes were slits. 'You were not there,' she said.

'No,' I agreed. 'But I'm here now, and you're here now, and so is Etienne. You are what's left. Christ,' I went on, leaning towards her, 'do you know how lucky you are to have a family? A husband and a son, a brother?'

My voice wobbled dangerously close to the edge, and I paused to draw in a breath.

'Fliss . . .' Angela reached a hand across the table towards me, but I shook my head.

'You would want a brother like mine?' Océane said in disbelief. 'A drunk, a coward, a liar?'

'Yes,' I said forcefully, 'I would. At least then, I'd have the chance to help him, and to mend things. You might feel angry with Etienne now, but imagine how much angrier you would feel with yourself if anything happened to him. You have the opportunity to put things right. Please, don't waste it.'

In the silence that followed, a flush of intense heat spread, uncontrolled, throughout my body. The only person I dared look at was Angela, and she was smiling at me with what felt like pride.

'This is the reason he drinks, isn't it?' Benoit said, turning first to his mother, and then to Angus. 'Because of the trauma he suffered?'

'There is always a reason,' Angus said gravely. 'But I think what your mother can't accept is why he chose that particular coping mechanism, when he'd seen first-hand how destructive it could be.'

Océane could only nod. She appeared to be close to tears.

'Ask him,' I murmured, then said it again, with greater clarity. 'Ask him why. He's still here; you still have time. I never asked my mother, and now – well, now I can't. I know more than I ever did before about what happened to my family, but I'll never know how alcohol came to play such a vital part in it all, because understanding the reason only solves half the puzzle. You have the opportunity to get the whole story, to work with Etienne rather than against him. I would give anything to have that chance – anything at all.'

Océane said nothing, and when I looked at Benoit, I saw the glisten of sorrow in his eyes.

'You make a very valid point, Fliss,' Angus said, and Océane threw me a watery smile.

'*Oui*,' she agreed. 'Some food for thought.'

'Why don't we change the subject?' I said, to a chorus of relieved sighs.

'Anyone heard any good jokes lately?' Angus asked.

'Oh, I have.' Sapphire shot up in her chair. 'Two cats are having a swimming race; one is named One Two Three, and the other Un Deux Trois – which cat won?'

We all waited.

'One Two Three – because Un Deux Trois cat sank.'

'*Mon Dieu*,' Océane groaned, but Angus and Adélard laughed.

'Dessert?' Benoit said tiredly.

He had prepared a vast strawberry tart, and also carried out platters of cheese and freshly brewed pots of coffee. I moved into Etienne's chair and fielded questions from Angus about the renovation. Sapphire, who was opposite, listened in keenly, though she was astute enough not to raise the subject of investment.

I told them about the volunteers, and how we'd managed to get a large amount of the cosmetic work done for next to nothing. The new guttering was close to being completed, and save for the murals, furnishings and finishing touches, there was nothing now preventing us from opening to the public in late summer.

'You've done brilliantly,' Angus appraised, and though I brushed off the compliment, it felt nice to have all our hard work acknowledged.

The candles had all but burned down by the time we called it a night. An exhausted Océane and Angus went up to the attic, where Benoit had insisted they stay rather than pay for a hotel, while Adélard woke a comatose Madame and took her and Sapphire back to his apartment. Angela tried to make a case for helping tidy up, but I shooed her to bed.

Soon enough, only Benoit and I remained.

'That's the last of the plates,' I said, stacking them next to the sink. Benoit half-turned, his arms wet to the elbows and coated with suds.

'I can't believe that entire tart went,' he said. 'I'd forgotten how much my dad can eat.'

'He's a big fella, that's for sure. How tall is he?'

'Around six-five, I think.' Benoit pulled a face. 'When I was younger, he used to refer to himself as "the BFD" – as in, "Big Friendly Dad". So friendly that he agreed to take Mum's name when they married. That's why I'm a Chapdelaine rather than a Gowling.'

'Breaking with patriarchal tradition,' I said. 'I approve.'

He side-eyed me. 'Are you saying you approve of my mum? Only, I got the distinct impression that you didn't like her much.'

'Oh, I do,' I said, pulling a tea towel off its hook. 'I think I understand her.'

'You certainly met her head-on.' He smiled wryly. 'She's not used to people doing that.'

'Well, you created the setting for that conversation to happen,' I pointed out. 'And you're the reason she's here – you refused to give up on this reunion.'

'And you told her how foolish she would be to give up on Etienne.'

I put down the glass I was drying and selected a dripping bowl from the rack. 'Anyone would think we make a good team.'

The straps of his apron were twisted, and a blob of cream had dried to a crust on his chin. I ached with the need to touch him.

'What you said to her, about taking the chance to make things right, it really hit her. My mother has a hard exterior; she wears her pain like a protective shield. A lot like you, in fact.'

I froze in the motion of wiping.

'And while it was incredible to watch you sticking up for Etienne like that, I couldn't help but wonder why you couldn't do the same for Lilah.'

I stepped back, shaking my head, ready to walk away. Benoit let the pan he was holding fall into the sink. Water sloshed over the side, soaking the floor and the tops of his trainers.

'You stand up for Etienne, but not yourself. You see the good in him, but none in your mum. You tell my mother she must forgive, when you can't seem to – not Lilah or yourself.'

'That's different,' I said, and Benoit threw back his head.

'No,' he said, 'it isn't – it's exactly the same thing.'

'Why do you do this?' I whispered. 'Why do you always push me so hard?'

My arms were clasped tight around me, and when he couldn't take my hands, Benoit gripped my shoulders instead, gentle yet firm, anchoring me to him.

'Because I care about you,' he said. 'My mother has carried around resentment her whole life, and it's corroded her, cut her through with this awful sadness, like a dark vein. I saw it in you the first minute we met, but I saw more, too. I saw someone who wants more than anything to let go of it all, to be free of all the hatred. I see how happy you could be, Fliss – glimpses of this passionate, kind, funny woman – and I want to help you be like that all the time. But I need you to work with me. Can you do that? Can you at least try?'

I was so close to saying yes, to melting into his arms, agreeing to anything and everything he said simply to please him, yet I was paralysed. Shame and guilt, grief and fear: each one lined up, a blockade past which I could see no route.

'It's not your job to fix me,' I said, feeling him deflate, hearing the sigh that escaped his lips. 'It's mine.'

49

I slept fitfully, kicking off the bedsheets only to wake shivering, plagued by nightmares from the past, and of a small boy with blond hair, his hand slipping through mine as I screamed his name.

When I awoke, it was to an urgent knocking on the bedroom door, and Benoit's voice.

'Fliss, are you in there? Something's happened.'

I lurched up, almost tripping in my haste to let him in. 'What?' I said, pausing at the strained look on his face. 'What is it?'

Benoit did not reply, though his gaze aimed deliberately upwards. Yanking a hooded top from the hook on the back of the door, I pulled it on over my pyjamas.

'Show me,' I said.

Benoit's shoulders remained hunched as he trudged up the stairs. There was pale dust all over his T-shirt, and more in his dark hair. When he reached the door to the morning room, he stopped, drawing in a long breath before turning the handle. I stepped around him, only to freeze in my tracks, trying to make sense of what I was seeing: a scene of total and utter destruction. The floor was covered in broken planks, great chunks of plaster and smashed items of furniture. There was a vast hole in the ceiling, a great gaping mouth that had coughed up the innards of the small loft space; wires trailed, and dust motes danced.

'How did—When did this happen?' I stuttered.

Benoit came to stand beside me. 'It must've been while we were all eating dinner last night. With all the music' – he shifted his feet – 'and, erm, lively conversation, none of us heard the crash.'

'Must've been some crash,' I said, moving cautiously forwards to peer through the hole. 'Thank goodness it wasn't your part of the attic.'

'I've already called Bernard,' he said. 'And Adé, although he didn't pick up.'

'Do you think this is because we put all that furniture up there?' I asked. 'Maybe it was too heavy for the boards.'

'What, a few old desks and a couple of armchairs? I doubt it.'

'Shit,' I muttered. Then again, with more feeling: 'Shit!'

'I know,' he said. 'Mega shit.'

'It *had* to be this room.' I groaned. 'First the damp, and now this.'

Benoit clenched his teeth.

'Has anyone else seen it yet?' I asked, but he shook his head.

'Not yet. I wanted you to be the first to know. Whatever happens next, it involves both of us.'

'What a relief nobody was up there when it happened,' I said.

'Could have been a lot worse,' he agreed.

'This will be fixable, though.' I turned away from the mess and faced him. 'Right?'

'Sure.' Benoit would not meet my eye. 'I mean, ceilings can't be all that expensive.'

'How much?'

Bernard's expression remained impassive. 'The damp from the walls has got into the beams, and there is a leak in the roof also.'

'I thought we'd checked the roof?' Benoit said, his words colliding with my own as I asked the same thing.

'From the outside, yes. But the recent rain . . . There must have been a gap we missed.'

'How bad is it?' Benoit asked, picking up a fallen board and grimacing as the wood flaked apart in his hands.

Bernard stroked his roughly stubbled chin as he considered. 'If you decide to patch it, which you can do, the cost will be lower, but it is my strong suggestion that you replace this section.'

'Of the ceiling?' I said hopefully.

Bernard huffed air through both nostrils. '*Non*,' he said. 'The roof.'

Benoit and I exchanged a stricken look.

'We do the roof first, and then recreate the loft – or,' Bernard mused, striding around the fallen pile of furniture, 'you could perhaps open the space, bring everything up, and do not have an enclosed space above.' He raised his hands. 'I think this could look nice, *non*?'

'Would that be more or less expensive?' Benoit said faintly.

Bernard raised a single brow. 'The roof will cost around twenty thousand euros – the rest? Maybe eight or ten more.'

I swallowed.

Even with the money I'd put into The Fitz returned to me, plus whatever was left of Etienne's donation, we would only just be able to cover it, and doing so would eat away all the funds I had earmarked for the first year of business. We could not open the guesthouse with empty bank accounts, but neither could we allow guests into a space that was falling apart around our ears.

'OK,' I said, and Benoit swung around, my name flying from his lips. 'What choice do we have?' I persisted. 'If the roof needs fixing, that's non-negotiable.'

Bernard came towards us. 'She is right,' he said. 'It is unfortunate, but I will do what I can to keep the costs down.'

We accompanied him back downstairs and bid him a dejected farewell before going through into the lounge. The blanket and pillows Benoit had used for his makeshift chaise-longue bed were neatly stacked on a low table, and an unfinished cup of coffee sat abandoned on the desk.

'I can't believe this has happened,' he said, collapsing on to one of the dining chairs and putting his head in his hands.

'I can,' I said mutinously. 'Things were all going far too smoothly.'

'This is going to set us back,' he said.

'Yup.'

'For how long, do you reckon?'

I did not want to tell him what I really thought, and so settled on: 'Too long.'

Benoit took his phone from his pocket and stared at it morosely. 'Still no word from Adé,' he said. 'Not that he can help us with this situation.'

There was, of course, one very easy solution. I could agree to sell my half of the house to Sapphire.

'I'm just going to go and get dressed,' I said. 'Will you be here?'

Benoit looked wretched as he raised his eyes to mine. 'Of course,' he said wearily. 'There's nowhere else for me to go.'

The house was still quiet. I had no idea of the time, but could only assume it was early. As I reached the middle landing, the bells began to chime, and I paused, counting silently along to seven.

I had told Angela that I couldn't stay in France because the house had been my mother's first, and now it felt as if fate was in agreement. I had allowed myself a glimpse at future happiness, only for the world to scoff at my audacity.

Sell, and I would be free of all of it – the memories, the hurt, the hope. Stay, and I would have no choice but to face them, each and every one, to sit in the emotions I had side-stepped my whole life.

The door to the bedroom had been left ajar, and I could see the painted flowers through the gap; their delicate blue petals blurred through my tears. Forgetting was never an option for my mum, though in choosing to remember, she had been unable to forgive. I did not have to make the same mistake.

The answer came then, and it was so simple, so utterly perfect, that I could have laughed. Within five minutes, I was dressed and racing back to Benoit.

'Come on,' I said, rousing him from a subdued state of self-pity. 'There's someone I need to see.'

He got slowly to his feet. 'Now? What about breakfast?'

'That can wait,' I said, beckoning for him. 'What I have to do can't.'

Adélard's apartment was situated on a narrow street not far from the river.

It took him a while to let us in, and he did so with a certain amount of disgruntlement, rubbing sleep from his eyes and yawning expansively.

'*Café?*' he muttered, in lieu of a greeting, stepping back from the door. He was wearing a knee-length green-and-white robe that had fallen open to the waist, his chest and legs bare.

Without waiting for an answer, he strode ahead along a shallow hallway and disappeared through a door to the left. A tap was turned on, and a machine whirred.

Benoit led me through into another room. It wasn't overly large, but the ceilings were high and the windows tall. One of the shutters was open enough to allow in a crack of pale daylight, but most of the light came from a lamp angled over a large, tan-coloured leather recliner. The floorboards had been varnished to a high shine, and there were a number of framed monochrome prints hanging on the off-white walls. Most of these, I saw, with a note of amusement, were artistic photographs of Madame, while the rest were French movie posters and abstract art. There was also a small piano, sheet music propped on its stand, and a coffee table loaded with architectural tomes.

I had just taken a seat beside Benoit on the sofa when Sapphire appeared, followed closely by Madame. Skittering on the spot in delight, the little dog scampered across to greet us and rested her bristly chin against my thigh.

'Hey.' Sapphire was also wearing a robe, though hers was made from deep red silk and was knotted far more tightly around her body. 'I thought I smelled coffee.'

Adélard came in holding a tray, which he lowered on to the table in front of us. '*Et voilà*,' he said. 'I heated up the milk.'

'*Merci*,' I said, reaching for a cup, ignoring the nervous tension that had begun to bubble in my throat.

Sapphire had sat down in the leather armchair, her feet curled up, head on one side, studying us with interest. I caught her eye and gave in to a smile.

'Is anyone going to talk?' Adélard said, as he stirred three lumps of sugar into his coffee. 'Or do we have to guess what is going on?'

'I have a question to ask,' I began, and Adélard leaned forward, confirming what I'd feared about him wearing nothing beneath the robe.

'You want me to be the best man,' he prompted. 'Of course, yes.'

'*Mon Dieu*,' Benoit said, shaking his head.

'Not that,' I said. 'It's not actually a question for you at all.'

'Ah,' he said, 'you want Madame to be the ring bearer? I will give her my permission.'

'Stop it!' I cried, through helpless laughter, and then, turning to Sapphire: 'I have a proposition for you.'

She sat up a fraction straighter. 'You do?'

'It's about the offer you made.'

'You've decided to sell?'

'No,' I said, adding, as her face immediately fell, 'not exactly. What I want is for you to invest in the business, become a partner in the guesthouse, alongside me and Benoit.'

'A partner?' she repeated slowly.

'Exactly. We'll draw up a proper contract, organise everything, split any profits we make – you can help us with the rest of the refurbishment. I won't even gatekeep too much, I promise.'

'Why the sudden change of heart?' she asked, and I glanced at Benoit.

'Truthfully?' I said. 'The bloody ceiling fell in.'

Her eyes and mouth widened.

'But all that did was give me the shove I needed. I would have come to the same conclusion anyway.'

Adélard put down his cup. 'So, you have decided to stay after all?' he asked, and I felt a burning in my chest.

'Yes. And I really believe that with the three of us on board, we can not only patch up the house but really transform it. Create somewhere that helps Libourne be more than a stopover, or somewhere people come only on market days. It's such a special place, and I want more people to know that.'

'I'm new to all this,' Benoit said, 'but Fliss has it all worked out. You couldn't hope for a better business partner.'

Pleasure every bit as warm as the frothed milk oozed through me. Sapphire stole a glance at Adélard, her fingers dancing up to disguise the twitch of her lips.

'Please,' I said, with such feeling that Madame began to whine along in unison.

'I'd need to see the business plan.' Sapphire said. 'But I dunno, it sounds like a no-brainer to me.'

Benoit punched his fist into the air. 'Is that a yes?' he said, and Sapphire laughed.

'That's a hell yes,' she said.

50

My first port of call when we returned to the guesthouse was Etienne.

He had not reappeared the previous night after staging his walkout, and I wanted to fill him in on everything that had happened. There was no sign of him in any of the downstairs rooms, and upstairs, I found nothing more than an unmade bed and heaps of discarded painting smocks. The shutters were pulled closed, and I opened them, blinking at the dust motes that swarmed. I made a mental note to move his bedroom up several places on the list of those requiring redecoration, then headed to the library. Etienne had grand plans to paint a chestnut tree mural on the blank wall, but he had yet to proceed further than a rough outline, and there was no sign of him having added anything new in the past few hours.

Out on the landing, I dithered for a moment, then hurried up the second flight of stairs to the scene of devastation in morning room. Bernard had returned and was staring up through the hole, a retractable tape measure in his hands.

'Have you seen Etienne?' I asked.

'*Non*,' he replied, frowning. 'Are you going for coffee?'

'Maybe later,' I said, turning away, distracted by the worry that was beginning to build.

Where was he?

I tried to be more systematic, taking each room at a time and calling his name as I went.

Angela yelped in fright when I barged into my mother's old bedroom. 'Do you mind?' she said, slapping her hands over her chest. 'I'm only in my skimpies.'

'Sorry.' I stalked past her into the en suite. 'I can't find Etienne.'

'He wouldn't very well be in there, would he? Probably off painting somewhere,' she added. 'Try not to worry.'

But I was worried. All of a sudden, I felt sick with it.

The Triffid Room was the next most obvious place to check, but the door was locked.

I hammered my fist against it. 'Etienne, are you in there? Open up, it's me, Fliss.' I pressed my ear to the wood, but there was no sound coming from inside.

'Is everything alright?' It was Angus, dazzling in a primrose-yellow shirt.

'I don't know,' I said. 'Have you seen Etienne? Did you see him last night at all?'

'No, I'm afraid we didn't. But I'm sure he'll be somewhere. Come on, let's go downstairs. I'll help you look.'

But Etienne was not in the lounge nor the kitchen; neither was he in the parlour, nor the courtyard. When I heard the front door open, I ran breathlessly into the hallway, but it was only Benoit, returning from the boulangerie with sticks of fresh bread.

'And he's not in the Triffid Room?' he said, when I'd explained.

'I can't get in there – it's locked.'

'That's weird,' he said. 'Let me put this lot in the kitchen, and I'll see if I can dig out the spare key.'

It was a hopeless quest. Every drawer we opened seemed to have twenty keys skittering around inside, but none that fit the lock. Adélard, who had arrived in his overalls as we pulled apart the dresser, suggested he take the door off the hinges.

'You can do that?' Angela asked.

'Of course,' he said nonplussed. 'But it is more likely that Etienne is not here at all. Perhaps he has gone out.'

I looked at Benoit.

'No,' he said. 'I think Fliss is right. There's a reason this door is locked, and we need to find out what it is.'

Adélard was on all fours, rooting through his case of tools, when Océane glided along the corridor. She had left her hair down, and it hung in soft waves around her exquisite face.

Angus chose that moment to puff his way up the stairs. 'Searched everywhere,' he panted. 'Not hide nor hair.'

There was a clunk as Adélard whacked the hinge pin with a hammer. Benoit hurried to help him, and before long, the two men were angling the heavy door out of its frame.

'There,' Adélard said, as I rushed past him into the room. 'I told you. He is not here.'

Etienne was not inside – but something far, far worse was.

The mural that he had begun, of my mother sitting in the square, had been ruined. Daubs of bright red paint were splashed across it like open wounds, and yet more had been hurled across the floor and over the surrounding walls.

Whatever hope it was that had given Etienne the strength to create something beautiful once more had gone.

51

'Oh, *non*,' Océane gasped, as she came to a stop behind me.

Benoit backed away, shaking his head. 'What does this mean? Why destroy it?'

Hairs lifted on the back of my neck.

'He's given up hope,' I said. 'That's what this means.'

'*Merde*,' Adélard muttered.

'We can't just stand here,' I said, tearing my eyes away. 'We have to look for him.'

'I agree.' Angus put his arm around Océane. 'Anyone have any idea where he might go?'

'The art gallery?' Angela suggested. 'He has a friend there, doesn't he?'

'And there are friends of his in Castillon-la-Bataille,' Adélard said. 'I will go in the van, ask if they have heard from him, then look around the town. There are many bars there also.'

Benoit paled. 'We should probably search all the bars here, too. Anywhere that sells alcohol. I can do that,' he said.

'OK, then I'll go around the shops, the town hall, the cafés,' I said. 'Angela, will you stay here, in case he comes back?'

'Of course, lovey.'

'What about the lake?' Océane asked. 'Would he go there?'

'Hang on,' I said. 'Has anyone checked if the car has gone?'

Benoit went to the window and heaved up the sash. 'No,' he called back, 'it's still where I parked it.'

That was something, at least.

'If you give us the keys, we can drive over to the lake,' Angus said, cracking his knuckles. 'I'm sure between the five of us, we'll hunt down the old scoundrel soon enough.'

As we filed out through the gaping doorway, I took hold of Benoit's elbow.

'Can I have that photo,' I said, 'the one of Etienne and my mum?'

He blinked rapidly. 'Of course – you want it now?'

'I thought I could show it to people, see if anyone recognises him?'

Realisation dawned and he leaned forwards, kissing the tip of my nose. 'Everything is going to be alright,' he said, and I believed it.

I believed it as I trawled the streets, as I stumbled over my French in shops and cafés, and as I saw tendrils of grey hair and ran joyously forwards, only to encounter another stranger. Nobody had seen Etienne in the Carrefour or the florist, nor at the train station or the boulangerie. Most of the people I stopped to ask were polite; a few knew Etienne by name, though none had laid eyes on him. The day had become ominously overcast, dishcloth clouds draped wetly across the sun. Sweat dappled my back and underarms, and my cheap sandals rubbed blisters on to my soles. A cat shot out from between two parked cars, and I stumbled, twisting my ankle on the raised edge of a drain cover.

How long had I been searching? I checked the time on my phone. Two hours had passed, and there were no messages from anyone else to say they'd found Etienne. With a groan, I limped back to the guesthouse. Angela and Océane were at the bottom of the stairs, and both turned as I approached.

'Is he here?'

Angela looked downcast. 'Sorry, lovey.'

'Angus is checking the hotels,' Océane said, her knuckles white as she gripped the banister. 'I felt sick in the car, and I thought that . . . I thought . . .'

'You're overwrought,' Angela soothed. 'Come through into the lounge and I'll fix you something sweet. Fliss? You must be famished.'

'I'm fine,' I said. 'I only came back to change my shoes.'

It took me some time to climb the stairs with my sore ankle, but it was a relief to be rid of the hated sandals. There was a bottle of water by the bed that had warmed to room temperature and tasted revolting. I drank it anyway, before refilling it from the tap in the en suite. My phone buzzed and I pounced on it, but it was only a notification from my bank, informing me that a Mr C. Fitzsimons had deposited thirty-two thousand, five hundred and seventy-eight pounds into my account.

The engagement ring he had given me was still in the small velvet box. I opened the lid, and the imitation diamond sparkled in greeting, though it needn't have bothered. It was the other ring I wanted, the gold band with its delicate blue glass flower. Delilah Sanderson had never once taken it off, not until the day she died. She had worn it to remind her of the son she lost, and there was only one person she'd wanted to have it after she was gone.

Of all the emotions I expected to feel when I slid it on, peace was not one. I recalled what Etienne had said, about the ring being a part of me, and for the first time understood what he had meant. The ring represented Felix, and he had been a part of me – more so than anyone else ever would or could be. Mum had merely been watching over him until it was my turn.

When I closed my eyes, I saw her. Not the ragged, embittered and broken woman I had clung on to for so long, but the woman she had been before grief took her from me: the lovestruck young bride in her wedding dress; the new mum with her babies in her arms. I did not need to remember her to know her, just as I had no trouble at all loving the twin who'd left too soon.

I bent my head and kissed the forget-me-not ring, my eyes shooting open as a bolt of realisation struck.

I knew where to find Etienne.

I had known all along.

52

Church bells were ringing as I made my way down the slope to the water's edge.

From above, the river was a silent companion to the town, its burble masked by the rumble of traffic, carried voices and the strains of music drifting out through open windows. On the bankside, that whisper grew to a roar.

Etienne was sitting with his back to a tumbledown wall, hunched form framed by scraggly hollyhocks, knees up to his chest, an uncorked but untouched bottle of red wine on the ground beside him.

'I've always admired those flowers,' I said, startling him out of his ruminative state. 'There's something pleasingly bolshy about them, the way they grow out of the tiniest patches of soil.'

He looked round in faint surprise, as if noticing the plants for the first time.

'Can I sit?'

Etienne nodded but said nothing.

I lowered myself down on to the dusty earth and stretched out my legs. 'You gave us quite the scare.'

His shoulders lifted as he grunted. 'How did you know where to find me?' he asked.

'*It was Lilah's favourite spot. She used to sit down on the bank, at the place where the rivers run together, sometimes for hours, watching the water.*'

'Intuition,' I said, 'and something Benoit once told me.'

He stared past me, towards water gilded silver by clouds. 'Why is he not with you?'

'Because he's out searching. They all are. In fact, I should let them know I've found you.'

I took out my phone, only for Etienne to put a hand over it.

'*Non*,' he said, with a shake of his head. '*S'il te plaît.*'

His skin felt cool and dry against mine.

'How long have you been here?' I asked. He was still wearing the linen trousers and shirt he'd worn for dinner the previous evening, his eyes dark hollows.

'I don't know.' He turned to face me. 'Many hours.'

'When I saw what you'd done to the mural, I thought that—' I stopped as the next word lodged itself in my throat. 'I was scared.'

He gave in to a frown that told me he was sympathetic, but not sorry.

'Why lock us out?' I asked. 'It took us a while to get in – Adélard had to take the door off its hinges.'

The corners of Etienne's mouth flickered upwards, a blink-and-you-miss-it smile that made my heart beat a fraction less erratically. If he could find amusement, then there was still hope.

'You know, I never got the chance to say sorry to my mum,' I said. 'I killed her son, and I never said sorry.'

Etienne patted my knee. 'What happened was not your fault,' he said. 'Lilah, she understood that.'

'I'm not sure if she did. I think she wanted to, but wanting and knowing are not the same thing at all. She knew I didn't mean to do it. *I* know I didn't mean to do it, but I still did it. It was me who gave him the chocolate, my action that caused the accident, and there is no getting away from that simple fact. Believe me, I've spent the past week or more trying my hardest, but the truth is there, immoveable and undeniable. It tormented my mum. I understand that now.'

'She loved you,' Etienne said gruffly, each word firm, ink stamps on a page. 'But the sadness, the grief . . .' He raised his chin heavenward. 'There are things that are too difficult to endure.'

'Is that how you feel?' I asked. 'Is that why you destroyed the mural?'

Etienne started to run his hands through his mess of grey hair, hands that shook and fumbled.

'I am tired,' he said, so vehemently that it sent a chill through me. 'Tired of thinking every day about my father, and what that brute of a man did to me; tired of the resentment felt by my sister; tired of this spinning circle of hurting other people and damaging myself. It goes around and around,' he went on, rotating his hand in agitation. 'The worst thing I have felt' – he looked at me in anguish – 'is bitterness. When Lilah died, I was sad, of course, but also, I was envious, because she had escaped her pain.' Tears tumbled out and he scrubbed them away. '*Ma pauvre chérie*,' he murmured. 'I miss her. I am tired of missing her.'

I squeezed my eyes shut to stem my own tears as he continued to speak.

'When Océane arrived yesterday, I thought for a moment that there could be some hope, but she has not forgiven me.' He lowered his eyes. 'Perhaps it would be easier for her, and for all of you, if I was gone.'

'Gone?' I looked round sharply.

Etienne nodded slowly towards the water, his meaning clear as he repeated the word again. 'Gone.'

I was struck by a primal rush of anger, and bunched my hands into fists. 'Do you know how lucky you are?' I said. 'To be alive. To have reached the age you are. It's a privilege.'

He dismissed me with an exaggerated shrug.

'I get that you're sad, that you miss my mum and that you're frustrated by your sister's reluctance to make amends, but that doesn't mean you get to check out. Somewhere in the future, there is a version of you who doesn't feel the way you do in this moment: a man who wants to live, to paint, to laugh, to sit by the water in the town he loves. You have to stay, for his sake.'

'I am a weak man,' Etienne said, sagging back against the wall. 'I have always been this way.'

'No,' I countered, 'you aren't. And you haven't. Think about what you went through as a boy. You survived that. You made a success of your art despite all the setbacks, and you have been here, sitting on this bank, for hours and hours, and you haven't taken a single sip of that wine.'

We both stared at the bottle by his feet.

'That is the opposite of weakness,' I said. 'It's strength.'

'I was not strong enough to stay,' he said forlornly. 'Océane is right. I was a coward.'

'You were a teenager – a boy who had been abused. Your father left you with no choice. And for what it's worth, I think Océane knows that, too. I think blaming you is what she does to deflect her own trauma. It's a lot easier to think history could have been rewritten if someone other than you had made a different decision – that lets you off the hook. But you can't go back; you can only try to move forwards. If you give up,' I went on, 'the pain just carries on and on. Stay, and there is a chance Océane forgives you. Leave, and you lose that chance.'

Etienne leaned forwards and draped his hands limply over his knees. 'Do you believe that she can forgive me?' he asked.

It was an easy question to answer. 'She wouldn't be here if she couldn't.'

'But her words—'

'Were harsh, yes. I know. But if she didn't care, Etienne, there would be no emotion there at all. The anger, it comes from regret. It's fuelled by something so much more complex than even she probably realises. I know, because I feel the same way about my mum. I'm angry with her, but I also feel desperately sorry for her. I feel guilty and helpless, and have no idea how to stop those feelings, but that doesn't mean I can't try. I have to try.'

A bee had landed on the neck of the bottle, drawn by the wine's sweetness, the rich scent of berries, the abrasive trace of pepper. Etienne reached across and, very carefully, removed it. The bee crawled for a minute across his palm, and then it spread its wings and took off across the water. Even that small life had purpose, mattered in a way beyond our understanding.

'I can't lose anyone else,' I said.

He tried to smile, but the gesture seemed to cause him distress. 'She was not afraid.' Etienne raised his eyes to the murky sky once more. 'Your mother, when she found out about her illness – death did not scare her. It was as if' – he frowned – 'as if she had been waiting a very long time for something, and it was hers at last. She was calm.'

'I don't think she ever knew peace, did she?' I asked.

'Not until the end,' he said.

'Do you know why she never tried to contact me? Why she wrote me a letter she knew I'd only read after she died?'

Etienne picked at a speck of dried paint on his trousers. 'I cannot tell you for certain,' he said. 'It is probable that she believed there would be more time, that she could wait a little while longer. But time ran out.' Scooping up a handful of dirt, he opened his fingers and let it fall to the ground. 'I feel the pain of that day.' He tapped his chest. 'And I do not know if I can bear it. It is too much for one person alone.'

'But you're not alone,' I said. 'I'm here, and so is Benoit, and your friends, and your sister. I know what pain is. I endured a childhood marred by a mother who shunned me, who drank and raged. I endured the loss of my father and shouldered the blame for it. I endured the man who was supposed to love me betraying me in the most public and destructive way, and I will somehow endure knowing that I caused the death of my twin brother. If I can endure all that, then you can endure.' I took his hand in mine, pulled it close to my chest. 'We can endure it together.'

The clouds parted then, and a shaft of sunlight broke through. It smiled across the water, spreading diamonds in its wake, illuminating the bankside, seeking out the place my mum had stood so many times before, and where we now sat.

To remember her.

53

Océane was waiting in the hallway when we got back. Having run straight up to Etienne, she slapped him very hard across the cheek, then collapsed, sobbing, into his arms.

'What is she saying?' I asked Angus.

He was leaning against the banisters, smile indulgent above his crumpled yellow shirt. 'A mixture of things,' he said, cocking his ear towards the torrent of French. 'She thought she might have lost him for good, and it scared her.' He paused. 'Oh, that's good. She doesn't want them to argue anymore.'

'She's willing to meet him halfway?'

Angus peered down at me, the kindness in his gaze reminding me of Benoit. 'She's willing to try,' he said.

With a singular thought in my mind, I made my way through the lounge and headed towards the kitchen, only to bump into Angela coming the other way.

'Oh, lovey,' she said, enveloping me in a quick hug. 'Are you OK?'

'Relieved,' I told her, and briefly explained what had happened.

'A whole bottle of wine, all day?'

'Not a drop,' I confirmed. 'I poured the lot into a flower-bed, so there are going to be some very drunk worms down by the river.'

'Adélard got back about ten minutes ago. He and Bernard are upstairs, rehanging the door.'

'And Benoit?' I said.

Angela winced. 'He got the train into Bordeaux, said he was going to search the bars there.'

'In Bordeaux? But there are hundreds.'

'I know,' she agreed. 'I told him that, but he was frantic, kept saying it was all his fault, that if he hadn't nagged his mum into making the trip then none of this would have happened.'

I took my phone from my pocket and scrolled to Benoit's number. The call went straight to voicemail. Either he had no signal, or a flat battery.

Etienne and Océane came in to join us. Seeing them with their arms tightly linked, Angela promptly burst into tears. 'Sorry,' she said, dabbing her eyes. 'Bloody menopause. I'm like a water balloon that's been used as a pincushion these days.'

'We've all been at it today,' confided Angus. 'Why don't I make everyone a nice cup of tea?'

'I should do that,' Angela protested, but Angus would have none of it.

'You sit down,' he said, steering her firmly towards a chaise longue.

I checked my phone. Still nothing. The message I'd sent Benoit, letting him know I'd found Etienne and that he was safe, had yet to be delivered, the single grey tick mocking me with its ambivalence. I had found one Chapdelaine, only to lose another.

'He definitely took his phone with him, didn't he?' I asked Angela. 'He wouldn't have gone without it.'

'Why don't you check?' she suggested.

I was halfway up to the attic before I remembered that Benoit had not slept in his own room the previous night. Once I'd ventured inside, I saw his charging cable curling out from its socket next to the bed. Had he managed to plug in his phone at all before everything descended into chaos? Unlikely.

Outside the Triffid Room, I came across Adélard, still in his overalls, screwing hinges back into place on the door. Bernard, who was on the other side, acting as assistant, poked his head around the frame and offered me a cheerful, '*Salut.*'

'Thank the Lord for you,' Adélard said. 'How did you know where to find him?'

'Just a lucky guess.' I explained about Benoit, and he nodded gravely.

'I told him not to go.'

'I wish he'd call,' I said. 'I hate the thought of him out there roaming the streets, thinking the worst and blaming himself. Maybe I should go after him.'

'To Bordeaux?' Adélard's eyebrows drew together. 'You will never find him.'

'Well, I can't just sit here and—'

The front door had opened below. Someone was in the hallway. Adélard and I looked at each other, both hurrying to the stairs in time to see the door to the lounge close. It had to be him.

I ran down, twisted ankle forgotten, and found not Benoit sitting beside Etienne, but a woman I vaguely recognised.

'Oh,' I said, unable to hide my disappointment.

'This is Madame Montagne,' Etienne explained. 'From the gallery.'

'Vanessa,' she said, with a polite smile.

Of course. I recognised the glasses hanging from a gold chain around her neck.

'It's all very exciting,' Angela said, passing me a chipped mug of tea. 'She wants Etienne to do an exhibition.'

'Since we sold the *Ville Lumiere*, there has been renewed interest in your uncle's work,' Madame Montagne told me.

My heart lifted at 'your uncle'.

'I am here now to persuade him to paint another collection. Perhaps you will help me?'

'Felicity has proven herself to be very persuasive,' Etienne said, with the ghost of a wink. 'But it will take some time. I have some work I need to do here before I can commit to anything more.'

Madame Montagne looked around, as if noticing the room for the first time. '*Oui*,' she said flatly. '*Tu fais*.'

Océane began to laugh, and soon enough, everyone else did, though I could not join in, not without Benoit. My hand drooped, and tea slopped out on to the rug. Angela rushed to take it from me.

'He'll check in soon,' she said, knowing without having to be told what was vexing me. 'You've done what you can; the best option is to wait here.'

They were all so relaxed, at ease enough to sit and drink their tea, laugh together while their nephew, their son, their friend, continued to torment himself.

I tried to call again, and once more, I could not get through.

'Have you eaten today?' Angela asked. 'Only, you look a bit peaky.'

'I'm fine,' I said, as my stomach gave a growl.

Angela's expression went from soft to stern. 'Come on,' she said. 'There are some leftovers in the kitchen.'

I traipsed through the courtyard after her and sat down heavily at the kitchen table, an ache in my jaw where I'd been clenching it. The bread was out, a knife still smeared with butter and coated in crumbs.

'Benoit knows,' I said, 'about Dad, about what happened the night of the accident. I've never told anyone outside the family before – I didn't even tell Charlie – but with Benoit, it's different.' I stared at my hands. 'I don't know, I feel like I could tell him anything.'

Angela closed the fridge door and set down a block of Cheddar and some tomatoes. 'You trust him,' she said. Not a question.

I nodded.

'Do you know why?'

'Instinct,' I said. 'Almost as soon as I met him, I had this sense that he was built from integrity, that he was honourable. You know what I'm like; usually, it takes me ages to warm up to people.'

'You think the world is out to get you,' she confirmed.

'I think the further away you are from the flame, the less likely you are to get burnt.'

'But not when it comes to Benoit?'

'No,' I said with a sigh. 'Not with Benoit. Whoever's voice it is I hear, urging me to do things, to take risks, to be brave, they're telling me that he is someone worthy of believing in.'

Angela cut herself a slice of cheese. 'Have you ever wondered if it might be Felix?' she asked. 'If it's his voice you hear?'

'No,' I said, my eyes hot. 'But I like the idea. I like it a lot.'

My phone lit up with a message. Benoit. At last. He'd seen my text and replied.

'What's happened?' Angela's eyes widened as I shot out of my chair. 'What did he say?'

'That he's on his way here.'

'Then where are you going?' she called, as I ran towards the door.

'To meet him halfway,' I said.

54

The square was near deserted.

Café tables sat empty, and pigeons dawdled, their neatly tucked wings the same mottled grey as the sky above. The mullioned windows of the town hall stared down at me with unblinking intensity as I crossed the cobbles to the old water fountain and eased myself down on to the pale stone surround.

The first time I'd walked through the centre of Libourne, I'd been full of impatience, my chief desire being to get in, get whatever I was owed, and get out again as soon as I could. That mindset felt alien to me now; the notion that I would ever find a place in which I felt more like myself was absurd. Libourne, with its quiet charm and faded splendour, had taught me what it was to belong, though my real debt of gratitude, of course, was owed to the people I'd met, those who had welcomed me in without question or judgement.

When the familiar shape of Benoit finally came into view, he did not notice me until I stood. Only then was his attention caught. With a raised hand, he walked slowly across to join me.

'Sorry,' he said. 'It seemed to take me forever to get here.'

'Me too,' I said, and his eyes flickered. So blue, so suffused with warmth. 'I wanted to come and meet you.'

'My phone died.' He held it up to show me the blank screen. 'I didn't realise until I got on the train how low the battery was, and I thought I'd better turn it off to conserve some power. That message I sent you, it took my last one per cent.'

'I feel honoured.'

'You're worth it.' He smiled easily. 'Thank you for finding him. Where was he in the end?'

'By the water,' I said. 'At the place where the rivers run together.'

'Of course.' Benoit groaned and bounced a palm off his forehead. 'I should have thought.'

'So should I,' I said. 'It took me hours, and then, I don't know, it sort of came to me. I was back at the house, thinking about my mum, and I just knew.'

He folded his arms as I talked more about Etienne, concern etching itself across his features.

'It's not all bad,' I said, when he began to pace up and down. 'He and your mum are speaking properly again, and I think he turned a real corner with the drinking today. I really do.'

'We could have lost him, though,' he said.

'We didn't, and we won't. But he is going to need our support.'

'*Our* support?' He looked at me. 'So, you really meant it when you said you'd stay?'

'I really meant it.' I sat back down on the fountain step, though Benoit continued to stand.

'I told you,' he said. 'Everyone falls in love with Etienne in the end. You fought a good battle, but I'm afraid your actions today have only served to confirm your defeat.'

I clutched my chest and pretended to keel over.

Benoit laughed. 'You're wearing the ring,' he said.

I fingered the glass flower. 'I thought it was time.'

'Time for what?'

'To forgive,' I said. 'The thing is, I do love Etienne. I love him despite all his failings, his mistakes, his struggles. I can see that he is more than all those things, and so was she.'

'And yourself?' he said gently. 'Can you see now that you are more than your past, and that whatever it is you feel guilty about shouldn't stop you from being happy?'

'I can see it,' I began.

Benoit came to sit beside me. 'I'm sensing a "but",' he said.

'But it's not here yet. It's on the horizon, and I know I'll get there – though when, I can't say.'

'That's fair.' Benoit rested his elbows on his knees and laced his fingers together. His jeans were frayed at the hems, the label of his T-shirt sticking out. It took every ounce of willpower I had not to tuck it away.

'Do you know what they call all this pale gold stonework?' he said, glancing at me.

I shook my head.

'Bordeaux stone. It's made from limestone and asteria, and there are hundreds of starfish fossils in it. Spend enough time looking at it, and you'll start to notice that it sparkles in the light. Etienne told me about it when I was a child – though, in my confusion, I took starfish to mean real stars. I thought that was why the guesthouse sparkled, because it had been built with stardust.'

I caught my tears before they fell, and Benoit missed them. He was staring straight ahead. Adrift, momentarily, in the past.

'That's why Etienne used the gold leaf in his paintings,' I said, and he smiled widely.

'I never thought of that, but I bet you're right.'

'I love that he's found his way back to it.'

'Thanks to you,' Benoit said. 'That mural he painted in your bedroom was the first beautiful thing he'd created in years. You woke something up in him, something that had been dormant for a long time.'

'I could say the same to you,' I said, heat creeping up from my chest to my throat. 'The night we spent together . . . I should never have said that it was nothing. It was so far from nothing. I didn't know that it could be like that, or that I could feel like that.'

'Like what?' he asked, leaning back, his shoulder a comforting pressure against mine.

'As if I was exactly where I was supposed to be, doing exactly what I should be doing.'

'You've never felt like that before?'

'Never. I've always either been two steps ahead of whichever moment I'm in, or five behind it, worrying about what's happened, or what's to come. But with you, that all fell away. I was so there, in the moment. And yes, when I went up to your room, perhaps I was seeking a distraction, but it wasn't only that. I thought – I hoped – that what we had would turn out to be different . . . special.'

'How do you feel now?' he said, the hand that was on his thigh straying closer to mine. 'About what happened? Do you regret it?'

'God, no. Absolutely not.'

'Good.' His knuckles brushed against my arm. 'Because neither do I.'

'The sky is beginning to clear,' I said. Looking up, I caught a glimpse of the moon, its face pale between curtains of ashen cloud. Come, perhaps, to check on the fallen stars that surrounded us, built, as Benoit had said, into the foundations of this magical French town.

My mouth was dry, and my chest tight, but I had to say what I'd come here to say. I took a deep breath and reached for his hand.

'What is it?' he said, filling the silence I couldn't. 'Fliss, look at me.'

I did as he asked, taking in the soft curls, the sprinkled freckles, that generous lower lip.

'You don't have to be afraid,' he said. 'Not of me, not of your feelings.'

I made myself meet his eyes. 'I'm not OK,' I said. 'With everything that's happened, I have so much I need to overcome. The grief, the guilt, how to reconcile my feelings towards my mum – it's going to be tough, working through it all, and it's going to take time. But there's only one person I want by my side while I do it, and I know it's a lot to ask, and you can say no, but I don't want to be completely alone in this. I need a friend.'

'A friend?' he repeated, turning the word into a question.

'That's all I can be at the moment,' I said. 'When we do this – if we do this – I want to do it right. I want to find my way to that bright spot of happiness on the horizon, and then, I want to bask in it with you. Do you think you can wait for me to be ready?'

Benoit's eyes were glassy as he cupped my face in his hands. 'Oh, Fliss,' he said. 'You make it sound as if I have a choice in the matter.'

'Is that a "yes"?' I asked.

'*Oui*,' he said, pressing his forehead to mine. '*C'est un oui*.'

55

Three months later ...

On a bright Saturday in late September, we opened La Fresque.

Word had spread through Libourne, and the locals were stepping through the propped-open doors by mid-morning, keen to take a house tour led by Jono and Rich. My cousins had been recruited for the weekend by a very pink-cheeked and excessively talkative Angela.

'*C'est magnifique!*' she kept proclaiming, while dabbing her eyes with one of Etienne's painting cloths.

'She's been learning French on some app,' confided Uncle Patrick, who was loitering in the hallway. 'Some bird or other. It's very demanding, tells her off if she misses a lesson.'

'My approach has been to speak as much English as possible, in the hope of wearing the natives down,' I told him.

'How's that working out for you?'

'It's not,' I said, and we both laughed.

In the lounge, Adélard had set up a makeshift bar on one of the tables, complete with themed mocktails, tiny paper umbrellas and cases of non-alcoholic wine.

'What are you calling this one?' I asked, taking a sip from a lurid yellow concoction.

'A Lady's Knickers,' he said slyly. 'Mango juice, lemonade, sparkling water and mint – so refreshing that you want to get it down as quickly as you can.'

'I see what you did there,' I drawled.

The courtyard door banged open, and Céline bustled through, looking harried. 'Paper,' she said. 'We are running out.'

'Third drawer down, right side of the dresser,' I told her. 'How's it going out there?'

She straightened up with the fresh stack of paper and used it to fan her face. 'It is busy. But why, I don't understand. He is making everybody look ridiculous, *non*?'

It had been Angus's idea that Etienne offer to do caricature drawings for guests, and having set himself up outside with an easel, he'd had a steady queue of customers all day.

There was a scrabbling of paws and Madame skittered into the room, followed closely by a hissing ball of enraged grey fluff.

'*Salut*, Minouche,' I crooned, scooping the cat into my arms. 'Is that incorrigible dog terrorising you again?'

'She, terrorising that beast?' Adélard exclaimed. '*Mon Dieu*. Now, I have heard it all.'

Minouche flattened her ears.

'I'll take her upstairs,' I said, going back out into the hallway and directing several newcomers towards the bar. It was impossible not to stop on the stairs and admire the new mural – a resplendent wisteria, every one of its petals rendered in painstaking detail. Bernard and his men had built an indoor rig of scaffolding for Etienne that allowed him to paint into the highest corners, and he'd spent hours perfecting it, often working through the night. I had lost count of the number of times I'd fallen asleep to the sound of his brush against the plaster, the low murmur of his voice as he hummed a song he loved.

In the library, I dropped Minouche into her basket and said hello to Océane, who was curled up on a reupholstered blue armchair reading a copy of *Le Monde*.

'What is your star sign, Felicity?'

'Taurus.'

'Ah,' she said. '*Taureau*. Stubborn.'

'Afraid so.'

She eyed me over the top of the newspaper. 'It says here that this is a good week for communication and' – she squinted at the page – 'getting something that you have wanted for a long time.'

'Well, I don't know what that could be,' I said lightly. 'I got the cat three weeks ago.'

Footsteps heralded the arrival of Jono and his next tour – a group of Americans he'd accosted in the street outside – and, after waiting to hear their collective gasp of awe when he took them into what had been the Triffid Room, I slipped away.

Benoit was exactly where I'd left him an hour ago, and he glanced up as I closed the kitchen door behind me.

'Whose idea was it to do hors d'oeuvres again?'

'Oh, that was all you,' I said. 'I'm afraid you only have yourself to blame.'

'Want one?' he said, gesturing to the table. 'You can choose from artichoke tartlets, Gruyère and caramelised onion straws, black olive tapenade on beetroot crackers, or *panisses*.'

I raised a brow. 'Say that last one again.'

'*Panisses*,' he said. 'Chickpea fries, very popular in Provence.'

'*Ooh la la*,' I said, popping one into my mouth. 'Oh wow, that is . . . wow.'

'I'm very glad you find my *panisses* so delicious.'

'I could eat your *panisses* all day long, but right now, I actually need to show you something. Can you spare five minutes?'

Benoit undid his apron and slung it on the hook. 'I can spare a lot more minutes than that for you,' he said.

Etienne was sketching exaggeratedly large teeth on to a caricature of Sapphire as we passed, and the two of them waved cheerfully. As a so-called silent investor, she had proved to be far from quiet, but her chipperness had chipped slowly but surely away at my more domineering edges. I did not need to control everything, and once I'd realised as much, life became far less stressful.

'Where are you taking me?' asked Benoit, as we reached the front door.

'When was the last time you took stock?' I prompted, checking for cars before crossing to the opposite side of the street. 'We've been so busy these past few months, what with getting the house done.'

'And choosing a rescue cat,' he put in. 'And making sure Etienne gets to his AA meetings on time.'

'And my addiction counselling course,' I added. 'That and the volunteering has taken up a lot of time.'

'But you love both,' he said, and I smiled.

'I really do.'

The day was still mild, lackadaisical clouds dressing a cornflower sky. Angela was right, the house was *magnifique*, the damp patches long since faded, the scaffolding and skip taken away. The marrow plant had been left to flower in its drain, and above it, the 'La Fresque' plaque shone in polished gold. Someone had even gone to the trouble of cleaning the ancient Renault, which was parked to the right of the entrance.

We stood side by side, gazing up at our home, allowing ourselves a moment in which to appreciate all that we had achieved. It was nothing short of miraculous.

'I got you something,' I said.

Benoit blinked in astonishment as I placed a tissue-wrapped oblong package in his open palm.

'Go on,' I said, when he hesitated. 'I promise it's not a desiccated mouse.'

'High bar,' he said drily, and slowly tore open the paper. 'It's a . . . spoon?'

'Not just any spoon,' I protested lightly. 'A Welsh love spoon. Turn it over.'

He did as I asked, a small exclamation escaping his lips as he saw what was etched into the wood. His name, and my name – and, on the bowl, the date we'd first met: 5 June 2025.

'It's made from teak,' I said. 'Resistant to water, so it should last longer than our roof did.'

Benoit's eyes shined.

'I chose a spoon because, well, you're a chef, aren't you?' I went on. 'And I had it made specially, so it would be one of a kind, just like you.'

'It's also beautiful,' he said, 'like you.'

'It's a promise,' I said, 'from me to you, that I will always be myself. Not a single thing more or less.'

'I don't know what to say.' Benoit fingered the delicately carved wood.

'You don't have to say anything. What I wanted to say to you is that I'm ready now. I don't want to wait anymore – and I don't need to, either.'

'Fliss,' he began, but I shook my head urgently.

'No, let me say it. I want to say it first.'

'OK.' He smiled.

My hands shook as I slid them into his, the spoon trapped between us. 'Benoit.'

He raised my fingers to his lips, pressed featherlight kisses on each in turn.

'I love you,' I said, the words barely audible.

He cocked an ear. '*Pardon, madame?*'

'I love you.' It came out in a rush. He laughed incredulously as I said it again, and then again, until I was bouncing on the soles of my feet, and suddenly we were kissing. We kissed as if nothing else mattered, as if time itself had paused at our behest.

Benoit wrapped me up in his arms and pulled me close against him. 'Is this the part where I say I love you too?' he asked.

'Better late than never.'

'What would you say if I told you that I had planned a surprise for you as well?'

'I'd probably tell you that I love you again.'

'Wait here,' he said, and ran back into the house.

My body missed him; every part that had touched him tingled. When he returned a minute later, all I could do was gaze at him. There was nothing inside me but felicity. No darkness at all, only the joy of contentment.

'Is that what I think it is?' I asked, glancing down at the tin of paint in his hand.

'You know how we couldn't decide on a colour for the external shutters?'

'They do look a bit bare,' I conceded.

'I'm glad you think so.'

Benoit put the container down on the pavement and I crouched beside him.

'I had to get this specially made, too,' he said. 'I wanted exactly the right shade.'

I knew what colour I would see when he removed the lid, and I loved him more in that moment because of it.

'Any idea what we should name it?' he asked. 'I thought you could choose.'

'Easy,' I said, as we smiled at each other. 'We'll call it Forget-Me-Not Blue.'

Acknowledgements

Every novel has its first scribbled note, and this one was conceived, rather befittingly, in Paris, where my good friend (and fellow author) Cathy Bramley and I had scarpered off for a chilly yet sunny day of exploring, food sampling, and general tomfoolery. By that stage, I had lost count of the number of readers who'd asked me if, and when, I was going to set a book in France, and so on that evening, with a glass of very good red wine in hand, I finally caved in to you all and outlined the plot of *The French Guesthouse*. I hope you enjoyed reading about Fliss, Benoit, Etienne, Adélard and – most of all – Madame, and that you have added Libourne to your must-visit list. I had such a wonderful stay there in the spring of 2024 (falling backwards off chairs aside) and can only hope I've done the town and its people justice.

Now – drum roll – to the thank yous:

To my agent, Alice Lutyens, who is fair and wise and hilarious – thank you for (gently) pushing me to believe in myself and my books, and to the wider team at Curtis Brown for their continued support and championing.

To Jo Dickinson, for her infinite wisdom and kindness, and for steering this novel – and me – through its edits, and to Kit Nevile for taking up the helm so brilliantly. I was extremely lucky to have a fantastic copy editor in Tara O'Sullivan, who has undoubtedly saved me from much embarrassment regarding my abuse of the French language, and an eagle-eyed proofreader in Helena Newton, who spotted all the tiny typos I somehow managed to miss.

Enormous thanks also to my Hodder & Stoughton team, including Alainna Hadjigeorgiou (for publicity), Ella Young (for marketing), Natalie Chen (for cover design) and Catherine, Sarah and Rich (for sales).

To all the authors who keep me motivated on the days when writing feels hard – especially Cathy Bramley, Katie Marsh, Kate Gray, Cesca Major, Tom Wood, Lisa Howells, Chris Whitaker, Louise Candlish, Tammy Perry, and Fanny Blake – and to my friends who don't guilt-trip me too hard when I vanish completely for months at a time – especially Sadie Davies, Tamsin Carroll, Ranjit Dhillon, Sarah Bedingfield, Gemma Courage, Ian Lawton and Vicky Zimmermann.

Thank you to all the librarians, bloggers, press reviewers, and booksellers – with a special mention for Grace and Grace at Waterstones Sudbury, who put my books in windows and on tables and buy delicious crisps for book club. You're the best!

Lastly, to my sprawling, dysfunctional, eccentric, love-infused family – the reason I never run out of novel ideas is mostly down to all of you, and I mean that as a compliment (I think . . .). And to my mum – I can't imagine a life in which we don't talk every day, about everything, from the serious to the sublimely silly, and it makes me feel like the most fortunate person in the world. Thank you for being you.

If you enjoyed *The French Guesthouse*, we hope that you will love more escapist holiday reads from Isabelle Broom.

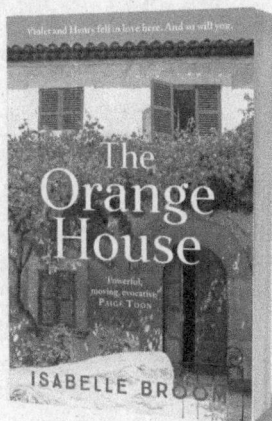